ADOBE DAZE

THE NEW WEST SERIES, BOOK THREE

TOM TATUM

WOLFPACK
PUBLISHING
— EST 2013 —

WOLFPACK
PUBLISHING
— EST 2013 —

The characters and events portrayed in this book are fictitious. Any similarity to real persons, living or dead, is coincidental and not intended by the author.

Text copyright © 2021 (As Revised) Tom Tatum

Published by Wolfpack Publishing

5130 S. Fort Apache Road, 215-380

Las Vegas, NV 89148

Paperback IBSN 978-1-64734-737-6

eBook ISBN 978-1-64734-736-9

ADOBE DAZE

CHAPTER ONE
BIG WHEELS

Trey Stuart's hands were on the leather covered steering wheel of his father's very nimble and dangerously fast black Maserati 650 GT coupe as the pump jacks in the New Mexico San Juan Basin's natural gas field flew by on Highway 550 north. The Ferrari engine's three hundred and ninety horsepower V-8 Atom motor sling shot the 650 GT to a 130 miles per hour. Trey passed a line of rugged oil and natural gas four-wheel drive white service trucks on a long-broken line straight about twenty miles north of Cuba New Mexico near Chaco Canyon. He tucked the Maserati back into the head of the line and continued speeding north toward Aztec, New Mexico, the home of a restored Anasazi underground kiva, which had been used by their priests for their secret religious ceremonies. Anthropologists now had confirmed human sacrifice in the kivas after a 400-year drought arrived around 1200 AD in the Four Corners region of New Mexico, Colorado, Arizona and Utah. Trey's parents Cooper and Judy had taken him to see the kiva at the National Monument when he was in middle school in Telluride near the family's YbarC ranch. It was western Colorado's largest remaining land and cattle operation. He was returning the Maserati to them after its annual oil change and check up at the La Scuderia garage in Albuquerque New Mexico where its specialized mechanics worked. It was a treat to drive it instead of a ranch pickup truck pulling a horse trailer.

Trey, who was twenty-six years old, had graduated from the University of Southern California and kicked around the Rocky Mountain West ski patrolling and as a pro extreme skier in the winter after graduation. His buff six-foot two-inch frame fit into the Italian black leather seats like a Le Man's driver in a race version. His dirty blond hair blew in the wind from the half rolled down driver side window. Serengeti driving glasses protected his blue eyes from the sun and dusty west. His tanned face accented outdoor good looks. The smell of the Colorado Plateau's sage covered high desert permeated the driver compartment. He had known the smell since it whiffed through the window of his ranch house bedroom into his crib. He thought about a cafe taco lunch with cold fresh lemonade in Aztec's old downtown next to the crumbling art deco movie theater. He had fantasized about buying and restoring it after minoring in film making at USC. The lunch stop was halfway home to the ranch for a Saturday night scotch with his father and a home cooked meal prepared by his mother and the ranch's cook. The cook also fed the cowboys in their bunkhouse dining room before they drove to nearby Norwood Colorado to drink, dance and play pool at The Lone Cone Saloon. It was late April of 2020, and the summer ranch crew was full up and ready to ride for the brand until the cattle were rounded up in mid-October. After roundup the grass-fed steers sold by the ranch's broker and were shipped. The YbarC only produced natural grass-fed beef. His family believed the past was the future for beef cattle that could not properly digest corn even though the federal government subsidized it. This forced cattle into the meat industry's feedlots. Trey slowed to forty-five miles an hour before he entered Aztec and his radar detector beeped loudly over the wind noise. A New Mexico State Highway patrol car was parked on a closed roadside café's sun faded cracked asphalt pavement's parking lot. He hit his power window button and rolled it up as he turned on the car radio to a Farmington, New Mexico country music station and smiled knowing the state cop knew he hadn't been driving the speed limit for the last two hours. But Trey also knew the oil and gas companies donated big dollars to the New Mexico Legislators and Governor to ensure many things. One of them was to let their service trucks speed unchecked to reach emergency well situations and keep the highly paid crews on schedule to cut their overtime pay. The black Maserati, like a Mexican panther, had moved in and out of the white service trucks with their radio aerial flags to identify them on the oil and gas company lease's sage lined dirt roads. But the mostly black state patrol car stayed on the edge of town under a shady cottonwood tree. He mused that life was in balance in the big empty western United States. Freedom still flowed like a raging river under the forever-blue sky, which was still punctuated with snow-capped mountaintops in spring.

Trey was finishing a beef taco lunch when his ponytailed black haired, early 20 something, kind of light copper waitress paused by his table to refresh his ice-cold fresh-squeezed lemonade. She was very easy to look at. As her brown eyes captured the light from the window she smiled asking, "That your black Maserati production sports car I see parked on the street out front?"

"Well kind of for today…I'm delivering it back to my father at his ranch near Telluride, Colorado. It was just tuned up in Albuquerque. You like fast cars?"

"I do. My dad restores old California drag racing hot rod roadsters. He lives in Durango, Colorado and resells them at car shows around the Four Corner's states. What's its motor's red line top speed?"

"Its motor is a Ferrari F-136 90-degree V8 with 4.2 liters producing 390 horsepower. It does 180 mph on Michelin Le Mans Z tires," he replied smiling. "Those specs in your pay grade?"

"Yes, they are. You staying here in Aztec to visit the Anasazi ruins where the priests cut out virgin girls' hearts to try and make it rain, or just stopping for lunch?"

"This café has been my parents' go to lunch stop in Aztec since I was a kid. Durango my next stop for a Second Street brew pub cold beer and then hop along to the ranch." Cooper replied ducking the gruesome kiva's history his parents hadn't mentioned to him on their visit.

"I'd love a ride in it. I'm off in a half hour and I'm planning to drive to Durango to see a college girlfriend and spend the night at my dad's house. How about you give me a ride if you'll let me test it out. I have drag raced a five-speed hot rod roadster since 16. My name's Maria Duran but most friends call me M, others the "go fast" girl."

Trey reflected a second realizing he was bored driving alone. "I'm

Trey Stuart. We can do that. I'm burned-out passing oil and gas service trucks and looking at sage. Meet me out front. I'll take a walk about around town...maybe find something for my mother's birthday present. You can leave from here?"

"My overnight bag is in my trunk. It's a 1977 Shelby Mustang my dad restored for my graduation present from Fort Lewis College in Durango last year. It will be safe behind the café tonight. The owner locks the back parking gate, and it has a surveillance camera to boot."

"Then you are my co-driver to Durango, but aren't the Colorado State Patrol merciless once we cross the border?"

"Not the local's back doorway through Hesperus to Durango. You know that route?" and she smiled deliciously adding, "I'll bring a couple of homemade flans from the kitchen with some Spanish brandy from the bar. There's a little park on the Hesperus River. It'll be a nice stop for some fresh riverbank ions."

A half hour later they pulled out of the parking place in front of the tin shed café as M gave Trey directions through Aztec to a county road that passed by the modern High School. They drove by a newly built subdivision on a low hill with its three-bedroom brick homes for the senior oil and gas company field production and servicing managers who reported to Houston or Denver hourly. It reminded Trey that oil and gas energy was pumped from 14,000 wells in the San Juan Basin, which straddled the New Mexico and Colorado border into pipelines for refining twenty-four/seven. It fueled the US's government, industry, transportation, military and heated its homes. It is the biggest top dollar industry in the entire world. The owners were wealthy, and its managers and workers are the top paid blue-collar workers in the US. Trey increased his speed as the Maserati's motor low throat rumbled as his view turned more rural with low hilly rocky clay soil covered with sage grass. The dwellings were now assorted doublewides in various stages of sun-baked peeling paint. The rough neck drilling crews lived in them between their six-day twelve hour on and off shifts at the drill sites. Their Jeeps, big-wheel pickup trucks, dirt bikes and speedboats on trailers were strewn like children's toys around their rental homes. They worked a prospect until it was drilled out, and if married wired money home every payday. Most were single and wild on days off, like the end of the trail cowboys who drove cattle to the railheads like Dodge City in the old west. Their work was plain old fashioned dangerous, and many died in fiery explosions or heavy steel pipe stem collapses on the drilling rigs.

Trey and M talked over the wind and motor's throaty rumble as she calmly rally-style navigated him through the twisty turney hill country on the narrow recently-paved deserted county road at 100-120 miles an hour. Her ponytail peeked out of a baseball cap that said NDRA Champion.

He asked, "You're a drag race champion?"

"I won the classic hot rod roadster class at the Nation Drag Racing Championships in my senior year in high school. My father was my builder and mechanic. The win was for my half Jicarilla Apache and half French mother who died of breast cancer that year."

M commanded, "T-junction coming in a quarter of a mile onto the State Highway to Hesperus along the river. Right turn." He brought the Maserati down to zero with its ceramic drilled disc brakes and pinned M to her seat as her full breasts strained at her light-blue cotton tank top, causing her braless nipples to outline in the afternoon sunlight. She said excited, "Wow, no six-speed down shifting…just brake to stop and accelerate up shifting…no brake fade," as Trey made the right turn from a dead stop.

He smiled, "Yes state of the art no fade Italian Brembo racing brakes, my father had installed for mountain driving, but he stuck with the old school six-speed manual transmission like his ranch pickups not a new paddle automatic shifter. Where's the riverside park you mentioned? We'll stop there for dessert, brandy and a driver change."

"A few miles up then take a left past the State of Colorado Ag Research Station…then two hundred yards of gravel road to the river. It's a grassy spot but no picnic tables. You have a blanket?"

"In the trunk in a carry bag. It's real Italian grey wool with the Maserati logo in red. I think my parents may still picnic and have some fun on it under the big blue skies when they travel the west…also a couple, sterling silver collapsible cups," he replied dead pan.

M laughed and said, "I think I like your parents already."

Trey and M sat in the shade of an old cottonwood tree with a ten-foot scaly bark diameter by the riverbank. Its spring leaves were still light green as the sunlight filtered through and the irrigation dam-controlled river gurgled by. The parked Maserati sheltered them from the view of any vehicles driving into the pocket park. They talked about college and life after it. M was waitressing to save money for a trip to Canada in her

Shelby Mustang in early fall. Trey said he'd been called back to the ranch after extreme ski racing and ski patrolling in the winter and was waiting for family work orders for the summer. As they finished dessert he toasted with brandy in their cups,

"To fast cars and their drivers, beautiful rivers and ranches."

M blushed, smiled and downed her brandy. Then she leaned over and kissed an off-guard Trey. Her tongue was warm, and her wet lips caressed his. She pulled off her tank top and freed her breasts. Her light copper skin was front lit by the west sun light filtering through the late spring pale-green cottonwood tree leaves as it reflected off the river water. Her body was sleek yet rounded like the Maserati's lines. She lay back and pulled off her running shorts. She pulled Trey onto her stretched out athletic body. Her hardening nipples pressed into his Jackson Hole Rodeo Tee-shirt as they lost contact with the spring world around them.

M wound the Maserati motor to its fifth-gear red line and passed a tricked out blue metallic painted big-wheel, hemi motored, pickup truck at 150 miles an hour on a long white lined straight away. Trey saw its rack of ten high-powered off-road search lights on its roof as they blew by it. It was jacked up three feet to run in the Colorado Plateau high desert sage at night with ten ply off-road tires on its two thousand dollar a wheel custom black rims. He reported matter of fact glancing over at M, "Looks like a couple rough necks taking their prize horse to a Durango saloon tonight to look for female companions."

He noticed a worried look as she brought the Maserati down to a hundred miles an hour and said, "Shit they're not rough necks. I've seen that truck in the student parking lot at college, and outside a popular bar on Main Street in Durango. My girlfriend says they are Mexican cartel drug dealers that control the flow of cocaine, meth, fentanyl and opium into the Durango area now that pot is legal. They are very bad hombres. If they're coked up, I hope my fast pass doesn't set their machismo off. I'll stay at a hundred miles per hour with your state-of-the-art radar detector until the final speed zone through some old buildings in a couple miles before our turn at highway 160 east into Durango." He reached behind the driver's seat and pulled his 9mm Glock pistol out of its holster and chambered a round as he moved it to the logo-matted floorboard in front of him. M shot him another worried quick glance.

Two minutes later, M braked the Maserati to thirty-five miles an hour in the speed zone as they passed a boarded-up, peeling, white painted store, a café and a few old-style German stone houses in the left over sleepy farm settlement. But before she could accelerate when the sixty-mile an hour speed sign came into view the big-wheel pickup truck filled the rear-view mirror at high speed and shot around them.

Trey noted the pass, "As my mother Judy would say, good riddance to the bad pennies." Then suddenly the big-wheel pickup brake lights came on and it slowed to a stop. She braked hard when it trapped them in their lane with no head on visibility around it for a safe pass. It loomed over them like an oil tanker.

"Fuck it's trouble. Get ready for action." M stated flatly.

A second later, the blue-jeaned, Tee-shirted, shaved-headed Mexican driver jumped three feet down to the pavement and ran to the back of the big-wheeled pickup truck as Trey brought the pistol up to dashboard level and opened his window. The Mexican driver lifted his sharp-toed, black armadillo-skinned cowboy boot and cocked his leg to kick out the Maserati logo on its silver grill. But M had quickly shifted into reverse and gunned the Maserati backward as his roundhouse kick missed. Wide eyed he hit the pavement so hard falling forward off balance that his chin spurted blood.

Trey said quietly, "Gamble a blind pass on the driver's side of the big-wheels now. The passenger just leaped to the pavement with a pistol in his hand."

"Green light that," and she shifted into first gear to accelerate the Maserati to 60 miles an hour in four seconds. Its right side race Z front tire crunched over the extended right hand of the Mexican driver lying semi-conscious on the pavement. But the passenger was now facing Trey's window at ten feet with his right arm raised to fire a shot almost point blank into Trey's forehead. M wheeled the GT Coupe left toward the oncoming traffic lane to use the big-wheel truck as a shield. Trey fired one shot through his open window into the hard-eyed Mexican's shoulder and his pistol fell to the pavement. He careened backward into the high metallic-blue tailgate of the big-wheeled truck and ate a boat trailer's silver ball hook on the way down to the black top. M had the Maserati beside the big-wheels as Trey fired a round into each driver's side ten ply off-road tire on the close pass. They were gone in four seconds and back in their lane safely when M accelerated to one hundred miles an hour.

"Nice shooting, Trey...you have another treat coming if you stay in Durango tonight since it's a very bad idea to stop...even though I want all of you right now."

"It's your precision driving that saved our heads. I'm in Durango with you tonight. I want you safe. I want more than a stop for cold brew pub beer too. But we need a hide out. They can't call 911 or the sheriff but they can text their drug gang. My best guess they will figure we are headed west for Mancos then Cortez to Arizona or north to Delores then Telluride in the Maserati but not east to Durango on highway 160. I'll take the mountainous route from Durango to Silverton then the Million Dollar Highway to Ouray to Telluride tomorrow once your dad picks you up."

"I don't want to draw them to my dad's house. He's too old for a gunfight, which he would get into the middle of with his shotgun to protect me. I'll text him that I had to pull a shift tonight for another waiter at the last minute. My girlfriend will take me back by the main highway through Farmington, New Mexico to Aztec tomorrow. I have the perfect hide away hotel. It's the Rochester on Second Street with a secured off the street parking lot beside it. There's a very expensive boutique restaurant across the Street. It's a tourist foodie hang out. It's not on the street drug dealers' beat."

He replied as she turned on to US Highway 160 ten miles east of Durango and merged into the afternoon local and tourist traffic. "I'm on expenses this trip with the ranch credit card...a perfect plan. A car cover is in the trunk too. But last one to the hot tub buys the first cold beer."

"I played college soccer, ski boy. You don't stand a chance." Then M moved the Maserati into an uphill passing lane to motor around a big-box store, double-trailered truck and an RV from California at 90 miles an hour. She grasped his hand briefly letting it drop on to her bare smooth thigh below her running short's line. She released it to shift gears and complete the pass. Snow-capped peaks loomed in the distant view as the Maserati reached the peak of its climb and dropped quickly into Durango. The fast car and woman had ruled this day in Trey's young life. The stories about his father's gun fights to save the ranch and his great grandfather's gun hands had guided his shots to their targets without remorse. His grandfather's polo pony was the lighting fast nimble 650 GT Maserati. He had been raised old western ranch tough in the rapidly changing new west.

CHAPTER TWO

DINNER BELL AT THE YBARC

Trey braked the Maserati down fast and turned into the YbarC's new-ly-paved blacktop driveway with horse manure accenting it in a few spots. He pulled it up in front of the rebuilt Colorado yellow-brick ranch house and turned the powerful motor off. It was like the ranch stallions of old that had been tied to the long-gone wooden hitching rail, which had presided over a shallow, pine-plank, watering trough. He surveyed the late afternoon western sun's lengthening shadows as he climbed out of the GT coupe. He checked the Maserati's doors, fenders and grill for blood splat-ters before walking up the well-worn granite steps as four generations of Stuarts had done before him. The first four often had pistols in leather hol-sters strapped to their waists. The first three had usually arrived by saddle horses, which they worked the vast rangeland on.

The first two were Mormons who had fought the Church and the Ute Indians for the land with its abundant water and grass. They answered to no one including the US government in faraway Washington and the church in Salt Lake City. They didn't call a sheriff because there weren't phone lines until 1940. They walked to the bunkhouse and ordered their gun hands to settle disputes and protect the ranch's women and children.

Their wives were strong southern Rocky Mountain frontier women who endured isolation and brutal cold winter blizzards while birthing and raising children. They finally had electricity after President Franklin Roosevelt created the Rural Electric Co-ops in 1935. Trey knew he was born into a rapidly globalizing world where beef cattle on illegal clearings in the vanishing Brazilian Amazon rainforest tried to compete with beef from the YbarC's deep grass mountain pastures because corrupt dictators willed it. The Brazilians were still murdering Indians for their rangeland.

He ended his pause and strolled across the natural pine planked front porch. He wondered about why the sudden call to the ranch for this family meeting on an early spring day. But he knew four generations of family meetings in the ranch house library meant that a change of course was usually the agreed upon outcome. His always trim and fit mom Judy met him in the entrance hall with a big hug and kiss as her beauty-shop black-haired ponytail swished in the air like her long dead NCAA champion barrel racing horse's had.

She gushed, "Hello, Trey, welcome home. A good drive, I hope," even though he had only been gone a few days.

He hedged, "As good as one can expect in the Wild West. The snow is still on the high peaks above tree line with rivers running strong with snowmelt. Range grass is greening up. It looks like Ireland in some spots. Good grazing for the early spring with good irrigation water for hay all summer."

She quizzed, "And Durango, how was that?"

He replied, "A stop with a new friend who has a fast car and wanted a ride in the Maserati."

She probed, "He help you drive it?"

He only nodded not wanting to get into a girl discussion with his always-curious mom. He turned and walked toward the library where he knew his father would be waiting in his new reclining Santa Fe style chair. He would be sipping on a neat Scotch already poured two fingers deep in an old pottery cup from the Highlands that had survived the ranch house fire forty years ago.

The tall still lanky, greying dirty blond, tanned Cooper in his late fifties rose from his new reclining chair to shake hands.

"I see the fast black stallion finally got you here."

Trey ignored his father's probe too. "A fast drive with the usual stop in Aztec for a tasty southwestern taco lunch with a flan dessert and then Saturday night fun in Durango. Albuquerque is a big bore with TV news dedicated to nothing but mostly drug driven crime. Sirens day and night, even on Nob Hill by the University where I stayed in a renovated, Route 66-deco style motel. It was nearing final exam time, so the students were scarce, but I ate in a hip Chinese restaurant and drank beer in a huge brew-pub. I even walked over to the University Museum to take in a retrospective show of Albuquerque and Taos modernist art. They were called the 1950's Transcendentalism artists. Very color driven southwestern modern art but no ranches, cowboys and horses."

Cooper replied, "A lot of good western scenic, cowboy, Pueblo Indian and Spanish village adobe village art is in Taos and Santa Fe. If my Ute Indian friend Joe Bear Spirit had lived, he probably would be painting down there and living at our ranch."

Trey perceived in a split second that the about to begin discussion would be the family's sprawling ranch 40 miles north of Taos on the flanks of Ute Peak. He had been apprehensive about this conversation for some time. But his parents were aging out of operating two big ranchos and he knew they wanted to die on the YbarC. They had saved it forty years ago from the Telluride National Bank and the early greed-driven ski town developers, which still wanted its land and water rights. They had spilled too much blood in the fight to save it in their twenties to ever leave. Their story was legend on the Western Slope of Colorado, so he sat down in his grandfather's cowhide wagon wheel armchair, which had survived the ranch house fire in the bunkhouse office. He waited politely to hear them out. He had no desire to manage the Ute Peak Ranch yet.

Cooper sat down after he handed Trey a crystal tumbler of 12 year-old Scotch. Judy returned from the kitchen with a cheese plate, crackers and a mound of fresh beef tartar. Trey, hungry from the fast twisty mountain drive and a night with M, generously helped himself. Cooper opened the family poker game hoping he had an ace in the hole but not totally sure.

"Son, time's come for me and your mom to slow down a little bit and work shorter days and weeks. As you know over the last three decades, we've turned the Ute Peak Ranch operation into a moneymaker with cattle, hay and private elk hunting. It has continued to appreciate in value with the growth of Taos and its ski resort. Maestas our long-time foreman treats it like it is his own. He's old-school New Mexico Spanish and we mostly stay out of his way these days. He'll be seventy-five on his next birthday, and he needs to slow down a bit too, although he'll die in the saddle. It's time for our family to take the reins again. Your mom says the books show the ranch is debt free. So, in short, we need you to move down to northern New Mexico and take over the operation of the ranch since it will be yours someday. That someday is in five years when I turn sixty-five. I've been running the YbarC since I was in my twenties because of my father's polo accident, which killed him when I was ten. Your mom and I will stay on the YbarC until we die, although you will inherit it on my death. I don't know if this comes as a surprise to you?"

Trey held his poker cards close to his chest. He was only surprised that he would inherit the Ute Peak Ranch when he was thirty-one years old. "You all both know I can operate the New Mexico ranch. I grew up on this one and summer worked it too. Maestas is a traditional foreman who shields us as much as he can from the New Mexico cultural politics and outright hatred by a lot of New Mexico Hispanics and Pueblo Indians. I know you all pulled out of the full-time operation of the ranch because of the old colonial Spanish families' Land or Death movement. Your former Spanish girlfriend Adrianna and her half Ute Indian son Joe Bear Spirit Jr. are still involved in the movement. And I read online that drugs are a bad problem around Taos including opium, coke and fentanyl plus the usual booze. Do I relish swimming in that ecosystem? No is the answer. But my duty is to the family and our business is land, water rights and ranching it since we don't have any oil or natural gas on our properties. So, I'll give it a fair try." And he shielded his ace as he thought about the possibility of long winter ranch nights with M in his bed. She was a modern western girl whose cultural roots could help him. He'd text her after dinner.

"Well, that sounds like a yes," his father replied as his mom turned her head away to hide a worried look.

"It's a yes for up to five years," he hedged. "Do I get a gun hand like my great grandfather had on this ranch?"

"Then what?" Judy asked looking slightly stricken.

"If it's a no go for me down there then sell the place and put the money in trust for me. I grew up on the YbarC and went to school in Telluride and college in LA. My friends are here and in LA but not in New Mexico. Life is simpler around here these days. We only have the white gold snow cul-ture to deal with although the Mexicans are returning as low wageworkers co-mingled with, I hear, Mexican cartel hard drug dealers. Colorado's Southern Ute Native Americans are getting rich on oil, natural gas and casinos. In fact, they could buy this ranch like other tribes are doing in Nevada and Arizona. I'm sure, though, I can ski Taos Mountain and hang with the young art crowd. They both always need a drink and a meal. I'll get a hotel room in town for Saturday nights like you did in Telluride, Dad."

Busted, Cooper could only agree. "That's in the ranch budget, for sure. Plus, now you have high speed Internet and cell phone service at the ranch house plus satellite TV. The wired world as your generation calls it. You grew up fly-fishing the northern New Mexico and Southern Colorado rivers, elk hunting on the Ute Peak and at rodeos in the summer both sides of the border."

"I agree the ranch is an outdoor paradise in a sea of land. I'll ride in three days after I wrap up some things in Telluride. Let's eat. I know mom has a big meal ready in the kitchen with a secret dessert pie." Trey downed his remaining Scotch with a gulp, rose and strolled purposely toward the kitchen in his $1200 pair of black handmade custom cowboy boots, which had been a college graduation present.

After a sexy good night text to M to set up a lunch stop in Aztec on Wednesday, he fell asleep in the same bedroom he had since birth, that was decorated with his high school ski posters and sports letters on its walls. Trey had wolfed down a pancake with eggs over easy breakfast. He was headed into Telluride in a tan Ford-150 ranch pickup truck. He had planned to meet his high school friend Nick, the son of his father's old friends Brady, who had helped Cooper save the YbarC ranch in the late 1970s. Brady had been the head of Telluride's Ajax Ski Resort's ski school for thirty years. He still sculpted too, and Judy and Cooper had a half dozen of his best pieces. Before lunch Trey wanted to do a little shopping at Telluride's spring sales for hip warm winter clothes for his Taos move. He had the Ute Peak Ranch credit card in his grandfather's sterling silver money clip with a thousand dollars in fifties from the house's safe his mom had slipped him. His first stop was a trendy ski shop on Colorado Blvd, which a former high school girlfriend Meg now managed. They stayed in occasional touch on Facebook. He also planned to invite her out to dinner after work. He was staying in Telluride for the quiet off-season Monday night to catch up on the local news. Trey walked through the shop's door and the very pregnant pretty ski racer Meg looked up from the cash register surprised smiling.

"Hello, Trey, welcome home!" as she swished her blonde ponytail.

A surprised Trey couldn't take his eyes off her hip, bare mid-drift flowered top. "Well, I must have missed a Facebook post or Snapchat picture. Congratulations are in order," as Trey, mused that he must have also missed her wedding too. Suddenly his high school and college friends were getting married and starting families. He reminded himself that no marriage and no children was his mantra for a long while.

"We're finally getting married in a small family ceremony next week. Then I'll post all. Big bash after the baby is born and I can drink again. You don't know Jeb. He took over coaching the Ski Club's extreme ski race program last winter when he retired from the pro tour. He's in a lot of ski "porn" films with big lines and jumps in Alaska and Canada."

"I raced against him but really don't know him. Count me in on your celebration. I'll look for your post. I'm off to Taos, New Mexico this week to take over our family's operation of the Ute Peak Ranch, but I'm always good for a Telluride party." He smiled after the word party and remembered for a brief moment some of his high school party nights with the very blonde and very athletic Meg.

She paused remembering Trey was the heir to a historic ranching and water fortune in two states. Life with Jeb would be more exciting than working on a ranch, but she knew it would probably be paycheck-to-paycheck living in Telluride's affordable worker housing.

He caught her blue-eyed drifting look. "I'm gone for at least five years. I'll miss the Telluride scene and my friends. It's a lonely job on a big dusty New Mexico ranch forty miles north of Taos. At least I can ski there in the winter. So please show me your winter sale – everything and help me pick out some hip clothes for trips to Taos. I've got a thousand dollars in my money clip and a ranch credit card to boot. I'll help you clear out the winter inventory."

Meg moved around the counter and smiled, "That'll be my best commission sale during the off season. Let's get started." She walked past him with her ski slope grace.

An hour and a half later he put four full, large, brown-paper bags in the pickup truck's half door rear compartment. Meg had told him that Telluride's town council had banned plastic bags. He affirmed that was way good because his family was tired of pulling them off their barb wired fence lines. She had given him a long lingering hug with her now full breasts and belly pressed into his chest and stomach when he goodbye kissed her on the cheek. It was a farewell as their young lives, that had once intimately touched each other's, moved into the future.

Trey stared across a table at Nick's carefully-trimmed full beard, the current rage in Colorado ski towns, and wondered if he was a mountain man in his last lifetime and then asked, "How's life in the refrigerator?"

A tanned Nick laughed and replied, "The snow zone's always great and the summer music festivals are overcrowded with star level talent. On your front, another local high school girlfriend just slipped away."

"I know, her bare midriff tells all. Meg just outfitted me for winter in Taos. And I was hoping to dine with her after our drinks."

"You moving to your family ranch down in New Mex that we used to shoot prairie rattlesnakes on when your dad turned us loose with twenty-two rifles and a Jeep at twelve years old?"

"Yes and no. I've got family orders to report there this week and operate it. Then it's mine in five years. I'd rather work the YbarC and hang in T'ride winters to ski. New Mex has lots of crime, hard drug and alcohol problems that are mired in cultural interface. But I guess everywhere has more of those problems now," Trey replied.

"That's not a problem in my mind as a real estate agent. Our clients are begging for ranches around here. With the acreage I remember your New Mex ranch has it must be worth millions of dollars near Taos with its ski resort and new airport for commercial and private jets." Nick asserted and added, "I can't make that in a life-time splitting commissions on condos and houses in Telluride with the other hundred and fifty plus agents."

"I can't deny that. Just come down and hunt elk with me and ski once in a while. I hear your dad's sculptures are appreciating. I assume you have some?"

"I've two and as the only child I will handle the estate. It sad but true his artwork will be worth a lot more after he dies. That's the fine arts collectable world."

"So what's the latest word on the street about more development in and around Telluride?" Trey probed.

"Bigger global money than ever targeting us for condo hotels, large houses, especially in town. The problem is there are almost no empty lots to build on in town. There's a Jeep street and people sidewalk jam at summertime lunches. And on the sidewalks, you can trip over a micro dog's leash and face plant concrete as it bites your ankle. Then every hot woman you meet on the street asks for directions to the Green Room to legally buy pot and walks off without even a thank you."

"And the YbarC ranch?" Trey probed again.

"Every developer wants its land and legendary senior water rights. Your dad ever going to sell it? It's probably worth a hundred million dollars on any given day."

Trey paused and carefully answered, "No, he's operating it until he dies in the saddle."

"Then what?"

"It's mine. I'm an only child too."

"And then?"

"I'll operate it and probably sell the New Mexico ranch if I still have it."

"That'll be unpopular in Telluride, I'm sure you know," Nick asserted.

"How unpopular?"

"Maybe way worse than when our dads saved it," Nick replied adding, "Big mean money wants the water and land or development slows a lot around the Ajax Ski Resort. I hear some awfully extreme solutions in boozy conversations."

Trey's eyes turned ice cold blue. "Keep me posted if one of those conversations goes over the line, especially if there's a threat against my mother. My father and his hands can handle their end. But I will go gun hand like my father Cooper and his Ute friend Joe Bear Spirit did 30 years ago if my mom is threatened. My grandmother's death in the ranch house fire forty years ago was arson caused in my father's mind...not accidental as the coroner ruled. Also get yourself a New Mexico real estate broker's license. The Ute Peak Ranch sale is yours exclusively if we sell it in the future. That's maybe a million-dollar commission for you at closing. Your family has always ridden for our brand," Trey said forcefully.

"I'm all in the YbarC poker game. Remember I'm a junior agent and I may not always hear everything moving on the real estate wireless network...too much encryption these days...not like the bar coke fueled talk of our dad's era," Nick replied.

"You'll hear more as you move up the pay grades. The box canyon walls still reverberate the news and gossip. Drink up. Time to hit the Sheridan Bar for a little pool and see if any women are looking for free off-season drinks."

Nick nodded in agreement. "Off season getting a little boring. The Bluegrass Festival women are still six weeks away." He tossed down a final shot of Tequila as Trey dropped a fifty-dollar bill on the counter and ignored M's text message on his iPhone alert. His cowboy boots were already moving out Oak's door on to the deserted gondola plaza.

Trey returned to the ranch on Tuesday morning at sunup. After a horseback cow calf check with Cooper, he returned to the ranch house to start packing. First, he texted M, 'Confirm I'll meet you in Aztec for lunch tomorrow noon. Can you get a few days off? I'm moving to my family's ranch at Costilla New Mexico 40 miles north of Taos to take over operating it. I could use some help moving in and we can spend some ranch time together. I miss you already. I'll drive you back, but in a ranch pickup. Hope you still like me sans the Maserati Trey.'

While he was packing his clothes in a North Face rolling duffle bag her text reply came in. 'That's major news. You're only two fast state highway pickup truck hours away from me now. I traded shifts…need to be back Monday at 10 am unless you put me on your payroll. Rounding up my cowgirl boots, spurs, jeans, shirts, hat and slicker. I can ride a horse too. A high school girl friend's family had a stable. I got paid to help her exercise the boarders before I got my driver's license. -M

Judy walked in as Trey deleted the text delighted that M could ride and drive fast. His mom caught his look, "Are your Telluride friends texting you goodbyes?"

"Not yet, but Nick and Meg are spreading the word. She's pregnant and marrying a famous ski film model. Nick is starting up the real estate ladder. He's my eyes and ears in Telluride like his father was for Cooper." And he didn't ID the text messenger.

"I always liked Meg but knew she wasn't a ranch wife to be after competing on the ski racing circuit. Can I help you pack?"

"Yes and no. I have my clothes under control. But what's the ranch house's cooking and bedding situation?"

"I've packed a box of new sheets, blankets, and pillows for the master bedroom. There's a washer and dryer there now. The housekeeper comes a day every two weeks from the nearby farm and artist village of Jarosa. Her name is Rosa Garcia. If you want her weekly, work it out. She bills me here. There should be plenty of kitchen utensils. The bunkhouse cook is on Monday through Saturday lunch. He will cook for you. Maestas lives in the foreman's adobe house near the ranch house but still has a family home on the historic Costilla Plaza. As you remember his wife died a few years ago but with you on the ranch he may stay nights at the Plaza more. The ranch house needs a makeover after we restored it thirty years ago. It's a historic adobe hacienda. Next Monday, David our local building contractor will meet you at 5PM. I've authorized up to fifty thousand dollars to repair, modernize and paint it. You're taking the two-year-old Ford F-150 red five-speed pickup from here. Maestas will go over the ranch's rolling stock and horses with you. All the ranch bills and invoices are issued or paid from my office here. However, you have a ranch $10,000 petty cash checking account with an ATM card at Taos bank." Trey low whistled to himself. He had grown up with his mother at the financial helm of the two big ranches. His father had never written a check or paid a bill and rarely even had cash in his pockets. Judy continued, "You start with a monthly three-thousand-dollar personal cash draw for operating the ranch. The ranch pays all operating costs including your pickup truck, food and housing. What you do with the draw is your business. You'll receive an annual cash bonus each December depending on each year's profits. I'll handle the ranch's various tax filings and payments. If you desire, I'll handle your personal tax filings and you pay them. Or you get a CPA in Taos. It's your call. That's the long and short of it. We'll work our other financial details as they pop up."

"Thanks, Mom. I'll get a CPA to handle my taxes," Trey replied exerting some independence. He continued, "And my estimated bonus in a good water year?"

"Thirty to fifty thousand dollars a year depending on cattle and hay prices."

"How about throwing in the Maserati for the winter months?" He smiled.

"It's your father's new toy and that's between the two of you."

"Well, that's a very comprehensive briefing. Thanks? I'm sure I'll have more questions as I settle in but I'm good for now. See you for lunch when I finish packing. Love you."

"Your position still that you may only stay up to five years? Your father is concerned about that," she stated.

"Nothing has changed on that front. This ranch and Telluride are my home. I'll see how New Mex goes. Nick is getting a New Mexico real estate license if I bail at any point, and we sell it." He turned to continue packing his rolling black ski duffle.

CHAPTER THREE

THE HIGH PASS MEADOW

Trey drove the red pickup truck hard through the tight uphill curves toward the top of the ten-thousand-foot high Cumbres Pass. The highway climbed past the 1880's narrow gauge railroad tracks. Its wood-fired tourist train belched a column of white smoke below them. M was nestled in the passenger seat in jeans and a Tee-shirt with her cowgirl boots off. Her big brown eyes followed the train's slow ascent on the steep grade. Trey's duffel bag, bedding box, saddle, ski and ranch gear was roped down in the pickup truck's bed. He had a repeating rifle behind the seats under M's weekend soft elk-skin leather travel bag. His Glock 9 pistol was under the fold down center seat console. The radio played country music with occasional weather updates and auto dealer commercials. Chevy pickups were on sale today the ads boldly asserted with 'get one while they last with no payments for six months' tag lines.

He joked to M, "They never advertise buy one and get one free."

M noted, "The train's curling white smoke makes you feel like you are in the old west. It's hard to believe that's how people crossed this pass from Chama, New Mexico to Antonito, Colorado before cars and pickup trucks to reach the San Luis Valley mines, farms and ranches. I wonder how many brides and women of the night made a one-way trip on this train."

"That's an interesting take on old west travel. I always thought about the trains hauling farming and ranching equipment, building supplies, mining machinery, horses, cattle, food, gamblers, gun hands, businessmen and soldiers," he replied.

"That's because you are all boy, not a girl. Your mind thinks of things that help own, build, feed, and protect us in the frontier Rocky Mountains. A girl's mind in the old wild west searched for family, a safe civilized community, love, and always survival."

Trey moved his right hand over the soft fabric covered console onto M's denim-covered firm thigh. "So why do modern women leave town to drive across this rugged pass in winter snow blizzards and summer monsoon thunder and lightning storms."

She pressed his hand lightly into her inner thigh as his fingers touched her jeans inseam. "It's still the same, Trey, in the New West. I haven't stopped thinking about you since our trip to Durango. Find a Forest Service road at the top of the pass and pull over in a pine tree grove by a secluded meadow. Let's breathe some pure, cool, high mountain air and stretch our legs and bodies. You can provide security for me from wild bears, mountain lions and rogue men while I taste your kiss and we walk. Now put your hand back on the steering wheel on these tight uphill curves."

The pickup climbed a final pitch to the top of the ten-thousand-foot pass that was surrounded by mountain snowfields on the above tree line grey rock faces. Trey turned it into a dry but rutted gravel road and slowed. Two hundred yards latter he turned on to a dirt track that ended in a grove of tall pine trees by a weathered wood plank cattle loading corral while M pulled her cowgirl boots on. The cattle were a couple weeks away from arrival to their high-altitude, deep, green grass summer pastures. He parked the truck by a snow cleansed rock fire ring left by the previous fall's elk hunters. He stepped down out of the pickup breathing the joy of the cool clean high air, which invigorated his body and mind. M opened her door, jumped down from the pickup and landed squarely in front of Trey as he rounded it. Her warm kiss found his lips as his cowboy shirted chest felt the outline of her breasts. They kissed a long minute before he said, "I don't have a blanket handy. It's in the taped-up bedding box in the back of the pickup. But we can make love cowboy style on the open range if you please. Just turn around drop your jeans to your boot tops after you unsnap and unzip mine."

"I knew you could figure out a solution to the no blanket problem to keep us off the hard cold ground."

She smiled as she unbuckled his handcrafted silver belt buckle and unzipped his ranch work jeans. She dropped them to his cowboy boot tops with his underwear. Her fingers teased him. She turned and braced her hands against the edge of the pickup's seat and said, "Your turn, cowboy. My panties are in my purse. I fantasied being in this high alpine meadow pine grove in my dream about you last night. I'm falling in love with you even though I'm not from your ranch world. Please remember if you make love to me that I'm not a lady of the night on the train but a would-be bride traveling up life's winding tracks." They heard the train's long whistle as it cleared the top of the pass and started its steep descent to Antonito Colorado.

He unsnapped her faded blue jeans, which dropped over her firm copper hips onto her boot tops. His hands found bare breasts under her Tee-shirt and they made love. When their bodies finally parted M whispered like the cool breeze, "Let's take a long walk in the meadow's refreshing spring air. That was perfect, Trey. Let's keep making it a perfect day as we descend the pass and drive to your ranch."

He replied, "I feel at peace for the first time in months, M. This will be our special get away meadow when we drive the pass." He kissed her again before they walked into the sunshine and the greening spring grass hand in hand.

Trey pulled the red pickup into the gravel horseshoe driveway of the sprawling 1850's adobe Hacienda as the late afternoon sun dropped to the west of Ute Peak. Six-foot high thick adobe walls with gun ports surrounded it. The front hand forged wrought iron gate began to creak open revealing the Hacienda's solid hand-carved wooden front door. He pulled into a gravel-parking place next to an almost antique car show maintained Chevy pickup.

M said, "Your ranch house could be a Spanish colonial museum. Are you going to really live in it?"

Trey sheepishly replied, "A bit different from my apartment I based out of in Breckinridge for ski comps. Mom says it needs refreshing and she gave me a big budget. I need your thoughts." The heavy wooden front door opened, and a sun-wrinkled faced, white sweat-stained cowboy hatted Maestas walked out to greet them, clearly surprised to see M.

"Let's say hello to Maestas the ranch foreman. He's run this operation for thirty years and is kind of a grandfather to me when I'm here. He'll settle us in with a tour. I haven't been here since I graduated from college. You want the guest room?"

"No, I'm sleeping with you. I want you close by not stumbling around in the dark to my room. Are there ghosts in the hacienda house?"

"Maybe and maybe not. It depends on whom you talk to. There was a Ute Indian raid on the hacienda when they attacked and captured the nearby historic fortress Costilla Plaza in 1852 taking 163 prisoners. There were deaths but Kit Carson's Taos militia tracked the Utes north to the now town of Saguache Colorado and surprise attacked them. They re-captured all the prisoners and returned the survivors from the ranch."

"That's all I need to know. Your bedroom. Let's not keep Maestas waiting any longer." She exited the pickup facing him face to face. Maestas froze when he saw M's exotic beauty and clocked she wasn't an Anglo ranch girl.

Trey said, "Maestas meet Maria Duran better known as M. She's here to visit and help me settle in. She's a stable-trained horsewoman too but not raised to work a ranch. So you'll need to help show her the 'ropes' so to speak with the ranch horses. First let's unload the household things from the pickup and then you can drive my saddle and ranching gear over to the tack room by the bunk house. Leave my guns for now in the pickup and lock it after we unload. Here's my spare key. Then show us around the Hacienda. It's my new home. You look good."

"Welcome, Trey, and, Ms. Maria. Cooper, and Judy called me and explained the changes in the operation of the Ute Peak Ranch to me in full. I report to you on ranch matters but Judy still runs the financial operations for now. Let's get your things into the Hacienda." His flat voice signaled he was not totally comfortable with the change of command. M was clearly a surprise and he wondered if Cooper and Judy knew about her.

Trey and M took their luggage to the master bedroom and Maestas followed them with the new bedding's box. While Maestas returned to the pickup for the remaining household items, they surveyed the room. Trey embarrassed said, "This is a dump. Peeling paint, cracked plaster, broken

Mexican floor titles and no King bed. A total makeover is in order."

M added politely, "Some wonderful Spanish antiques that could use a real cleaning, and great Taos art, but sun-faded droopy curtains, worn out pillow covers and bedspread, a dusty record turntable, a pink princess phone and the eight-track music cassette player and more. Time for a clean up and throw out."

"We'll start tomorrow moving my parents' stuff to the guest room and give the builder marching orders to remodel this room first and I'm sure its bathroom too. Let's go meet Maestas for the tour."

They followed Maestas through the hacienda's 12 rooms that formed a square around its enclosed central plaza with a flagstone veranda. When they reached the kitchen Trey commented, "Every room needs plastering and painting. There are cracked floor titles everywhere. The windows need to be modernized and replaced by Anderson with built in screens and most of them enlarged."

"You need a flashlight to see in here," M asserted and Maestas frowned as she added, "And the overhead fans look like they were in the Vietnam War movie I saw."

They walked into the kitchen and M was actually startled. "This is a dangerous disaster with fire ready to strike. Frayed wiring is tacked onto the adobe walls to the 1950 era appliances. Do they even work? Can I even make coffee and toast in here?" Maestas frowned again.

"You're in charge of the kitchen remake. Write it up tomorrow. I want it Maserati modern. I'll order a complete rewire and remodel of this adobe dump from the contractor. Some of this wiring looks eighty years old from when the REA electric co-op wired this place. We probably have glass fuses. I just checked the fire extinguisher. It was last checked and refilled fifteen years ago. It has zero pressure. My mom and dad modernized the ranch operations and made it profitable by saving dollars on the house since they mainly lived in Colorado at the YbarC. I'd rather move to a hotel room in Taos to manage the ranch than live in this dazed adobe," Trey asserted to no one in particular.

Maestas did not comment and led them into the library that had red streaks in its well-swept polished hard mud floors. M's mouth dropped open and she asked, "Is this a hardened mud floor with decorative red paint in it? Any of the 1960's Taos commune hippies hang out in here before your parents bought the ranch?"

Maestas answered, "Yes, it's a hardened mud with ox blood floor and some say the Indian raider's blood in it from the 1850's the Old Spanish way."

M lifted her cowgirl booted feet high off the floor one at a time backing out of the library. She quietly said, "My mother was half Apache who was born sixty miles west as the eagle flies. That could be her ancestors' blood I'm walking on. This is Spanish barbarism. I can't be in this room."

Trey swooped her up in his arms and carried her through the low arched doorway bumping his head. "It's gone tomorrow at sunup. Maestas, get two ranch hands and the impactor to tear it out. Then take it to the far reaches of the west facing canyon on Ute Peak and spread it so the wind blows it away. The house tour is over. M, let's take a sunset walk around the ranch buildings. Maestas, please send the bunkhouse cook over with our dinner and set it on the dining room table by seven. We'll take care of the rest tonight. Thank you for the tour. No wonder Judy gave me a budget to remodel this place on arrival. It's a Spanish colonial relic." He put M down as Maestas walked out of the kitchen and her tears rolled off her cheeks onto Trey's cowboy shirt. She cried pressing her face into his chest:

"Now you know what it's like to grow up part Apache Indian, part Spanish and a little French. They all scalped each other around here in the old west." And more uncontrolled tears flowed.

Trey asked M to stay and meet with the contractor to go over the remake of the kitchen. He agreed to buy out her Monday café shift for $150 and charge it as a consulting fee to the Hacienda remodeling account. As they completed the walk through with David, the well-muscled forty-something building contractor said, "These are the first round of remodeling orders."

"I'm sure there will be more after you start work, with change orders. Write up a contract and I will sign it and scan a copy to my mother. Are there any questions or other thoughts? What is your ballpark cost?"

David replied, "At least $90,000 plus another $10,000 for change orders. Judy approved a budget not to exceed $50,000. What do you want to cut? Modernizing the windows is a major expense. It's probably $50,000."

"Nothing, I operate the ranch now and this place is an adobe dazed dump. Judy will pay it all or I'll move to the Taos Inn. Have her scan you a counter signed contract after I sign mine. Ute Peak Ranch is moving into 2019. This is just the beginning of changes I am going to order ranch wide.

I need you to start yesterday so you can roll men and equipment on Monday a week. Start on the master bedroom and bath first. Make sure you order everything on M's kitchen equipment list first thing. Bring the contract over ready for me to sign by Wednesday close of business and I'll see your crew on Monday 8 am sharp." David looked happy to have a bigger contract and Maestas was silently stunned. Trey led M out of the kitchen by her hand and they walked out onto the Hacienda's interior plaza into the spring sun.

M asked, "You're double your mother's budget. Is that wise? You and I could live with two or three phases of remolding as long as the kitchen, bathrooms, master bedroom and guest bedroom get done first."

He answered, "You are very thoughtful, but I didn't request this family assignment with no input at this time in my life. She will approve it, or I live in Taos and commute here. There's plenty of money in the ranch's bank account to pay for the work that should have been done annually and not deferred. Plus, my mom is a businesswoman. She knows if I decide not to operate the ranch for five years to own it outright that the remodel of the Hacienda will help sell it. The sale money will be held in trust for me."

"Let's get a couple horses and take a sunset ride. It's too beautiful an afternoon to waste in adobe darkness," M suggested. She didn't want to intervene in a potential money battle between Trey and his mother.

He kissed her and led her back into the Hacienda and out its side door toward the tack room. He picked out riding gear for her and told a cow-hand to saddle a horse for him and one for M. They walked back to the red pickup truck where he retrieved his repeater saddle rifle in its handmade leather horse holster. A seasoned rugged faced cowhand met them at the Hacienda gate with two Paint horses.

Trey asked, "Are these fast sure-footed ponies?"

"They are, sir, our two best riding range horses. The 17-hand high stallion Big Spots is for you. Your lady's mare is Blue Satin the best riding horse on the ranch. Your mother Judy rides her when she is here. If you're riding into the sunset keep your eyes peeled for a big male mountain lion. He has been spotted this spring hunting the antelope in late afternoon coming out of the low west sun. They can outrun him but you all can't."

As Trey rigged his saddle rifle he replied, "I've got it covered but I don't want a big cat pow wow, so we'll be alert. We're riding over to the Rio Grande River Gorge where State Line Road meets it. Was the cat seen over there?"

"No, usually on the south side of the mountain. A person never tries to outthink a mountain lion," the cowhand replied.

"I don't," agreed Trey. They mounted and rode off due west, throwing up dust.

A half hour later, they were sitting on a warm flat-topped black basalt rock overlooking a four-hundred-foot drop into the Rio Grande River Gorge. The snowmelt's high spring runoff made a dull roar through the class three rapids below them. The horses were tethered behind them to a lone errant leaning steel fence post.

"Beautiful spot. How can we ride down there?" M asked.

"Not enough time before nightfall and a better trail drops in north up the Gorge a few miles where it shallows out near the Lovato Bridge. This old trail's a little steep. It's for sheep and shepherds to walk in and out to ford the river," he replied as the sound of a vehicle came toward them. Trey walked back to his horse and pulled the saddle rifle out of its holster as a dented fifteen-year-old blue Dodge pickup truck approached them. He stood next to M and chambered a bullet. "Hopefully, they are sightseeing to look into the gorge. If not and trouble starts, drop behind the rock. Hopefully it doesn't."

"Roger that."

The pickup came to a stop and after a long couple minutes a sun-bleached, sandy-headed, teenage boy and black haired, ponytailed girl popped out. They were clearly surprised to see people at their after school hangout spot. The freckle faced boy said, "Howdy, you from around here or are you lost riders from the airbnb house in the sage north of the road."

Trey replied, "Newly arrived but from around here. I'm Trey Stuart and this is M, my girlfriend. I've moved down here from Colorado to operate the Ute Peak Ranch that my parents own. We're out for a sunset ride."

"The UP they call it around here. I'm Rick This is Annie, my girlfriend. We're freshman in Alamosa Colorado at Adams State College. I play quarterback there. Annie's a soccer player. So, you're Cooper Stuart's son. My dad operates the Jensen Ranch just across the border. We grow a lot of alpha hay. If the UP is short some, we cover your winter-feed shortfall. Is Maestas your foreman still? His nephew's a hand on our ranch."

"Maestas is our long-time foreman...good to meet you." Trey lowered his rifle. "We'll mount up and return your sunset spot. We've got a bit of a ride before dark." Annie blushed as M knowing smiled. "Any local scouting reports for our ride back?"

"If you see a low flying twin engine airplane then ride to cover so they can't spot you. The Mexican cartel drops drugs usually due west across the gorge on federal land but sometime on this side. Big-wheel pickups are waiting in the cottonwoods along the irrigation ditches or in the dry Rio Costilla riverbed over here. If you get too close they'll shoot a warning shot at you and worse. They raped a girl in Annie's high school class who was late riding home alone at sunset after her horse threw a shoe." M blanched and Annie looked away saddened.

"You be careful too," M added. "I know their kind. I went to College in Durango. They hung around the Main Street student bars." She did not want to reveal their Maserati shootout, so she added, "I hope you're armed when you're out here." They both nodded as Trey and M mounted and spurred the Paints into a gallop toward the hacienda.

M smiled at Trey. "So I have been promoted from kitchen consultant to girlfriend since my riding is as good as my driving all in one day."

He smiled, "That's my thought but only if you want to be. It's not a family assignment like operating the UP. You handle Blue Satin like you handled the Maserati."

"I'm all in for girlfriend. Let's work these ponies a little on the way back. Look out for mountain lions and low-flying planes too. Then we wipe down these sweaty ponies at the stable followed by a shower together and a cold beer in the hacienda living room." She spurred her Paint horse to a full gallop.

CHAPTER FOUR

HOME ON THE RANGE

Two weeks had passed since Trey had dropped M off in Aztec when he heard her Shelby Mustang's motor growling as it closed in on the hacienda. They had texted and talked back and forth daily while Trey took charge of the ranch operations and supervised the remodel. His mother had approved the $110,000 budget but his father had refused to talk to him about it or anything else since then. M had worked fourteen straight cafe shifts to get a week off. He spurred his Paint horse and raced the black Shelby Mustang to the horseshoe driveway. He pressed the wrought-iron-gate's new remote opener in his faded-blue work-shirt pocket and followed the car into the hacienda's parking area. Suddenly M did a semi-circle spin and braked it to a dusty stop that sent gravel flying. The Paint horse reared but Trey brought the stallion's front hooves down safely. His look at her was not one of amusement.

M scrambled out smiling. "Oops, I'm in trouble now. Am I fired as girlfriend for forgetting range ponies hate hot rod spins? Do I have to sleep in the haunted guest room?" Her wit and smile won Trey's heart. He dismounted and kissed her long and hard.

"I have to remember to watch out for mountain lions, low flying airplanes and now your hot rod Shelby Mustang. Life's been very cowboy around here while you've been gone. I'll tie Big Spot up next to the Mustang and they can get acquainted. Let's go in and check out the remodel. The workmen just left for the day. The kitchen is halfway complete, and the master bedroom and bath are done. The dining room's a mess. We'll have to eat in Red River tonight at Texas Reds, the best steak house around here."

"Start the tour and please get me some ice-cold water. I had to toss a leaking organic corn water bottle out the window on the way over." They walked through the heavy wooden front door into the living room. It was a montage of scaffolding, paint drops, stacked cut titles, electric saws and a slight fresh paint smell. A windowless opening in the high ceiling great room had been enlarged. The hole was covered in thick plastic waiting for a ten-foot-wide custom Anderson framed window with sliding screens.

"Wow, Trey they are on it." And she walked toward the kitchen. She exclaimed. "A perfect stainless-steel stove and double door refrigerator. Once they install the hood over the stove then I can cook you a meal. I love the all-new Italian tile floor. It's just as I imagined for a Maserati kitchen look. That empty hole over there is for the new stainless-steel sink, garbage disposal and dishwasher. They're doing a great job. No worries. Let's see the master bedroom." He handed her a cold bottle of Fiji water from the refrigerator.

"Follow me but watch your step because they have paint drops everywhere and have cut electrical conduit troughs into the adobe walls. The bedroom has in-floor radiant heat now under the new Spanish tiles."

"Wow and a king bed too." And she back flopped onto it pulling Trey down onto her and kissed him hard.

An hour later, they finished showering and dressed for the Texas Red's steak dinner. A smiling ponytailed tight-cut cowgirl shirted M said, "Now that was my best welcome back ever."

Trey countered, "Your best welcome home on the range ever. This old hacienda is adopting both of us. And Blue Satin's resting in her stall waiting for you."

"We'll ride tomorrow after I tackle the antique Spanish dresser, chest and armoire with a little tender love and natural pine cleaning oil I brought. Now I'm hungry. I've eaten nothing since breakfast but an energy bar. We'll take the Shelby Mustang and cut the drive time. Grab two cold beers from the fridge and it's go-fast time."

Trey and M had been riding two hours checking the extreme southwest corner of the ranch's grazing land and part of its summer herd of Black Baldy cows and calves. He was impressed by the health of the cattle on dry land pasture spring grass. He looked up as he heard the sound of an airplane engine, which was not unusual. The recently modernized Taos Airport's flight path north to Denver, Alamosa and Colorado Springs was near the west boundary of the ranch. He hand-signaled M to rein in her paint horse and stop beside him.

"Let's watch the plane because it's lower than the normal flights I've seen over the west side of the Rio Grande River Gorge except for three Apache military helicopter gunships practicing low flying attack runs. They're from the Air Force Academy in Colorado Springs according to the ranch hands."

"Should we look for cover as the teens suggested?" M asked with an apprehensive look.

"Not yet, it's holding a due north route and there really isn't any place to hide horses on this two-thousand-acre open pasture this close to the Gorge, which is four hundred feet deep here." Five seconds later, the twin engine airplane banked sharply east and dropped lower to cross the Gorge as it headed straight for them.

"Follow me. There's an old travel trailer about a half-mile south, that my neighbor uses for his cowhand when they summer graze across our fence line on New Mexico State lease land. The green gate to it is unlocked so our ranch hands can look for cattle that sometimes escape. Spur Blue Satin." And he took the lead at full gallop.

The silver-grey twin-engine airplane crossed the Gorge and screamed in low. A large tan canvas wrapped bundle fell from its passenger side door and landed two hundred yards from them. The plane went over them at 300 feet off the ground as it pulled into a steep climb over the San Luis Valley and headed east toward the mountains. They rode their horses at full gallop and Trey hoped the sure-footed range smart Paint horses didn't panic as the airplane's prop wash hit them like a dust devil. The Paints snorted but kept their fast gallop along the five-strand barbwire fence line as the green gate loomed. Trey hand signaled as he slowed his horse to dismount and open the gate. M pulled her horse up beside Big Spot and took the reins from Trey. He dismounted quickly, released the gate chain and swung it wide open. Then he looked up too late. A big-wheel stripped down roofless twenty-five-year old metallic brown Ford Bronco had emerged from behind the beat up silver cowhand's trailer, It was racing at 60 miles an hour across a rough ranch track toward the open gate.

"We're out of here east inside the ranch's fence line." He remounted and they swung the Paint horses hard left and spurred them.

Fifty yards down the fence line on the ranch road Trey glanced over his shoulder as the Bronco charged through the gate and turned to follow them. Suddenly the passenger stood up and fired five semi-automatic rifle shots at them. Trey shouted to M, "Go fast." Then he reined in Big Spot to a perfect dismount stop and pulled his saddle rifle out from its holster. The high clearance Bronco was slow coming out of its ninety-degree turn. He fired a heart shot, and the passenger went limp, falling backwards into his seat as his rifle flew into the air. M heard the shot and glanced back just as Trey remounted and rode hard to catch up to her. The Bronco driver broke off the chase, turned and raced through the sage at forty miles an hour to recover the tan canvas covered bundle that was beeping loudly. Trey caught up with M a half mile down the fence line. They brought their horses to a stop.

Trey said, "Call 911." M pulled her iPhone from her jeans hip pocket and punched it in. After a few long seconds she reported,

"There's no signal here."

"Fucking sage squatters blocked the new cell tower. Something about imaginary radiation, Maestas told me." He pulled his mini binoculars from his cowboy shirt pocket and glassed the Bronco.

"The driver is loading the canvas bundle into the Bronco. It's not a burlap bag pot bale. It's too small. Hard drugs for sure like cocaine, fentanyl, meth and heroin the Taos newspaper says is out of control around the county. Dismount and we will use our horses for a shield. My guess he will drive hard for the green gate to escape. We're out of the chase. He may have the AR 15 high volume round semi-automatic rifle the passenger was firing at us. I couldn't see if it landed in the Bronco. Zoom in your iPhone eleven video and film the Bronco while I keep my rifle sight on him."

"The passenger isn't moving, and his shirt is blood red. He has long black hair," M stated matter of factly.

"I fired a heart shot. We were dead if he kept spraying AR-15 rifle rounds when they closed in on us," he replied without remorse.

"Good decision. I guess you learned to shoot like that growing up on a ranch?"

"By ten years old. No 911 calls on a big ranch. You ride and work alone a lot."

"He's driving toward the gate. I have the Bronco in full frame." M added.

Through his binoculars Trey picked up a white late model SUV with a black cattle grill guard approaching the open green gate.

"Swing the camera to the white SUV approaching the green gate. OMG it looks like a Sheriff's vehicle with its rack of lights and long radio antenna. Maybe we have help but how?" M continued to iPhone video as he kept glassing the two vehicles. They stopped side by side after the Bronco crossed through the gate, which obscured the SUV's logo.

"It's not help…the deputy is looking right at the bleeding passenger and they're talking. The dirty deputy is covering the drug drop just like in the movies. Secure your iPhone and we'll ride hard into the sage on a game trail back toward the ranch that the SUV can't follow. Pull up your bandana in case he has a camera. The game trail ends at a deep arroyo that comes off Ute Peak a mile ahead. We'll hide in it until we're sure they're gone. Then we ride back to the ranch and figure out what to do next. One thing I know for sure they will not drop drug shipments across our ranch's side of the Gorge again. You good to ride?"

"The answer is yes. Good thing I drag raced. This all happened so fast you don't have time to think about it…just react. I've watched a couple toasted dead drivers pulled out of fiery crashes. We'll debrief at the hacienda," she replied.

"And not even a hint to Maestas or the cowhands. I don't want them involved and possibility targeted. Now I know why these shipments are going unchecked. The question is how to stop them, and that will take some thought." And he spurred his horse toward the mountain and to the safety of its deep arroyo. They reached the edge of the arroyo and listened for the sound of vehicle engines. Trey glassed the green gate area with his binoculars.

He reported, "No sight or sound of them. Let's rest the horses and try to figure out our course of action. I'm tired of being attacked by Mexican cartel drug dealers. Could you ID their faces while you videoed them?"

"The drug dealers both looked Hispanic, maybe the one you shot part

Indio. I couldn't tell if they were locals or Mexican cartel. The deputy was too far away and stayed in the SUV with the window rolled down, but he was backlit. No ID was possible." She replied continuing, "The bloodied shooter never moved except to bounce with the Bronco. My best guess, he's dead. They made no effort to bandage him up to rush him to a hospital. We can look at the iPhone video tonight."

"His body will probably be dumped into the gorge. How could either of them explain the cause of his condition at the Taos Emergency Room or to the State Police with a Taos flight for life helicopter crew out here? Then they will split up once the drug shipment is secured in a safe house, which could be one of a thousand adobe houses countywide either occupied or abandoned. The question is will they lay low and wait to see if we file a police report. Or will they be proactive and look for us, figuring we might have seen the Sheriff's Department logo on the SUV doors and might bypass the local law enforcement agencies and go to the Feds…FBI or DEA," Trey outlined.

"And if they are proactive, then will the deputy probe the UP ranch or ranches around it? There is no way he could ID us at that range from the SUV without binoculars, which I never saw him use. The Bronco driver was too busy driving fast on rough ground in sage to ID us except maybe that we were riding Paint horses," she replied concerned.

"I agree and dead men tell no tales, which rules the shooter out. So I'll have a cowhand horse trailer the Paint horses tonight and drive them to the YbarC. I'll tell Maestas my father called me and needs them. I'll text my father there was an attempt to rustle them here. He knows purebred Paints bring top dollar. We'll cut your week's visit short here using the hacienda construction as an excuse. Tomorrow morning we'll pack a couple of my fly rods and camping gear in the Mustang and head north for Pagosa Springs Colorado to hot spring and fly fish. We'll also visit my father's former Spanish girlfriend Adrianna and her half Ute son Joe Bear Spirit Jr. in nearby Tierra Amarillo. I haven't seen them in a decade, but father wants me to visit them. I'll explain more of their history on the way. Your thoughts?"

"You think we're safe in the ranch house tonight?" she asked.

"Safer than traveling tonight. We don't know the extent of the dirty local police network to protect the drug drops. It probably extends across the border into Southern Colorado, which is along our route. It's better for us to travel during the day on busy highways. We cross the Taos County line and New Mexico border eight miles from the ranch house into Costilla County, which I hear is the most corrupt, drug ridden and poorest county in Colorado. My guess is that the plane is dropping drug bundles on both sides of the border in the sage flats on the west side of the Gorge. Also I'll post a cowhand on hacienda watch tonight on the excuse some of the new windows are not installed," he stated.

"That all works for me. So what next?"

"The horses have had a good breather. Let's ease them back to their stalls and rub them down. Then we'll have a drink with a soak in the new hot tub in the master bathroom…clothing optional." He smiled, adding, "Since we're confined to quarters tonight. I was going to take you to dinner in Taos."

"Only if you get rid of that doggie look." And she trotted off on Blue Satin.

M pulled the Mustang into the 1960's style Hot Springs Motel's parking lot in Pagosa Springs Colorado around noon and they checked into room 112 for three nights. After they unloaded the luggage and fly-fishing gear into their room they drove into town for lunch at a small town café with two big picture windows. After lunch as M pulled out of a Main Street parking place

Trey asserted, "The best pimento cheese sandwich on the planet. We'll hot spring tonight. Now we're going drive to Adrianna's office in Tierra Amarillo, which is about forty-five minutes south of here. She texted me back that she was in her office this afternoon until five. She manages the Land or Death Foundation that succeeded the Allianz. It's been trying to return the 20,000 original Spanish settlers in New Mexico there the stolen land grants they received from the King of Spain. In 1967 the Allianz members attacked the courthouse at Tierra to free a member from jail. It got out of control after a deputy sheriff was wounded. They burned the courthouse and its deed room. On the way out of town some members kidnapped two FBI agents. All hell broke loose with the New Mexico National Guard, US Army soldiers, Jeeps, tanks and helicopters deployed countywide. The FBI arrested dozens of the Allianz members including its leaders who went to prison, and the movement was crushed…kind of. Adrianna entered the jail during the attack to help secure original deeds

and the FBI later arrested her years later after she broke up with my father. A New Mexico judge threw her case out of court. Cooper has stayed
in touch with her for thirty years after he and my mother bought the UP
ranch. That's the long and short of it. Be warned the Foundation wants to
return the seventy per cent of land in Northern New Mexico they believe
has been stolen from the original Spanish settlers since the US took the
Southwest from Mexico in 1848. That's the short version of this hundred
and seventy year ongoing saga."

"Does the Foundation and Adrianna want your family's UP Ranch returned to the original northern Taos County Spanish families?" she asked.

"Yes, but its technically legally complicated because its land grant
was Mexican and granted in 1844 only four years before the US conquered the Southwest. The US Congress later patented our deed after
the Civil War to cement its legal status in American courts. There's a
long-standing disagreement between my father and Adrianna on this issue. I'm sure she'll raise it. Be warned it's a rattlesnake pit. Has your
father ever mentioned it?"

"Not in my memory. His family was originally from Pueblo Colorado when it was in New Spain. They were not farmers or ranchers. They
forged wrought iron products like gates, wagon wheels, door handles,
shutter latches and more. They even built freight wagons that replaced
the ox carts that traveled up the Camino Real from Mexico City to Taos
and on to Pueblo. They repaired the Spanish Toledo steel lances and
swords the garrison soldiers and Conquistadors fought the Indios with,
including the Apache."

An hour later, Trey rang the doorbell camera by the security locked
heavy wooden door with its hand carved Spanish cross panels. The old
adobe brick building had once probably been a mercantile store he guessed.
The building had been recently plastered with mud and straw the Spanish
colonial way. After a moment, a striking Spanish woman of sixty plus
years old in a black ankle-length dress appeared when the door opened
blocking his view into the room behind her. "Trey, you look like a young
Cooper. I'll meet you out on the veranda under the cottonwood tree."

"You are Adrianna then? I was last here with my father when I was nine
years old, he reminded me."

"I am," and the door closed. Trey walked to the side of the high
walled building and sat down on a wooden bench in the shade of a giant

cottonwood tree.

A few minutes later, Adrianna walked onto the faded Mexican tiled veranda followed by a young twenty something Hispanic man with a trimmed black beard holding an iPad. She opened the meeting but did not sit down while pacing back and forth slowly.

"Meet Juan, an intern at the Foundation. He's a first-year law student. He grew up here and plans to return to help with our legal fight to recover the stolen land grants. Cooper called to tell me you were taking over operating the Ute Peak Ranch. I told him that was a bad idea, but he insisted we meet anyway. It'll have to be brief because there is an important meeting with an aide to the new woman Hispanic Governor of New Mexico in our conference room. My son Joe Bear Spirit Jr. is chairing it."

Cautiously Trey framed a reply wishing he had Maestas with him. "Thanks for meeting with me on short notice, Adrianna. Good to meet you, Juan. Please meet Maria Duran a friend of mine who prefers to be called M. Maestas, who you know, remains the foreman of the ranch but couldn't come and says hello."

Adrianna's brown eyes looked straight into M's eyes. "You, M, are Trey's girlfriend, I think, and like my son part Spanish and Indio I would guess…maybe Apache not far from here. I was once Trey's father's girlfriend. Keep your brown eyes wide open and protect your heart from your Anglo ranch boyfriend. They all ride for their family's brand."

M was caught off guard but countered with strength, "I'm a modern Four Corners woman. I can choose whom I date. My mother was part Apache from the reservation thirty miles north at Dulce. I'm sure you have driven through it. Your Spanish families stole her tribal land before the Americanos stole the Spanish King's Land Grants. Her ancient people actually chose real Land or Death. The Spanish and the Anglos imprisoned or murdered most of them. Your fight is for stolen Native American land. I think we need to leave, Trey. She is not on either of our sides." Trey stood and waited for Adrianna's reply, fearing it was shark-feeding time.

"So you have abandoned your father's Duran name to fight for the Indios and the Anglos. You can drive her out of here now, Trey Stuart. I told Cooper sending you to run the Ute Peak Ranch was a mistake. With Maestas running it at least the community felt it was mostly in Spanish settler hands. I have told Cooper many times he can leave it in trust for the Foundation at his death. Juan is setting up a land trust for us. Now that I

see this part Apache Indio woman is in the game our gloves are off. I can't
control the Land or Death movement's members reaction to you managing
the Ute Peak Ranch. Juan, please walk them to their car."

Trey pulled M to her feet and replied, "I'm disgusted by your veiled
threat. I agree with M that neither the Spanish or Anglo's have a better
claim to ancient Pueblo Indian or Apache or Ute land in the Four Corners.
Your old boyfriend Cooper always has said that's why we have title insurance on the Ute Peak Ranch. If either the Spanish colonial settlers or
the Pueblo Indians can prove a legal claim to it in court, we'll collect the
money and ride into the sunset. Until then, I operate the Ute Peak Ranch."
He pivoted holding M's hand as they followed Juan to the Mustang. "Time
for a hot spring at our motel."

M angrily gunned the Shelby Mustang spinning it 360 degrees and
spraying gravel onto the Foundation's wooden front door. Trey saw Juan
jump behind an old model light blue pickup truck out of the corner of
his eye. She hit the blacktop edge of the highway and aired the Mustang.
When it landed, she accelerated to a hundred miles an hour past the right
turn into Tierra's rebuilt courthouse. Trey shouted over the roar of the
motor, "Slow down, please. The left turn to Los Ojos village is next. You
don't want to hit any of the ladies driving home from work who spin the
Spanish Churro sheep wool at the co-op there and loom beautiful rugs
and clothing. I'll buy you a wool scarf for winter riding on the range if
you can make the turn."

M slowed but drove past the turn. "I hate bribes, Trey. Don't try one
again even to take my heavy foot off the pedal. I won't wear wool anything
from Spanish sheep that are grazing on stolen Apache hunting land. But
you can buy me a French wool scarf anytime you please or Paris lingerie
and dresses. That's where one of my grandmothers lived." She smiled,
calming down and slowing to the posted speed limit of thirty-five miles an
hour seconds before the radar detector went off. As a county sheriff's patrol car passed, she added. "That was close. The attempted bribe worked."

"Luck with us. Google Paris shopping on the Internet is my next stop.
Do they have French lingerie models on the sites? Let's cruise back to
Pagosa Springs. When you get north of Chama New Mexico you can run
hard to the T turn into Pagosa Springs. Then it's dinner bell time at a small
restaurant in an old house on the way to the motel. Next, we enjoy a very
long relaxing hot spring. You have a French bikini."

"You'll have to wait for a visual answer. I'm all in. Fuck waiting for Chama. The sheriff's car is headed to dinner. I'm hungry too." She gunned the Mustang to 120 miles an hour adding, "I'll slow at the Chama speed zone in case a state patrolman is running radar there."

After a candlelight trout dinner M turned the Mustang into the motel's driveway as Trey suddenly ordered, "Don't park in front of our room. That restored blue 50's Chevy pickup truck was parked in front of the motel office was in the Land or Death's Foundation parking lot. While you were busy spraying the Foundation's front door with gravel, Juan took cover behind it. Pull over in the parking lot as far from our room as possible and cut the lights. Let's watch and wait while we pretend to make out."

"We don't know how to pretend to make out. Trying to could cause us not to watch carefully enough. So let's just wait." She laughingly replied as the Mustang came to a stop. Just then two heavy set Hispanic men walked out of the motel office glass door and headed toward their room. The short mustached one had a room key in his hand. When they reached their room door the taller one with a full beard pulled a pistol out of his black leather jacket pocket while the shorter one unlocked the door. They entered the darkened room, closing the door behind them.

"I guess the desk clerk is part of this too. Time to surprise them. Call 911. Give them our room number 112." He pulled a Glock 9 out from under his seat.

Relieved Trey was not intervening with his pistol in hand she called 911. "The Pagosa police are on the way. The dispatcher said stay in the car. Please do not confront them. They are armed and dangerous."

A minute later, with its siren blaring a police unit pulled up in front of their room. Two uniformed officers exited their squad car with grim looks. Their pistols were drawn. They stepped to each side of the door's frame and the one on the left twisted the doorknob and pushed it open. A shot rang out through the open door and blasted out the police car's windshield. The two men burst through the door with their pistols blazing. The two policemen fired in unison and gunned both of them down. The men went down hard onto the motel sidewalk as their pistols skidded under the police car. A pool of blood started to form instantly beside their bodies. The short one was grasping his shoulder and screaming in pain but the tall one in the black leather jacket lay still face down.

"Fuck them. They came to ambush and kill us," Trey said as M burst into tears grabbing his hand. He continued, "This'll take all night to sort out. The fucking dumb SOBs. Juan the intern is toast if I see him around here. He heard me say we were staying here when he walked us to the Mustang. He's in law school and he set us up to be possibly murdered. He's the only one who knew where we were staying tonight. The local teen Hispanic front desk clerk is naive too. She'll do hard time for giving them a key to our room. Look to your right. She's running across the parking lot toward a beater car." But before she could reach it a second arriving police car leading a paramedic ambulance turned in front of her and cut her off. A woman officer jumped from the still-moving police car and grabbed her as she let out a blood-curdling scream.

Trey and M walked over to the officers who were yellow taping the crime scene while the paramedics attended to the two men on the pavement. "I'm Trey Stuart and this is Maria Duran who called 911. We are staying in room 112. We saw the short man walking to our room with a key in his hand and the tall one in the black leather jacket pulled his pistol from a pocket. Then he unlocked the door and both of them entered. The motel desk clerk must have given the key to them and told them we were out of the room. Your officers just grabbed her as she ran toward a beater car in the parking lot."

"You and Ms. Duran stay put. This is now an officer involved shooting investigation. These men aren't robbers. They are involved with the Land or Death Movement over in Chama and Tierra across the Colorado state line. They threatened to kill and beat up a Texas rancher on his summer grazing land just south of Pagosa on the Colorado side of the border a month ago. They're out of county jail on bail. We have their pictures on our dashboard iPad. You own a ranch."

"Two as a matter of fact."

"Where?"

"One near Telluride Colorado and one I just started operating for my family in Costilla New Mexico."

"Well, Mr. Stuart you just started operating trouble with the New Mexico place. Northern New Mexico's a hornet's nest they say. We're just trying to keep the trouble over the state line. A person might consider selling out and moving back to Colorado. This Land or Death group wants it all back from the Anglos and the federal government for the Spanish settlers' families in these parts. If Ms. Duran is your girlfriend or wife, she's not safe anywhere but Taos and Santa Fe alone. You know or have contact with any of the Land or Death people?"

"We just met with Adrianna, the Executive Director of the Land or Death Foundation this afternoon in Tierra. Thirty-five years ago, she was my father's girlfriend when she owned the Bistro Restaurant in Telluride. I saw the 1950's restored blue pickup in the Foundation's parking lot when we drove out. It's parked in front of the motel office." Trey deliberately withheld Juan's name.

"That complicates things." He ordered another officer to secure the blue pickup.

"Mind if we hang out in the hot springs, since we're staying at the motel, until you need a statement?"

"That's an odd request, but no. The police chief with a detective and the DA are on the way over here. You both are material witnesses. So you and Ms. Duran go sit down on the office couch and toss me your car keys."

"That sucks. We were looking forward to moonlight hot springs before closing at ten. It's included in our room rate," Trey said deadpan trying to break the tension.

"Look, Mr. Stuart, it's me and James that just shot those two men who were laying in wait to either threaten you or maybe even kidnap and murder you because you have a ranch across the state line. Now we know you both met with the Foundation today. According to the medics one of the assailants is deceased and the other one has a severe shoulder wound. We'd both rather breakup the usual late night bar fight and go off shift than do paperwork all night and all month long. I repeat, give me your ranch pickup keys. Take your girlfriend and sit on the couch in the office until we take your statement. Also, I advise you to call the Best Western down the street and get a room for the night. This one is a crime scene."

M stepped between them knowing a big rancher's son like Trey didn't take orders well from anyone in any town. "Let's go, Trey. We'll pull the blinds and make out." Her smile broke the tension, and she handed the officer the keys adding, "It's my restored 1977 Shelby Mustang parked way over there with Colorado plates."

"A Shelby Mustang. If we run the plates, are you from Durango?"

"I could be."

"We've received calls on alleged highway passes at over 140 miles an hour between Pagosa and Durango by a black Shelby Mustang with a black ponytailed woman driver."

"There are thousands of Shelbys in the US and millions of black-haired girls and women with ponytails. Let's go, Trey." They walked toward the office where a crowd was converging behind the yellow tape police line with iPhones Instagramming it all. As Trey scanned the front of the crowd, he saw Juan with tears in his eyes.

He walked toward him. "You little fuck, see what you caused?" He started to go after Juan but thought better of it when M grabbed his arm. Juan turned and walked through the crowd and disappeared. He hoped Adrianna had no knowledge of Juan and the Foundation's members' trip to the motel. He made a mental note to try and get an answer from her.

CHAPTER FIVE

RODEO DAY

Trey and M pulled into a dusty graveled parking place in the last row with mostly aging ranch battered pickup trucks at the Sky Hi Rodeo grounds in Monte Vista Colorado. A large cottonwood tree shaded the red pickup truck when he cut the engine.

"Well, cowgirl, it's good there was one good parking space left because my physic parking mostly works. This rodeo is sold out."

"Take your hand off my bare thigh so we can get to the rodeo opening on time and before some cowboy walks out here looking for his extra rope," M replied as she pulled the blue denim skirt down to her knees.

"We have two box seat tickets waiting, thanks to my father's long-time foreman on the YbarC. Tommy Lee's aunt who farms and ranches in the San Luis Valley can't attend this afternoon. Her husband had a horse wreck on the range when a neighbor's potato irrigation rig's sprinklers cut on suddenly and spooked his horse. The fall broke his shoulder but fortunately not his neck."

"My mother always said farming is way more dangerous than ranching. I believed her until I met you." A roar went up in the arena as the early Saturday afternoon sun beamed down on the high mountain-accented, dusty southern Colorado landscape. M continued, "Move your cute cowboy butt or we'll miss the rodeo queen's ride with her princesses into the arena."

Trey replied, "Follow all those blonde-headed pre-teens in plaid shirts eating pink cotton candy from the rodeo's carnival rides across the highway. They're headed toward the box office by the entrance."

As they walked into the arena, twelve high school aged girls thundered onto its packed dirt floor on their perfectly trained mounts. Their horses were shampooed, brushed, and glistened in the sun. Their saddles were leather soaped, and ponytails of assorted colors blew straight out from under cowgirl hats as they galloped straight backed in the saddle behind the rodeo queen. Each one held a pole with a sponsor banner in her right hand as she reined her horse with her left one. They circled the full rodeo arena stands counterclockwise with their hopes and dreams tucked under their cowgirl hats. Most of them were lean junior, tanned-faced barrel racers who rode strong in the saddle guiding their trained horses with one hand at speed. Their eyes blazed in the western sun like their mothers before them as they rounded the arena and stopped facing the American flag, which the rodeo queen held high on its pole. This was their dress review by the local community. It was the reward for long hours of barrel racing practice on isolated ranches and farms on countless days in the strong spring west wind, hot summer sun and cold fall days after school. Their horses were one with the riders and would protect them in any struggle with man or nature. Their teenage cowboy-hatted boyfriends present and future sat atop the rodeo competitor's fence line and yearned to make out with them in their battered ranch pickup trucks under the ancient cottonwood trees in the back row of the parking lot. But they all had to rodeo first. They like the queen and her court had to ride thousand-pound horses and bulls at full speed in the arena with the wind in their faces and the roar of the crowd in their ears. Flying hooves and horns brought death to the edge of their young athletic bodies as rodeo unfolded in the arena like their lives would. Eight seconds or less on a rodeo stock bull could bring death in the arena as blood pulsed from a young bull rider's horned heart. But as the local high school singer struggled with her high notes in the National Anthem all eyes were on the queen and her court. All the crowd's hearts were committed to the rodeo riders' afternoon of valor on the fenced arena's tan sandy dirt floor.

Trey and M found their front row, smooth-planked bench seat in a box for four. They settled in just as a bareback bronc rider broke out of the green steel gate straight across the arena from them. His horse tried to make him weightless as it bucked all four hooves off the dry sandy soil. M adjusted her gold-rimmed aviator sunglasses she used for hot rod drag racing. Trey tipped his cowboy hat down to shade his eyes and watched for the rider's score. It was a high 79 and the crowd applauded vigorously. The next rider broke the gate and the crowd focused on his bucking horse. A tall, tanned, slightly-stooped, grey-haired, heavy-set man and in a grey cowboy hat, jeans and a western cut denim sports jacket slid into their box and sat down next to Trey. He said, "I'm the very retired Commander Jumbo Roberts of the Colorado State Highway Patrol. Your father called me about your move down to the Ute Peak Ranch across the border. He asked me to keep an ear and an eye open for you. I retired to a small horse ranch near here but still have access to the state police Intel reports and law enforcement gossip along the Southern Colorado and Northern New Mexico border."

M's head turned and she stared icily at Jumbo as Trey replied,

"You are held in high esteem by my father and mother for your help in saving the YbarC from the criminal developers and their lackeys at the Telluride National Bank plus solving Joe Bear Spirit's murder. So far, I'm making out OK operating the ranch including its hacienda remodel. Meet M, my girlfriend from Aztec and Durango."

As M's face muscles tightened, Jumbo replied, "Most of the Southern Colorado State Patrol knows Ms. Maria Duran. Her state patrol radio handle is Mustang Sally. She run that Shelby Mustang flat out, still? Her pony-tail, big brown eyes and smile have been getting her off for years when we could catch her. She tell you that to keep her driver's license from being revoked for life she has taught high speed driving at the Colorado State Patrol Academy for two weeks each of the past five years?"

M blushed. "I haven't yet, sir." Trey fought back laughter.

Jumbo continued, "Well it depends what the definition of OK is, I guess. There is a State Police interagency Intel report out of Durango that a Mexican cartel drug gang we are monitoring with the DEA has a hit out on a black ponytailed driver and passenger of a go-fast Maserati Coupe that tangled with a dope-running big-wheel truck near Hesperus Colorado. The Durango Hospital has a record of one of them being treated for a suspicious accidental gunshot wound. Cooper took me for a ride in his Maserati Coupe last year when I visited the YbarC. You two know anything about that?"

Trey looked at M and she replied, "I drive the Shelby and Trey the red pickup out in the parking lot."

"Then there's a Taos County Sheriff's report on a couple ranch hands who allegedly interfered with a drug bust along the northern Rio Grande Gorge on or near your ranch, Trey. They want to interview them."

"None of my cow hands reported anything like that to me," Trey snapped back too quickly.

"You sure? Cooper wondered why you shipped him two Paint horses when I called him to warn you that there are Mexican cartel drug flights west of your ranch across the Rio Grande River Gorge. Were any of your cowboys riding those Paints?"

"Not that I know of," Trey hedged.

"Then there is the police shoot out at your room in the Pagosa Hot Springs motel after you both visited Adrianna at the Land or Death Foundation in Tierra, I assume Cooper probably asked you to do that without getting a police Intel update on the organization's current actives from me."

Trey replied flatly, "Yes, he did, and it turned out badly."

M frowning added, "Very badly. The police told us we could have been killed or kidnapped."

"That's correct, Maria. The movement is heating up again with a new biography book out about its deceased leader Reyes Lopez Tijerina and his pal the deceased Baltasar Martinez. It chronicles the theft of the original Spanish settlers' families' ranch and farmland after the USA took over the Southwest from Mexico. The Colorado State Patrol has Intel files on them since 1967 when they often crossed the border to hold meetings to stir up trouble, which led to the raid on the Tierra courthouse. Do you know how they found out where you were staying, or did they follow you?"

Trey laughed. "M was driving the Shelby and it was dinner time. They didn't follow us."

"I wish it was funny, but a local cop had to kill one of them. Once more, how did they know where you were staying?"

M tearing up grabbed Trey's hand, "A legal intern heard Trey say 'let's take a hot spring after dinner at the motel'. We didn't tell Adrianna where we were staying in Pagosa Springs. His name is Juan."

"Trey, it's mostly not your father's day anymore or mine around these parts. I suspect you are as tough and good with a gun as he is. The Mexican cartel will kill anyone who interferes with a hard drug shipment. Illegal

Mexican cartel drugs are being pushed more than ever now that pot is legal in both states. Corrupt county deputy sheriffs spring up to help them as fast as we catch and jail them. A deputy who starts at $20,000 a year with little training takes $100,000 to protect drug shipments to buy a house for his family. So far, the state police in both states are clean but the DEA is watching everyone more closely now that pot is legal. The DEA is concentrating on hard drug shipments including fentanyl...a stone-cold killer. So you two need to lie low on the ranch for a while. I'll let you know when things cool down after we bust the cartel in Durango. Warn your cowhands to stay clear of the airplane drug drops and report any they see to the DEA in Santa Fe. The FBI and DEA are working on it. It's not a good idea for M to continue driving from Aztec to the ranch alone. If the cartel intercepts her, they will rape and kill her to get at you. Stay away from the Foundation and Adrianna. Enjoy the rodeo and the dance. It's good to be young." Jumbo tipped his hat and slid out of his seat.

"You're hired to help with the horses, manage the remodel and teach high speed pickup driving to the ranch hands. Call the café tonight and resign," Trey said smiling.

"I accept. Your wet dreams have come true. No more iPhone sex."

She hugged Trey. "Now, let's watch some PRCA rodeo. The program says Steer Wrestling is up next."

"You want to go to the Rodeo Dance tonight? The radio says it has an Austin country music band."

"Dancing would be way fun. I'm all in."

"Then I'll call the Best Western for a room. I can bribe the hostess at the steak house next door to it for a table. We'll celebrate your new job." And M kissed him hard as the first steer wrestler's horse broke the barrier cleanly.

A week later, Trey and M were driving the red pickup over a dusty hard packed ranch road onto the flank of Ute Peak. They were looking for a break in the high boundary barbwire fence line so they could repair it. A cowhand had reported an old Spanish family's neighboring ranch's cows had grazed across it, in search of grass and water. The cowboy who was on horseback had pushed the cattle back out of fence cut but didn't have patch wire to repair the break properly. Maestas had reported to Trey it was an annual occurrence and he believed the five-strand barbwire fence cut was deliberate. Trey wanted to confirm it himself so while Maestas was at a family funeral in San Luis Colorado for the day he decided to repair it. He and M both had been mostly ranch bound for a week partly because of Jumbo's warning and because of the final stages of the hacienda's renovation. They were ready for a day on the range in fresh air.

After the sage turned into the evergreen Pinion and Jenifer trees, they parked the red pickup and walked along the fence line for a quarter of a mile south and found the break. "It's a cut for sure. That's up to a year in jail and a fine in New Mexico. Problem is who cut it? Is it by a neighbor or an elk horn shed hunter or an illegal poacher? Without a witness the brand inspector can't even make an arrest even if neighboring cattle have used it to cross the fence line. Maestas warned me an accusation against a neighbor, Spanish or Anglo, without proof could lead to violence worst case. Plus with the Land or Death Foundation on the resurgence I don't need more trouble. So let's patch it up." He dropped the shoulder strapped leather bag he was carrying with repair wire and a fence tool adding, "New Mexico's a fence out state so it's my ranch's legal duty to repair it."

"I've never patched barbwire, only electrical auto wire, so tell me know what to do," M stated.

"Put on the small size rawhide gloves and safety glasses in the leather bag. You'll hold one side of a cut strand of barbed wire while I attach its end to the splice and stretch fence tool. Next, I'll attach the other cut strand of barbwire to the fence tool. When I start to stretch the cut barbwire ends with the fence tool to splice them together, you must step safely back away from the fence line. If the wire snaps out of the tool before or after the splice is completed its barbed whiplash could cut you badly. Stay alert, we will repeat the process five times starting with the bottom strand of cut wire."

"Got it."

He pulled rawhide work gloves from his jeans' hip pocket and put them on. Then he picked up a cut bottom strand of barbed wire. He spliced one strand of wire at a time carefully and moved up to the fourth line. M settled into her routine. Working on cars with her father had given M a cautious natural grace with her hands for the mechanical repair of the fence. After Trey tightened the splice of the fourth strand of barbwire it suddenly snapped and whiplashed back onto his work shirt's sleeve, but its sharp barbed end missed M who had stepped away.

"Whoa!" she exclaimed, "That was heavy duty. Are you OK?"

"Yes, This's why we work in long sleeves on the ranch no matter how hot. It's only a tear not a cut. After I splice the top strand, we're done here. Then we'll drive this fence line a half mile each way from the repair and check for any other fence damage, human or animal."

"Roger that."

After a hot afternoon of walking and splicing a couple of broken top strands of elk damaged boundary fencing, they returned to the red pickup and stored the fence repair bag. They drank cold lemon sodas with Taos Energy Bars. After the refresher snack they drove farther up the ranch road to the end of a late 1930's mule-drag logging road through sage, pinion and juniper trees on the eastern flank of the extinct one and a half million-year-old volcano to view the farming and ranching valley below them. An eight-foot-deep dirt walled and grey black basalt rock strewn arroyo brought the pickup to a sudden stop.

Trey said, "I forgot about this arroyo. I haven't been up here in years. Let's take a short hike up it. As I remember, its rocky sandy bottom is a gently sloped climb up the mountain for a half-mile or so. Then we can climb out of it for a great view of this part on the ranch and the valley from eight thousand feet high. We can see the Great Sand Dunes in Colorado from here."

"I'm good for no more than a half mile up. I'm not a hiker by trade," M replied wearily after an afternoon on the fence line.

"I'm good with that too. Then downhill by foot and pickup truck to the hacienda for a cold beer, dinner and a hot tub?"

"A perfect plan." M smiled.

They climbed out of the pickup truck onto thin soil with circular light green gamma grass pods interspersed with the invader sage. Trey found an elk trail down the steep bank of the arroyo, and they carefully hiked into it. They continued up hill in their thick-soled tan leather cowboy work boots. Its narrow basalt rock strewn bottom was interspersed with grey sandy patches, which were littered with shiny black chipped obsidian rocks. Trey stopped and picked up one of them and showed it to M. "Indians on the mountain in waves have worked these chipped rocks over the past ten thousand years. They are unfinished or broken bow and spear points used for hunting and as weapons. They wash down the mountain in snowmelt runoff and summer monsoon thunderstorm torrents of water."

"There have been people living on this mountain that long?" M asked.

"Maybe longer but only hunting and making obsidian weapons and tools that long. There's no water on this solid volcanic rock mountain so they lived in the valley around it and hunted around a twelve-thousand-year-old lake left by the end of the ice age as it melted and retreated. The mountain was surrounded by shallow water. We find their perfect sharper than steel obsidian points around its dry boundary banks. Folsom Man, the oldest group killed the big, tusked mammoths down below us."

"Very interesting, so these nomadic hunters were here before the Anasazi who lived around Durango and Aztec in stone house settlements."

"Try eight to nine thousand years before the Anasazi lived in the Four Corners area in rock walled settlements and farmed irrigated corn," he answered. Suddenly his eye caught the low afternoon sun's glint from a small rock several yards up the arroyo and he signaled M to follow him.

He picked up the rock as she stopped by his right side and bumped the Glock 9 pistol in its black leather holster. "What kind of rock is that?"

"Gold bearing quartz," he replied. My father made me take a geology class in college. He said it would come in handy on the ranch. The question is how'd it get into this pocket of broken basalt, red pumice and chipped obsidian?"

"You have any ideas from your class?" she asked.

"We didn't study prospecting but took a couple of field trips. It either washed down the arroyo or an elk picked it up in its hoof and tracked it up down. My parents told me rumors abound that a sixteenth century Spanish colonial gold mine is hidden on the mountain or another mountain near by perhaps Saint Antonio Peak its twin across the Rio Grande Gorge. Let's follow the first "bread crumb" up the arroyo and see if it's a trail toward an exposed weathered vein or just a random quartz rock. You good to uphill scramble on this loose volcanic lava rock and sand?" Trey picked up the quartz rock and stuck it in his pocket. "I'll assay it in Telluride when we return to the YbarC for a visit. Too many loose lips in Taos, my father has cautioned."

She replied, "For Spanish gold and a higher view of the southern San Luis Valley my sore feet and legs are all in. But only for another two hundred yards up or so."

They silently climbed carefully step-by-step eyes on the ground through the slightly curving arroyo when suddenly a black as a moonless night raven appeared and circled above them. It sounded an alert as they walked up to the near wilderness part of the mountain. They spotted two more small gold bearing quartz rocks in the now shaded arroyo, which they left in place on their breadcrumb trail. Near a basalt rockslide above them Trey's boot hit a weathered piece of leather protruding from a sand bar on a bend in the arroyo's south bank. He knelt as M approached from below him and carefully started clearing away the sand around it with his fingers. She watched silently as his fingers gradually cleared six inches of sand around the weathered leather strap. The raven circled lower and squawked a warning. A very tarnished piece of silver metal emerged as his fingers cleared more sand around it. "Careful, it's very old silver metal probably held together by its tarnish," she warned.

"Very careful," he replied. When it came loose, he lifted the leather strap with its silver buckle that had a barely visible tarnished Spanish Cross stamped into it. "It's proof the Spanish explored the mountain but the question is which era of them? Was it Coronado's army scouts in 1640 or later Spanish colonial miners, or Spanish sheepherders and settlers? I need to get this to a former professor at USC for carbon dating. Hopefully, he will do it for a recent alum."

"A piece of a bridle maybe?" M mused as he carefully picked up and put it in his left jeans pocket for safekeeping. "Let's keep moving. We're losing daylight quickly," she reminded him. They both started up the arroyo at a faster pace but with eyes still on the dark shadowed arroyo bottom. The arroyo suddenly ended at the middle of a massive basalt rockslide about fifty-feet wide and a football field long. They carefully walked to its edge.

"Don't step onto it. One loose rock could send you tumbling and start a slide that could bury you."

"Thanks for the warning. I've never seen anything like it. In Colorado, the rockslides are sandstone or granite with dangerous large and small boulders that can break loose and roll. Plus, very dangerous above tree line spree," she replied.

"Maybe this slide was set off with black powder to hide an abandoned Spanish colonial mine entrance. The 'breadcrumbs' may be washed down from under it by snowmelt and thunderstorms. It could be a trap with hollow places under it to kill intruders who cross or probe it and set off a slide like a snow avalanche? Or both? It doesn't gut feel or look natural," he concluded. They both heard a soft crack above them as the raven swooped noisily above them. They looked up in unison and their eyes focused into the shadows on the grey rockslide. Above them the largest male mountain lion Trey had ever seen on either ranch was quietly crossing it one padded paw at a time toward their edge of the slide. They stared in silence as he pulled the Glock 9 from its holster.

He whispered, "I wish I had the saddle rifle I left in the pickup truck." They remained silent and still as the mountain lion crossed without loosening a rock. At the slide's edge above them he turned his head away from them and his paws thundered into the ponderosa pine and blue spruce. After a long minute, the big cat's paws were silent.

Trey still alarmed, said, "We quickly have to cross the slide twenty feet apart so he can't circle back down on us from the ponderosa pine trees without re-crossing the slide and sounding an alert. Once we're on the south edge of the slide we'll walk down to the arroyo bank and back to the pickup quickly before it gets totally dark. I can't stop him with the pistol…maybe scare him. He'd tear my neck jugular out before a pistol bullet, even to his heart, could bleed him to death. He's twelve feet nose to tail tip. I'm first then you follow. Scamper up to safety if I set off even a small lava rockslide."

"Let's set our intentions for a good crossing like a safe quarter mile drag race," M replied while making the sign of the cross.

He silently stepped onto the unstable rock. He moved quickly but sure footed across it. At the quarter point of his crossing route, she started across the slide, moving faster with lighter footing. Trey paused as he heard a paw hit a bush on the north side of the slide above him. "He's above us in the trees maybe twenty yards. Keep moving and don't look back." Moments later, he reached the edge of the slide as M closed in a step behind him. "Scramble carefully but fast down the arroyo edge; I'll walk drag and keep an ear out for the cat. If he re-crosses the slide or moves toward us across the arroyo, I'll shoot to kill or scare if I miss."

"Roger that," she replied in a whisper. "Wish I had a sure-footed Colorado mountain horse though."

Trey walked behind her his Glock 9 in hand ready to shoot if the big cat managed to cross the arroyo under the slide from the trees to attack them.

Step by step with an occasional missed but not fatal one they descended in silence as the light faded to dark on the mountain. He listened for the big cat until they reached the safety of the pickup as the last orange rays of light disappeared to the west. They climbed into it slamming both doors and rattling its windows. He pulled the short-barreled repeating saddle rifle off its rear window rack and chambered a bullet. He handed it to M.

"We're downhill in low four-wheel drive to keep the brakes from burning out. I doubt the cat will attack a ranch pickup truck but lower your window and shoot at him if he appears in the headlights. Watch for cat ears. I don't want him to leap through a side window. There's not enough room on this bench seat for all of us." He laughed and put his Glock 9 between them.

"I've never fired a rifle, Trey."

"It's like the western movies. Lever in a bullet. Then point and shoot off your right shoulder. We'll start pistol and rifle target shooting lessons at the ranch tomorrow."

The pickup motor sprang into life and he slalomed it downhill over the rough ranch road at fifteen miles an hour. When they reached the ranch's main gravel road, he shifted into two-wheel drive and a cloud of dust chased them toward the hacienda.

As they drove through the hacienda's main gate, M said, "I never want to cross that slide again and I really don't want be that near a big cat on foot either."

"Not even for gold?"

"No, not even for gold," she stated emphatically.

"Let's see what the carbon dating says. If the strap end is very old and my dad's retired mining geologist friend in Telluride confirms this is gold-bearing quartz then I want to investigate the slide area. I'll need a geo guy and a miner or two to work it with me. There are plenty of unemployed ones at Cerro and Questa with the molybdenum mine closed. It's not a job for novices stumbling around in cowboy boots." He laughed at that image to break the tension.

"For now, a cold beer and dinner is in order followed by a hot tub," M replied.

"You start diner while I brief Maestas on the fence repair plus the lion's size and its behavior. I need his thoughts on the lion's possible interest in humans. The cowboys will need to be alerted. If there are any other close sightings or a calf kill, we will have to hunt and kill the cat. He's very mature. If he is losing eyesight and hunting speed, then he's very dangerous. Slower humans can become his prey. There're no retirement centers for old mountain lions."

"That's nature," M replied. "Some old drag racers whose reflexes slow don't make a retirement center."

After dinner, Trey and M were in the steamy hot tub bath in the master bathroom. She teased, "I'm undusted and all nude. How are you keeping your hands off me?"

"Since maybe that's an invite for hot tub sex, I'm all in," he replied with a smile as his hand found a warm wet inner thigh under the bubbling hot water.

"It's not a maybe invite. It's a real one," and her hand dropped under the bubbles. She added, "Let the fun begin," and kissed him.

CHAPTER SIX

HIGH TIMES IN TAOS

M who pulled the Shelby Mustang into a parking place in front of Taos's traditional western paintings gallery.

As she cut the engine, Trey said, "Let's take a look in here first. The ranch received an invitation for art gallery openings tonight. The paintings feature old west scenes that my mom and dad like. I'm looking for a thank you present for them for approving all the renovations to the hacienda we requested. Hopefully, a good one is in the show."

"Next let's drive over to the gallery in a metal warehouse building where the pop-up modern art show is opening with a late night rave party. We need something for the hacienda's living room and our bedroom that is now art," M requested.

"That's the plan then. How did you hear about it?" he asked.

"On the K-SOLAR radio station. When will you give the painting to your parents?"

"They have asked to come to the ranch in a week or so to see the completed renovation and probably discuss Adrianna's Foundation's Pagoda Springs incident. Jumbo probably called them after the rodeo. And it's time they met you."

"Do they know I'm living at the ranch with you?" she questioned.

"They will when I confirm the arrival date with them."

"Wow that's a big step in our relationship."

"It's time."

"I'm good with it. Let's get them the right painting."

They walked into a buzzing gallery filled with mostly grey-haired people in southwestern garb accented with mostly old-school Indian turquoise, tarnished silver jewelry. Many of the men wore custom made beaver cowboy hats with no sweat stains or creases. Their expensive leather cowboy boots were custom made too.

Trey scanned the room and said softly. "Western art collectors have gathered here. The cowboy hatted men with wrinkled tanned faces and rough hands are running old family ranches that go back in some cases to before the turn of the century in Texas and New Mexico. The other ones probably have never cut a calf on horseback for branding and if they did it was in childhood on a ranch. They are doctors, attorneys, bankers, oilmen and trust funders. I see a of couple of trophy wives too."

"I've never been to an adult gathering like this; just drag strip awards parties. The men and women have grease under their fingernails and oil stains on their clothes. The only art shows I have attended were in college where a couple of my girlfriends exhibited student works, not horses and cows. Some in fact were nude models real and abstract. One was a portrait of me in a tight white Tee-shirt with an oil-streaked face after a local drag race."

"I want it. Where is it?"

"In Durango at Jill's house. She'd sell it to you faster than I can make a drag strip run. She's a starving artist waiting tables to paint. I'll text her to hold it and next trip through Durango it's yours," she replied smiling.

"Done deal. Let's chat and view the art."

After a half hour of looking at cowboys, outlaws, stagecoaches, Native Americans, Pueblos, adobe villages, horses, cattle, and wildflowers, with plastic wine cups in their hands they paused in front of a new west old west brightly colored painting of running horses.

M said, "I like the spirit of this painting and it's kind of abstract style."

Trey agreed, "Me too. It's a modernization of the way an Indian painter Kicking Bear depicted the horses at Custer's demise at the Battle of Little Big Horn. I saw it at the Buffalo Bill Museum in Cody.

Wyoming. The price is right for us. The artist must be new to the western art scene. Let's red dot it and pick it up tomorrow. Then on to the other show."

"Perfect."

After a quick taco dinner in a small white-walled adobe restaurant, M pulled the Shelby Mustang up in front of a small rusting tin clad warehouse building. A wall of electronic music from its open door met them as they walked toward it.

"The right place." M smiled.

"This is going to be an eight second bull ride. Hang on for the buzzer," Trey quipped.

They walked into a boiling room of chatting and dancing Taos youth. Pot wafted through the air. The front wall was hung with electronic backlit flashing modern graphic and abstract art. The attendees were clothed in everything from colorful oil paint splattered jeans and Tee-shirts to daringly short mini-skirts with halter-tops. Their iPhones were videoing the scene. Most of the men were not clean-shaven and many women had tattoos and color in their hair. The crowd's passion for art flowed up to the roof's open eves. The DJ was on a round polished steel stand in the middle of the room with twenty thousand dollars' worth of electronic music equipment and speakers.

"This isn't a student or adult art show!" M exclaimed.

"It's like nothing I've ever been to. It's way fun. Let's take in some art and ease into the scene. iPhone pieces we like." Trey led M by hand down a long wall. Abstract nudes, graphic oil painting and multi-media pop art covered the sidewall. M stopped in front of a bright graphic painting. It featured a young woman with long dark hair in a tight crotch length white Tee-shirt leaning on the long fender of a mauve-yellow 1970's muscle car. Above her braless breasts was LOVER in red letters. Her left arm was extended, and her hand pointed a six-shooter pistol past the front windshield of the car off the frame line into nothingness. M simply said, "This is the one. It's a perfect expression of the danger blind love can bring a woman whether it's a too fast car or a man."

Trey paused as he considered the painting and M's reaction to it. "Is the pistol pointed at her boyfriend?"

"No, it's pointed past the car she loves too."

"Could it be pointed at me?" Trey startled asked.

"I hope never." And she pressed her body against him and kissed him hard.

After her arms released him, Trey smiled saying, "iPhone it. Let's take it up to the desk by the door and pay the tattooed woman in the black body sock dress for it. Next, stash it in the Mustang's trunk. Then let's return and look at what appears to be electronic art in the darkened back of the building and dance."

"I'm paying for this one. You can buy one for the hacienda living room if we find it later." She took it off the wall and led him toward the battered metal desk through the rave dancers.

When they returned to the building, the DJ was blasting his sound out to the dancers. They danced into the art crowd. Trey and M had never danced together but it wasn't their first rodeo. They swirled into the anarchy on the floor surrounded by the visual art. After several back-to-back numbers by the DJ, they danced out of the crowd at the darkened back of the building to catch their breath and escape the pounding on the concrete floor.

"It felt good. I miss dancing. We all went out dancing most Saturday nights in Durango," M said.

"Same for me at USC. Lots of dancing at the clubs and house parties."

"Look at the art on the dark wall. It's electronic like the music. One is a three D hologram. Several are lit from behind with LEDs and are changing colors and scenes. Let's look at them close up," she said into his ear. They approached a long, tall, painting of the universe with the moon, planets, and stars. Colored layers faded in and out revealing a dynamic colorful universe. Trey read the white card under it using his iPhone light.

"It has a fiber optic panel behind the canvas. See its electrical cord. It's called new media fine art, the card says. It's by Kathryn Tatum a Taos artist."

"I love it. It's a modern abstract expression of the night sky we see at the ranch!" she exclaimed.

"The night skies are one of the reasons we live in the Rocky Mountain West. It's perfect for the hacienda living room with its high viga ceiling. I'll buy it and charge it to the renovation expenses. I bet my mother and father will love it too. Let's go up front and get a red dot on it. We will have to pick it up next week in a ranch pickup truck after they crate it. It's too long for the Mustang."

They maneuvered through the dancing bodies and Trey wrote the gallery manager a check for two thousand dollars and arranged for a pick-up day. Then they stepped outside for a breath of fresh night air under the Taos stars. A thin male stranger with short black spike hair slid out the door behind them and said, "I'm the artist who painted LOVER you bought. Thanks, it's rent for a month. There's an after party in a friend's studio at midnight. It's in an old adobe art studio off Kit Carson Street near the Plaza. Here's the address on his card," and he handed it to them and slid back into the door.

"Well, our first Taos Saturday late night party invite. Let's go and meet some locals. We'll stop at the La Fonda Hotel on the Taos Plaza first and get a room for the night. Our family always stays there. I'll show you the infamous 1930's D H Lawrence paintings in its office. He painted them in Taos," Trey said.

"Who's D H Lawrence?" M asked.

"Let's dance some more first then head over to meet him too, Trey said.

M led him back through the open door.

The elderly desk clerk, with a cigarette dangling from his lips, who was a retired cowboy, trailed portable oxygen behind him as he led Trey and M to the owner's office. He knocked twice and the door opened. Saki, the never-married eccentric owner, who was wearing a royal blue English smoking jacket, smiled. "Well now, it's the very good-looking Trey Stuart in an adult body. Who is the exotic beautiful lady on your arm?"

"Well, sir, that would be M," a disarmed Trey replied, smiling.

"So step in for a neat Scotch while the very modern M views the D H Lawrence paintings before her bed time. I presume she has read his books."

"Well, no but I want to meet him through his painting," M replied quizzically.

He stepped back into the small office and sat down behind his desk with an open bottle of fifteen-year-old Scotch on it. Trey led M by the hand into the office as she looked up at the eight large paintings that depicted nude men and women having sex in varying scenes. Her eyes locked on the painting featuring an orgy scene.

"OMG, Trey, these are amazing. Did he really paint them in the 1930s? Are his books written like the paintings? I can't believe he wasn't hung on the big cottonwood tree in the Taos Plaza. They are the essence of exotic sensual sex. Who were his models?"

"I'll let Saki tell you about them after he pours me a Scotch. Do you want one too?" Trey replied.

"I do."

Saki handed each of them a crystal tumbler of neat Scotch. M walked up to the orgy painting, her eyes focused on its chaotic lovemaking.

"My dear M, if I may call you that, or should it be Maria, I presume?"

"M."

"Delightfully modern. D H wrote near Taos in a log cabin for a couple summers. He and his wife arranged sexual encounters with many of the local artists and their collectors. He used these scenes in the novel he wrote here, and he painted them. They were beyond the cutting edge of the world's Avant-guarde cultures including bi-sexual relationships. Let your eyes tell you his stories. Please do read a book or two. His works were once banned in most the countries of the world and his freedom and life were threatened. Today, movie theaters show films like 'Last Tango In Paris' but it was DH who lit the path."

M moved slowly from one painting to the next, sipping her Scotch. Trey and Saki caught up on Taos' happenings and the Stuart family. Saki had no family and avoided the subject. When the tumblers were empty, Trey rose. "Time for us to let Saki retire."

M smiled and replied, "Us too. The paintings work. Good night, Saki. Trey's all mine for the night." She led him hand in hand out of the hotel office and up the stairs to their second-floor room off the lobby. They made wild love in a salute to DH.

Cooper and Judy were finishing an early sunrise breakfast at the YbarC headquarters house on a blue bird, southwestern Colorado, summer day. Judy drank the last sip of her coffee.

"I talked to Trey, and he invited us down to the Ute Peak Ranch to visit him and check out the renovation of the hacienda." Cooper laid down his iPhone after checking cattle future prices and his opening stock share prices.

"Then it's time to visit him and check on the ranch operations. I also want to talk to Maestas and find out when he wants to retire. If it's sooner rather than later, he needs to start training a new foreman and top hand. He's been both for years. Did Trey say anything about returning the two

Paint horses? We can trailer them down."

"Nothing on the Paints so I guess they stay here for now, but I want to find out why? It doesn't make a whole lotta sense they can be stolen from the hacienda's corrals by the bunkhouse with cowhands everywhere on the ranch day and night," she stated matter of factly.

"Me either. But I can't figure out what the either is."

She paused and replied, "There was a subliminal edge in his voice that only a mother could pick up. A detachment from me I've never perceived before like I'm no longer the female center of his universe."

"Well maybe it's because you're no longer fixing him pancakes and fried eggs with fresh squeezed orange juice. Bunkhouse coffee is rough."

"Maybe, but we'll see. I'll text him this morning that we'll arrive sunset Friday night for the weekend. I don't like driving to the UP after dark because of the wild horse herd that crosses the highway near the hacienda's entrance road. We've nearly hit it several times over the years. Or we can air charter down with the new pilot over at Telluride airport since the Paints seem to be visiting us a while longer."

"Let's skip the charter this trip. It'll be a good six-hour summer drive through the mountains in the Maserati. We'll lunch at that little café in Aztec New Mexico on the way down. Once we get an update on the Adrianna situation with Trey, we'll meet her for lunch at the Elk Horn Café just south of Chama New Mexico on the way back. I don't think it's a good idea to stop at her office. I'll also ask her to bring Joe Bear Spirit Jr. with her. I've always hoped he and Trey could be friends in adult life."

Judy replied, "We both miss Joe Bear Spirit. He was an inspiration to the Southern Ute Tribe and us. It seems many of the very good die young. Thanks to his early work on the tribe's treaty water rights the new diversion dam on the Animas River at Durango sends their res water for irrigating crops. Since his death, the Southern Utes have fought for all their rights. The Supreme Court ruled in their favor on the fracked natural gas royalties from the wells on their res. It's said they are the richest tribe in the US. The chief Joe worked with has set up a well-managed investment fund for them. They have a casino too. I've heard from the owner of Marie's bookstore in Durango where I shop that they may have as much as three billion dollars invested."

"The Denver Post runs story after story that says the eco groups in Colorado want to stop fracking oil and natural gas just as the Utes are making real money after they were stripped of most of their land to mine gold and silver. They were never given a dime in royalties from mining in Colorado. The tribe is very clear today they will pump natural gas on the res regardless of anyone in Colorado's opinion about it. They have the best attorneys in the state today. The tribe just built a solar plant to supply the casino, school, Tribal Headquarters and a museum where some of Joe's paintings hang with electric power. I often wonder about Joe's work in the Ute spirit world."

"Well put. It's time for a road trip. Where are you and Tommy Lee riding today?"

"We're checking the cattle on the close in north mountain grazing. It has been a little dry this summer so far. We want to check the grass to see if it's time to rotate them to another grazing area."

"I'll see you for a late dinner at sundown. I'm doing our quarterly taxes today and then book club in Telluride. It's a good place to keep an ear to the ground on the resort's development politics. Trey's last visit might come up."

"See you at sundown. Pick me up a good bottle of bourbon while you're there. I want to give it to Jumbo Roberts for watching Trey's back. We'll meet him for lunch on the way back if Adrianna refuses." He finished his black coffee and started the ranch workday at six a.m.

The volcanic basalt gravel crunched under Trey and M's hiking boots as they made their way out of the steep, narrowing arroyo on an elk trail. It was near where their gold-bearing quartz rock had been discovered. They were high on the old volcano's flank. The terrain was too dangerous for their cow horses, which were tethered 500 hundred feet below. He volunteered, "The assay report says the quartz rock we found a couple weeks ago is gold-bearing. But it cautions that it may have washed down the arroyo either in thunderstorms or in the spring snowmelt. However, there is a chance that an elk or deer or sheep or cow could have carried it from anywhere on or around the mountain in a hoof. Unless we discovered it at or near an exposed quartz vein it is long odds on finding its origin. The report also said there are no recorded findings of gold-bearing quartz on the mountain, only obsidian from a weathered vein and red pumice from an exposed vein on a basalt volcanic vent which was trench mined at an unknown date."

"So an animal could have had it stuck in a hoof like a piece of gravel in a Jeep or pickup tire with deep tread?"

"Exactly, and for many miles in any era they have lived here but probably after the ice age which was 12,000 years ago. The volcano the US Geological Agency estimates is 1.2 million years old. So it's a tough geo puzzle that may elude human history."

M asked, "So why are we grinding up this old volcano on foot then?"

"On a hunch the basalt slide we crossed a couple weeks ago could be man made by Spanish colonial gold miners. It could conceal a mine tunnel at the point of the quartz vein. On a summer visit to the ranch, I attended an USGA lecture in Taos about the mountain. A government geologist said there is something mysterious about this old cinder cone volcano. I figure it's worth a hike on a perfect summer day. If we don't find gold, you'll get some great views of the ranch and the valley as we climb higher. Plus, you get to break in your new hiking boots."

"The breaking in part may be a problem. My feet are already starting to hurt," M said with an exaggerated grimace.

"One step at a time until we are above the basalt slide where my field glasses picked up a rock outcropping. We can check it out for any sign of an exposed quartz vein or other quartz rocks."

A half hour later, they were a safe distance above the slide, approaching the mostly weathered basalt outcropping. At its downhill edge they paused for a Taos energy bar chased with water.

M complained, "My feet hurt...no mas."

"I read you loud and clear. We'll slowly work up the outcropping's ragged edge. It's only thirty yards or so. If we don't find anything, then a short rest and down we go."

They hiked up on the loose volcanic soil against the outcropping a yard at a time with M's eyes on the ground and Trey's on the rugged wall. Halfway up Trey stopped by three sage plants that surrounded a tall bush growing against the basalt wall. He paused and carefully pushed them away from it as M watched. The top of a rounded archway came into view slowly as he pushed the bush down with his hiking boots. M gasped as she moved up to help him. A three feet high arched tunnel entrance came into view.

"Wow," exclaimed M. "Is this an old Spanish mine tunnel entrance?"

"It's definitely a Roman Spanish arch opening cut in the rock. Old

Anglo mine tunnels are square topped for cut timber supported entrances. Hand me the LED high beam flashlight in your hiking backpack. Let's take a look see as Maestas says," as he bent down. M handed him the powerful flashlight and he pointed it into the dark cavity. The light beam penetrated about ten feet of darkness where it picked up a dull dusty glint surrounded by dark grey basalt walls. "I've got a glint of probably metal about three yards or so into the tunnel. I'm crawling in headfirst. Hold my ankles and if the tunnel starts to cave in yank me out using your downhill gravity as I push out."

"Trey, that's a big risk. Shouldn't we get a cowboy or three to help out and maybe a mining tunnel engineer?"

"Probably but it's not that far in. Also, give me my safety glasses and the yellow hardhat in my backpack. I borrowed it from the contractor's crew at the hacienda. Only your arms in the tunnel, not your head. Silence now. Sound waves can cause a cave in just like they cause snow avalanches."

Trey inched into the tunnel carefully on his stomach as M loosely held each ankle. He controlled his breathing, remembering college yoga classes taught by a former California college girlfriend. Inch by inch he crawled into the low tunnel, stirring up dust. He pulled his red bandana over his mouth and nose. When M could no longer grasp his ankles safely, he stopped. He stretched his right arm and hand as far as he could reach. His fingers touched metal and then old dry leather. They wrapped around a leather strap, and he slowly pulled the dull silver colored object toward his face. A dusty Spanish armored steel chest plate emerged a foot in front of his shielded eyes He wasted no time in retreating backwards out of the tunnel when a small rock rolled off the wall toward him. M pulled his legs to help the hasty exit until the yellow hardhat emerged from the tunnel opening chased by low dust cloud. He came up on one knee and pulled the tarnished amour out into the daylight.

M whispered, "It's a Spanish amour chest piece just like the one I saw at the History Museum in Santa Fe on a high school field trip."

"You're on it. It's like the ones in the crusade movie. See the Spanish Catholic cross in its center?"

"Did you see anything else in there?"

"No, but the flashlight beam followed the tunnel floor in deeper. When a rock the size of an adobe brick fell off the wall above the amour as I pulled it toward me, I bailed out. Thanks for guiding and pulling my long legs. We will need a team to explore further into the tunnel. I want to talk to my father and mother first. We need their input. Until then it's our secret."

"Roger that, if word gets out it would start a gold rush across your ranch boundaries that could be uncontrollable. Then there's all these State and Federal Antiquities Acts I learned about on a visit with my mother to Mesa Verde National Park. Who knows which group will try and claim it?" M was interrupted by a ping on the ground when Trey lifted the chest plate as he stood up. They both stared at the ground where a gold coin shimmered in a ray of sunlight through the pinion trees. M picked it up. A Spanish cross-appeared on its brightly lit side. "OMG it's the real thing. Not a plastic one I used to get in Cracker Jack boxes at the Caribbean pirate's movies."

"It is indeed," Trey replied in awe continuing, "The rumors my parents heard, from the old Spanish families around here when they bought the ranch, about Spanish gold and amour on the mountain are true, although Maestas down played them. Cooper always said where there's smoke there's fire. He and Judy rode and walked this mountain a lot but never found a trace of either. He even invented a game for my boyhood friends and me to search for the lost Spanish gold on the mountain. We slept well after those treasure hunts."

"Let's rest and have another energy bar with water then down we go to the horses with the treasure. I can wrap the chest plate in my bedroll we brought in case we were stranded by dark. We'll sneak it into the hacienda and hide it and the gold coin in the large gun safe until your parents arrive Friday night. It's a second big surprise for them. Me and Spanish gold."

Trey joked, "Maybe the Spanish left it for your dowry to go with your fast horse the Shelby Mustang."

"Maybe they did," M replied blushing and kissed him hard.

Cooper and Judy parked the Maserati on the street in front of the café's window in Aztec New Mexico on the way to visit Trey. A dark-haired young lunch waitress showed them to a table by the window and gave them menus.

"I'm Anna, I'll get you cold water while you look at our menu, but I can't help but ask if that is M's boyfriend Trey's Maserati or just a look alike?"

Cooper and Judy both had quizzical looks on their faces as Judy answered probing, "My son Trey drives it from time to time but it's ours. He ate here about six weeks ago on his trip back to our ranch near Telluride Colorado. Is M here today?"

Anna chirped innocently, "No, Maria who we all call M quit her job a month ago after she didn't return from her boyfriend's ranch near Taos. She texted me last week that she had seen some amazing art in Taos and is very happy over there. She hasn't come back to visit us yet because a couple Mexican drug dealers in a fancy big-wheel pickup truck from Durango have been looking for her and your Maserati for some reason she didn't disclose. She drives a fast-restored black Shelby Mustang that is the envy of the oil and gas boys around here. I guess I've maybe talked too much but the drug dealers were in here again last night. I'll be back for your order."

Cooper replied, "Please bring us two cheese enchilada specials and ice teas our usual. Thanks." After she walked away, he said in low voice, "I ordered quickly so we can talk before she returns. This is obviously very serious. Two Mexican maybe cartel drug dealers looking for Trey's secret girlfriend we just found about. She drives a restored Shelby Mustang that sells for $100,000 plus on a waitress salary. They are looking for the Maserati and presumably Trey too."

Judy, with stress and concern in her voice, replied almost in a whisper, "I told you I had an inkling that Trey was concealing something in his phone conversation with me. Call him now. We need to know if we're in danger driving the Maserati around here."

Cooper called on his iPhone but there was no answer, so he left an urgent message for Trey to call back as soon as possible.

"He must be out on the ranch in a cell phone dead spot. I'll try to reach Jumbo Roberts and see if he knows anything about M or the drug dealers. I need his advice on whether we should drive the Maserati from here to the UP ranch."

"Good thinking." Jumbo answered as Anna delivered their plates. "Hello, Cooper what a pleasant surprise. I didn't think I would hear from you until lunch on Monday."

"Well pleasant it may not be, but a surprise, yes," and he recounted Anna's information.

"I was going to talk to you about an incident that the Maserati, Trey, and M were probably involved in near Aztec six weeks ago but not witnessed. I assumed wrongly you and Judy had met M or Maria Duran. Start eating your lunch while I call and get a New Mexico State patrolman to shadow you to the ranch. The waitress is probably ok, but the drug dealers may have a Mexican kitchen connection, who has called them to get a reward; I'll be back to you. Stay on hold."

Judy listened with her ear near the iPhone, "Whoa, horse, this is serious! What has Trey gotten into this time?"

"We'll find out when Jumbo comes back on the line." He took a half taco bite.

"I'm back…listen up. When you see a New Mexico black state patrol SUV pull up across the street from the café, pay up routinely then walk out the front entrance to the Maserati. If anyone and especially a Mexican approaches, you all move to the street side of it. Flash a Vee finger signal with your hand that is concealed behind the coupe. The state patrolman will call for back-up and intervene. I know you have a pistol in the front passenger side but only use it if and only if one is pulled on you all before the trooper can reach you. This is a very dangerous southern Colorado Mexican cartel gang out of Durango. The Colorado State Patrol is days away from a sweeping arrest of them with the DEA."

Judy asked, "Is M part of the gang? Is that how she affords a $100,000 car?"

Jumbo replied laughing, "OMG no. She's a twenty-two-year-old recent graduate of Fort Lewis College in Durango with a lead foot. Her father restores old hot rod drag racing cars. He restored her Shelby. She was a National Drag Racing Champion at 17 in its class. In lieu of jail time for leading the Colorado Patrol on a very dangerous high-speed chase she teaches our cadets at the State Patrol Academy fast driving. She's the equivalent of a champion barrel racer like you were in college, Judy, but in a go fast car."

"Wow that's a lot to digest. But why the drug dealers?" Judy asked.

"Colorado. State Police Intel thinks that the Maserati with M probably at the wheel tangled at a very high speed with a big-wheel, high desert running, drug pickup truck on the back route to Durango through Hesperus where you turned to Aztec today. Coked up Mexican cartel egos probably kicked in. There was a chase and a Mexican that DEA is tracking showed up at the Durango hospital on a Saturday night six weeks ago with a shoulder wound. Precisely a Glock 9 wound."

Judy volunteered, "That's the unscheduled night Trey spent in Durango on his way back to the ranch with the Maserati."

Cooper added, "He had a ranch Glock 9 in it."

Jumbo stated, "And he could target shoot lights out by six years old at the YbarC."

"Yes," is all Cooper could add as saw the state trooper's black SUV pull up about twenty yards down the street from the Maserati. He added, "Trooper's here. We're on the move. Thanks."

They paid the waitress with a good tip and walked out normally to the Maserati. As Cooper approached the passenger side door and pushed the key to electronically unlock it, a young Mexican approached them. He had a worried look as he stopped.

He said in broken English, "I cook here. M my friend. Cartel kill me if I didn't call and say fast black car here they look for. They wait for you outside of Aztec both ways. Get help." He walked away.

Cooper walked to the street side of the Maserati and signaled the state patrolman who exited the SUV and approached with his hand on his pistol holster. Cooper repeated the cook's warning.

The patrolman replied calmly, "I'll shadow you at a safe distance with back up on standby at Chama. He'll follow you to the Colorado border. Keep your Glock 9 handy, but if a shootout occurs don't hit me in the crossfire. I hope they think you are being followed for a chance for me to write a speeding ticket. We don't want to tip our drug investigation. Your distress signal is a triple brake light flash. If I have to intervene, I'll write them a speeding or reckless driving ticket then follow you to just west of Chama. When you return to Telluride take Independence Pass through Aspen. Don't return through New Mexico. Do not drive the Maserati in New Mexico or around Durango unless and until Jumbo Roberts says it's safe. We're doing this favor for him." His eyes scanned the street and he walked back to the black SUV.

"We're out of here now," stated Judy, "before I get really angry at my son."

"You can't," replied Cooper. "Jumbo, Joe Bear Spirit and the old Ute Medicine Man saved me form worse fates." He pulled out onto the street with the black SUV following them.

Fifteen miles outside of Aztec in the sage flats dotted with pump jacks the state patrol SUV followed a quarter of a mile behind them. Cooper kept an occasional bead on him in his rearview mirror. Judy scanned both sides of the roadside ahead of them. Suddenly without warning a late model big-wheel green pickup truck emerged from a sage surrounded dirt road onto the state highway with a too close high-speed turn behind the Maserati. Cooper softly touched the brake pedal three times flashing his brake lights and then pushed the metal race type pedal firmly. The Maserati accelerated from seventy to one hundred and twenty miles an hour in four seconds. The big-wheeled blue pickup truck faded in his rearview mirror on the long straight stretch of broken yellow line black top.

Judy, looking into the side mirror, said calmly, "The passenger is holding a pistol out of his window. Go to one fifty."

"Roger that," he replied.

"The state patrol SUV with lights flashing is closing on them fast. The pistol is back inside the pickup's window. The trooper may not have seen it. They're falling off us. Slow down to one hundred. The trooper has pulled them over. I see his backup's flashing lights closing in fast. Back to ninety and out of here."

"That was close. They were ten feet from hitting our trunk lid when I accelerated away from them. We would have spun out of control and rolled," Cooper said.

"Their high steel front bumper with its four top mounted running lights filled my passenger side view mirror. I hope the two troopers can handle them."

"They can. The drug dealers will figure he nailed them for reckless driving by roaring onto the highway out of the sage and almost hitting us. He probably didn't see the pistol, but the troopers will assume they're armed and dangerous. He'll stall writing the ticket until back-up arrives." Suddenly a county sheriff's white sedan came into view a mile down the road with lights flashing and a siren screaming into the air over empty sage flats. Cooper slowed and pulled the Maserati as close to the edge of the pavement as possible. The sedan screamed by them toward the now out of sight state patrol pullover behind them. Cooper said, "He's covered. Additional back up was close. The cartel boys will take the ticket quietly to avoid a drug arrest if the trooper searches their pickup. Both sides want to protect their cover, interestingly enough. Anyway, keep our Glock 9 handy."

"Roger that, Cooper…to the ranch where at this moment in time I want is my hands around my son's neck, but I'll calm down," she asserted.

"You have to handle this carefully with him. We can't publicly or privately cut his legs out from under him with the responsibility of running the ranch. He now has a live-in girlfriend whom we've never met. That solves the ranch's isolation for him but adds another dimension to our relationship just like when you moved to the YbarC," he replied.

"I know. She's taking my bridling from the nest. I need to meditate on all of this until I spell you at the wheel."

After a gasoline stop in Chama, Judy took over driving and she turned at a tee junction toward Antonito Colorado across the Cumbres Pass. She drove toward one of the earth's most beautiful high mountain passes with the highway following the narrow gauge railroad up it. Millions of green pines and Aspen covered its sides below tree line, while summer cattle grazed on its high grassy meadows. When the Maserati passed the rail yards on the edge of Chama, a New Mexico State Patrol black SUV pulled off the shoulder of the highway to follow them to the Colorado border. He fell in behind as they crossed the bridge over the cold blue water in the Chama River.

Judy commented, "I guess we can't pull over at our favorite spot in the blue spruce trees by the old corral at the top of the pass on a perfect deep blue sky day."

"Don't tempt me." The Maserati accelerated out of town past the old glider plane's narrow paved takeoff and landing strip.

Judy parked the Maserati at the hacienda's hand carved wooden front door. Maestas walked over to greet them in the low west sun, which highlighted the shadowed soft angles of the adobe's rounded corner edges. Judy and Cooper opened its low doors and stepped out slowly standing up.

"Se buena for you to come here. It has been a long tempo. Much is happening. I want to talk about things. Some of it's dangerous around aqui I think. I'll take your bags and show you the new guest room. The hacienda is very beautiful inside."

"We'll carry our soft luggage. The trunk is very small. You look well, Maestas," Cooper replied.

Judy looked around the front of the hacienda with anxiety on her face. "Maestas, where is Trey? I told him we would arrive near sunset."

"They, I mean he's riding back from the south grazing area," Maestas mumbled just as two horses and riders galloped through the hacienda's front gate, throwing up a cloud of dust. The riders saw the black Maserati, reined in their horses but still made a tight pass by Judy, Cooper and Maestas. The dust cloud drifted over the black car and the group.

"Whoa," Trey shouted as the sweating horses came to a stop by the corner of the adobe hacienda. He and M dismounted, and walked over to Judy, Cooper and Maestas as the low sunlight filtered through the dust back lighting the scene. Trey smiling said, "You're early. Welcome. Say hello to Maria Duran or M, as she prefers to be called. She rides and drives like the spring wind. She lives here with me. She's been my secret partner in the renovation of this old adobe dump. A tour is in order."

A dusty disarmed smiling Judy spoke first, "Well hello, M, if I may, you sure can handle a range horse. I want to ride with you. Trey, I can't wait to see the hacienda. The new large front window looks great. Well worth the expense."

"Trey told me you were a champion barrel racer plus that you do the ranch books and would know the cost of each renovation item. We tried to get the best deals around here but it's not Albuquerque."

Cooper, who was taken M's natural beauty and riding, added, "I thought the outlaws were chasing you and your range ponies. M, it's good to meet you. Trey, please help us with a small box and a couple cherry pies in a cooler your mother baked. The box has a modern toaster oven for your new kitchen. They are on the Maserati's back seat. Then show us to the new guest room. Maestas, take the ponies and have a cowhand cool them down. Trey, I have a good bottle of bourbon for cocktails. We'll sip a glass or two while we tour the hacienda with you all."

"You all look a little dusty so splash a little water on your faces in the new guest bathroom." Maestas took the reins from Trey and M rounded the corner of the hacienda with the horses. The low Northern New Mexico sun's magic hour light splashed the faces of everyone in their cowboy hats and denim work shirts.

With bourbon in glass tumblers, they toured the renovated hacienda before dinner. The bunkhouse cook had prepared ranch rib eye steaks with baked beans and coleslaw. M opened a bottle of New Mexico red wine from a Dixon vineyard near Taos as they all sat down.

Judy opened the conversation. "Great job, both of you. I always imagined that this old adobe ranch house could be modernized and returned to its original splendor. We just were never here long enough with the money to tackle it. A toast to your work and the hacienda." Wine glasses clinked as Trey and M smiled.

Trey said, "We have a little thank you present." M pulled the brown paper wrapped painting up from the side of her chair and handed it carefully to Judy. "Our present."

Judy removed the paper and smiled, "Perfect for our bedroom at the YbarC. I love the artist's modern approach to painting the horses but it's not too abstract like the new media fiber optic painting in your bedroom."

"A toast to our new painting." Cooper raised his wine glass.

"Let's enjoy these fresh ranch steaks."

When the plates were nearly empty, Cooper stated, "Maestas indicated there was danger on the ranch or near the ranch?"

"Yes, and we were going to discuss it with you because I assume you'll see Jumbo on the way back to the YbarC. So here goes." Trey told them about the drug drop that crossed the Rio Grande River Gorge onto the ranch, which caused the shoot out that, put him and M in extreme danger. He said he shot the drug gang shooter but couldn't confirm he killed him. Finally, he told them about the deputy sheriff's surprising arrival on the scene as they watched from safety in the shallow arroyo on horseback.

"So that's why you shipped us the two Paint horses you were riding to the ranch. Have there been more drug drops on the ranch?" Judy asked, very alarmed.

"The cowboys haven't reported any to Maestas. They've seen more low altitude flights across the Gorge but farther west from it…none over the ranch," Trey replied.

"Have you reported the flights to the authorities?" Cooper quizzed.

"No," M interjected, "it's too dangerous. Some are corrupt in northern NM and even Southern Colorado like the deputy in the SUV we saw at the drop. He escorted the topless brown Bronco sage runner off the ranch, which had the wounded or dead shooter and the drug bundle in it. Jumbo Roberts told us at the rodeo there was a cross border drug running investigation underway but to keep our heads down around here."

A surprised Judy asked, "Did he happen to mention a Durango Mexican cartel drug gang was looking for a black Maserati and you, M, plus you, Trey, too?"

"Whoops!" M chirped. "That's on me."

"Yes, a big whoops, my dear," Judy replied with a serious frown on her face. "Your waitress friend Anna tipped us off at the Aztec café that the Mexicans had been in looking for you last night after she saw our black Maserati parked on the street. We called Jumbo and he explained the situation as well as he could. When we returned to the Maserati, your Mexican kitchen worker friend met us on the sidewalk and told us he had tipped the cartel off or they would kill him. Jumbo had the New Mexico State Patrol follow us to the Colorado, which saved us from a big-wheel, pickup surprise attack outside of Aztec. After Jumbo's information about your drag racing career M and your work with the state patrol cadets, I have to assume you were at the wheel of the Maserati when Trey shot and wounded a cartel drug dealer."

"You're right. I made a stupid high-speed pass to impress Trey and kind of protect the Maserati's windshield from the gravel the big wheels throw off. I guess I'm probably off your future daughter in law's list?"

"Not yet. Trey, you did the shooting yes or no?" his mother demanded.

"Yes, the passenger had a pistol and pointed it at M after they blocked the highway to force her to stop. I shot him in the shoulder to wound him and cause him to drop his pistol. He did. M wheeled us out from behind the pickup truck to safety," Trey replied.

"You're still on my future daughter in law's list," Judy said to break the tension.

"You're my son all the way. You could always point and shoot a pistol like the gun hands of yore on the YbarC," Cooper stated.

"I can if I have to, plus a rifle," Trey replied.

"So since this is a tell all catch up dinner, are there any other kind of odd or key things we need to know about your activities both on and off and the ranch?" Cooper asked.

"Well kind of," Trey replied. "We found a mine tunnel entrance with an old Spanish arch over it on the mountain inside the ranch boundary. I crawled in my body's length against M's advice and pulled out an old Spanish amour breastplate with a cross on it and a solid gold coin a couple days ago. They're hidden in the master bedroom. No one knows about them but us. We're planning to take you on a ride-hike to the tunnel tomorrow so we all can decide what to do. Other than that, the ranch is having a good summer with plenty of grass for the cattle."

"Do you two ever just take it easy and keep your heads down?"

Cooper asked.

"We do," blushed M, "but that's classified." Trey couldn't hold back his laughter.

Judy, blushing stated, "Dinner adjourned. Cherry pie in the beautifully remodeled living room."

On Saturday morning after a sunup breakfast Cooper, Judy, Trey, M, and Maestas rode out to the western grazing pastures near the Rio Grande River Gorge. They all had saddle rifles on their range horses. The riders approached the green gate where the drug runners and the deputy sheriff had trespassed onto the ranch the afternoon of the drug drop and reined up. Trey re-briefed everyone including Maestas for the first time with all the details at his father's request.

Cooper concluded, "We can't let our cow hand's lives be put in danger."

"What do you and Maestas recommend? One, they are already fully aware of the airplane drug drops across the Rio Grande River Gorge so they ride with saddle rifles and pistols. Two, ranch orders are to pull back from any airdrops as far away from the Gorge as possible. Three, every cowhand rides with a fully-charged walkie-talkie and cell phone to call or text Maestas first and me second if they can't reach Maestas," Trey stated.

Cooper suggested, "Four, chain lock the green gate and give the cowhands a key to it to use to gather stray cattle. Five, you, Trey, and Maestas ride with binoculars to see if you can ID the airplane's tail number if it's visible. Trey, stay in weekly touch with Jumbo Roberts to see if any progress is being made by law enforcement at the county, state or federal level to stop the drug drops. Also set up a secure way for you to contact him about ongoing drug drop activity. Finally, operate the ranch on the assumption everything that can go wrong will go wrong with these drug drops. I don't want anyone on this ranch caught in the crossfire. Only seasoned cowhands ride these west pastures in pairs. M, it's your call if you ride with Trey out here."

"Then these are the posted orders. I will write them up," Trey stated.

"I'll be Trey's paired rider. The state patrol cadet trainers taught me how to shoot a pistol and I'm now rifle target practicing with Trey," M asserted as Judy looked up in admiration.

"I rode with Cooper during 1989-90 range war on the YbarC. Also, here after we bought this operation to back him up when we were cowhand and money short. Good that you're willing to ride with my son," Judy added.

"Settled then," stated Cooper, "The range grass and fences look good, Maestas. You can return to the headquarters and brief the hands. We're taking a ride over to the mountain with Trey and M for our picnic lunch." He spurred his horse.

The sun arched at summer high noon when the group tied up their mountain shoed range horses close to the hidden tunnel entrance. Judy laid out a rolled wool saddle blanket and spread their lunch on it. After lunch she bagged garbage and stored it in her saddlebags. Trey led them on foot toward the tunnel entrance while carefully checking the trail for new human footprints or animal activity. He saw some elk and deer scat thirty yards from the tunnel entrance. Closer fresh mountain lion scat with its blood streaks was on the trail. He pointed to it and in a whisper said, "We have a mountain lion following the elk and deer...last night. Dad, keep your saddle rifle ready. I hope it's not in the tunnel." The group moved step by step carefully up toward the tunnel entrance but so did the mature mountain lion tracks in the dry rocky soil. Cooper hand signaled them to stop about ten yards from the sage covered tunnel entrance and he raised the saddle rifle to his shoulder. They all heard a hiss from the tunnel. Trey hand signaled a retreat back down the trail as he and M pulled Glock 9's from their holsters and chambered a bullet. Cooper sidestepped carefully on the dry dusty basalt rocky trail with his rifle pointed at the hidden tunnel opening until they were back at the horses. They were snorting fear.

"Let's ease the horses down the mountain. They sense the lion. I'll ride drag with my rifle in hand and, Trey, you lead with a saddle rifle. M holster your pistol. It's too dangerous to shoot off a descending horse in a group of riders...only in old westerns with blanks and stuntmen," Cooper ordered in a strong whisper.

Ten minutes later, they were riding a rocky arroyo edge off the mountain. It was dangerous footing for the horses, but they couldn't risk the cat jumping a rider and horse in the still six feet deep narrow trench. A half hour later, they reached the mountain's grassy, sage-specked flank and rested in the saddle while the horses nibbled on the pale green circles of the rocky soil's gamma grass pods.

"There was no sign of mountain lion scat or kill bones in the tunnel's first ten or so feet and none on the trail to it last week. I think it's a mature male because there are no kitten tracks. He followed our scent, to the tunnel entrance. Lucky for us it was only a cornered hiss warning. A female with a kitten would have come out of the tunnel like a rocket propelled grenade to protect it. So, you only got to see the sage concealed entrance, Dad, and, Mom."

"That we did," Judy replied.

"Do we explore the tunnel with a team including a mining engineer? I showed you the assay report that confirmed the small quartz rock we found in the arroyo is gold-bearing," Trey asked.

Cooper reflected and replied, "Let's hold up on that. There's a retired mining engineer from Ouray Colorado, which is across Ajax Peak from Telluride. I have ridden the ski lift with him. He's currently consulting on reopening a closed silver mine there. He would probably sign a non-disclosure agreement for a consulting contract. I'll feel him out. The tunnel is on our ranch so the claim can't be legally jumped. News about the tunnel could set off a treasure hunt on the mountain across our fence lines. Word of the Spanish gold coin and armor would be like throwing gasoline on a campfire. There are eco groups against new mining or re-opening old mines in the New West. There are conflicting state and federal laws on who really owns the found artifacts. In our will, which you will execute there are a few of the YbarC's secret antiquity finds. You can decide how to handle them."

"Fair enough," answered Trey. "Let's enjoy a blue-sky relaxed ride back to the hacienda. The horses have worked hard enough today."

"Second that," Judy and M said in unison.

Three days later, Cooper sent a simple coded text to Trey.

"Lunch with the WHALE good. He'll monitor situation/keep us posted until then watch out for eagles. Don't get a speeding ticket." Trey deleted it from his iPhone after he read it to M. He reviewed the new ranch written operating orders with Maestas and posted them on the bunkhouse bulletin board.

CHAPTER 7

HOT ROD DIRT DRAGSTERS

M and Trey were in the Tech Inspection tent at the Hot Rod Dirt Drags by its hard-packed, eighth of a mile, dirt drag strip near Monte Vista, Colorado on a warm May day. M's father fired up the motor on the chopped and channeled metallic cobalt blue 1934 modified Ford Roadster dragster. Its black stock car dirt track tires on wide chrome-plated rims were brand new. Pete had built it for M to race at the event on Saturday. It was entered in the unlimited class with a highly modified Edelbrock super-charged motor that ran on ninety percent nitro fuel. The inspection official checked it with an iPad list of the drag race requirements for the unlimited class. Trey and M chatted with her aging, dyed-black-haired father Pete Duran as he waited to answer tech questions.

"Thanks, Dad, for trailering the Roadster over for me. It looks very fast for dirt. I need a practice run in it this afternoon when the track opens. I've only raced your classic restored unmodified T 1933 Chevy in this event," M stated clearly.

"Mr. Duran, or I guess I should now call you Pete as you requested, how many horsepower does the engine produce?" a concerned Trey asked,

Pete's brown eyes darting, answered, "Three hundred and ten horses with the super charger but these oversize dirt track stock car racing tires will provide the traction stability it needs for an eighth of a mile. It's in the night race tomorrow under the lights at lower track temps. M can run practice after lunch to get the feel of it on dirt. A couple times if necessary. I want to sell it at the car show auction Sunday, so I need M to light foot the run but still win."

"I'll take good care of it, Dad. My over-the-top lead foot days have ended," she replied.

Pete gave her a surprised quizzical look. "You sure that's a winning attitude? If not, I will pull the race entry and just sell it in the car show."

"No way, but I won't deliver you a blown motor or broken dragster from a dirt race. Besides, your Roadster has fifty more horsepower than any of the posted entries. We'll get a winning elapsed time with a safe speed above the record 140 miles an hour," M stated.

The aging, grey-bearded, baseball-capped inspection official said, "That's sixty horsepower more than any other unlimited class entry. I passed it, but I hope your suspension can handle the weight of the wide dirt track stock car tires. They will grip the dirt good no doubt, but we don't have a rule, you know, on tire size as long as they are new or in good condition. Yours are new. I need your signature as builder, and M's signature as driver, on the iPad line. It's good to see M back after three years. She's still the youngest driver to ever win a class here."

Trey said, "Smell that Monte Vista barbeque over at the smoker by the white trailer. Lunch is on me with baked beans and potato salad. This part of Colorado's San Luis Valley has the second biggest potato crop in the US. Let's eat our share before M's test runs."

After a mouth-watering lunch with other drivers, dragster builders, motor mechanics, entry sponsors and general car nuts, they walked over to their pit. M changed into race gear in the nearby women's drivers' tent for two practice runs. Trey found a seat in the sparsely filled, grey aluminum portable bleachers by the start line and waited for the first practice run. After Pete completed a final tune check with his laptop. M eased the dirt strip dragster out onto the track to the left lane for its solo run. Her pink helmeted head was below the Roadster's roll bar and she wore a fireproof blue racing suit. Her black-gloved hands grasped the steering wheel. She rolled the car back and forth warming its cold tires. It threw up loose dirt. She pulled it up to the starting line and waited for the timing light to go green.

When it did, she accelerated the dragster into a startlingly fast straight fast line as its side exhaust pipes roared into the life. It tore down the strip with only a rear wheel wiggle near the finish line. A small electronic time board flashed a speed of 134 miles an hour. Its caption said fastest time of the day. The small, mostly race crew, crowd clapped in approval.

Trey heard a crew chief type below him say, "Back to work, boys. She's faster than our Bonneville Salt Flats Lake time. Pete brought an automatic pistol to a six-gun fight. His girl has a hair trigger start."

Trey met M in the pit after the Roadster was towed back. She was in a heated conversation with her father. "Detune it. There's too much torque for the dirt. You saw it get loose near the finish. I almost pulled the parachute, but I got it straightened out. Otherwise sell it at the car show Sunday."

"I think you warmed up the tires too much. Maybe caked the treads. Dirt stays cooler than pavement. We'll clean the tires and practice run again," Pete countered.

"No, we won't. Detune it. Cut the horsepower by forty horses, lower the compression and torque. I'll only drive it one more time and that's in the race tomorrow night. I have a new life now with Trey and the ranch. I'm not rolling it and exploding into flames at 140 miles or more an hour with nitro fuel in the tank. You've got an all-night job, Dad, to make final inspection. Maybe your wrench pal Billie will help if you pay him. I will if you won't. See you at breakfast at the Best Western Manor Motel. Trey and I are watching the classic movie Hot Rod from our room's picture window that faces the Manor Drive-In Theater screen. The rooms have a sound box from the Drive-In." She grabbed Trey's hand and pulled him toward the pit exit. When they reached her Shelby Mustang in the mostly empty parking lot, a few teenagers surrounded it. After she answered all their questions, popped the hood, and the teens started to depart, they got into the Shelby Mustang. She gunned the motor and spun it three hundred sixty degrees spraying gravel. She straightened it out and sped toward the open gate. A few cheers went up from the event Tee-shirted teens.

"You're angry at Pete?"

"You damn straight. He put me in an over torqued dragster in an eighth of a mile dirt race because he thought he could get away with it and set a record. I almost lost that dragster out there before he could sell it Sunday. I'll drive it tomorrow with less torque and still get the speed and elapsed time I need to win. So, let's go back to the Manor Motel for a hot tub and a shower."

"I have a good steak house in town for dinner. After dinner, it's watching Hot Rod at the Manor Drive-In Theater Motel in bed with you."

"Way better than in the back seat of a car at the Drive-In movies I heard about in our parents' days. We'll sleep in and sunbathe by the pool. I drive tomorrow night after sunset."

"Your plan is perfect," he replied as the Shelby Mustang roared onto the state highway.

As the bright orange horizon sunset faded revealing the clear night sky, car headlights were turned on along both sides of the dirt drag strip. The lighting was marginal but good enough for M's projected five second run at 140 miles an hour finish line speed. Trey leaned down and kissed her hard before she pulled her pink helmet on and her racing goggles down. Her black ponytail peeked out below her helmet line. His hand scraped the coarse material of her fireproof suit as he stood up.

"Go fast, M, but I need you back in one piece."

M answered, "The revised inspection report states Billie and Dad knocked thirty-seven horses out of the motor and therefore enough torque to let my tires grip better for 5 seconds and change when the blonde lady waves the checkered finish line flag. If I pull the parachute after the finish line don't worry, it's because I'm blind on the drag strip's dark run out. Got to go. I love you, cowboy." Pete and his helpers rolled her out of the pits.

Trey, sipping a Coke Billie had spiked with bourbon, walked over to the grandstand and found a high seat to watch the entire eighth of a mile dragster race. M had the right lane start by the bleachers with the Bonneville Salt Flats land speed record holding Lake Dragster black coupe in the left lane. This was a one run match race for the class championship, winner takes all. He noticed a lot of betting going on in the bleachers with cash being held by third parties in wads. High tension saturated the cooling summer night air as the sunset's last pale orange glow line exited the western horizon. The first orange-hazed night star appeared. Both dragsters rolled their tires a few times and backed behind the starting line. Pete was behind the portable, ranch steel fence line by M's cockpit. He looked around tensely at a crewcut Billie in his grease-stained overalls who looked back with a frown Trey noted.

M's dragster's motor roared through its un-muffed straight pipes with nitro fuel flame flares lighting the starting line. The starting light flashed green, and M roared off the line first with a perfectly timed start. Her drag racer accelerated to a hundred miles an hour midway down the dirt strip as the car headlights strobed between the two charging machines. M had a half a dragster lead as her speed rocketed. Trey was transfixed on her silhouetted pink helmet under the glistening polished chrome roll bar. The crowd roared in support of their favorite. Trey saw M's dragster's rear wheels wiggle again twenty yards short of the finish line as Billie screamed noooo! into his right ear. Her dragster veered sideways toward the other lane at over one hundred and forty miles an hour. It went airborne as the parachute opened and flew over the Lake Dragster at the finish line. The checker flag blonde lady dived in the dirt. The crowd screamed in unison and some burst into tears.

Billie blurted out, "Pete screwed her. He only cut half the horsepower and torque she asked for. He lied on that final inspection report."

Trey was in shock as he jumped to his feet and ran down the bleacher's metal bench seat tops, jumped the fence and ran down M's empty lane. Sirens wailed as emergency vehicle lights flashed red and yellow. Trey saw flames flare from the M's wounded dragster's exhaust pipes as it crash-landed on its side. While he ran, a stream of white fire-retardant foam from a fire truck hose was sprayed onto the burning dragster, covering it like a puffy comforter. M, blinded by the foam with her broken hand unable to pull the release on her safety harness, suddenly felt strong-gloved hands under her armpits. She heard her tight safety harness release the pressure across her chest below her breasts. She blacked out. Trey, running full speed, saw Pete reach two firemen in full gear who were dragging a limp M away from the burning dragster. As he started to cross into the empty outside lane near the finish line, someone grabbed him from behind and pulled him to the ground.

"Stay down, cowboy, this isn't a bad bull ride…it's going to blow!" He saw a police badge sparkle in the dirt filled corner of his right eye as he hugged the drag strip's hard dirt surface.

M's dragster blew sky high when the nitro fuel tank exploded, throwing flames a hundred feet into the night air as onlookers screamed. The sirens intensified as more foam was poured onto the burning machine. Trey's compression-stung eardrums heard the patrolman rise and run toward the burning dragster. He gathered himself mentally and his adrenalin forced him back onto his feet and he ran toward where he last saw M. The flames had abated as he passed the dragster and felt its heat field. He saw M on a stretcher that was being slid into a red, white-topped, red-bodied EMT ambulance with Pete at her side. He heard an EMT yell to a policeman.

"Secure this area, the medical helicopter from Alamosa hospital's trauma center is on the way. It needs to land by us and fly her out ASAP."

Trey ran by the policeman before he could start unspooling yellow tapeline. He reached Pete, pushed past him and jumped into the ambulance's back open door. M weakly grasped his trembling hand. Pete started to step up into the ambulance.

M murmured to the middle aged EMT, "Keep Pete out. Let Trey stay with me." She lied, "He's my husband." The EMT outside the open door forcefully pushed Pete back.

Trey whispered, "How do you know about the horsepower lie?"

"I saw the RPM's go too high about four seconds off the line but it was too late to power down. I hoped my ride's rear wheels' grip would hold the dirt until the checkered flag and I could pull the chute. The big tires were too heavy, and the weak suspension vibrated them loose at over 140 miles an hour. That's all I remember as I went into the air and pushed the chute button. Tell my father he's fired forever," and tears came to her smoky eyes and rolled down her bright red smoke-streaked cheeks.

"I will. Billy confessed to me as you went airborne. I love you even though you smell like a charred, Cub Scout campfire hot dog with a singed ponytail."

He asked the EMT, "Can I fly with M in the helicopter?"

"No, only the emergency trauma doc and a flight nurse on this bird. Too much weight if you're added and they need room to work." He changed M's IV. "We're going to put Ms. Go Fast back together again for you. Out of here, the helio is landing. Tell the state patrolman you are her husband and he'll give you a fast emergency lights-on escort to Alamosa Hospital that'll be fifteen minutes or less."

M, voice fading, whispered, "I ache, I can't move my right arm and hand much and a couple tiny burns are lit up above my fire suit collar. I'll live for you." M closed her eyes. The heart monitor beeped and the EMT gave her a shot and then pushed Trey out of the ambulance door. He jumped and landed in front of Pete and Billie.

Pete blurted out, "You tell her?" as Billie winced.

"No, I didn't but she saw the RPM's go too high near the finish line, but it was too late to pull the chute. She figured it out. I told her what Billie said about your false inspection report that she checked before the drag race. She whispered to me to fire you forever, so you are fired!" Trey said, raising his voice.

"Crew chief and dad?" he asked with tears finality in his eyes.

"Both, I assume, but you can talk to her after she recovers. It's clear she doesn't want you at the hospital. M's unconscious and they're fighting to save her life. She promised me she'd make it. I'm driving to Alamosa behind the investigating state patrolman. I'll call you with an update. Goodbye." Trey walked away stone cold mad at Pete.

After a moonless night, white-knuckle drive in M's Shelby Mustang behind the Colorado State Police car escort to the Alamosa hospital a frazzled Trey bounded up the steps to the second floor ICU nursing station. An on-duty head nurse looked up and calmly asked, "What can I do for you, young man?"

"I want to see M...I mean Maria Duran," an out of breath Trey blurted in a stressed voice. "Why's she in Intensive Care?"

"Are you next of kin?" the nurse asked. We downloaded her medical records from Durango and they only list Pete Duran as her father and the family member to contact. No mother or siblings." She stated clearly.

"I'm her boyfriend Trey Stuart. We live together at my ranch near Costilla, New Mexico about an hour away." Tears came to Trey's eyes as his voice started to break. "Please let me see her. I followed a state patrolman here after they loaded her into the medical helicopter."

"I don't think I can until her father arrives."

She paused as the ruggedly handsome uniformed state patrolman reached the ICU station. He took charge of the situation with a hand on Trey's shoulder.

"Trey Stuart's cleared to see Maria Duran if you are allowing visitors at the state police commander's request. Maria or M as we call her told the EMTs her father is banned from visiting. When asked why not, she told them to talk to Billie, a member of her pit crew at the Monte Vista Dirt Drag Races. I have to open a criminal investigation and will also need to talk to her when she's strong enough. Billie and the dragster inspection official alleged her father falsified the dragster's motor horsepower and torque specs, which is a violation of the event rules. Worse than that, he did not tell M, the driver. That lack of information may have led to her almost fatal accident. What's her condition?"

"Serious on the edge of critical but because our pulmonary doc that's the lung specialist won't arrive until noon tomorrow, we're keeping her in ICU as a precaution. We don't know if there's undetected lung damage from the nitro fire and smoke she inhaled. Physically the emergency room docs have stabilized her broken hand and arm. After she's out of ICU, a hand and ortho surgeon will operate and set them with pins. I don't want her to talk so please hold your police interview for now. At your commander's request regarding Mr. Stuart, I will go into her room and ask her if he may visit," the nurse stated matter of factly. She made a note in her room log and then walked through the ICU's door to M's room.

"Thank you, officer," Trey said, relieved.

"Accepted but we all respect M. Her high-speed driver training has probably saved trooper's lives andor injuries. She needs your support now. Her father may have committed a very serious crime, but we owe him, like any citizen, a full and fair investigation. The Alamosa County DA will have to decide if criminal charges are brought. When and if did you know about the falsified Inspection Technical Horsepower Report?" the trooper probed.

"I was sitting in the bleachers next to Billie when the dragster wiggled like it did on its Friday practice run near the finish line. This time it skidded sideways and flew into the air. He blurted out Pete falsified the inspection info and didn't cut the horsepower. M argued with Pete after the practice run. She told him to cut forty horsepower plus the motor's torque or she wouldn't race it."

"Do you know when and how she found out?" the trooper asked.

"She told me in the ambulance she saw the RPMs go too high near the finish line just before the wiggle. That it was too late to power down and pull the chute unless she could steer the dragster straight across the line. Then it went airborne. Billie confirmed her guess when the EMT's got her to the ambulance." Trey struggled to hold back tears.

"You are a material witness. Please stay in Alamosa until Monday for an interview with me and a meeting with the DA if necessary." The

ICU nurse opened the door and signaled Trey to come through it. He followed her to room 212.

"Be very calm with her and supportive. She needs your love more than anything in the world. Betrayal by a parent is a deadly sin and I have seen it kill a patient. Trauma healing can be as much medical as psychological." She opened the room door and walked Trey into it. M looked up, with tears in her eyes, in a sea of tubes and monitor lines to machines with screens.

She said in a weak whisper, "You're here. I need you. I love you. I want to ride the Paint horses with you."

"I love you, M. The docs and nurses will get you unhooked from all these machines in no time. They just want to make sure that the fiery nitro fuel fumes are out of your lungs. The clear blue sunny western sky and pure air on the ranch will do the rest. You can rein your Paint horse with one hand the way you ride." He bravely held back tears.

She softly replied, "Hold my hand and kiss me on the cheek."

Trey looked at the nurse and she nodded yes. He took her hand, pulled off his summer straw Stetson cowboy hat and steered his dirty blond matted hair through three lines. He gave her a long kiss on the cheek and then he whispered in her ear. A wan but delicious smile came to her lips. She said softly, "I need to rest, I'm very sleepy. Can Trey stay with me?"

"We need to keep you isolated while you rest until the lung doctor checks you at noon tomorrow. We're protecting your lungs from infection from heat trauma. I'll get Trey settled on a couch with a blanket in the guest waiting room near the nurses' station."

Trey stood up and followed the nurse out of the room as M nodded off. After the nurse settled Trey on the couch with a pillow and blanket, she said, "If I may ask, what did you whisper to get that smile and bring her heart beat back to a strong normal beat on the monitor for the first time since she arrived here?"

"We would make love beside her Shelby Mustang on our picnic blanket in the grassy park by the Hesperus River like we did the first day we met as soon as she was ready to drive it," Trey replied with total loving innocence believing M would be well soon.

The seasoned nurse had a tear in the corner of her eye as she said softly like the mother she was in daily life, "Love is an amazing healer. Please get a little sleep. Tomorrow is a long day for Maria and you. This place wakes up early. You can get breakfast downstairs a six a.m. Just let the nurse's station know where you are. Give us your cell phone number too. Do you have someone to look after your ranch? You may be in Alamosa for a while."

"Yes, Maestas my foreman and our cowhands will operate the UP ranch. OMG! I need to text my mom and dad. They just met M but returned to the YbarC near Telluride. They can return and help."

"Do it please. Maria doesn't have a mother as you know. You'll need female help for her while she recovers on a big ranch like yours. Big ranches surround Alamosa and I don't have to tell you they are tough boy's clubs that all operate on the code of "cowboy up" for the brand and ride hard." She exited.

Trey pulled his iPhone out of his smoky jean's hip pocket and texted Judy, "M in bad crash at her Dirt Strip Drag Race. Now in Alamosa hospital ICU. I'll need you at ranch to help her when she gets out of hospital, nurse advises Dad may want to help Maestas too. I may be in Alamosa for a while. Know more at noon. Trey. Bring Paint horses." He fell asleep in the dark room on the hard couch. His cowboy hat was on a cowboy boot top beside it.

Dawn came early as a hungry Trey ate bacon, fried eggs over easy, sausage and a stack of pancakes in the busy hospital cafeteria. There was a low din as doctors, nurses, and assorted personnel came on and off shift. Patients' relatives, friends, and children ate breakfast waiting for visiting hours to start after the weekend on-call doctors made their rounds. A few of the relatives looked like they hadn't slept much in days. Cowboy hats speckled the dining room. His iPhone buzzed a text; "We're on the way in a half hour straight to hospital. I've called Alamosa Best Western and have a suite with two bedrooms reserved open ended. See you in six hours or so. Paints being trailed to ranch by a cowhand tomorrow. Love, Mom".

As Trey finished his breakfast the night shift ICU nurse stopped at his table, "M had a good night. She rested well and her oxygen absorption is much better with a normal heartbeat. The lung doc will see her by noon. Betty is the ICU day nurse. I told her you are cleared to visit M. By the way, I'm Amber. See you in twelve hours."

"Thanks, Amber, for everything. My mom just texted they are on the road."

"Good parents," and she departed. Trey finished his coffee and walked out of the lobby into the clear, early summer morning, high Colorado Plateau cool air. He checked the Shelby Mustang and made sure its security alarm was on. He called the Manor Motel and had the desk clerk check them out and store their luggage. The clerk asked, "Are you M's boyfriend?"

"Yes."

"Tell her everyone in the lobby at breakfast hopes she is ok. She's all anyone is talking about."

"I will. I'll ask the hospital to issue a press release on her condition as soon as they can for the Dirt Drag Race crews and fans. Thanks for asking."

He briefed Maestas by iPhone and walked back toward the main entrance door where a satellite TV truck had parked. A TV newswoman with movie star looks had a mike in hand and the cameraman had a high-tech camera on his shoulder. She stopped Trey. "I saw you by the Shelby Mustang. We were told the badly-injured woman driver who races by M drives it. Are you on her crew? Is she still in ICU? We're rolling sound and picture."

"I'm her boyfriend, Trey Stuart," he replied surprised not knowing what else to say.

The TV reporter raised her logoed mike and looked straight into the camera lens. "I'm Tracy Miles for Denver Channel 1 sports news. Durango Colorado's famous young woman national drag racing star is in intensive care at the Alamosa Hospital behind me. I'm with Trey Stuart, her boyfriend. Trey, what is her condition? Was she badly-burned when her dragster exploded into flames? Have you talked to her today? Her fans are praying for a fast recovery."

"She's resting from the traumatic drag racing accident and resulting wreck with a nitro fuel explosion. She's listed in serious but stable condition. Her fireproof body suit and modern pink helmet with goggles protected her from burns except for a slightly singed ponytail. A specialist will exam her lungs this morning so we should all have an update by afternoon."

"We have a tip from an event official that her father who's her longtime mentor, dragster builder and crew chief, filed a false technical specs report. The official has reported it to the Colorado State Patrol. Did that lead to the accident?" she asked point blank.

Trey paused considering his answer carefully, "You will have to get the event official's opinion on that. I'm not qualified to comment on what technically caused the dirt dragster's accident. I know it wasn't M's driving ability. I saw the dragster's rear end wiggle near the finish line in her only practice run on Friday afternoon. I know she ordered her crew chief, that's her father, to cut its horsepower and torque for the Saturday night race under the lights. I saw it wiggle the same way again Saturday just short of the finish line. She had the lead, but it went airborne and rolled over the dragster in the outside lane and exploded after it landed. The brave EMTs did an incredible job getting her out of the burning dragster, and helicopter medical team flying her. They all saved her life. We both thank them from our hearts."

"Have you talked to her father? Is he in the hospital with her?"

"No and no." His iPhone buzzed signaling a text. He glanced down, "Gotta go."

The reporter said to the cameraman. "We use it all and edit the iPhone footage of the crash that was emailed to us over part of it. This is breaking news; please get it up to the bird and down to the station ASAP. It's the lead story today on the five o'clock news."

Trey trotted to the ICU nurse's station where Betty was standing. "You Trey Stuart?"

"Yes,"

"Follow me. The doc got here early. With the Denver TV News crew and local newspapers here, he'll have to hold a press conference. He's ready to brief you both." She led the way to room 212. Trey's heartbeat raced when he reached M's bedside. She looked up at him and reached for his outstretched hand.

The doctor with a gown over his golf clothes calmly stated, looking at both of them, "You're going to get to walk the aisle if that's in your future plans, and ride the range together. M's lungs are mostly clear of nitro fuel fume burns and smoke damage. There're only two micro damage spots on the c-scan. At her age with some special rehab and your ranch's fresh air they will regenerate in time. You owe your life and future good health to the EMTs who pulled you out of the burning dragster. The medical helicopter team kept your traumatized heart beating and flew you here in record time. The bone doc will operate to pin your arm and hand back together. We're the cleanup batters now."

M cried happy tears as Trey kissed her cheek. She softly asked, "Can I drag race again? When can I ride my Paint horse on the range with Trey?"

"Lung-wise I don't want you around nitro fuel flames, thick smoke or chemical fumes for at least a year. Then maybe you might want to consider drag racing retirement. It'll be your call. We'll MRI your lungs, hand and arm. I'll set your rehab schedule and let you know when large gulps of fresh range air are good for you. The bone doc will set your broken bones' rehab schedule and determine the damage to your reflexes that could affect drag racing if any. So, I want you and Trey to work together to heal your body and mind in a patient manner. I recommend some counseling. You both have suffered a very traumatic event. I know Trey, and maybe you too, come from a Western buckle up and ride banged up culture as soon as I let you out of this bed. You might get away with it mostly bone wise, but your lungs are full of micro tissue, and if they can't breathe properly for you then worse case you could have an unpleasant life as you gasp for air. You're a smart, talented woman and a star driver so I know you're listening. See you tomorrow. One more night in ICU as a precaution until I evaluate the MRI."

"Thanks, Doctor," M said softly, and Trey tightened his grip on her good hand.

The Monday MRI report confirmed that M's lungs had three micro burn spots that would heal with proper rehab and rest. On Tuesday she had surgery and the doc put six small pins in her right hand bones and a two-inch plate in her forearm near her elbow. A nurse trimmed off her singed hair and she was moved to a standard hospital room. The docs ordered two weeks of intensive outpatient physical therapy in the Alamosa Hospital after her Wednesday release. Trey met with a Colorado State Highway Patrol detective who was assigned to M's case and repeated what he knew. The detective also interviewed M after her surgery. Judy volunteered to stay with M at the motel for the two-week first phase rehab so Trey could return to ranch but commute nightly to be with M. Cooper headed back to the YbarC for the busy early summer hay and cattle ranch work. The Dirt Drag Race Event and the National Drag Racing Association suspended Pete and Billie for life pending a full investigation.

Trey led the way as an orderly pushed M out of the hospital's main door in her wheelchair. Judy pulled up her pickup truck to the curb's ramp. A restored purple chopped and channeled hot rod coupe roared

up behind Judy and slammed on its brakes laying rubber. Pete ducked
out of the chopped top coupe and charged toward Trey and M, yelling,
"Your fucking boyfriend has destroyed my livelihood and your drag
racing career! I told you to stay away from rich boys and any boyfriends. Drag racing is your boyfriend. I'm going to cut his dick off and
take you back to Durango." Pete, who reeked of whiskey, pulled out
a switchblade knife and snapped it open. Trey stepped in front of him
and M burst into tears. The orderly who was pushing M's wheelchair
pushed his mike button and called for hospital security. He spun the
wheelchair and pushed M back toward the door. M gasped in a thin
voice, "No, Dad. Leave please."

Judy pulled her Glock 9 from under the driver's seat and opened the
pickup door to exit. The armed hospital security raced through the entrance door and threw a drunk Pete to the ground, knocking the knife out
of his hand. It skidded under the hot rod coupe. Judy pushed her pistol
back under the seat and ran after M into the hospital lobby. A stunned
Trey said to the armed security guard, "Keep him down. I'll watch your
back until the police arrive." A siren wailed near the entrance to the hospital parking lot. Pete remained face up on the sidewalk with the security
guard's pistol pointed at his heart.

He shouted. "This isn't over, Trey white-boy. You'll never steal my
Indian girl."

Trey coldly replied, "You almost killed M. Come near her again and
I'll settle it with you."

A white Alamosa police sedan pulled up lights flashing. The first officer
out of it handcuffed Pete and held him on the pavement as he struggled to
free himself. The other officer opened the hot rod coupe's passenger door
and ordered a shaking Billie out at gunpoint. He semi crawled out from
under the coupe's low roofline and raised his hands high.

Billie muttered, "I'm not part of this shit show. Pete made me come
at knifepoint. Thank God he can't own a gun as an ex-con. He's been
drinking all night."

Trey filed the new information about Pete and asked calmly,

"Pete, how can you treat the best daughter a father could have like
this?" He walked back into the hospital lobby to comfort M.

Late afternoon after Pete was jailed, Trey, M, and Judy accompanied by a local attorney and the arresting Alamosa police officers went before County Judge. She issued a temporary restraining order against Pete from being within one thousand feet of M and Trey. After the hearing, Judy drove a still very upset, tiring M to the Best Western Motel while Trey met with the assistant DA for an update on Pete's and Billie's arrests.

The young serious woman ADA informed him, "Billie will be released on bail bond after his preliminary hearing on Thursday because he had no criminal record. He'll be charged as an accessory after the fact, which is a misdemeanor criminal offense. The DA will seek a no bond jail hold for Pete until his trial for the attempted assault on you, assaulting the hospital security guard plus resisting arrest. The DA will also oppose a bail bond release of Pete because he has an FBI arrest felony conviction for aggravated assault and battery with deadly force on the Apache reservation in Northern New Mexico. He pled guilty and served three years' probation. Pete has had a clean record since his probation release so a good attorney will eventually get him out on bail bond before his trial. I advise you and M to leave Alamosa even if her rehab is not completed. Off the record the Sheriff's Department is stretched thin and it will struggle to enforce the restraining order in a county the size of Rhode Island."

Trey asked, "Do you know the details of Pete's probation?"

"No there's no record of any conditions on it, which is unusual. The DA speculates that maybe the FBI used Pete as a drug informant on the drag racing circuit in that era for the probation only sentence. The DA asserted that some drag racing team owners were rumored to be laundering drug money. If Pete was still an active FBI informant, the DA would have been called already. He hasn't been."

A very troubled Trey returned to the motel. He decided to tell M and Judy that Pete would remain in jail for now. He would cross the bail bond bridge if and when it materialized with M. He wanted her to focus on her critically important hand and lungs rehab for the next two weeks. In the meantime, he would check out rehab facilities and therapists in Taos and Santa Fe. He planned to commute from ranch and stay with M at the motel nights while Judy drove her to rehab every day.

CHAPTER 8
TWO PAINT HORSES AND CHAOS

Trey returned to the motel after his first day back on the ranch and took M and Judy to dinner at a family run, old style, Chinese restaurant. It had patched, aging, pleated, red Naugahyde booths, black ink, Chinese mountain paintings on rice paper, and lights with Asian painted, rice paper shades. Their shared meal was Mandarin style on a bamboo top turntable. After they returned to the motel, Judy retired to her room. Trey and M each had a bedroom in their suite. M's cast hand and arm needed pillow elevation and plenty of space, so she slept alone in a king bed on her back. They sat down on the ranch house style, pleated, brown leather couch. He turned on the Denver Channel 8's TV news to watch the weather forecast. The ranch needed a week of sunny weather for its first hay cut. A commercial for the new aluminum body, Ford pickup truck ended and the anchor came back on air. He introduced a live report from Tracy Miles in Alamosa. Their eyes shifted to the screen in unison as footage of M's wrecked, burned out, dirt strip dragster was on screen. "Maria Duran or M as she is known on Southwestern drag racing circuit has been released from the Alamosa Hospital after successful surgery to repair her broken hand and arm. The hospital spokesperson reported her body and lungs suffered no permanent nitro fuel fire injury damage. She added M's doctor stated her lungs need a rest from drag racing's nitro fuel exhaust flames so she will not race again for one year. She underwent surgery for her broken forearm and hand with rehab to follow. The doctor, on a lighter note, said the ends of her cinched ponytail that were outside of her fireproof pink helmet would grow back in a month. She wears the pink helmet in memory of her Apache mother who died of breast cancer."

Then a picture of her father's mug shot appeared. "On a darker note, Pete Duran, her father and crew chief, has been arraigned and held for trial in Alamosa Colorado. The DA alleged that he falsely altered the horsepower and torque specs for the dirt strip dragster on the final signed technical inspection report for the Saturday finals race. M, its driver, requested a substantial reduction in horsepower and torque after the practice run on Friday. He concealed this fact from M. The DA alleges this material fact caused M to lose control of the dragster and almost kill herself, the driver of the dragster in the other lane, and the finish line checkered flag lady when it rolled over in the air above them." The iPhone footage of M's dragster in the air ran on the TV's full screen. "Added to this charge today was Pete Duran's knife assault on M's boyfriend, Trey Stuart at the Alamosa Hospital. Mr. Stuart is the son of Colorado ranching legends Cooper and Judy Stuart. They operate the historic YbarC ranch near Telluride Colorado. Mr. Duran also assaulted a hospital security guard and resisted arrest. He has a previous federal court conviction for assault and battery on the Apache Reservation in Northern New Mexico and served three years court ordered probation. Pete Duran is being held in jail without bail bond until his preliminary hearing. His attorney stated he will request bail for Mr. Duran at the hearing. The attorney stated that Colorado Law has no statutes that cover technical information provided to a dirt drag racing event and they will fight the charges. Channel 1 tried to contact M and Trey for comment, but the DA will not disclose their location because a court order is now in place that restrains Pete, her father, from coming less than 1,000 feet from them. Channel 1 will continue to follow this breaking story from Alamosa." Trey hit the off button on the TV's remote skipping the weather report as M burst into uncontrollable tears. He put his arm around her carefully to console her. His iPhone text alert buzzed, and he crossed the room to pick it up on the entry table.

"Your father saw the TV story. He watches channel 1's weather report like you did at the YbarC. We'll talk at breakfast. love Mom".

He texted back, "Roger that, we saw it too". He texted Maestas, "Watch the Channel 13 Albuquerque New Mexico TV weather report tonight regarding hay cut weather".

M asked with tear-stained cheeks. "Who was that from?"

Trey white lied to ensure more crying did not hurt her lungs.

"Mom texted saying goodnight. I texted Maestas to watch the weather report on Albuquerque TV news at the bunkhouse. It's first hay cut time on the ranch. We need a few days of dry weather. Bedtime for you unless you want to phone your father at the jail."

"No, not now. He almost killed the other driver, the flag lady and me. He risked the first responders' lives. He's probably ruined my reputation on the circuit even if the lung doc clears my return. I spent an hour going over my personal racing notebook logs I take to all driver race event meetings. There're three other races where the technical reports stated peak horsepower doesn't match the final top speed. I guess that he expected I could handle the extra horsepower and torque on the blacktop drag strip surfaces. I have always dodged his drunken bouts after my mother died. The FBI arrested him for beating up her Apache reservation's health clinic Native American doctor after she died from breast cancer. He was drunk. My mother was a peaceful woman who crafted beautiful pottery. Her early death is not an excuse for his drinking and violence. Bedtime."

Trey followed her into the bedroom and to help her undress since she only had a working left arm and hand. He quipped with a doggie smile, "This is my favorite health care job," as he unsnapped her vintage Rockmount Ranch Wear cowgirl shirt.

"I like the shirt's sound…snap by snap."

M giggled, "Now unsnap my bra and take it off. Then unsnap and unzip my jeans. I'm not wearing panties. We need to figure out an on my back position with my wounded arm and hand outstretched to make love. I asked the docs if it was ok. They both blushed and said very careful sex but no drag racing and horse riding. Get out the Sexual Secrets Book in the bedside table drawer. Judy gave it to me. She found it at the used bookstore downtown the Adam's State college students frequent. The cover's tattered so it must work. Open to the page 34 illustration. I think I found gold there. You'll know how to do the rest. I need Tantric energy as they call it in the book. It releases healing enzymes. I need lots of them, plus it looks way fun sensually." She laughed for the first time since the crash.

A blushing Trey replied, "You both are amazing women." He opened the drawer and pulled out the book. He opened page 34 and iPhone photo'd it for quick reference. He unzipped his boot cut jeans.

"I like that zipper sound. Now kneel on the bed close to me so I can touch you with my good hand and we'll have fun working on our positions. Leave the bedside lamps on for my broken arm and hand's protection. Let's enjoy our first Tantric yoga style love making."

Two weeks later, Trey returned to the hacienda with M and Judy. After they unloaded M's luggage, she asked to go to the horse stables to visit the two Paint horses. She brought two red apples for them from the motel's breakfast buffet table. They stopped at each stall, and she fed each one an apple with her good hand. "They're wonderful, Trey. Can I have Blue Satin as my very own?"

"Yes, you can. She's purebred with a working ranch horse name. Big Spot is a stallion that still stands stud and Blue Satin is a mare that still bears foals. Because they had the same mother, they can't breed with each other. Their relationship is platonic."

"Blue Satin will be my girlfriend on the ranch."

"I'll have the ranch attorney do the bill of sale and attach her breeding paperwork to it. She'd like to have a girlfriend too in cowboy club here. She'll take good care of you in the saddle with her satin smooth ride. Paints are very smart, and their linage comes from the original Spanish Conquistador's warhorses. They are a combination of the Spanish Andalusia and Arabian breeds. The Spanish called them Pinodos. The Pueblo Indians bred them after they took them in New Spain's now New Mexico's 1680 Pueblo Indio Revolt. They called them Mustangs. Before the revolt in 1680, a Pueblo Indian was put to death if found in possession of a horse. Later Anglos bred them with Thoroughbred horses. They are strong and sure-footed. They'll run until they drop dead to save their rider's life. You experienced that in our getaway from the errant drug drop."

"I'll treat her so well my Shelby Mustang will be jealous," and she smiled from her heart.

Trey helped settle M into the hacienda's remodeled master bedroom and rearranged some of its furniture so her arm and hand would not bang into it. He put a roll of clear tape and a box of small garbage bags on a battered TV tray by the shower and hot tub. The doctor had advised sliding her arm and hand into a garbage bag to her shoulder and taping it tight under arm was the best way to protect its cast in a shower. She placed a pair of kitchen scissors on the bathroom counter for Trey to cut it off after he helped towel her dry. The doctor advised it would work for the hot tub but to rest her arm on its top edge. He warned no bubbling water on the cast. Trey had his old ski race training stationary bicycle shipped UPS from the YbarC and set it up in the master bedroom as part of her rehab. The Sexual Secrets Book was in the top drawer of the bedside table with her Ibuprofen pain pills. Upside down yellow post-its now marked nine pages of explicit illustrations and text. M had scheduled late afternoon rehab three days a week at the medical center in Taos. Trey planned to drive her there two days a week and the bunkhouse cook one day a week when he shopped at the supermarket. The doctor barred her from one arm and hand driving. After lunch, they finished setting up the hacienda for her recovery.

Trey said, "Tomorrow night I need to go to the Cattlemen's Association Water emergency meeting. Ninety percent of the ranch's irrigation water is from deep aquifer wells for growing hay plus watering the cattle. The remaining ten percent on the east sections is snowmelt ditch water from the Association. I need to attend the meeting with Maestas. With my mom returning to the YbarC tomorrow by charter plane and Pete out of jail on a $100,000 bail bond secured by his classic hot rods, I'm worried. Even with his ankle bracelet and the judge's order not to leave Colorado, I will assign a cowhand to watch the hacienda until I return. You both will have hot walkie talkies."

"Thanks, I hope he doesn't violate the restraining order, which the judge transferred to New Mexico too. I know his alcohol problem well. Better safe than sorry. Billie texted me he is staying with his brother in La Vegas, Nevada until the trial is over. Pete threatened Billie if he testified against him. He's still a wildcard."

"Done then. You rest and I need to get out on the ranch and check the newly cut hay storage. We'll need it all for the mother cows this winter. It's 20 below zero on this ranch many nights plus wind-chill. They need a lot of calories to stay warm."

"That's very cold. Do we get some R and R away from here in a warm sunny spot?" M lobbied.

"Absolutely."

Trey and Maestas walked into the Cattlemen's Association pine paneled meeting room as the white-haired Spanish rancher and Water Committee Chairman gaveled the meeting to order. Every head in the room had a sweat-stained cowboy hat of various vintages. Some had an oil stain, and others had a break in the brims. They were a black, white grey mix of beaver and rabbit felt or summer straw cowboy hats. Most of the members had come straight from their cattle's summer range or hay fields to the meeting. It was a bank boardroom meeting, and water was the cash in the vault. Trey was a little embarrassed to be wearing a custom made all beaver felt black dress cowboy hat with a Rockmount Ranch Wear white-pink pin striped shirt and clean jeans when eyes turned to see the new ranch operator in the valley. Maestas nodded to the members and chairman. He and Trey sat down in the back row on peeling repainted dented metal folding chairs. The chairman and the other two officers were on a three feet high riser above the room in high backed, worn, black leather chairs behind a white-cloth covered, folding banquet table with rust spotted legs. The room settled and the chairman said, "Let's start the emergency meeting, rancheros. First let me introduce Trey Stuart, who is with Maestas, whom most everyone here has known since childhood. Mr. Stuart is operating the Ute Peak Ranch for his father Cooper Stuart who you know from his occasional attendance at water meetings over the past thirty years."

More heads turned and there was a murmur around the room as he repeated it in Spanish. "Get to know Trey after the meeting. You all know his ranch's contracts pay well. Many of us have fenced, graded roads, put in gates over the years to help his cowhands and make extra money for our ranches…now to our emergency business. Read the one-page document our attorney prepared that the secretary is passing out. One side is in English, and one is in Spanish. If you ancients have bad eyes from working in the sun too many years, please have your neighbor read it to you. Ancients, there're pamphlets in English and Spanish on the office counter about laser eye surgery in Santa Fe. It works. I had it last year and can read again."

Trey and Maestas each took a one pager. Maestas read the backside in a low voice in Spanish to his very old neighbor who had a weathered face that was all cracked, sun-trenched skin. Trey was shocked when he finished reading the legal memo, so he read it a second time.

The chairman called the meeting back to order as angry voices quieted but angry eyes stared at him. He said in a firm voice, "The new owner of the Diablo Mountain Ranch is Bill Tibbetts from Texas and his attorney has contacted us and said they are cutting off the Association's irrigation water flow from our reservoir. It is located on his ranch but the water in the reservoir is deeded to you, the Association's water user members. The dam's reservoir gate releases the water into the Rio Costilla River. It flows to the diversion dam near here and then through the mother canal to your ranches and farms. They are alleging they own the headwaters of the river because it flows through their ranch. Our attorney says it's settled New Mexico Water Law by the State Engineers Office and courts that the snowmelt water in the reservoir belongs to the Water Association's members. Therefore, it can flow freely down the river from the reservoir gate to the diversion dam. You own the water. Your second cut hay crops will die without it. They plan to cut it off in a week. Our water attorney is going into state court to get an injunction stopping them. They also plan to lock the entrance gate to our road that crosses their ranch by easement that the Ditch Rider needs to operate the reservoir. We have a customary easement for it on the original Mexican Land Grant where the reservoir is situated."

An Old Spanish member stood up, "We'll take our rifles, open the road gate and size the reservoir if the courts fail us as they always do on land and water rights. No Texan can do this. My family defeated them when the Texas Republic invaded New Spain before the US Anglo's defeated Mexico and stole New Mexico and southern Colorado. Since then, the Anglos and their courts have stolen seventy percent of our families' Spanish and Mexican Land Grant ranches, farms and water my son says, who is the new state historian. Only guns will stop them. I move we adjourn the meeting and go home and clean our hunting rifles. If our attorney fails in the rigged New Mexico and Anglo Federal Courts, then we fight to death for our water. All in favor stand and this meeting is adjourned."

Trey was taken by surprise as the whole room stood around him including Maestas. Eyes turned toward him as he remembered the stories of his father's fight to save the YbarC water rights and Joe Bear Spirit's death fighting for the Southern Colorado Ute Water rights. He knew from childhood, water was life in the arid southwest, and he jumped to his feet. The chairman pounded his gavel adjourning the meeting. Angry ranchers and farmers clustered in groups as a worried Maestas led Trey out of the room's exit.

He said in a low voice, "You need to leave with me. Old Anglo crooked court crimes against some of these families will surface tonight after the meeting in the parking lot and nearby bar. Any Anglo will do for a young Hispanic man to start a fight with or worse, take a shot at to defend his grandfather's honor. Alcohol mixed with drugs these days and fueled by revenge is a bad combination." Maestas quickly led Trey to the ranch pickup and they pulled out of the full parking lot of pickup trucks.

A week passed by quickly after M started rehab in Taos. Maestas monitored the Water Association rumors and the rancheros' emails in Spanish. Trey monitored the legal emails in English. The routine ranch work continued daily while the second crop of hay was being irrigated on the ranch's center pivot circles, which were fed by the deep wells drilled into the San Luis Aquifer. Trey had been monitoring the electric bills for the well pumps during the first hay crop. They seemed high, so he had the ranch's accountant pull ten years of irrigation well pump electric bills. They had gone up 35% during that period. He had been following the use of PV Solar panels for producing electricity for water pumping online. With the federal government's solar tax credits of 30% it seemed to be getting cheaper every year to install a solar system for each well. The only remaining obstacle was that the irrigations rigs worked all night when it was cooler as well as in the daytime when it was sunny. He'd recently read an article that solar electric battery storage was getting better and cheaper. He talked to a small ranch neighbor who was using PV Solar panels with their direct current water pump to fill stock tanks for his cattle to drink 24/7. He got a positive report, so he called the local solar company in Taos that advertised on the Solar Radio Station. The owner set up a meeting with him and Maestas for the next day to Trey's surprise. He had been looking for a big ranch to put all its well pumps for cattle and irrigation water on PV Solar electricity systems with battery storage.

Over dinner Trey reviewed his solar plan with M.

"You want to accompany me in the red pickup tomorrow while I tour the wells with the solar guy and Maestas? I can duct tape a long pillow to the passenger side door to protect your broken arm and hand from surprise rutted ranch road bounces."

"Yes, I'm going stare crazy in the empty hacienda all day long."

The next day at noon when the sun was high in the southern sky the caravan of three pickups with Maestas in the lead left the hacienda for a tour of the eight ranch wells. The group had already looked at the hacienda and ranch headquarters buildings and mutually decided it was a "no brainer" to put them all on PV Solar electricity with battery storage. Don also recommended a plumbing company that could install a solar panel hot water system to augment the hacienda's new propane powered radiant in floor heating system and its household hot water.

Trey said to M, "If the evaluation by the solar guy works solar well site-wise, I'll send his proposal to Judy and our accountant to evaluate numbers with the federal tax credit benefits. We could install the hacienda system immediately and at one ranch well for a test after our third cut of hay in early October. It would be ready for next year's irrigated hay season. If the test well solar system works, then we expand it to the other wells. Your thoughts?"

"It's great forward vision on your part. Your family already raises natural beef on both ranches and solar is eco-friendly electricity. Since I've been recuperating, I listen to the Taos Solar Radio station. They talk about it daily, and global warming caused by carbon dioxide. They say there's too much coal-fired electricity being used in this region, which has perfect solar conditions with 330 days a year of sunshine. We use nitro fuel in drag racing, which is corn grain-based alcohol. It burns clean with no carbon dioxide, just good old H_2O exhaust for classes like the fast Funny Car dragster's three-second quarter mile runs. At one drag race I drove in Phoenix the nearby Arizona State University engineering students raced an electric-motor-powered prototype with solar panels on its roof against one from Cal Tech in Pasadena. They hit 40 miles an hour by the finish line so there's still more work to do. I had dinner with their driver, an engineering student, who hit on me after I won my class. His line was they needed a driver like me, so I bit. He said his crew's average IQ was 170. I picked up his iPhone and snapped a selfie of myself with my phone number under it slash M driver. I told him to have their crew chief call me when they doubled their top speed, and I could make a difference off the line. If he calls me while the docs don't want me in nitro fueled dragsters I'm all in to driving a solar electric powered one. The future is here with more battery powered electric cars and one just set an electric powered land speed record at the Bonneville Salt Flats at 321.831 MPH. They can put amazingly high RPM torque into each wheel with its own separate electric motor."

"Wow that's a lot to digest. When can we use electric pickups on the ranch? Do I have competition at U of A?" Trey asked deadpan.

"Not for at least a couple decades out here for high altitude cold weather work pickups and long-haul trucks that transport twenty tons of hay per delivery. They will be available if and when battery storage gets a lot better and cheaper. Plus, you can charge their batteries with PV solar panels. Concerning the electrical engineering student driver, he wasn't my type. I skipped the after-race awards dinner and party because I had been up all night with Billie solving my dragster's fuel feed problem."

"We're at the first well. Step down carefully after I open your door. The ground's bone dry right now until the monsoons come. You're the ranch's mechanical electrical hand from now on. These solar panel well systems have to work mechanically too with their DC current solar electrical water pumps. Each well needs a fixed amount of water flow a day in gallons pumped. Let's get the evaluation process started."

On the way back to the hacienda, Trey reviewed his notes with M as he drove. "If the PV Solar company's construction numbers and the ranch's well service company's estimated the cost of replacing the AC electric well pumps with DC electric pumps is reasonable then we'll send to Judy and her accountant."

As soft late afternoon summer breeze blew through the pickup's rolled down windows, M said, "It's so beautiful. I want to make a picnic lunch on Saturday and ride my Paint horse with you. I'm strong enough after three weeks of rehab to rein her with one hand. We'll ride them easy and cover my casts with bubble wrap just in case. I'll even use a riding helmet I picked up in Taos after my last rehab session. I need to move my body in nature again."

"You calling the ortho doc on this?"

"No, but my rehab woman says try it at your own risk. Just don't land hard on the casts if you fall off."

"Let's ride then. The Paints need exercise. They are the most intelligent horses I've ever ridden. Your mare will take care of you. I also fear this Water Association fight is going to flare up soon and that might eliminate my picnic time."

"Has the court ruled yet on it?"

"On Monday, the war drums say."

"Will the Texas rancher obey a New Mexico Court order?" she asked.

"I wouldn't bet on it. They act like they own New Mexico and even call the old Spanish settlers like Maestas' family Mexicans to their face," Trey said grimacing.

"Then what happens?" she asked concerned.

"Guns and men with guns pointing them at each other. One trigger finger mistake and bullet chaos!"

"Are you going to be a man with a gun?"

"I'm weighing that decision. The ranch's water rights in question are only a minor part of what we use for irrigation. However, there is the Western principle of water theft. They say around the West, whisky is for drinkin' and water is for fightin'."

"You really believe that? I don't want to lose you. Isn't Joe Bear Spirit's murder over water enough for the Stuart family? The businessmen in Durango say money runs uphill toward water. Your family has plenty of money to buy more water. They only have one you to take over their ranching empire. I have only one you to produce an heir if we marry." M went silent.

On Friday Trey emailed the solar proposal to his mom to review and forward to the ranch accountant. Judy email replied that it would take a couple weeks to evaluate the project and she would also use it as a stalking horse to evaluate PV Solar power for the YbarC. She added a local solar company in nearby Ridgeway Colorado had contacted the YbarC. Saturday morning brought Twitter chatter about the Water Association's pending court ruling.

M mounted her Paint horse by stepping onto a foldable campstool with Trey's hands on her waist. Maestas stood on the opposite side of the horse to catch her if she rolled off the saddle. The scheme worked and they walked the Paints out of the hacienda entrance and turned them toward the northwest side of the ranch with the sun to their backs.

M reported, "My bottom feels good in the saddle, my legs are strong, and my boots are gripping the stirrups. Blue Satin is riding easy. We can trot in a few minutes once I'm completely settled in the saddle. The wind feels good on my face with the sun on my back."

"That's great news. I'll continue to lead with the stallion because he'll take out any surprises like a prairie rattlesnake or a jackrabbit attack. We're headed toward a family picnic spot I haven't visited in years.

We'll toss our blanket there with the collapsed nylon campfire chairs. What's for lunch?"

"You and the rest is a secret," she seductively whispered.

"Too bad you can't gallop," he said laughing.

Just as M tired, they rode into the picnic's grassy clearing, which was surrounded by Pinion and Juniper trees on three sides near an arroyo. He helped M dismount and hobbled the horses. "The old pine plank picnic table is gone so it's blanket time." He spread it out perfectly.

"Time for your treat, cowboy. Pull those jeans down and lie on your back knees open." A few minutes later, Trey came in ecstasy with his eyes staring into the deep blue sky. M said, "Time for red wine and my special lunch. Please get the lunch sack and bottle of wine that are in your saddle bags."

She laid out two Irish cheddar cheese and organic salami sour dough bread sandwiches, fresh seaweed salad, two large dill pickles, and cold baked beans. "Eat up, lucky cowboy, I stopped at the Taos holistic supermarket with the bunkhouse cook after rehab. He buys their natural apple wood smoked bacon."

"I'm all in. This sandwich is insanely good. Please shop there every week."

"I can but it costs more than the regular supermarket," she explained.

"It's worth every dollar for the taste and quality."

After a restful lunch, Trey helped M mount Blue Satin with the collapsible campstool, and they rode out of the clearing. A very low airplane motor's noise caused both Paints to snort. Trey quietly hand signaled M to rein her horse to a stop. He pulled his binoculars from his saddlebags and glassed the airplane as it dropped a large bale wrapped in a bright blue nylon tarp on the other side of the Rio Grande River Gorge. "It's a drug drop. We'll ride our horses back into the clearing and wait for the airplane to depart. Hopefully, no one in the air or on the ground has seen us."

"Roger that. Blue Satin is a little nervous. Let's ride back to the hacienda once the airplane is gone."

"Roger that."

An hour and a half later, they walked the Paints through the front gate. Before they could dismount, a County Sheriff's white SUV pulled into the open hacienda gate and braked too fast, throwing up gravel and dust. It spooked the horses. M barely got Blue Satin under control as she reared-up on her hind legs. Trey jumped off Big Spot and swatted his rear end to send him to the horse barn. He took M's reins and led Blue Satin away from the SUV so she could dismount with his help.

The deputy got out of the car and shouted, "Don't walk away from me. Keep those Paint horses here."

Trey lost it, "Get off my ranch unless you have a warrant to be on it. You spooked M's horse. Look at the cast on her broken arm and hand. You could've killed her driving through the hacienda gate at high speed."

The deputy placed his hand on his holster, "I'm here to question you about," and he stopped realizing he couldn't link himself to the Paint horses during the drug drops and shootout on the ranch.

M held Blue Satin's rein tightly in her good hand and whispered to her.

Trey stated calmly, "Unless you have official business and a warrant, please leave the Ute Peak Ranch." Two cowhands with pistols on their hips rode sweaty horses through the open gate and reined them in. They reported to Trey. "We just saw a low flying airplane drop a blue tarped bale west of the Gorge when we were fixing a fence break. This white Sheriff's SUV was watching it outside the ranch's southwest green gate. He stop here to tell you about the drug drop?" The deputy caught off guard dropped his jaw.

"I don't know? He hasn't stated his business. You can ask him." Trey replied.

The deputy trying to recover said, "I can't discuss official stakeout business that may or may not have happened off your ranch boundary." His radio in the SUV squawked giving him an exit excuse, "I've got to go but I'm warning you to stay out of official Sheriff's Office business." He climbed back into the SUV and backed out of the gate slowly, talking on his handheld radio.

The lead hand said, "That's deep bullshit. He was glassing the drop. We quit repairing the fence as Maestas ordered us to if we saw a drug drop and rode into a nearby arroyo for cover. We couldn't see the drug pick-up across the Gorge, but we heard a vehicle's motor over there after the airplane circled west and departed. Then we heard the deputy sheriff's white SUV drive south from the ranch gate. Once there were no more motor sounds in the air or on the ground we rode hard back here."

"Thanks, you did the right thing. Report it to Maestas on Monday. Stay clear of that deputy. Here's a fifty-dollar bonus. Enjoy a good dinner at the steak house tonight across the Colorado border in Fort Garland just west of the turn onto US 160."

"It's got a good bar. Thanks. See you Monday," and they rode out of the gate.

"Trey, the deputy saw us riding the Paints two months ago. Somehow, he or the pilot saw them today. After he secured the drop area and drug pickup, he must have driven straight to the hacienda."

"You're right. It's about an hour the long way south around the ranch on rutted roads most of the way. He almost blurted out he saw us on the Paints during last drug drop but realized that would link him to the drug runner I shot. In the space documentary I saw last year the crew radioed mission control, 'Huston we have a problem'." He frowned deeply as M grasped his hand.

He mused out loud, "This must be the violent Mexican cartel drug smuggling we see on the TV news or read about on our iPhone news every day. They ambushed and murdered a convoy of Mormon women and children from their 1940s ranching settlement in the mountains of Northern Mexico two days ago. The news said there could be 50,000 cartel murders in Mexico this year. This paid off deputy is putting all of us at risk on the ranch and our neighbor's ranches. I'll call my father and Jumbo once I wash and brush the Paints. You get some rest."

"Roger that. I'm a little hot and very tired." She handed him the reins and walked toward the hacienda with a worried expression that Trey had never seen before.

Trey put the horses in their stalls and fed them oats. He iPhoned Jumbo. "Hello, Trey, you calling about the drug drop a couple hours ago?"

A surprised Trey asked, "How do you know about it?"

"There were eyes on it. Did a Taos County deputy come to the hacienda in a white SUV?"

"He did after our picnic near the Gorge. He saw the Paint horses but shut up when he realized that would put him at the scene of the drug drop shootout on the ranch."

"He's made you and M?"

"Yes, she's very scarred. I believe a drop could get out of control again and someone on my ranch or a neighbor could be killed."

"We have a wiretap they're planning to hit you both if the Paint horses are yours. The deputy visually confirmed that this afternoon. There are corrupt deputies on both sides of the border. The DEA's planning a no locally involved police agencies' cartel take down on the next drop. Its date is unknown at present. You and M should depart immediately for the YbarC where I can have the Colorado State Patrol protect you both."

"I probably can't until I know the outcome of the Water Association's court ruling Monday. M's in rehab in Taos."

"Your ranch has Association water? That's a hornet's nest."

"I know."

"Stay out of it. You're not from a Spanish settler's family. Post armed cowboy guards around the hacienda and headquarters buildings 24/7. You both leave by charter air tomorrow morning from the ranch's airstrip for the YbarC. Don't call your father until you all are in the air. Cooper is too old for another gunfight. No more rehab trips for M to Taos or Alamosa. But please charter-fly her to Telluride if you stay. Your cowboys work armed. I'll call you when I know more. Encrypt your iPhone for calls and texts and don't call anyone on hard lines." He hung up. A stunned Trey walked into the hacienda and reported his and Jumbo's conversation.

M stated clearly, "I'm here if you stay. I'll do my rehab on Face Time with my PT and she can Snapchat me video of new exercises. Give me a shotgun. I heard they are point and shoot to kill guns."

"I'm staying until the Water Association's issues are solved. I need to save face with all our neighboring ranchers and farmers. Maestas can't keep carrying my family's load. I'm the owner and operator."

"Then we stay," M asserted. "I'm Spanish and Indio so I have two dogs in this fight."

Trey walked out to the bunkhouse and stopped the two cleaned up cowboys from leaving for their night off in Fort Garland.

He white lied, "There's been a Ranch Watch alert that one of the drug-running big-wheel pickup crews robbed a ranch house across the gorge and stole a pickup truck. You're on rotating twelve-hour security shifts around the hacienda and head quarter's buildings until Maestas returns Monday at six a.m. for the bunkhouse weekly work meeting. Patrol with pistols and rifles. Bring a bunk house bird-hunting twelve gauge shot gun to the hacienda with a box of shells," Trey ordered.

"We're on it." Trey wearing a holster with a Glock 9 walked out to the hacienda's iron gate and pushed the close button. After it clanked shut, he pushed its electronic jamming lock button. When he returned to the bedroom, M was napping. He quietly placed the loaded shotgun in the corner of the room near its hand carved wooden pine door.

S unday morning came early with tension in the air. The two well-armed weekend hands rode out of the gate on fast horses to check the cattle. Trey called Maestas and briefed him about the deputy sheriff incident. He set a bunkhouse meeting with all the cowhands at six a.m. Monday sunup. He and M walked around the headquarters area and checked all the buildings. Nothing seemed out of place. They had a quiet lunch, and she took a long nap. The hands rode back mid-afternoon and reported the herd was grazing with no apparent overnight disturbances. Trey opened the Monday sunup bunkhouse meeting with a report on the Saturday drug drop he and M had witnessed. He and the weekend hands described the deputy's strange behavior.

Trey carefully chose his words not wanting to reveal his Jumbo Robert's call adding, "I have an alert the big-wheel drug pick-up crew burglarized a house and stole a ranch pickup truck on the west side of the gorge. I also have a tip the drug cartel has threatened to kill anyone in our area that interferes with a drop, and that the deputy may be on the take to cover the drug drops. Continue to ride or drive back to the safety of the ranch headquarters if you see a drug drop. Do not interfere even if the drug drop airplane crosses the Gorge and flies over the ranch. Maestas will assign you all a night and daytime security shift at the hacienda and headquarters. Ride with a pistol and saddle rifle and patrol here with a pistol and shotgun. I'm working with law enforcement to get the drug drops stopped. The town of Jaroso Colorado across the border is too, according to an email I just received from an artist group. I realize this situation is not part of your job description so if anyone wants to quit the outfit please do so."

There was a chorus of no's.

"Thanks, Maestas hand out the weekly work assignments."

After Maestas completed the range and hacienda's security assignments he and Trey walked over to its office. Trey said,

"It's worse than I told the cowhands. There may be an attempt to kill me and M now that the deputy has linked our Paint horses to the first drug drop."

Maestas guessed, "That's why you shipped them to the YbarC. Word in the village across the Gorge these are dangerous men. Everyone is scared of them. They are Mexican cartel bad hombres working with the old drug gang in Espanola, New Mexico. You and Maria should return to the YbarC for now. I'll keep the ranch secure."

"I'll consider that if the Water Association court ruling is favorable. I guess we'll know today. I feel I should help if it's not."

Maestas replied, "It won't be favorable. A young cousin of an Association member is the judge's clerk. He wrote the judge's decision this weekend. There's no injunction. There will be a long court fight like always. Once it's announced, the chairman will call an emergency meeting tonight."

"I'll contribute money to help pay the Association's attorney's court fight."

Maestas starkly replied, "That's good but it'll be used to get members out of jail too. The plan is to seize the reservoir, the dam's water release gate and its road with guns at sunup Tuesday. The members can't lose their second hay crop. Returned Veterans from Iraq and Afghanistan will help plus an old one from Vietnam. I'll represent the ranch."

"No, I will. My family owns the water. I need you to manage and secure the ranch. Please take this check over to the chairman at the Association Headquarters," and Trey wrote it for $1.000 dollars.

"I will, but send Maria to the YbarC. I don't want her hurt if you're at the reservoir."

"She doesn't want to go but I'll set up a charter flight for this afternoon. Secure the air strip at three o'clock."

Trey called a former Alaskan bush charter pilot in Telluride and set up the flight. He followed with a call to his family's physical therapist and set up an appointment for M. He walked over to the master bedroom where she was spinning on the exercise bike. "News has gone from bad to worse. Maestas says the drug runners are very dangerous Mexican cartel men. Our neighboring ranchers and villages are asking law enforcement for help but getting none. The court ruling is going against the Water Association today and the members will seize the reservoir tomorrow at sunup. I need to help them or Maestas will and it's not his fight. He'll manage and secure the ranch but wants you to go to the YbarC because of your poor mobility. A charter flight will pick you up at three O'clock on the ranch's airstrip. I've set up rehab for you in Telluride with an old family friend.

We'll call Judy to meet you. Our cover story is your doc wants your rehab moved to Colorado when the casts come off. Telluride has some of the best rehab in the state because of skiing injuries."

"I don't want to leave you, but I understand. I can't put Maestas under the pressure of guarding me with you off the ranch. I'll pack." Trey called Judy.

M was in the YbarC's house guest bedroom at sunrise on Tuesday morning and Trey's red pickup was parked at the reservoir road gate with forty or so armed Water Association members all wearing assorted colors of faded bandanas like old west outlaws. A grizzled cowboy with a young cowhand stood facing them with rifles in hand. Both were backlit by the sunrise behind their blue jean jacketed backs. The tanned wrinkled faced Association chairman walked up to the locked chained reservoir road gate carrying a heavy steel cutter. The two cowhands raised their saddle rifles.

The chairman said, "Members raise your rifles but hold your fire." Forty plus rifle stocks were raised onto strong shoulders and sighted on the two cowboys. The chairman continued looking straight into the rising sun at the cow hands in the silence while an early summer morning breeze rustled the Aspen trees. "This is not your fight. Lower you're rifles. Get on your ATVs and leave."

The grey bearded Anglo cowhand with tension in his voice replied, "We have orders to shoot to kill from the owner if you all open the locked gate and trespass onto the ranch road until the court in Santa Fe settles the dispute."

The chairman said calmly, "Are you ready to die behind the gate? Lock and load." Forty plus high-powered hunting rifle bolts and saddle repeating rifle levers snapped in unison as the sharp metallic sound echoed in the nine thousand feet high tight valley. Trey levered a bullet into his saddle rifle's empty chamber. His finger tightened against its trigger. He had ridden with the rifle since twelve years old. He held his breath as his eye hardened onto a target.

The older cowhand slowly pointed his gun barrel toward the gravel road surface as the young clean-shaven one turned and walked back to his ATV. "I'm not dying today for the half-cocked usually drunk new owner. I've rode this ranch thirty-two years. There's no question in my mind the Association owns the reservoir, the water in it and this road." He turned and walked back to his ATV. They gunned the ATV motors and roared off as the Association members cheered when the chairman cut the lock. Rifles were put back on safety as the members jumped into the fifteen or so pickup trucks and a half dozen ATVs. They drove through the open gate toward the reservoir.

The chairman selected four members with ATVs to man the gate. He informed them, "The New Mexico State Patrol and the Taos County Sheriff will be here sooner rather than later even with no cell phone signal up here. Do not lock the gate but keep it closed. Do not point a rifle at them even if they insist on driving up to the reservoir. We'll secure it and I'll open the dam's gate to release irrigation water into Costilla Creek. Do not let anyone else drive through the gate but the law." The four hand-picked senior members nodded with battered cowboy hats bobbing.

Trey unloaded new barbwire spools from the tailgate of his red pickup. Two young veterans from Iraq with other members begin unspooling the coils into a defensive perimeter around the dam's gate and across its earthen bank top. Other members began filling sandbags and building gun positions along the top of the dam. A few bulletproof vests of various military vintages were handed out. Three large outfitter's canvas tents went up on the north side of the reservoir. One had a cook stove tin pipe. Rifles begin peeking out of completed sandbag positions.

The chairman walked up to Trey, "Thanks for the check for our attorney and the barbwire. You're an Anglo whose family purchased a ranch that came with Association water rights. This is our fight not yours, so you don't have to stay. I hope cool heads prevail...there'll be guns pointed in both directions. Leave if you want to."

"I'm all in. My family has always defended its water rights. When this is over, I'll sell my ranch's Association Water rights to an original Spanish settler's member for a fair price. We don't need the Association water rights with our modern aquifer irrigation hay practices. This is dangerous and expensive to defend them. I'm staying," Trey replied.

"That's fair enough. Keep your head down though. Let the highly trained and disciplined boys who have recently been discharged from the Army and Marines point the guns while I negotiate a deal. We've been through this scenario right here four decades ago right after Vietnam. Heads up, a member father and son are here who recently inherited a small ranch near Costilla are part of the Land or Death movement over in Tierra. The father was in the courthouse raid in 1968. They are my wildcards. The Allianz is still seeking revenge and their land grant farms and ranches back."

"Roger that," Trey replied without expanding the conversation.

Mid-morning the first New Mexico black State Patrol SUV followed by two County Sheriff's white SUVs arrived at the road gate. The chairman radioed down to send two state patrolmen and the sheriff with one deputy up to the reservoir. When the lawmen protested, he reminded them they had to have a warrant to enter the Water Association road and dam. Since they didn't have one the terms were agreed to. The law enforcement caravan arrived at the dam and stopped in front of the coiled barbwire. The deputy stepped out first with binoculars and glassed the entire scene, stopping to zoom in occasionally. He stopped on Trey's exposed head behind a sandbag. Trey realized to late that he was the deputy that had been at the hacienda on Saturday afternoon. He ducked behind the sandbag and hoped the deputy didn't recognize him. He had dropped his bandana around his neck while he worked stacking the sandbags. After the deputy briefed the sheriff and patrolmen on his walkie-talkie they all stepped out of the two SUV's with rifles or shotguns in their hands. They tossed a modern police walkie-talkie up to the chairman's sandbagged position and the parley began. Trey listened to the open walkie-talkie in the chairman's hand.

The sheriff opened the negotiation. "Mr. Chairman or Mr. Silva if I may call you. I know and every northern Taos County native knows that the Water Association owns the reservoir, the water in it and the road to it. But the new Anglo District Judge in Taos was out maneuvered by the Texas ranch owner's high paid attorney, and he kicked the case up to Santa Fe state court to avoid making a decision or staying a decision. That said the Association seizing the road and reservoir with guns is a problem until the court rules. The Texas owner is all over the right-wing social media alleging discrimination and armed insurrection in Taos County and New Mexico. It's bad for summer tourism and the governor is upset. She's an Albuquerque woman who doesn't know irrigated hay from weeds. That's why the state police are here. I need you to stand down until the court can rule even if an expedited hearing takes a month."

The hairmen replied, "In this matter it's Mr. Chairman, I'm acting in my official capacity. In a month, all of our member's second hay crops will be dead without water so we'll guard the reservoir gate until the case is heard."

The sheriff replied, "I've been ordered by the governor to remove you. The state police are here to supervise your withdrawal."

The state police captain shouted, "You have one hour to pack up and leave." It was a miscalculation. A volley of shots fired into the reservoir water rang out as the lawmen hit the dirt with weapon's ready to fire.

The chairman stood waving a white flag and said into a bullhorn, "Hold your fire. Let the lawmen withdraw. The state patrol doesn't have any jurisdiction here, only the sheriff does, our attorney says."

"We're withdrawing. You have overwhelming force. I'm sure the governor will take over now," the sheriff stated.

"We're here until the end of irrigation season or a court order in our favor. Tell the gov to put the state court in high gear."

The extremely aggravated state patrol captain stated, "Fire shots again and we'll bring overwhelming force."

Laughter came from behind the sandbags with a shout, "We have decorated war veterans behind the sandbags. Besides our Hispanic cousins in the state patrol or the National Guard won't fire on us. Adios." The sheriff stood up and signaled everyone back into the SUV's and they departed.

Cooper asked M at lunch, "I just read a news flash on my iPhone that the Water Association that provides some irrigation water to the ranch has seized its reservoir with guns. I texted both Trey and Maestas and got no reply. I suspect you're not really here just for rehab." Judy's eyes opened wide.

M replied, "Yes and no. Trey is at the reservoir. Maestas didn't want to be responsible for me on the ranch without Trey or traveling to rehab in Taos. Local tensions are running high because of the situation."

Judy honed in. "The water or the drug drop situation or both."

M answered, "Both, Trey called Jumbo after the latest drug drop Saturday, which we watched during a picnic while riding the Paint horses. A deputy came to the hacienda and ID'd the Paints after we rode in. Now he knows we saw the first drug drop on the ranch side of the gorge while riding the Paints."

Cooper stated, "That's really why Trey shipped them to the YbarC."

"Yes."

"OMG the deputy is working with the drug gang!" Judy gasped.

"How are you certain about this?" Cooper asked.

"Jumbo confirmed it," M admitted.

"Why didn't Jumbo call me?" Cooper demanded.

M looked for a diplomatic way out but was trapped. "He said you're too old to get into another gunfight."

Judy demanded, "Is there more?"

"Not that Jumbo will allow us to discuss. We have encrypted our iPhones. Jumbo can't take your call," M revealed.

"Or won't?" Cooper replied.

Judy countered, "So there's more?"

"I'm flying to New Mexico today," Cooper replied.

"Don't," both Judy and M replied. M added, "Trey and Jumbo don't want you there."

Cooper's iPhone rang and he talked to a cowhand. "Why is there a state patrolman parked at the YbarC's front gate?"

"Oops, I kind of forgot that might happen. Jumbo says they have a cell phone intercept discussing a Mexican cartel hit on Trey and me after the deputy left the hacienda. There's a major law enforcement raid planned by the DEA and FBI for the next drug drop but the date's not certain yet."

"That's another big oops!" Judy burst into tears as M kept a stiff upper lip. Cooper stared out the dining room window while Judy recovered her composure.

"You poor woman there's a cartel hit out on you and a restraining order on your father. How do you bear it?" Judy asked.

"My mother was Apache. She taught me to be brave."

"I'm flying down to the ranch."

Judy said firmly, "Not until our son or Jumbo calls you." Cooper stood up and walked out of the dining room his cowboy boot heels thumping against the pine floor. Judy grasped M's trembling good hand. M silently thanked her Apache gods that Judy and Cooper had not asked about the details of the first drug drop. She didn't want to be the one who told them their son had killed a drug runner in the shootout.

After a restless night's sleep Trey woke up at sunset in his bedroll after sleeping under the stars on a moonless night by the reservoir. He rolled it up, put it in the red pickup and walked over to the cook tent. The smell of bacon, elk sausage, eggs and coffee permeated the air. He sat on the slope of the dam's bank and savored his hot breakfast in the cool morning mountain air.

"Man your sandbag positions and pull up your bandanas. The state patrol and Sheriff's Department have arrested the Association members guarding the reservoir road gate and are following an armored vehicle up the road in SUVs," a bullhorn boomed. Trey walked over to his sandbag position balancing his half full, hand-painted, trout tin plate in one hand and rifle in the other. He sat down behind the sandbags and finished breakfast. The law enforcement caravan arrived in a flurry of motor sounds. A state patrol spokesman with a bullhorn announced:

"You have until noon to pack up and leave." He retreated into a camo painted surplus military armored vehicle that Trey had seen on TV in urban riots. The law enforcement contingent deployed along the sides of their SUVs. There was no reply from the chairman as silence set in.

Trey's iPhone buzzed and he answered it looking over his sandbag's top for a repeater aerial. The armored vehicle had a dish.

M said, "Hello, I've called every four hours with no luck."

Trey in a whisper replied, "We're surrounded by heavily-armed lawman in a tank-like vehicle but it has a cell phone repeater. Hello, I miss you. The ground was hard sleeping but the country breakfast was first class. The coffee's cheap but hot."

"You spoiled man. I'm settled in the YbarC's plush guest room with rehab in T'ride as Judy calls it this afternoon. But after the state police security car arrived at the ranch gate, I was forced to tell most all under tough questioning by your father and mother."

"I understand. What does most all mean?"

"Everything but your shooting incident during the first drug drop."

"Good and Dad wants to come over and is pissed at me and Jumbo."

"Really pissed, but Judy and me stopped him."

"You've formed an alliance with my always level-headed mother already."

"Yes, she's worried about our lives."

"Tell them what the old western movie's call a 'Mexican Standoff' is going on at the reservoir, except the Mexicans are mostly old Spanish settlers' family members. The new Albuquerque woman gov has over-reacted because of the New Mexico TV news reports of potential lost summer tourism. If there is a shootout and Water Association member vets from twenty-two to eighty die, then tourism will really be lost. So nothing's going to happen unless there's a wildcard shot. I suggested to the chairman last night to tell our attorney to petition the Santa Fe court for an emergency hearing this morning since I'm paying most of his legal bill. He sent a messenger by foot over the mountain on a hunting trail to the nearest ranch house with a phone like in the old westerns. We're safe for now, but the deputy that came to the hacienda was here with the sheriff yesterday. He may have ID'd me."

"Stay clear of him."

"Roger that."

"I'll Instagram you a risqué photo if you're really bored."

"I love you but don't. The armored vehicle dish may be able to intercept it and since you look sixteen, we'd go to jail for sexting."

"Funny man. I've got to go. Judy just honked."

"Brief them. Skip the deputy. Try me again tonight."

Noon came and no one had moved more than a few feet on either side. Nothing happened so lunch runners moved about on both sides. The southwest summer sun continued to bake everyone. The Association member vets wore their bullet proof vests with ammo belts over bare chests like in Vietnam and Iraq TV news reports. After a fresh rolled Taco lunch Trey pulled his cowboy hat over his eyes and placed his head on a low sandbag ledge and took a nap while silence prevailed except for an occasional afternoon wind gust. He was jolted awake by a bullhorn announcement.

"The New Mexico Court Of Appeals will hold an emergency hearing tomorrow at nine a.m. Now pack up and return to your farms and ranches."

The chairman said over his bullhorn, "Bring me the court's decision in writing. If it's favorable, we'll go home." Silence descended on the scene again. Trey texted M, 'Court hearing tomorrow AM. Watch Denver news tonight. If this doesn't end by tomorrow night, I'll reconsider the pic. Hope iPhone holds out. Forgot solar charger. Turning it off'. He turned onto his side and continued the nap.

Day three started the same with a beautiful sunrise and a hearty breakfast. Trey walked around the entire reservoir for exercise out of boredom. He returned to his sandbag emplacement with his rifle's ammo clip in his shirt pocket. He didn't want to be the one who fired an accidental shot. He

TOM TATUM

daydreamed about a hot shower, cold beers and M's return to the ranch. He turned his iPhone on with maybe an hour's power at noon guessing the emergency court hearing would take about two hours. He got a signal. The lawmen had not figured out he was piggy backing their repeater. He checked his iPhone about one o'clock and it was on the low power indicator. It vibrated and he cupped his hand around it hoping to conceal it against his ear. M announced, "We've been monitoring the Santa Fe New Mexican newspaper online. They just published the court's decision. It ruled that the new Texas owner has no rights to the reservoir water or to close the road to it. The state engineer's office settled the water issues four decades ago in favor of the Water Association. The court has enjoined the ranch owner from interfering with the Water Association's right to release the irrigation water."

"I'll tell the good news to the chairman." He turned off the iPhone but as he looked up, he realized the Association member from the Land or Death movement had heard the conversation. Trey started to crawl over to the chairman's sandbag position to deliver the news, but the Land or Death member blocked him when he suddenly stood up and fired a shot at the state police's armored vehicle. A volley of shots rang out from the lawmen that hit his sandbags. Trey, still crawling low, put his hands on the shooter's legs and pulled them out from under him knocking his rifle out of his hand. Trey pulled his white Tee-shirt off and stood up waving it in one hand and holding the other one high with the cell phone.

He yelled at the top of his lungs. "The Court in Santa Fe ruled the new ranch owner has no rights to the Water Association's reservoir water and the road belongs to the Association. Hold your fire everyone please. The new ranch owner is also enjoined by the court from interfering with the Water Association's irrigation operations. We won."

The chairman stood up waving his white flag and turned to secure the Land or Death member who was on his knees reaching for his rifle in the dirt. Trey saw the deputy sheriff step from behind his white SUV. He had a rifle on his shoulder pointed at Trey's heart. He dived for cover behind the sandbags. There was a loud bang as the shot went over his sandbag wall. The Land or Death member recovered his rifle, aimed it over the wall and shot the deputy sheriff in the head killing him instantly. The chairman continued waving his white flag.

He shouted into his bullhorn, "Hold your fire. We won."

The Land or Death member aimed his rifle at the chairman and started to press the trigger. A single shot rang out from a state patrol sniper, and he fell backward as his head exploded. A Water Association member yanked his son's rifle out of his hands. A long minute later a cheer went up from the Association members as the state patrol commander stepped out of the armored vehicle with his bullhorn.

He stated clearly. "I just talked with the state attorney general. The court has ruled in favor of the Water Association on all issues. I have a printout of the decision." He waved it in the air. "Everyone, eject your gun's ammo and secure your weapons on their safeties. No more hothead pot shots. Your chairman can walk down here under his white flag and read the decision to you from his copy." Five minutes later, the chairman raised his hand with a victory signal while the EMTs worked on the deputy and the Land or Death member. They were eventually both body-bagged. Trey sent a text out to M that the siege was over, and he would call her from the ranch with more news. His iPhone died.

Trey emerged from a hot shower, wrapped a white cotton towel around his waist, poured a Scotch and walked into the master bedroom to wait for dinner. He iPhoned M.

"Hello, Trey, you're a hero. Maestas called Cooper and told him our cell phone call ended the standoff."

"It almost ended the standoff without bloodshed. It's good Jumbo had us encrypt our iPhones because there is more to tell. A Land or Death movement member overheard our call and fired a shot at the state patrol armored vehicle. The chairman had worried he had come to start a war. I tackled him on my way over to tell the chairman the court's decision. Out of the corner of my eye I saw the deputy sheriff who came to the ranch aim his rifle at me. I dove behind a sandbag as he fired a shot that missed me. Then the Land or Death member shot the exposed deputy in the head. A state police sniper shot the Land or Death member when he aimed his rifle at the Water Association chairman."

"Is the deputy dead?"

"Yes, both of them. I hope this takes the heat off us, but I'll call Jumbo tomorrow. They say in the old west, dead men tell no tales. The Land or Death member's son was with him. He saw me tackle his father to try and stop a heavy casualty gunfight. This won't go down well with Adrianna's Foundation's hardcore members. Leave this detail out when you brief my father and mother, please. Only tell them the deputy was shot and killed in a flare-up."

"So when can I come back?"

"When Jumbo green lights your return charter flight," Trey said firmly.

"I'll keep my iPhone in my jeans hip pocket on vibrate. I'd like to vibrate your bottom right now. I'm resting in bed with only a towel around my waist after a hot shower." M teased adding, "If the start light flashes green, I'm very fast off the line."

"The bunkhouse cook just knocked on my door. My steak dinner is waiting. Please tell my dad I'll call him tomorrow. Love you."

CHAPTER 9
A GREEN LIGHT RESTART

Trey iPhoned Jumbo at sunup. "Good morning, Trey. I heard you helped stop a shootout at—"

"I did what I could, sir, but an older Land or Death member who is now a Water Association member killed the deputy sheriff who came to the ranch last week and ID'd the Paint horses. A state police sniper killed him. So cutting to the chase, can M return from the YbarC?"

"When I heard that, I knew you would call so I checked with my FBI source. They intercepted a cell phone transmission calling off the hit on you and M since you all can't ID the deputy in court... dead men tell no tales. The cartel drug gang doesn't want to create unnecessary heat on their operations around the drop zone. Nothing concerning the cartel is risk free but it's your call to let her return. You left out that the deputy shot to kill you?"

Trey ignored Jumbo's query. "Any word on the next drop?"

"No."

"M is airborne."

"Just keep her off the west side of your ranch near the Gorge, please, and out of the black Shelby Mustang."

"Roger that." Trey red buttoned off. He texted an order for her charter flight to the ranch's dirt strip from Telluride. He called M and confirmed her flight time. Then he briefed his dad and warned him the Land or Death's Water Association member's death would not go well with Adrianna's Foundation members. He spent the rest of the day checking the range cattle with Maestas.

The charter tail dragger airplane from Telluride threw a cloud of dust a hundred feet into the air as it landed on the ranch's dry dirt and range grass airstrip. When the prop stopped, M opened her door, stepped onto the wing and hopper off into Trey's waiting arms. After a long kiss he helped the pilot unload M's luggage and a box of homemade desserts and chocolates from his mom. After the airplane took off into the prevailing southwestern wind and afternoon sun, he and M drove to the hacienda. She did an hour of home rehab and took a nap while Trey returned to ranch work until near sundown.

M greeted him at the door, "You look dusty and I'm sweaty from rehab. Let's take a quick shower together before dinner. I put it in the oven to stay warm. There's a bottle of red wine airing out."

"Sounds perfect." They walked into the master bedroom bath and stripped down. M put her healing broken arm and now cast-less hand into a garbage bag. Trey taped it tightly. They walked into the large brightly Mexican titled shower and soaped each other down, which led to shower sex. He sat on the modernized shower's built-in tile bench as she straddled his powerful rider's thighs. The hot water splashed over her shoulders and onto his chest. They toweled each other off, dressed and walked to the dining room for a steak dinner followed by Judy's homemade cherry pie.

Trey asked, "Does my dad suspect I shot a drug runner during the first drop gone bad?"

"Not that I could tell. He didn't link the dead deputy to more than that he ID'd us on the Paint horses during the first drug drop and figured we could ID him. He trust's Jumbo's intel. He told me to stay off the range alone and both of us away from the Gorge," she stressed.

"That's easy for you but hard for me on the Big Ditch issue. How's your rehab coming?"

"Good, my hand's cast was cut off in Telluride after my rehab session. They prescribe aggressive hand therapy developed for ski racers. I have limited home rehab arm and hand exercises. My outpatient therapy plan has been scanned to Taos for three days a week sessions. My arm's cast is two weeks away from coming off."

"We'll move into the La Fonda Hotel for the three days and two nights each week. That also limits our exposure on the ranch while we gauge if cartel is out of our lives until the Feds take it out."

M answered, "Then I'll set rehab up for Tuesday late afternoon, Wednesday and Thursday early morning so we're only in Taos forty-eight hours."

"Good. I'm sure we can find plenty to do including sample the local food scene. The Tempo section of the weekly Taos newspaper has art, film, music, and more listed every day and night in the summer tourist season. The Police Department patrols the town, but the County Sheriff's headquarters is at the modern courthouse. We'll keep our ears open. Townies like to gossip unlike ranchers who keep their heads low and their lips sealed."

M asked, "Can we tour the Taos Pueblo? It's a thousand years old. My Apache mother's tribe used to raid it."

"I haven't toured it since childhood with my mom. Let's do it," Trey replied.

"And hear some live music?" she asked.

"I'm all in on that. I miss college concerts and summer music festivals in Telluride."

M said laughing, "On that note help me clear the table."

On Tuesday morning, Trey drove an older ranch pickup to Taos for M's rehab. He didn't want to use his red pickup in town because the dead deputy may have seen it parked in front of the hacienda. He had the Paint horses shipped back to the YbarC as a precaution. He didn't want them ridden on the ranch or grazing in its corrals. They checked into the La Fonda Hotel on the Taos Plaza in their cowboy and girl clothes with Spanish leather luggage and a saddle rifle. They caused the usual stir with the tourists in the lobby. The rule in Taos was never leave a gun in a pickup truck overnight. He drove M to her rehab in a medical complex by the modern hospital and drove to a local hamburger stand for green chili cheeseburgers with spicy fries. After rehab they drove past the new county courthouse and jail. He did a double take when a white Sheriff's

SUV pulled out, but it turned the opposite direction. At the hotel, M scanned the Tempo.

"A Pueblo Indian band is playing at a bar across the Plaza tonight. It's a hip-hop band. They could be fun, and I could use a good margarita."

"I'm down for that," he replied using rapper slang from college days.

"Good, I'm going to nap. Rehab lady says rest heals," M replied.

"I'll camp in the hotel's guest only mezzanine lobby in a leather chair and manage the ranch from my iPhone. Nap well." Trey departed, happily enjoying a routine day. At eight o'clock they walked across the Plaza and down a cobblestone street to a two-hundred-year-old adobe building. After a New Mexico style red chili scrimp dinner and margaritas, the PO.10.CEE band cranked up with maximum musical energy. The young Taos Pueblo band members wore hip Tee-shirts and jeans. They sang rap hip-hop lyrics in English and the Tewa language.

When they took a break, M said, "Those guys are way good. Better than the Navaho hip hop band that I heard in Durango. It's great to be in town for a night."

"They're sensational. New wave Pueblo Indian music without feathers, beads and fringed buckskin," Trey replied just as one of the young band members jumped off stage.

He overheard them and stopped at their table, "You like our music. If you live around here, tell your friends. We need more local support to get gigs at the Taos music venues."

M was intrigued, "Can you sit with us during your break. I'm M and Trey is my boyfriend."

"It's short...OK for a couple minutes. I'm Tony 5017. The bar wants the audience to order drinks but not wander off." His eyes noted she might be Native American, as he sat in an empty chair.

"Are you Apache?"

"Yes, my mother is. Trey is a hundred percent rancher."

"Are you from Taos?" he asked.

Trey answered, "My family operates a ranch up on the Colorado border near the old volcano by the Gorge."

"My grandfather says big elk there. The ancient Pueblo people hunted on the old volcano before the Spanish came."

M added, "I'm half Spanish too."

"I'm a quarter, most of the Taos Pueblo has some Spanish blood and names too," he replied.

Trey probed, "You have a manager or agent and record deal?"

"We're our own manager but we're on a small Taos label. You can buy a CD after the show or listen to us on Spotify and Apple music. Our problem is the old people at the Pueblo don't like our music. They want all Pueblo music and dance to be traditional."

M said, "Trey, I'd like to talk to Tony and the band more. Can they visit the ranch?"

"Good by me. We can take them riding. Pueblo Indians are famous horsemen."

Tony smiling said, "My grandfather taught me to ride but two of our members are pickup truck Pueblo Indians and one will not ride on stolen Anglo or Spanish land. I'll come. Leave a cell phone number with the bartender and I'll text you for directions." The drummer hit a beat. "That's my cue." He hopped up toward the stage, slapping outstretched hands on the way.

"I'll leave the ranch's business card at the bar with our names and our cell numbers. If he texts us, we'll text back directions," Trey said.

"Leave my cell number off. I don't want to send a smoke signal that I'm a groupie that's interested in him. This band is young and on the road. It plays on Indian Country Radio Stations, in Pueblo Casinos and Reservation music venues. I'm sure very attractive rural Indian Country Radio listening girls chase them."

"Not you?" he asked.

"I'm over touring band musicians. Durango's bars and clubs had plenty of them. They always hit on attractive Indian girls as they sampled Southwestern groupies. Kind of like the Mountain Men of the frontier days. It's not my scene, especially when a lot of them were too drunk and too high to fuck according to my college girlfriends. I want to learn more about the Pueblo and its secret kiva religion's practices. My mother's ancestors raided the Taos Pueblo for slaves, which they sold to the Spanish settlers. They called them farmers not warriors like the Apache, but they feared the secret Pueblo's kiva spiritual ceremonies. I want to pick Tony's mind." She stopped talking suddenly.

"That's a lot to chew on as the cowhands say. You're not letting me in on all of your thoughts. There weren't any Native American girls in Telluride or at college in Los Angeles. You're the first one I met."

"Drop your card off at the bar. I want you all to myself tonight. We're out of here before the last set ends and the town police make their rounds." Trey sensed the Pueblo conversation was over and he walked over to the bar. He scribbled the info onto the ranch's business card.

At sunrise, Trey awoke as the Taos Plaza came to life below their corner room's open window. He looked over at M who was asleep nude on top of the sheets. Her body picked up the hue of the east sun as it rose over the Sangre de Christos Mountains lighting the Taos Plaza. Their clothes were strewn all over the hotel room's hand-made carved white wooden Spanish style chairs and writing table from another era. When he rolled onto his side to look at her backlit silhouette the well-worn bed springs creaked.

M opened her brown eyes and whispered, "Make love to me in the east sun, which brings life to all beings, animals and fish on earth each morning."

After breakfast, Trey drove her to rehab. They agreed to take the afternoon group tour of the Taos Pueblo and eat lunch in a Pueblo café listed in the local tourism guide. M wanted to learn more information about the Pueblo before Tony 5017 visited the ranch. Trey noticed she avoided any discussion of the Kiva religion. After rehab they stopped at the ranch equestrian store where she picked up a pair of brown deerskin leather riding gloves to protect the healing hand. They drove to the Taos Pueblo and parked in the intercept tourist lot. A sign stated no vehicles were allowed in the Pueblo's historic plaza area. At the ticket office they paid for the afternoon guided tour and were given directions to the café. They ordered fry bread with spiced ground beef and were sipping lemonades when Tony 5017 walked out of the kitchen with a brown paper grocery bag of delicious smelling food.

He chimed, "We meet again. My aunties own the café and prepares the food. You should have asked me for a morning private tour last night. I can't take you this afternoon. The band's leaving for the Hopi First Mesa in Arizona to play tomorrow night."

M replied, "I didn't want to impose on you before we had a horse-back ride. I don't know how an Apache unmarried woman is received here these days."

"Among the old ones not well and you know why. Among my generation, you, like all modern Indian Country women, men and children are good here except the Hopi priests." He stopped mid-sentence when a horn honked three times and he darted out of the café with a goodbye. "Gotta hip hop, that's the band's van. Road trip day."

Trey asked, "What's with the Hopis? I've visited their three mesas. They make stunning Kachina dolls in costumes they dance in. Judy bought a bear dancing with a bow and arrow."

M in a low voice dodged, "I wasn't allowed to visit the Hopis when I was a young girl. I only knew Apache girls when I was young. When I was a teenager, I mostly met Ute girls whose two Colorado reservations flank Durango. A few of them were classmates at Fort Lewis College. We all were occasionally treated badly by white redneck boys. We alerted each other to the ones we considered to be violent physical threats. They were mostly from the natural gas field roughneck families. The oil and gas drilling crews assault and rape Indian Country girls and women all over the west. The Indian casinos have made it worse than ever," she stopped talking as their lunch was served by one of Tony's middle-aged aunts.

They toured the thousand-year-old Pueblo, which they were told is a United Nations Heritage site. The thirty something Pueblo woman guide spoke in perfect English as well as Tewa. She told them the history of the Taos Pueblo. The group's first stop was by the Rio Hondo River that ran through the middle of the Pueblo's plaza with its multi-story adobe brick buildings.

She lectured, "The ancient living quarters in the building are maintained by their resident families. No electricity, natural gas, phone lines, or running water are permitted in the buildings. All the heat and cooking is with firewood from Pueblo forests and water from the river. Mostly older traditional members live in the dwellings. You cannot enter them unless invited by a family member."

A teenage tourist asked, "Can they use cell phones?"

The guide dodged, "I can't answer that question." The group then stopped at the river.

"This pure snowmelt water comes from the sacred lake above the Pueblo on the mountain above us. Only Pueblo members can visit it to practice our spiritual ceremonies. We all must go on one special day each year. President Nixon returned ownership of the lake to the Pueblo. The Spanish King's gave the Pueblo Land Grant status including the sacred lake. After the American conquest of the Southwest from Mexico the federal government's Forest Service stole it. He is remembered well here still." There was a murmur from the group of tourists.

As they passed a gap between two buildings, a woman in the tour pointed to a ladder emerging from underground. It emerged through a round hole in a dirt covered log roof.

She asked, "Where does the ladder go? Can I climb down it?"

"No, it's a kiva a special underground spiritual room. Only members of the kiva society may use it. Our spiritual practices are secret and cannot be discussed with non-Taos Pueblo members. They are conducted in our Tewa language. Only two Pueblos speak it. You all cannot leave the central Plaza area on this tour or walk into the gaps between the buildings or climb into the kivas."

Another tourist said, "We stopped at the reconstructed kiva at the National Monument in Aztec New Mexico yesterday. Is this kiva like it?"

"That's a stolen Anasazi site. It was reconstructed by white government archaeologists without the permission of the ancient one's spirits. We do not enter the Anasazi dwellings or kivas out of respect and fear of the spirits. Let's move on, please."

"I want to know more about this kiva stuff from you?" Trey whispered.

"I cannot discuss anything I may have heard about it unless you are my husband," she whispered firmly into his ear. "And please remember my mother is Apache not Pueblo. Follow the group."

The guide stopped by a battered screen door in front of a ground floor dwelling. "You may enter this shop. The family that lives here makes beautiful silver turquoise jewelry that is sold worldwide and many other craft items." M led Trey into the shop as he ducked through its low door.

They browsed the two battered antique glass topped counters and M asked an elderly wrinkled woman, "May I try on this bracelet?"

The woman nodded yes and took it out of the counter. M put it on her wrist. Stars and the moon in turquoise and other precious stones peeked out of the shiny hammered silver.

M turned her wrist toward Trey's eyes. "This is an exceptional piece. It'll bring good fortune from the universe."

"It's yours. It's beautiful and fits your wrist perfectly. My mom would say it was waiting for me," Trey replied. M handed it to him, and he read the price tag, which was on a string. He had seen a Visa/Master Card sticker on the screen doorframe, so he handed the old woman who nodded approval his credit card. She pulled out an iPhone with an Intuit credit card reader and walked to the screen door where it picked up a wireless signal.

Trey noted, "I guess that answers two questions. Cell phones are used for commerce in the Pueblo buildings."

"And the other?" M asked.

"The old women craft maker will trade her goods with a young Apache woman."

"But not her Pueblo grandson's hand in marriage. Her great-great grandmothers could have been captured or raped in an Apache raid," M said starkly. "She probably believes her bracelet will help me atone for my ancestor's violence."

"I hope it heals your arm and hand too."

"It will. I felt its power from the universe." The old woman smiled at them and silently handed M the bracelet as she blessed it in Tewa for its new journey with M.

M in Apache said, "Thank you for forgiving me for my mother's people's violence against the Taos Pueblo. I'll protect its power." She repeated it to the old woman and Trey in English, and they exited.

They walked behind the tour group toward the remains of a burned-out roofless adobe church. Trey said, "You are a very complex woman."

"It's because I live in three cultures and speak three languages. That can never change. My love for you is simple and love is the same in all three of them. Remember that is our foundation stone." M said with a smile letting the sunlight shine on her bracelet as its gems sparkled.

Trey said, "I remember the burned-out Catholic church from my childhood tour. The US Cavalry cornered the rebel Pueblo Warriors in it and turned their cannons on it murdering men, women and children as it burned. Not a pretty white man's story of conquest."

"It's not your story like the Apache raids on the Taos Pueblo are not my story. As long as we do not repeat the bad cultural behavior toward another being or animal it will not be our story. Let's go now before the spirits are stirred up in the burned-out church."

Trey picked up M after her early morning rehab and they drove back to the ranch with a stop for herbal medicine.

She reported, "My rehab physical therapist says my arm and hand are healing quickly. I can now drive and ride using both hands. I have to wear the riding gloves to protect my healing hand. I need to elastic bandage wrap my arm to avoid bending my elbow suddenly and jarring the mending bone break. If or when Tony texts, you set up the horseback ride."

"I still don't want you driving to Taos alone or in the Shelby Mustang."

"I totally agree. I asked her about the policing and crime situation around Taos since the Physical Therapy Center treats every kind of injury including gunshot wounds and sexual assault. Her unguarded answer was not good. She warned me as a part Native American woman to be very careful. Violent sexual assault on and off the Pueblo happens too often. On the Pueblo the FBI has jurisdiction and most cases are not ever prosecuted. Off the Pueblo there's little police protection of its women members and other Native Americans in New Mexico in general. She believes the FBI, the federal courts and its prosecutors to not pursue many rape cases. She has rehabbed several violently injured women of all races. There is even a non-profit group fighting violence against women in Taos."

"And drug violence victims?"

"Yes, if they survive the shootings," she added.

"Not a pretty picture. My parents have always lived an isolated, mostly part-time life on the ranch here. They spent very little time in town. There were no drug drops on or around it before we stumbled into one. I don't even remember a cow being rustled. I guess the outside world's headlines are here. Maestas always screened out the tension between the Spanish ranchers and other water rights holders. I'll watch your back and put a pistol in your car. There's always one in all the ranch pickups. It's under the driver's seat in this one." He added with urgency, "Look in your side view mirror. A white Sheriff's SUV just pulled out of the road to DH Lawrence's cabin and is following us. We'll pull over for a taco in the next town to see what happens." Trey turned on a radar detector. It beeped.

"He's definitely tailing us. I learned that tactic from the State Police Academy. I taught them moving high speed chase pursuit driving when a fugitive suspect they were tailing made them and took off at high speed," M stated.

Five minutes later, they pulled into a café in a battered adobe building. They walked into it and sat in a table by the 1950's front picture window. They watched the Sheriff's SUV back into a parking place in front of the bar across the street and he walked into it. They ordered lunch and ate it. The SUV didn't move.

When they were back in the pickup, Trey tensely said, "Watch your side mirror to see if he pulls out behind us."

A minute later, M reported, "He's tailing us again."

"Keep your eyes on him. I'll drive directly to the ranch and skip our ice cream pick up at the gas station. Call Maestas on your cell and ask him or a cowhand to meet us at the ranch road's entrance gate."

"Roger that."

Trey drove the speed limit the rest of the way to the ranch. M reported the Sheriff's SUV had dropped back but was still tailing them. The radar detector did not beep. Trey was relieved to see the main ranch gate on the left side of the highway with a pickup parked inside it. He pushed his turn signal lever well in advance of the open gate.

M reported, "He closing on us and just turned his flashing lights on." Trey slowed for the turn as M said, "He turned them off and is passing us."

After Trey was through the gate, he said. "He saw the ranch pickup inside gate and broke off the tail."

"He didn't want a witness. This is pure intimidation," M replied.

Trey stopped by the cowhand's pickup and rolled down his window. "Lock the gate and follow us to the hacienda, please."

"Yes, sir."

"I'll call Jumbo," Trey said. He iPhoned Jumbo from the hacienda's living room. After he and M recounted the Sheriff's SUV's tail on speaker phone Trey asked, "Was he following us for security?"

"No," replied Jumbo, "Remember I told you the DEA does not trust some of the local law enforcement in your area. We have had no contact with them. This tells me there are more and probably bigger players above the dead deputy in Northern NM. I'll pass this on. Stay on the ranch as much as possible. Drive armed and M travels only with you. I'll call back if and when I have any news."

CHAPTER 10
PROSPECTING FOR GOLD

Trey and M settled into a routine at the ranch as her arm and hand improved with daily physical therapy. Summer ranch management filled Trey's long warm days until the last dim rim of pale orange light faded away on the western horizon. When he surfed the national news at day's end, the cities on the Pacific Coast seemed like remote islands of frenzied high tech non-stop business that was changing life on the ranch. Packages arrived from Amazon with everything from ranch equipment parts to kitchenware. M shopped for French lingerie, dresses and jeans on the Internet. Animal husbandry supplies and parts for the pickup trucks came almost next day to the bunkhouse office. All this made life on the ranch more productive without trips an hour or two away to pick up supplies, spare parts, food staples and just about everything the ranch consumed. Trey bought a hundred shares of Amazon stock for his 401K that his accountant set up. It made the ranch more isolated without social interaction during the outbound stops. The satellite TV dish beamed the world into the hacienda's living room with hundred plus channels. The news media's massive urban political tilt's projected chaos made little sense while riding the summer range in pristine air under a deep blue sky. Chatter about corruption in the Ukraine or war in Afghanistan was so delinked from the southwest rural ranching areas it made no sense why the USA was involved. Reports of billions of wasted war dollars angered the ranchers and cowboys who believed the tax money should be used to fund modern irrigation systems to conserve water, improve local schools and provide rural health clinics, hospitals and more. Rural families tired of relatives and friends dying on long emergency medical trips to hospitals. It seemed only the farm country Iowa presidential primary every four years was all the media cared about and reported on from rural America. Trey had started to notice most of the news media conversation except for Albuquerque TV was eastern urban jibber jabber. Only tornadoes and blizzards made the national news in the Rocky Mountain West.

Trey's iPhone chimed its rodeo chorus after a late veranda dinner. "Hello, this is John Moore. I never heard back from you about my assay report on the gold bearing quartz you sent me," a deep clear voice stated.

Trey replied putting the iPhone on speaker, "Well that's true but we've been busy on the range and otherwise. Hold a second and let me see if M, my girlfriend, can ride and hike to the area where we found it. She banged up her hand and arm drag racing."

M listening replied, "I'm all in. I'm going stare crazy in the hacienda."

"You heard her. When can you come down to the ranch? Will you sign a Non-Disclosure Agreement if you find anything of significance?"

"I've got a couple days that opened up this weekend. Are you both available? Have a Non-Disclosure Agreement for me to sign? I've checked a satellite map of your area and it's possible there were illegal secret colonial Spanish gold mines. Have you found a tunnel entrance since I sent the report?"

"After you sign an NDA, I'll brief you on what we know currently. Text me your arrival time and I'll text you, directions to the ranch's hacienda. Thanks for getting in touch. See you."

M asked, "You trust him? Your father said to lay low on the Spanish leather and silver as well as the tunnel's location."

"Cooper did indeed say that but since we're confined to the ranch for now, let's use his availability to learn more about what we found up there. I could always use a gold mine old or new with the cost of ranching going up annually. Even though we own all the ranch's mineral rights there is no current information that leads us to believe there is oil or natural gas under the ranch, so gold works. Let's all take a look see."

"Fair enough. Let's ride," M smiled. "Tonight, let's go to bed early after a hot tub bath. I'll sleep in my new Parisian white cotton shorty nightie that just arrived from Amazon. It's perfect for the warm summer nights we are enjoying."

"That's the best idea of my dusty work week. Let's get it started with a cold beer."

John Moore arrived at the hacienda at ten a.m. on Saturday morning and signed the NDA agreement. He was a no-nonsense seasoned mining engineer. At noon, the party on horseback approached the high arroyo where they had found the original piece of assayed gold-bearing quartz. Trey decided to ride the sure-footed quarter horses higher up the arroyo's bank so M could avoid a long hike on slippery volcanic soil to the basalt rockslide and tunnel entrance. He and John had saddle rifles on their horses, and M had a light Glock 9 pistol in a hip holster. Occasionally John dismounted and walked into the deepening arroyo to pick up a small rock, which he put into a canvas bag with a leather shoulder strap that was red-stenciled ROCK SAMPLES. When they reached the dangerous basalt rockslide's edge Trey signaled to rein in the horses.

"Let's tie the horses up here and then we hike up to the old Spanish tunnel entrance we found, after John evaluates the slide."

John replied a little surprised, "You didn't mention you had found a tunnel entrance, but I carry a hard hat in my backpack always. I explained at the hacienda I work with a team that searches for lost Spanish colonial gold mines."

"I wanted to show you the slide first. We had to cross it to lose a big male mountain lion after we discovered the gold bearing quartz rock. It's dangerous footing," Trey replied.

"Looking at it you're both lucky it didn't slide. I assume it was dry when you crossed. When monsoon rainwater or snowmelt gets under the basalt scree it causes liquefaction. When a booted foot strikes a rock, it can slide loose and send you tumbling, which in turn can start a big slide kind of like a snow avalanche. Tie the horses away from it so their hoof vibrations don't reach the basalt rocks. Then I'll inspect it but not cross or walk on it for now."

"Roger that," replied M with a frown as images of their crossing it to escape the big cat flooded her mind. John walked up about fifty yards of the slide's edge snapping iPhone photos, and picked up small pieces of basalt for his rock bag. Trey and M ate roast beef and Swiss cheese sandwiches chased with New Mexico soda drinks while he worked.

When he walked back down to them, he stated, "This slide is man-made and maybe two hundred years old. There's a black powder blow line across it ten feet below its top edge. The basalt scree is probability tailings from a mine tunnel under it. I have a sample rock from the blow line that we can analyze for powder burns. I will carbon date the black powder's age at my assay lab. It's probably Spanish black powder brought up illegally from Mexico City for an unlicensed gold mine. It was blown to hide it from Spanish Colonial tax inspectors from Taos or Santa Fe or possibility after an Indian attack nearby to hide it. Now for my lunch and a soda, then show me your tunnel entrance."

M replied, "Wow!"

Trey led them up the side of the rocky basalt outcropping above the slide to the low tunnel's entrance, which was hidden by the sage and high bushes. John did not spot it until Trey pushed the sage aside.

He said, "That's a classic Roman arched Spanish colonial mine entrance into the volcanic basalt rock face. If it follows a gold vein that was exposed, it may be connected to the underside of the slide. It reinforces my theory the miners blew the tailings to cover the main mineshaft. They covered this tunnel entrance with brush to conceal it. They probably never returned, and a couple centuries have passed. It's well hidden. Have you been in it?"

"Yes and no. I crawled in my body length with a flashlight."

"Did you find or see anything?"

"I found a Spanish gold coin and a Spanish armored breast plate with a weathered leather strap," Trey replied.

"Is there a date on the gold coin?" John asked.

"Not that we can tell," M replied.

"Can I see the coin when we return to the hacienda?" he asked.

"No, it's not there. It's secured elsewhere for now. I can email you an iPhone photo," Trey replied.

"Good, now I want to crawl in and take a look see before I bring the team up here to explore the slide and the tunnel. You might be a very rich rancher."

M asked, "Isn't that too dangerous without your team?"

"Maybe, tunnels into this solid basalt are usually very stable. I only have fifty feet of rope with each end tied to one of my feet so you two can pull me out. My max trip is twenty-five feet. Help me rig. No talking or shouting into the tunnel. Sound vibrations will echo and can bring down loose rocks. No one's been into this tunnel probably for two hundred years. Here's my device that will send a signal to a satellite and activate a rescue. Push the red button if the tunnel caves in."

John pulled out a helmet, climbing rope, a LED headlamp, knee and elbow pads, high-end safety glasses and a titanium rock pick from his backpack. Trey and M helped him rig. He left a portable folding shovel with Trey. The exploration went into low gear as Trey held his breath. He belly-crawled a foot at time into the tunnel. His headlamp beam bounced into the black void. M let out the rope with her good hand. The strong wide light beam bounced from wall to wall to wall to ceiling in the tunnel as John belly-crawled a foot at a time into the old tunnel. The tension built with John's forward movement. He reached the wall where Trey had found the gold coin and armor. He carefully dug up the loose soil with a short knife, putting a sample into a large zip lock bag. He continued minute after minute deeper into the tunnel as M's heart raced. Suddenly twenty feet into the tunnel a foot long thin basalt rock broke from the ceiling and bounced off John's helmet. He flashed his LED beam as deep into the tunnel as possible exposing a shadow of an iron form. He hand-signaled for Trey to pull him out as he pushed crawled back to the entrance. There was another thump on the dirt floor back farther in the dark tunnel and he sped up his departure. Booted feet emerged from the tunnel entrance and Trey grasped his legs. He carefully dragged John to safety as a loud thump echoed from the tunnel entrance.

A dusty John sat up, "Well that was a little too exciting. There's a long crack in the tunnel ceiling about twenty feet into it that's shedding basalt rock. It will need to be shored up before it's safe to explore farther into the tunnel. At the end of the fifty-foot light beam I picked up an old pine log timber support beam with probably an iron wheeled low wooden sided gold ore cart. The dry, New Mexico mountain air has preserved it. Hopefully, the soil samples I took will show traces of gold ore dust. The tunnel drops a couple of degrees and bends left a couple of degrees. It's maybe following a mined out volcanic gold vein. It's dry as a bone. This mountain is volcanic rock solid with no water veins or springs flowing through it. That means the tunnel has never flooded and should be safe to shore up with jacks. I'll need an experienced colonial exploration mining team to follow the tunnel deeper into the mountain."

Trey replied, "That's a lot of good information. When will your sample rock reports and carbon dating be completed?"

"A week or so. Let me get onto my feet and please help dust me off. After I jot down some notes, we can make our way down to the horses and a hot shower."

M replied, "Trey and I will take some iPhone photos of the area around the tunnel while you write up your notes. We'll look for arrowheads or point clusters as the locals call them, which could indicate an Indio attack. We'll be back in fifteen minutes." A few minutes later, M stooped and picked up a broken obsidian point. They examined the area around it and found small cactus plants.

Trey said, "Time to return to John and get off the mountain. This point was probably a missed bow hunting shot at an elk or deer. There's no sign of a battle with the miners. We'll keep it and let Maestas ID its vintage. He has a point collection at his house."

"It has been an amazing day!" M reflected.

Trey and M were eating Sunday brunch in the hacienda's interior courtyard veranda under an umbrella that shaded a Spanish style, hand forged, black, wrought iron table. John had left before sunup without waking them. They were listening to Jazz music on a Taos Radio station when the DJ cut in with a special bulletin. They both stopped eating while he read it, "Two Federal Bureau of Land Management rangers were ambushed west of Tres Piedras and the Rio Grande River Gorge in Rio Arriba County early this morning. They were flight for life to Albuquerque Presbyterian hospital where one was pronounced dead on arrival. The other ranger is listed in critical condition. A BLM spokesperson will only say they were investigating illegal grazing on federal land. However as most Taosinos know the Land or Death Movement from nearby Tierra Amarilla has long claimed their family's Spanish Land Grant communal grazing rights were stolen from them by the federal government as well as Anglo ranchers after the seizure of New Mexico by the US government in 1848 from Mexico. This appears to be another Allianz battle in the war against the federal government, which was started by the Land or Death's Movement in the 1967 Courthouse raid at Tierra Amarilla. The members wanted to regain the 600,000 stolen Spanish Land Grant ranching and farming acres from the original Spanish settlers after New Spain became New Mexico in 1852. The legendary Reyes Lopez Tijerina and Baltasar Martinez led the raid. Tensions have been rising again since two members of the movement attempted to murder Trey Stuart and his girlfriend M in Pagosa Springs Colorado this spring. Trey operates the Ute Peak Ranch in northern Taos County. M is a famous drag racer from Durango Colorado. One of the movement's members was killed in the shootout with the Pagosa Springs police. The other one has jumped bail after he failed to appear in court on attempted murder charges. We'll keep you informed. The FBI has been brought in to lead the investigation with the New Mexico State Patrol. The Sheriff's Department in Tierra Amarilla has refused to be involved. It's rumored some of its officers may have family members who belong to the movement. More local news at noon. Now let's listen to Miles Davis."

Trey, who was angered by the report said, "We need this publicity like a bullet in our heads. The FBI will be at the hacienda's gate in no time. They hate the Allianz and the remaining Land or Death members from the 1967 courthouse raid and rebellion. The FBI crushed it with the US Army. They still want to arrest Adrianna for her part in it. They also probably still want to arrest my father for leading the battle in Telluride against the corrupt Cortez Colorado uranium czar and ski developer."

M replied, "History repeats itself, or does it?"

"What do you mean by that?" Trey asked.

"Or did the BLM rangers stumble into a drug drop or pick-up across the Gorge near Tres Piedras? How far away is the ranch's southwest boundary from the ambush site?" she asked.

Trey replied, "Twenty miles as the crow flies. That's an interesting theory. Maybe the wounded ranger can shed some light on it but probably not if it was a blind ambush at sunup. The movement won't talk to the FBI. They don't care who shot the rangers even if it wasn't one of their members. A dead BLM ranger is a victory for them. The drug runners are safe at home base if they shot them. If an FBI agent shows up while I'm on the range, refuse them entry to the hacienda until I return. I'll post a cowboy at the gate."

"Roger that. They treat Indian women half or whole like shit. They let the rapist run free in reservation and Pueblo towns. I'd empty my pistol before I'd be alone in the hacienda with an FBI agent."

"Your mother raised you tough like Cooper raised me. Let the cowhand keep them out. I don't want to have to visit you in jail."

"Roger that too," M replied.

"Now let's enjoy our brunch on a rare day off. The hacienda walls will keep any intruders out. I want to discuss a rafting trip in the Rio Grande River Gorge along the ranch's west boundary before the water drops too low. And as soon as your arm is healed."

"Let's finish brunch and then you're my dessert." M's smile was mouth-watering delicious.

Monday morning came early as Trey and two-cowhands rode hard out of the hacienda gate. Their horses threw up a dust cloud as twelve hooves pounded the dry summer soil. Three saddle rifles bobbed in stained tan leather scabbards. Maestas had advised Trey to check the cattle in the southwest pastures of the ranch after he heard the ambush radio news report. He wanted to make sure there hadn't been an airplane drug drop on the ranch side of the Gorge and that the boundary gates were chain locked. Trey had him post a cowhand on hacienda security duty to watch for the missing Land or Death movement member who jumped bail, and to intercept any arriving law enforcement officers including the FBI. Their ride was hard and fast to the ranch's southwest corner. They found the gate locked and the barbwire fences were up. There were no signs of a drug plane drop and pick up. The mother cows and calves were grazing and nursing peacefully. It was an idyllic early deep blue-sky summer day. They ate beef jerky chased with pristine cold aquifer well water while the horses rested and drank from a stock tank. The conversation was range easy until Trey's walkie-talkie buzzed, "Trey, M over."

"Trey over, what gives?"

"Our cow hand Mike is holding two bogies at the hacienda gate. Can you return?" A bogie was their code for FBI and other federal agents.

"Roger that. Tell Maestas that all is quiet on the Southwest corner. Beautiful day to ride the range but I'm on the way." Trey gave the cowhands their work orders for the rest of the day. He mounted his horse. "Get'ie up. We're galloping home. You get extra oats tonight."

Trey reached the hacienda gate with his horse sweating profusely in the high summer morning sun. There was an unmarked black SUV blocking the gate with multiple aerials on its top. Two hard faced agents in dark suits were pacing back and forth. A tense Maestas was inside the locked gate with the cowhand. Trey dismounted and held his horse by it reins to start letting it cool down.

"What do we owe your visit to?" he asked.

An irritated fiftyish, crewcut, grey-haired, FBI agent replied,

"We'd like to interview you and Maria Duran about the ambush of two BLM agents yesterday. We believe the Land or Death Foundation may have been involved. We know that they tried to ambush you both after you met with Adrianna at her office earlier this year." Trey's iPhone rang.

Jumbo whispered, "If the Feds are at your HQ, it's a fishing expedition. Send them on their way." His iPhone went dead.

"I don't have anything to add to the Pagosa Springs police report nor does M. The county prosecutor's office is handling the case. The Taos radio reporter said the surviving movement member who was at the motel jumped bail. I've posted old fashion cowhand security at the hacienda to make sure a round of lead meets him if he shows up here."

"So we can't interview you both?"

"No and no or enter the hacienda without a warrant. Adios, I need to cool my horse down ASAP," Trey replied calmly.

"You don't want to help us investigate murder?"

"We have no information on it period, except what we heard on the radio at brunch yesterday. M does have a speculation. Could it have been a drug plane drop or pick-up that the BLM rangers stumbled into, which are plaguing ranches on both sides of the Gorge. I just checked our southwest pasture this morning with two cowhands and found no signs of a drug plane drop or pick up in it or any open gates on the boundary fence."

"We can't comment on the ongoing drug trafficking investigations in Northern Mexico," the senior agent replied.

"Or arrest them because ranching families and cowhands are at risk. We have nothing else to tell you but please solve this tragic murder and stop the drug plane drops. If we hear anything that's relevant on the barb-wire wireless, we'll phone it in." Trey pointed to their car door.

They walked over to it and slammed their heavy black SUV doors and pulled away. Trey asked Maestas to open the gate and he gave his horse's reins to Mike the cowhand. He issued afternoon range orders to Maestas.

M opened the front door and met Trey with a hug.

He whispered, "Jumbo called and told me to lose them because they were fishing." They disappeared through the heavy wooden front door into the historic security of the thick-walled fortress adobe.

An hour later, Trey's iPhone signaled a text. It was from Adrianna. He read it. 'FBI at my office re: the Tres P shootings. Alleging that you implicated the Foundation in it by refusing an interview and threatening to kill the Foundation member who has jumped bail'

Trey texted back, 'I refused an interview because all I know about it is the Taos radio report. Nothing to add except I pressed them to end drug plane drops here. For the ranch's safety my cowhands have shoot to kill orders if the bail jumper shows up. You can put that on your barbwire wireless. -T He Rockie-Talkied Maestas who was at the bunk house and ordered a 24/7-armed cowhand posted at the hacienda until further notice or capture of the fugitive.

CHAPTER 11
WAR CHIEF

Trey's iPhone rang early just after sun-up the next morning while he and M were making love. Since she was on top, M rolled over the bedside table and answered it breathlessly with a smile, "Trey Stuart's Ute Peak Ranch headquarters office. Who may I say is calling?"

"Eagle Feather the War Chief of the Taos Pueblo. I would like to speak with Mr. Trey Stuart."

"Please hold a second while I pass his iPhone phone to him Mr. War Chief Eagle Feather." She handed the iPhone to a surprised Trey.

Trey who had only read about the war chief in a Taos News Legends of Taos story took a deep breath and in a strong voice replied, "Good morning, sir, what do I owe the pleasure of your call?"

"I will be brief, Mr. Stuart, I would like to schedule a secret meeting with you at the Taos Pueblo this afternoon. I can only tell you it pertains to the drug plane drops near your ranch. The Pueblo would like to discuss stopping them with you. Please come to the Pueblo's Tourist information and ticket office at four pm this afternoon. Ask for Juan Four Elks who will bring you to me. He is a Korean War veteran. Are you available today?"

Trey paused as a listening M signaled thumbs up. "I will see you at four pm, sir."

"**W**ar chief drug drop powwow, what do you make of this?"

"The cartel is supplying hard drugs to a dealer on the Pueblo just like they do to the Ute Reservations around Durango. He knows whom deals and supplies the drugs on the Pueblo but is afraid the FBI, BIA or the sheriff may all be corrupt. They could sell him out to the Mexican cartel and he or a family member might be murdered. My mother said this is how it works on the res."

"Why me? How does he have my iPhone number?"

"The art gallery has it as well as Tony. The gallery carries Pueblo artists. Plus, you are an Anglo or white eyes rancher therefore you distrust the federal government like the Pueblo."

"How could he know we intercepted a drug drop?"

"The presumptive dead gunman in the drug recovery brown Bronco might be Taos Pueblo member. If so, he knows you are tough like a war chief and assumes you tried to stop the drug pick-up," M replied.

"Then the meetings on. You want to go with me?"

"I can't. It will be in a very secret place maybe even the Warrior Society's kiva. Women are not allowed. Remember when we visited the Pueblo, I refused to tell you much about its kivas and specifically the Hopi people. The reason why is my mother told me the Hopis and maybe other Pueblos were still sacrificing young maidens in the kiva ceremonies during the spring to bring rain for the blue corn when she was a girl." Trey's blue eyes hardened.

"I'll go shopping near the Plaza at the woman's store for some very sexy summer jeans and a top or two or three. I'll need your American Express card. The jeans are two-hundred-dollars a pair. My ranch wages won't cover them like my tips did. Now let's reenact waking up again. Except this time, you're on top."

Trey climbed down a lodge pole pine ladder with Aspen rungs into the darkened kiva that a ponytailed, slightly limping Juan had led him to in a corner of the Pueblo. His eyes adjusted to the low light slowly. His cowboy booted heels hit the hard packed dirt floor. A flaming torch lit the underground room with its stacked, grey, flat stonewalls. The still air was cool and its smell ancient. He blinked one more time to clear his eyes. The war chief sat on a stone bench built into the wall. Another Pueblo warrior sat next to him with his fully cast upper arm and shoulder in a sling. Their dark brown eyes pierced the low light as they locked onto his blue ones. Juan hadn't followed Trey down the ladder, but a shaft of sunlight pierced its round opening and bounced off the kiva's floor. The war chief hand signaled Trey to sit on a stone bench across from him. Trey had slipped a knife into his right boot and a small black Glock nine pistol into his cowboy cut, Justin, brown leather jacket's concealed pocket in the inner lining. His iPhone was not receiving a signal so no 911.

The shadowed war chief said, "We have invited you to the Warrior Society's kiva not the Blue Corn Farmer's kiva. We are the protectors of the Taos Pueblo. Our Tewa language is spoken within these underground walls. We both will speak English for your benefit today. Jonathon Runners Feet sits next to me. You shot him on your ranch."

Trey's blue eyes signaled alarm as his right-hand fingers opened ready to draw his pistol. "He's not dead from my bullet but why not? Is this a revenge meeting?"

"No and no," answered the war chief continuing."He was wearing his bulletproof army vest from the Iraq War. When your bullet hit him square in his warrior's heart spot it knocked him backwards into the high roll bar, which broke his arm and shoulder. He fell forward hard into the Bronco's dashboard and was knocked out."

"But as a warrior he must want revenge?" Trey stated.

"Not against you, only the Mexican cartel and its gang leaders from Taos, Espanola and Albuquerque. He realizes now that it was wrong for him to sell drugs to the children, women and men on the Pueblo. He's working with the Pueblo's cacique medicine man to cleanse his spirit." The old, ponytailed, wrinkled, brown faced cacique stepped out from behind the stone alter. He was dressed in ceremonial clothing but remained silent. He had a brightly-colored parrot feather pushed across and through his ponytail.

Jonathon spoke, "Forgive me for trying to kill you and the woman who rides like the wind. It was wrong of me to shoot at you to protect cocaine, Oxy and meth. I became an addict after I returned from Iraq. I tried to erase the war memories with drugs. It was not a warrior's war. You are a true warrior. You rode like the wind and shot like a Comanche from your horse to protect the woman and your land."

"Apology accepted even though you could have killed M and me plus our horses. Now may I depart?"

"You can but hear us out first?" the war chief asked, continuing.

"The cartel will kill Jonathon my son and others on the Pueblo if we go to the crooked white eyes…the Bureau of Indian Affairs, FBI and your sheriff. We know who runs the Mexican cartel in New Mexico. They are allied with the same families that have sold liquor illegally to all the Pueblos and Reservations throughout the state since the Americans first came. They are very powerful, and they reach into the Governor's office, the BIA, the FBI office in Santa Fe and many county Sheriff's offices around the thirteen Pueblo's. Their leader is a powerful banker named Smith Jones in Albuquerque. His bank takes the drug money. We need you to help kill him. We will set up a meeting with him and the cartel in the Pueblo. You will have a kill shot at them with two Pueblo Warrior Society members who were snipers in Iraq. We will help you vanish into the night. They will never bother your ranch or the Pueblo again. Their drugs are killing many of our Pueblo members. The cartel is like the Spanish catholic priests and soldiers who sealed the Taos Pueblo's war chief, cacique and warriors in this kiva during the 1600s and pumped in burning hot pepper fumes to murder them. Popay our great cacique ended their reign of terror when he led the Pueblo Revolt in 1680 and drove the Spanish soldiers, catholic priests and settlers out of New Spain that is now New Mexico."

"That's a lot to think about. I'm not an assassin or sniper but as you know a good shot. I want the drug drops stopped. My cowhands and the woman M who rides and drives like wind are in danger. The FBI blew me off yesterday on the drug drop investigation. I know at least one deputy sheriff was dirty. He covered Jonathon's drug drop and later threatened me. He was killed in the Water Association's shootout at the reservoir. I'm told the DEA is investigating the airplane drug drops but nothing has happened to stop them. Let me talk to M and I'll get back to you. Call me at sunup in seven days from now on my iPhone at the ranch. Ask if I have a Palomino stallion for sale. If I say no, then game on. Please have Juan lead me out of the Pueblo."

Trey met M at the still-deserted Taos Inn's back patio for an early dinner. Her large logoed shopping bag signaled a successful trip. She was wearing new designer jeans with a yellow blouse and looked fashion model hip. After they ordered, he outlined the meeting and the war chief's offer. She looked at him with her brown eyes wide open.

"That's more dangerous than any drag race I've ever driven in. Let's let this request ride the wind for a while and wait for Jumbo to tell us what the DEA and the state patrol plan is. Your meeting summary didn't mention the state patrol as a corrupt law enforcement agency. If there's no law enforcement action to stop the drug drops, or if there is another one on the ranch, then maybe we have to consider the war chief's game plan. Remember you are a white eyes outsider on a thousand-year-old Pueblo. The Pueblo Warrior Society members have no obligation to protect you. If the plan goes badly then the war chief could easily use you as the fall guy and hand you over to the FBI, which has criminal jurisdiction on the Pueblo. My mother said the FBI did little or nothing to protect the people on her reservation from illegal alcohol and drug sales. Remember they told you the Pueblos have been drowning in alcohol and now drugs since the Americans conquered the Spanish in New Mexico in 1844. No government law enforcement agency has stepped in to stop it. Also remember the war chief's son shot to kill us. The war chief and the BIA doctor who treated him at the Pueblo medical center did not question him about how he was injured and therefore report him to the FBI. His apology to you is suspicious to me as an Apache. I love you and do not want to lose you."

Trey's face finally relaxed. "That's sound thinking on your part as usual. I have every right to take defensive action on my ranch to protect you, my parents and the cowhands. His son had no right to shoot at us on the ranch. Fuck his apology. The Iraq War is just another excuse for soldiers to drown in alcohol and drugs after their return home. The US government is tossing them into the wind like Vietnam, my dad says. We'll stay on the ranch for now but defend it with maximum deadly force."

M replied, "Remember the war chief and his son believe they have every right to shoot at you on the ranch. It's the Pueblo's stolen hunting land."

"So I could be in a crossfire on the ranch from both the Spanish whose king took it from the Pueblo and its Warrior Society who fought the Spanish to get it back in 1680. If I die in a gunfight against the cartel on the Pueblo it's a win win for them."

"Perversely, it's exactly that for you as a white eyes and me as your Apache girlfriend. Taos is drenched in blood for land. The US army seizure of the Pueblo is no different than the Apache raids on it."

"Can this beautiful land ever escape its dark past?" Trey mused.

"The hard-core Apache's say no and the Pueblo caciques say no," M retorted. The waitress arrived and placed two loaded plates with two Cowboy Buda margaritas on the table. After she departed, M proposed, "A toast to the ranch, our love and my new jeans. As long as you're with me, both the Spanish and the Apache have their land back. Let's eat these chili rellenos while they are hot."

"I haven't thought of it that way, but true. You can take it back without firing a shot. Can I help pull your new tight jeans off when we get back to the hacienda?" Trey asked laughing and tossing down a big Cowboy Buda gulp.

"That's why I'm wearing them, Trey. They'll distract your thoughts from the war chief's real game whatever it is." M smiled like a mountain lioness who had just pounced on a deer.

Two days later at breakfast, Trey's iPhone rang and it was John Moore on the line.

John asked, "My team has had a project cancelled and is available tomorrow to explore the mine for two days. Does that work for you all on short notice?" Trey paused and considered that he had not heard from Jumbo.

"Come on down. I'll get a couple of cowhands to help get your equipment up to the mine tunnel entrance. Can you all ride? Do you need bunk house space?" he asked.

"We can all ride. The four of us will bring tents and sleep overnight on the mountain to be more efficient. You can loan us a cowhand though for mountain lion security. We'll see you at the hacienda tomorrow at 7a.m. sharp."

"That'll work. See you all tomorrow," Trey replied. He put his iPhone on speaker and briefed M along with Maestas about the plan.

After he hung up, M said, "Are you going to warn them about the drug drops?"

"No, they're high on the side of the mountain, which blocks their view of the drop zone. They'll have an armed cowhand with them overnight plus us during the day. I'll take our bed over sleeping in a tent on volcanic soil by the mine tunnel entrance."

She laughed, "Is it really the bed or just me?"

"Busted, it's really you. Let's get set for the expedition. You need to

find the bunkhouse cook and get provisions and water set for two days.
I'll find Maestas and arrange for horses and pack donkeys to meet the
pickups by the mountain…plus the cowhands. It'll be like the movie
Treasure of Sierra Madre."

"Roger that, trail boss. If we find a big goldmine, can you sell this dusty
place, and we can retire to the beach."

"No, but we'll let Maestas operate it and surf Costa Rica winters for a
year or two or three until he retires." Trey smiled.

"I'm on my way to find Cookie," and M was out the door.

John Moore and his geology mining team arrived at seven a.m. as promised at the hacienda gate. Maestas met them with two cowhands each
with a pickup truck after they parked their two SUVs. One pickup trailed
four horses for the mine team and the other one two horses for the cowhands. They loaded their equipment and camping gear into the pickups
and drove to the mountain on a sunny morning. Trey and M had left at
sunup on horseback. They trailed two pack donkeys to the trailhead to
the mine tunnel. Maestas stayed at the hacienda to secure it and oversee
ranching operations during the two-day mine exploration. The fugitive
from the Pagosa Springs motel shooting was still on the loose. When the
pickups reached the top of the ranch road near the tunnel entrance the mine
search and camping equipment was strapped to the donkeys' packsaddles.
Each mining team member was assigned a saddled horse for the ride to
the tunnel entrance. Trey and one cowhand led the single line procession
with the mining team in the middle with M and a cowhand riding drag.
Each cowhand trailed a donkey. It was a slow careful ride up the mountain
on the loose, rocky, volcanic soil. The horses and donkeys were range
sure-footed and kept an even pace up the mountain with the experienced
riders. When the line of riders reached the tunnel entrance area the cowhands dismounted first and secured the donkeys' lead lines to a pine tree.
Then the riders dismounted, and the cowhands hobbled the eight horses so
they could nibble on the mostly gamma grass on the mountainside. Trey
and M led the mining team up to the tunnel entrance with their hand carried equipment while the cowhands unloaded the camping gear and food
from the donkeys' packs and set up the double tents.

At the mine tunnel entrance meeting, John stated, "Trey, you and M
stay at the tunnel entrance. Please do not enter it. I'm setting up a transmit-

ter for you, which is attached to a spool of wire we will unroll as we descend into the tunnel for communications. Our lightweight digital Rocky Talkies may lose their signal path out of the tunnel to you as we drop into it. We'll clip the Rocky Talkies with carabineers to our belts to talk to each other and you also. If there's a cave in, please do not enter the tunnel. Call the Taos County Sheriff for Search and Rescue members who were trained in mine rescue at the now closed Chevron molybdenum mine in Questa. Have your cowhands guide them up here with their rescue equipment. We are taking lightweight, hardened steel, telescoping roof jackets into the tunnel. They can brace damaged timber roof supports. If there is a cave in, those of us who are uninjured on the tunnel entrance side will come out to you. If any of our team is trapped in or on the other side of the cave in, we will wait for search and rescue to help us. Our large first aid kit is by the transmitter but we each have a pocket-size one. If we radio an injured team member is coming out, call 911 and request the medical helicopter from Taos Airport to fly as close as possible to the tunnel entrance. There is a collapsible stretcher at the campsite. We will be in the mine probably the rest of the day, but our exit will be no later than 6 p.m. Special lunches and water bladders are in our back packs Any questions?"

Trey asked, "How often will you update us after we lose the Rocky Talkie signal?"

"As we can over the hard line to the transmitter but every fifteen minutes plus or minus," John replied.

Trey replied, "We'll stand by here and monitor your communications. Safe exploring."

John strapped on his hardhat with an LED spot lamp on top of it, as did the other team members. They crawled into the tunnel five feet apart, one after the other. Their packs had the collapsible steel roof jacks attached to each side of them.

M asked, "Wow these are brave men. What are you paying them?"

Trey answered, "A thousand dollars out of pocket expenses and a 10% royalty on the gross value of any gold ore mined or the sale stashed gold coins and Aztec icons."

"So, they have an incentive to explore the old mine shaft at a high standard since they have a fair piece of the pie," M stated as a cowhand walked toward them.

He reported, "The camp is set up and Rip will stay for security."

Trey replied, "Return with your horse and pick up tomorrow at 5 p.m. Please tell Maestas that M and I will be down for dinner by eight p.m. tonight assuming all goes well. Report everything is on schedule up here."

Trey and M sat by the radio and monitored the team's communications as it worked a yard at a time into the tunnel. Their radio conversations signaled they had stopped at the cracked ceiling beam, which had shed some small roof rocks near John Moore on his solo trip into the tunnel.

Ten minutes later, he reported to Trey, "The steel roof jack is in place and the sagging, square, hand-hewn pine roof beam is holding. We're starting the descent around the ten-degree sloping corner. So far there are no visible signs of gold ore."

"Roger that," Trey replied as Rip arrived with their lunch and reported, "The camp's set up. I'm staying for the night. I'm on Rocky Talkie to you all on ranch channel 105."

"Thanks, please remember the non-disclosure agreement you signed to work up here. Total silence about the exploration of this old tunnel we found until it's explored."

"Got that straight, boss. Don't want to start a stampede across your fence lines. Treasure hunters have combed this mountain for two hundred years as rumors have flown." He turned on his cowboy boot heels and started down the mountain.

M said, "Treasure on the mountain is a local story all over the Four Corners, from lost gold mines to hidden Aztec gold sent up from Mexico when Cortez invaded Mexico City."

Trey replied, "Yes, even my father alleges he and Adrianna who he dated before my mom, found a mine tunnel high in Utah's La Salle mountains above a family friend's ranch that had a skeleton guarding the tunnel's entrance. When he returned the next year a winter avalanche had caused a landslide that covered the entrance. He said rumors of hidden Aztec gold in the La Salle's had been around in his grandfather's lifetime."

"You know where Cooper's tunnel entrance is?"

"Yes and no, he has the compass coordinates from a helicopter trip over the area, which he won't discuss. They are in the safe at the YbarC ranch house. I want to check coordinates out someday. It's on the back burner."

"One lost gold mine at a time is enough," M replied.

"You got that right. They say there's one a mile or so up the Bear Creek drainage from downtown Telluride. An old miner showed up from time to time at the Sheridan Bar with high-grade gold nuggets. He was shot in back for a pocket full of them. No one has ever found the nuggets' source."

M said, "We're not hearing Rocky Talkie conversations."

Trey replied, "Something is blocking the line-of-sight transmission."

Five minutes later, John Moore's voice crackled over the hard-wired transmitter. "Tunnel turned again 10 degrees with 4-degree slope. We see an old wooden push ore car thirty feet ahead that is blocking the tunnel. We'll inspect it first and then decide if we have to take it apart to continue farther into the mine. We'll be on the transmitter every fifteen minutes. You're not responding on the Rocky Talkies."

Trey pressed the send button on the transmitter's mike and replied, "Roger that." He released the button. "Let's lunch before the next report."

Inside the tunnel John's team began disassembling the old ore cart after they photographed it. The dry, even temperature air in the tunnel had preserved the iron bolts. With a little WD-40 their wrench removed one bolt at a time. It took an hour to remove them all and stack the wooden frame and panels on the tunnel's sidewall. They collected dust samples from its inner planks for testing. They took a small piece of a pine plank end for carbon dating as well as a hand-forged bolt. Then they ate their lunch of dried fruit chased with apple juice in squeeze containers. John said to the team, "This confirms ore or treasure may have been hauled out of this tunnel. The dust samples from it should tell us what kind of ore. So far it looks like the miners found an exposed thin stray gold vein in this approximately 1.2-million-year-old volcano according to the US Geological Survey. Next, we'll see where the tunnel takes us. Be extra careful. The Spanish colonial miners may have left the ore cart in its blocking position to warn of danger beyond it when they departed as well as hide it for their return. They clearly never returned. The Spanish cross that's carved into its front side panel confirms this is a colonial mine legal or illegal. Keep your eyes and ears wide open. I have placed my lithium battery-powered digital pocket seismograph on the tunnel floor behind us. If the tunnel starts to shake it will sound a screeching alarm. If it does, we start an orderly retreat."

Three voices quietly echoed, "Roger that." They started crawling on hands and knees deeper into the tunnel in a single line.

Trey and M received reports over the transmitter every fifteen minutes or so. Trey gathered dried Pinion and Juniper branches for the mine team's cook out and campfire. M read the annual rulebook changes for NHRA racing for her class. With her arm and shoulder nearly healed, she was considering drag racing her Mustang again. M had decided she still needed a life outside of the ranch. One of the cowhands had told her about a local teenage Spanish mechanic who was a prodigy with motors and cars. He was already rebuilding vintage muscle cars from the junkyards and family farm stashes near the ranch. She intended to contact him after the mine exploration was finished. As the clock ticked toward six o'clock, the sun disappeared to the west behind the mountain. It cast a longer and longer giant shadow across the wide valley below, which reached for the hacienda.

The transmitter squawked. "Trey we're turning around and backing out of the mine. Our LED headlamps continue to disappear. Our transmitter cable mark shows we're 350 feet into the tunnel. We've installed six of our roof beam jacks. We just cleared a small rock pile under the last one. I'll review our digital trajectory line once we get back to camp but I believe we're approaching the top edge of the basalt shale slide on the mountain's face. We've only found a hand-forged iron hammerhead and no other artifacts or equipment besides the Spanish ore cart. See you soon."

"Roger that," Trey replied.

M said, "That's a football field plus inside this old volcano. It's not for me."

"I agree. I like riding under the big blue open sky."

"It seems odds are getting longer that we don't surf Costa Rica," M stated a little sad.

"Maybe not for a whole winter but a month after the fall cattle sale. It's too soon to assume there's no remaining gold. Once they come out, we'll carry the firewood down to the camp and ride to the hacienda in daylight. I can taste cookie's charcoal broiled ranch T-bone steak with a local baked potato after a hot shower."

"I'm all in on that plan as long as the shower includes me. I'm dusty dirty too." M winked at Trey.

At the hacienda after they exited a hot shower with large bath towels wrapped around their tired bodies, Trey's iPhone chimed. Cooper asked, "How did the mine tunnel exploration go today?"

"The team made it in 350 feet. They found a Spanish colonial ore cart, which they will carbon date plus assay dust samples from it. No gold ore or anything else of importance. They put up six steel telescoping tunnel ceiling beam jacks. They go back in at eight a.m. tomorrow."

"They believe it's safe to re-enter the tunnel again then?"

"Yes."

"And you do too?" Cooper asked.

"Above my pay grade. It's John Moore's call. M and I monitor the hard-wired transmitter for progress reports and in case of an emergency. We have specific protocol emergency instructions for a cave in or injury. We are barred from entering the tunnel."

"Call me when they complete tomorrow's exploration. Thanks."

M looked at Trey quizzically, "That was Cooper?"

"Indeed, it was. Maybe he's thinking about some Fiji surfing with the gold profits. He was in the Peace Corps there. Put some clothes on for the veranda featuring sunset steaks and cold beer."

The east sun filled the tunnel entrance area with eight a.m. morning sunlight but the late-night Albuquerque TV weather report future cast was for afternoon thunderstorms on the ranch and the mountain.

After Trey briefed John on the weather report he replied, "We have seen no sign of water flow or tunnel roof leakage. This old volcano is rock solid." He smiled at his geology quip.

Trey replied, "The old Spanish ranchers say there has never been a spring on the mountain and the arroyos carry off all the rain and snow melt water. The tunnel entrance is well above the nearest arroyo and its entrance area slopes downhill."

"We're going in but alert us if there is a thunderstorm so we know it's thunder echoing into the tunnel entrance." The team disappeared one by one into the mountainside.

The cowhand standing by Trey said, "With that weather report, Rip and I'll pack up the campsite gear and donkey pack it back to the hacienda with our horses ASAP. The mining team's horses will be at the campsite hobbled. We'll leave our ranch pickup and yours with their horse trailers at the trailhead. You and M can drive the miners back to the hacienda."

"Works for me. Just bring me a tarp to cover the transmitter area and keep us dry."

"Roger that, boss, but remember lightning can get real mean up here."

"I've heard that. We have to man the transmitter in case of an emergency. Bring me a saddle rifle too since you're pulling out. I only brought my Glock pistol."

"Will do."

The morning passed slowly with routine reports from John while the big white cumulus thunderclouds slowly built over the mountain.

Trey said, "The old Spanish ranchers say the mountain has a hat on it when the clouds build up and to get the hell off it because the lightning is deadly."

"I agree," M replied.

He set up the blue, heavy plastic cloth tarp and staked its sides down tent style. He dug a shallow drainage ditch around it with a portable camp shovel. M brought him basalt lava rocks to form a low table to set the transmitter on with the saddle rifle. He put a garbage bag over the transmitter. He pulled rain pants and jackets out of his backpack for himself and M. Right after lunch the transmitter squawked just as thunder and lightning struck a quarter mile from the tarp.

"We're near the end of the tunnel where it has caved in. Or its other entrance was blown in under the basalt rockslide, which I now believe was a tailings dump too. It's too dangerous to explore any farther. We haven't found any gold ore, coins or more mining equipment. They probably mined out a thin vein."

Trey replied on the mike as a thunderclap almost deafened him. "Then get out…all hell is breaking loose out here in the thunderstorm. Lightning just struck a hundred feet from the tunnel entrance."

"I heard it over the mike. There's one other find. A skull with a colorful Aztec priest's parrot feather pushed through the eye sockets. The feather is like the ones they found at nearby Aztec and Bloomfield NM in the Anasazi kiva ruins."

"What's it doing in the tunnel?" Trey asked, amazed as M flinched in shock and shouted into the mike, "Don't pick it up, it's the sign of a curse."

John replied, "We already bagged it and are bringing it out. It's your property. It's worth $100,000 to a collector or museum." A major ear-shattering, thunder-lightning bolt hit the basalt shale slide on the mountainside above the mining team. "A lightning bolt just rattled the basalt slide area and set off static electricity in here. Our seismograph warning signal just went off." Trey and M heard the siren like sound over the transmitter. A second lightning bolt struck close to the tarp and a bolt of static electricity hit the transmitter and sparked an electrical fire in it. Rain blew through the tarp's uphill open end, soaking the transmitter and it went dead.

"Fuck, we have no communication with them!" Trey yelled over the storm.

"Dial down your calm meter, Trey. They've set off the Aztec curse. We all need you at full strength to survive the day," M stated with no emotion.

"What's the Aztec curse you're talking about?"

"The Spanish colonial miners probably found an Aztec tunnel the priest's slaves' dug when they fled Cortez to bury and secret gold religious sacrifice icons in. The skull with the parrot feather was put in the cave to warn any Pueblo Indian intruder away. Their priests visited the Pueblo kivas with these feathers. The Spanish miners examined the skull, set it down and continued into the mine. The curse activated and they may be buried under the slide. John and his team are in grave danger in the tunnel."

"How do you know all this?"

"It's Jicarilla Apache legend. The Aztec priests' warrior protectors killed some of my mother's tribal warriors as they pushed up the Rio Grande River, which flows on the other side of the mountain."

Trey reported, "I saw a parrot feather in the Taos Pueblo kiva." Suddenly a bolt of close lightning shook the earth and in the flash Trey saw something move in his peripheral vision.

"M do you see something moving near the tunnel entrance?"

She looked hard through the blowing sheets of rain with her racing eyesight. "It's a large, wet, mountain lion moving toward the tunnel entrance to seek shelter."

"It's a dead one," Trey said. He picked up the saddle rifle, aimed and fired a shot behind the lion's shoulder blade into its heart. He levered another round into the repeating rifle and the lion turned to pounce the fifteen feet to M. He shot it between the eyes, blowing a hole into its skull as its back hind feet wobbled. It staggered and collapsed a couple feet from her. Trey shot it in the head again at point blank and slashed its throat with his hunting knife killing it.

A stunned M cried out in shock with the bleeding lion's head near her cowgirl booted feet. "The Aztec curse, Trey. Thank you for your shot. The priests' spirits sent the mountain lion to kill me as revenge because I told you all about the curse before it could kill the mining team. We wait to see if the mining team survives."

"Is there a possibility they won't?" Trey asked.

"A very high possibility they haven't. It's a strong ancient curse to protect the sacrificial Aztec gold icons that may still be under the rockslide.
If they're not out by 6 p.m. then you call search and rescue as John stated
in his protocol." Another thunderclap in the distance boomed as the storm
moved across the valley toward the hacienda. M shivered in her rain suit
as Trey reloaded the saddle rifle. Lightning struck near the old fortified
hacienda under a violent grey-black sky.

In the tunnel, John made a series of quick decisions. He pulled the skull
with the parrot feather out of his pack back and laid it where the team
found it. He photographed it and said, "We leave the skull and feather
here, curse or no curse. It's not what we were contracted to find. The transmitter is dead possibly hit by lightning. Tie the transmitter line to the skull
through its eye sockets. If Trey or a museum wants it, they can pull it out
of the tunnel. If anything happens to us it will mark our stop search point.
Leave the roof jacks in place as we exit. Let's move at full careful-scram-
ble speed out of here."

The seismograph siren continued to scream at full volume. The team
started its crawl scramble about 500 feet from the tunnel entrance according to the mark on the transmitter line. Their LED headlamps made eerie
patterns on the tunnel's sidewalls and roof. John led the tight line of the
other three miners. They stirred up dust from the mine floor, which filled
their nostrils. John stopped the scramble with a hand signal and ordered
over the Rocky Talkies, "Put on your N-95 dust face masks." They all
pulled them from their backpacks, sipped some water from their tubes to
clear the dust out of their mouths, and carefully put them on. John hand
signaled forward, and the line continued to scramble.

Trey watched the area around the tunnel entrance with his saddle rifle
in hand. M watched the tunnel entrance and the transmitter line to see if
it jiggled as the thunderstorm moved away. They could hear the arroyo
below them roaring. Rainwater continued to run four inches deep through
the tarp's floor area. Suddenly a rogue lightning strike with an immediate
thunderclap deafened them when it hit the basalt slide area on the mountainside as the rain subsided.

"That was a big flash and close. It would have fried us if it hit the tunnel
entrance area," M reported.

Trey replied, "The mountain gods have been with us today. We have been narrowly missed a half dozen times by these violent lightning strikes. I totally understand why the old Spanish ranchers say leave the mountain when its cloud hat forms. This big standalone rock attracts violent lightning thunderstorms."

M replied, "I'm never coming back up here when I see the hat."

Inside the tunnel the lightning strike sent a shower of roof rocks down on the team.

One of them hit the trailing miner on a gloved hand and he screamed in pain. "My hand's broken." The line stopped. The team member in front of him pulled his first aid kit from a cargo pant pocket and gave him a powerful pain killer pill. Then he crossed tape around the top of the hand and wrist.

John said, "Prepare to move," but as he pointed his headlamp forward it revealed a ceiling timber was sagging. He looked at the transmitter line and said, "The line marker says we are at 325 feet from the entrance. Get another roof jack in place on this beam and we can restart our exit. It's still probably too far for the Rocky Talkies to transmit but I'll try anyway. "Do you copy us, Trey or M?" Nothing came back. The two team members behind him scrambled by carefully to place the roof support jack. John checked the broken hand and added some tape from his first aid kit. The wounded team member grimaced in pain.

At the tunnel entrance area after the rain stopped, Trey dragged the dead mountain lion into the pine trees. He left it for the grey foxes and crows to scavenge. He didn't even want its hide at the hacienda. It was an evil spirit. He dropped the tarp onto the wet ground to use it as a pad until the team came out of the tunnel. M worked on the radio, blowing dry air from her mouth onto its buttons and switches to no avail. She blessed it and said, "RIP." They both listened for their waterproof Rocky Talkies but received no transmissions. Trey's military style waterproof digital watch's time moved toward six p.m. He tried his iPhone one more time, but they remained in a wireless dead spot.

M asked, "Should I drop down to the wireless hot spot and iPhone Maestas to get the cowhands to meet us at the pickups?"

"Too dangerous for you to go without me. The dead male mountain lion could have a mate this time of year. The wet rocky footing will be dangerous until more of the rainwater runs off. Plus, you couldn't cross the arroyo until it gets shallower where the pickup trucks are parked. You'd be swept to your death. I'm worried about riding the horses down from the campsite. Even their footing will be dangerous. We may have to lead them down. We wait together."

M replied, "That's fine by me."

In the mine the roof beam jack was finally in place but only after two larger basalt rocks fell narrowly missing the two-team members. John ordered the team to move under the beam one at a time five feet apart with the member who had the broken hand going first. They carefully reached the other side and regrouped into a single file line.

John said, "Now we move out of here but check the roof jacks and roof beams with your head lamps as we go. I don't trust this tunnel anymore after the storm with tons of water coursing down the mountain. It's forty-five minutes until six p.m. when Trey will call for Taos mine search and rescue. Let's move out. Follow the transmitter line."

The scramble crawl started as the lead member winced in pain. Thirty slow minutes passed until the team reached the first roof beam jack where they had lost the Rocky Talkie signal to Trey and M on the way in. John hand-signaled the team to stop before they scrambled under the beam, and he searched the ceiling with his headlamp. It was sagging badly, ready to break.

He Rocky Talkied Trey, "John and team over to Trey and M."

A relieved Trey replied, "Copy that, where are you in the tunnel? Is everyone ok? The lightning took the transmitter out."

"We are at the first roof jack about fifty feet from the tunnel entrance. We haven't crawled under the roof beam yet. It's sagging badly probably from the storm's concussion sound waves and maybe the jack point pressure has made it worse. There isn't a safe placement spot for a second jack. It could bring the whole tunnel roof down and seal us in here best case or crush us worst case. One team member has a broken hand from a rock fall."

Trey replied, "Do you want us to call for mine search and rescue?"

"Negative on search and rescue but positive on an EMT ambulance if you have an iPhone signal."

"Negative on an iPhone signal. I can't risk sending M alone down to the pickup trucks where we get one."

"I'll start the team under the roof beam one at a time and each one will scramble straight to the tunnel opening. Have the large first aid kit ready. Shine your LED spotlight into the tunnel to help us exit faster. I'll send the two uninjured team members out first and I'll follow the injured one out. Go." He hand-signaled the team to start out. The first team member carefully moved past the jack and scrambled toward the tunnel, but the beam creaked from his vibration. John radioed, "Team member one on the way."

He sent the second one through as the beam sagged more.

"Team member two through." John said to the injured member,

"I'm going under the beam first and will stop just past it. Follow me to it. I'll reach back to you and pull you through with your good hand. We'll keep scrambling toward the tunnel entrance."

John crawled under the beam as it groaned and sagged more. He reached back and extended his arm and hand carefully to the injured team member who grasped it. John started to pull him through, but his wobbly crawl scramble caused his leg to hit the jack. Its vibration went through the steel-telescoping jack to the sagging, old, dried-out pine, roof beam. It snapped with a loud crack that echoed out of the tunnel entrance just as the other two-team members reached it.

Trey requested, "M, help me pull these two out." A cloud of dust raced toward the tunnel entrance, blocking his spotlight's LED beam. John yanked the injured team member from under the collapsing beam as the mine tunnel roof cracked and started to collapse. John continued to scramble out of the tunnel with one hand pulling the injured team member, but a rock hit his legs.

He screamed in pain. "My left leg is broken."

John whispered, "Crawl on you good knee while I pull you out." The dust cloud blinded his headlamp's beam. John followed the transmitter wire on the mine floor toward the tunnel opening.

Trey and M pulled the two-team members to their feet outside of the entrance.

Trey asked, "Should I crawl in to help John with the injured guy?"

"No, it's too dangerous. The roof beam probably broke starting a rock fall. They both may be dead under tons of basalt rock. Pray," the senior team member replied. M crossed herself. John continued to drag the injured miner through the dark, dust-choked tunnel two feet at a time as he heard more tunnel roof cracks and rock fall behind them.

M helped the two miners on the tarp and gave them the first aid kit to clean and bandage small cuts on their faces from their scramble. Trey pointed his LED spotlight into the thickening dust cloud in the tunnel. He started to hear scrambling sounds echoing on the tunnel walls. Suddenly there was a rumble and a boom from a massive rock fall in the mine. Trey saw a gloved hand appear out of the thick dust cloud and he reached into the tunnel. He grasped it pulling John almost out. The injured miner screamed in pain as a rock fell onto his good leg, breaking it. He stopped scrambling forward, but John still had one of the miner's hands. Trey stretched his arm into the tunnel and grabbed the injured miner's other hand. They yanked the screaming miner's body a foot at a time through the tunnel entrance. M grabbed Trey's cowboy booted feet, pulling his shoulders and cowboy hatted head out of the tunnel entrance. The injured miner's yellow safety helmet emerged as the roof collapse accelerated toward the tunnel entrance. The dust cloud blinded everyone. Trey, John and M blinded by dust grabbed the injured miner's arm pits and yanked him past the tunnel entrance as he whimpered in semi-conscious pain. Small basalt rocks rolled out of the tunnel entrance as they pulled him to safety onto the tarp. The tunnel opening's Spanish rock arch collapsed. Suddenly the dust cloud stopped flowing out of the mine tunnel entrance as it sealed itself.

John and his wilderness medical team member started triage on the wounded miner. Long minutes later, his hand and both legs were bandaged and splinted. John gave him a morphine pill to kill the pain.

He asked Trey, "Please head down to your iPhone reception point and get the Taos medical helicopter to the meadow by pickup trucks. I've detected some internal bleeding in his upper leg. An artery may be damaged. He could bleed to death internally. M can guide us down. Two of us will carry him down on our portable stretcher. M and I will ride and trail the two extra horses with our backpacks on them."

"Roger that but M, who's a very experienced horsewoman, will make the call on riding down to the pickups and or trailing the horses with your equipment packs down. The terrain is dangerously slippery. The arroyo is running fast up to and maybe over its banks in places. My cowhands can collect the horses and your backpacks later. I'll iPhone Maestas for four cowhands to meet us with two four-wheelers ASAP. I'll ride down as fast as possible on my sure-footed horse. I grew up in the saddle. Adios." Trey turned and walked down the trail toward his horse.

John helped the other two team members load the injured miner onto the stretcher and they started the difficult trek behind M. Everybody's footing was slip and slide. When they reached the five horses, which were hobbled and nibbling wet grass they sat the stretcher down on a flat, wet, grassy spot. M's eyes surveyed the trail below them with her mini binoculars. It still had water coursing down it in places. She could see and hear the arroyo roaring below them.

She said, "Since you have to walk the stretcher down, we'll leave all the horses here. The wet trail with its loose, basalt, rocky volcanic soil is still very dangerous for their footing with less than cowhand riding skills. Leave your backpacks too but bring the first aid kit and wear your safety hats with their spotlights. Stay as far away as possible from the side of the arroyo bank at all times. The runoff is fast, up to and maybe over its banks in places but its water level will drop fast now that the storm is over."

John replied, "Roger that. Let's start moving."

Trey's sure-footed horse reached the wireless signal area and his iPhone beeped to life. He could see the pickups a football field below him in the small grassy mountainside meadow surrounded by sage. The arroyo water level was dropping but still too dangerous to cross on horseback or foot. He punched in 911 and a police operator answered.

"I'm Trey Stuart operator of the Ute Peak Ranch near Costilla. We need a medical helicopter ASAP to rescue a hiker with two broken legs and a hand. He had a bad fall off a cliff face in the violent thunderstorm up here on Ute Peak. We believe he may have a torn artery in his upper leg and could bleed to death." He stated to protect the tunnel site. "My GPS app is approximately 41" 21"12.2N2"10'26.5E since I'm riding my horse. It's west of State Highway 522. The pilot will see a landing zone by a red pickup and a white pickup. I'll mark its center with my blue rain suit. Three men are carrying him down off the mountain on a makeshift stretcher."

"Roger that, Mr. Stuart. I'm calling the medical helicopter at the Taos airport. The emergency flight medical crew should reach you in twenty-five minutes with a flying time of fifteen minutes straight up the valley. Will you be in iPhone range?"

"Roger that."

"I'll keep you posted, and the pilot will have your number. Over and out."

Trey continued on horseback until he was parallel with the pickups.

The arroyo was running a fast four feet deep and its banks were dangerous, washed-out mud. He maneuvered his horse up to its sidewall. The
paint steadied and he slid it down the elk trail. It struggled for footing in
the rushing water but finally found some. Trey spurred hard and pointed
it up the five-foot high, arroyo wall's muddy path. It strongly surged up
and out of the arroyo, but its hind hooves barely held on the bank's edge
as wet soil crumbled under them into the rapidly-flowing water. Trey
spurred the horse hard again and its powerful front legs pulled him out
of danger over the arroyo wall. He reined the horse in by his red pickup
and whispered into its ear, "Brave boy…extra oats tonight." The Paint
horse whinnied in agreement as he dismounted. His cowboy boot heels
sank into the wet rocky soil as he walked to the pickup truck and opened
the door after pulling off his blue rain suit. He got a LED flashlight that
had a red strobe, out of the glove compartment. He walked to the middle
of the meadow and crisscrossed his rain pants with its jacket and basalt
rocked it to the to the ground. He turned on the flashlight to its strobe
position and faced it straight up toward the clearing blue sky. His iPhone
chimed. It was the pilot.

"Over to Trey Stuart."

"Trey Stuart here at the landing zone which is marked by a blue cross
with a powerful red strobing LED flashlight."

"We're flying at 100 nautical air miles an hour and a hot five miles
out. Is your injured patient at the LZ and alive?"

"Negative on the LZ but coming down on a hand carried portable
stretcher."

"Roger that and let me know when he arrives at the LZ. I'll circle a
couple times as the helio descends. Is the blue cross staked to the ground
securely, so I don't pull it up into my props?"

"Only loose basalt rocks on it."

"Then pull it after the first circle above the LZ."

"Roger that."

"Over and out." Trey iPhoned M but there was still no answer.

M looked up and saw the helio approaching the landing zone as the two
pickups came into view below her. The injured miner was unconscious,
and a large hematoma had formed on his left leg's groin intersection.

She iPhoned Trey, "M over."

Trey replied, "Medical helicopter a couple minutes from landing. Are you in visual contact?"

"Yes, about a hundred yards out. Will continue to descend as fast as possible. The patient is unconscious. Major internal bleeding."

"Get him to the arroyo trail crossing. Water has dropped to three feet but still running fast. Hold there and two of us will come down our arroyo side, cross and help handle the stretcher with two of your team members. We'll have to lift him above the water once the stretcher is partially down the bank. The uphill bank will be more dangerous. Rope him to the stretcher."

"He's already strapped to it,"

"Roger that and out."

The red helicopter circled for a second time and slowed its descent. It landed dead center in the LZ as its blades gradually whirled to a dustless stop. An EMT and a flight nurse exited the open side door and ducked under the blades.

The EMT ran toward Trey and shouted, "Where is the victim?"

"Coming down on a game trail on the other side of the arroyo on a portable stretcher."

He quizzed, "You all just happened to have a portable stretcher on the hike?"

Trey responded. "At our camp site because we were scouting steep rocky terrain and a cliff face. Two ranch donkeys carried up all our gear. We will meet the stretcher on the other side of the arroyo. Water's dropped to three feet but still fast. The four of us can get him across it but the banks are muddy dangerous."

The paramedic replied, "Good plan. I'll get our gurney out and we'll transfer him to it on the helicopter side. The flight nurse has a blood transfusion rigged for him inside the helio."

Trey had hobbled his horse, but the helicopter's landing made him nervous. He removed the hobble and tied the reins to the red pickup's bumper. "No hobbling into the chopper blades, boy."

M shouted, "Ahoy, Trey," breaking the tension. He ran toward the arroyo as the paramedic followed in his waterproof hiking boots. They stopped at the top of arroyo bank when the stretcher team reached the other side with M.

John shouted across the roaring water, "His pulse is fading fast.

He's strapped in."

The EMT responded, "We'll cross and get him to the helio gurney. We'll need to lift him shoulder high above the water."

He and Trey slid down the muddy bank and carefully stepped through the rushing water. It reminded Trey of fly-fishing in his waders. They reached their arms up as two miners each took one side of the stretcher while John held its two end handles. They slid it out over the bank as Trey and the paramedic each grasped a handle shoulder high. Then all three of them slid down the bank keeping it mostly level as Trey and the paramedic walked it backwards across the arroyo. Trey and the paramedic slid their handles on to the top of the bank and the pilot gradually pulled the stretcher onto the grass as the team in the water pushed it. One of the miners lost his footing and splashed into the rushing water. He yanked his side of the stretcher down. The other four men struggled to right the stretcher as the victim started to roll under the straps toward the edge. Once the stretcher was on the grass the flight nurse rolled the gurney to it. Trey helped EMT transfer the victim on to it. The nurse gave him an adrenalin shot. John helped M cross the arroyo and Trey pulled her up the bank with one hand. The paramedic and the nurse rolled the gurney to the helio, sliding it through the side door.

The pilot shouted, "Clear the LZ. I'll start the blades for lift off as soon as we close the doors." Trey scrambled behind the red pickup where M and the team were standing.

He said, "Good job everyone. There are water bottles in both pickups and energy bars in the glove compartments. The cowhands will be here soon with two more pickups. The cowhands will get your backpacks before dark and bring them down to the hacienda. A shower, dinner and beds are waiting for you. We're out of here in these two pickups once I detach the horse trailers."

The medical helicopter roared into life and its prop wash blew them sideways. Trey and M's cowboy hats went airborne. Trey's horse strained at his reins. It lifted into the air and banked, turned toward the Taos hospital while M calmed the horse.

CHAPTER 12

CAT AND MOUSE

The afternoon after John and his team departed the ranch, he reported to Trey that the injured team member was out of ICU at Taos Hospital. The doctors expected him to make a full recovery. He emailed Trey the iPhone photo of the skull with the Aztec feather piercing its eye sockets. Cooper and Judy arrived late afternoon from the YbarC. Trey and M met them on the hacienda's veranda for cocktails. Trey and M gave them a summary of the tunnel exploration.

Cooper asked, "Can I see the Aztec feather photo?"

"Sure," replied Trey and he opened it on his iPhone. Cooper and Judy viewed it and he asked, "Are you going to share it with an Aztec scholar or a museum?"

"What's your opinion on that issue?" Trey asked.

"It'll invite another exploration of the tunnel, probably from the slide side this time. It will bring treasurer hunters onto the ranch. What are the theories on how it got there if any?"

"Fuzzy but John speculates the Aztecs' priests who came up the Rio Grande River fleeing Cortez dug a tunnel that is now under the basalt rockslide. They sealed solid gold sacrificial icons in it. They left the skull and feather, M says, to warn of a curse and departed back to Mexico City. The Spanish conquistadors slaughtered the Aztec king and his priests on orders from the Catholic Church. They never returned to New Mexico. No Spaniard did until Coronado came up from Mexico City looking for gold. He followed the Rio Grande River north and camped on our ranch by the Rio Costilla near the mountain. He claimed all of now New Mexico and southern Colorado for Spain. Based on John's carbon dating a Spanish prospector and miners found the sealed tunnel entrance. They used black powder to blow it open, but it caused the basalt rockslide and resealed it. John found and carbon dated Spanish black powder residue that dates to late 1600s. The mining cart's wood sample dates to that period also. What's confusing, there were no traces of gold on the cart's wood plank sample or gold ore dust in the tunnel from a mined vein. He believes the Spanish miners engineered the new tunnel from the entrance that we found. Its route was calculated to intercept the old tunnel entrance under the basalt slide. John's team explored the new tunnel until they intercepted the skull with the feather in the original Aztec tunnel. The Spanish miners may have found the gold icons before the curse activated causing the Aztec tunnel roof's cave in just past the skull and feather. He believes the wooden mine cart was for hauling the gold icons out through the Spanish miner's new tunnel. They may have left with or without the gold icons. They may be buried just past the skull with feather under the cave in with the Aztec gold. Now both the old and new tunnel's roofs have caved in sealing them with hundreds of thousands of tons of volcanic basalt rock," Trey concluded.

Judy asked, "M, how do you know about the curse?"

"My mother's Apache ancestors were attacked by Aztec warriors who were guarding the priests as they moved the gold icons up the Rio Grande River. The priests used the parrot feathers for spiritual power. Placing one through the eye sockets of a skull indicates a sacrificial curse."

Cooper speculated, "A dig to reopen the now completely caved in tunnels would cost millions of dollars and set off worldwide treasure hunting publicity including a reality TV show to help finance it. If there were Aztec gold icons, they may be gone. The miners would not have reported them to Mexico City to avoid the Spanish king's taxes. They simply would have melted them into bars to sell illegally. The Spanish Catholic priests had ordered all Aztec and Inca gold icons melted down into ingots for transportation to Spain. They believed that the icons were the devil's work. I don't think we want to cause that event. It would destroy our ranch and damage the mountain."

M added, "Plus reactivate the curse, so I agree."

Trey asserted, "I repeat all we have is a bunch of ifs and maybes from John except the carbon dating. John did not find a trace or atom of gold or gold ore. I agree let the ranch and mountain sleep in peace."

"So be it," added Judy.

"Let's drink some of the 18-year-old Scotch I brought you, Trey, while M and Judy drink the margaritas I mixed. Judy made the salsa for the corn chips. Let's enjoy this beautiful summer evening and sunset on the veranda."

The next morning, Cooper and Trey saddled up at sunup and headed out to check cattle. They planned to ride all day in the south and west pastures to check the boundary fences for cuts. As they rode through the hacienda gate, a Taos County Search and Rescue pickup stopped and they reined in their horses A buff, forty something, crewcut, tanned man stepped out. "I'm looking for Trey Stuart."

"I'm him and this is my father Cooper. What can I do for you?"

"You made the 911 call for a medical helicopter rescue on your ranch on the mountain's flank, correct."

"Yes, your pilot and the medical flight crew did a great job," Trey replied.

"There seems to be some confusion in the rescue report. The 911- call recording says the injured man fell from a cliff band while exploring it. But his nurse said he kept talking about a tunnel in his heavily drugged state. The hospital says a Colorado company named Geo Exploration's workmen's comp insurance policy is paying the helicopter medical rescue and the Taos Hospital bill. So, what gives?"

Trey replied, "That's easy we were exploring what we think is an old Indian cave under a ledge on the mountainside looking for artifacts and chipped obsidian rocks from a nearby vein. He lost his footing near its entrance and rolled down a forty-foot cliff bank. The team carried him on a portable stretcher to the helicopter's LZ that I set up."

"Mind if I see the cave site?"

"We do. It's on our ranch and it's private property. We don't want it disturbed. Plus, it's summer and we're busy with cattle operations so I can't help you. I'm told your medical helicopter rescue bill will be paid in full."

"I'm sorry you don't want to cooperate, but I know the New Mexico State trespass law for private ranch land. I'll be on my way." He departed with a frown.

Cooper asked, "Why did you tell 911 it was a fall not a tunnel cave-in injury?"

"Because the medical helicopter response would have been the same. However, when word got out around Taos County about a 911 medical rescue injury call caused when an old mine tunnel caved in on the ranch's mountain land we would be fucked. The ranch would have been overrun with treasure hunters," Trey replied.

"Can they get a search warrant?"

"No because the medical helicopter rescue and hospital bills are being paid by John's company insurance, which is all that matters. He signed a non-disclosure agreement on the operation, as did the injured team member. They specialize in top secret old lost gold and silver mine exploration work including the Spanish colonial mines in the Southwest."

"Smart on the NDAs on both parties' behalf. Let's ride," Cooper concluded.

M and Judy decided to visit Taos during Cookie's grocery trip and look at art while he shopped. They stopped at the gallery where Trey had bought the horse painting for Cooper and Judy. While they were looking at the newest art, the clerk who sold Trey and M the painting approached them.

She said, "Welcome back, M. The Taos News says your ranch had a helicopter medical rescue on Sunday. Is the injured cowhand ok?"

A surprised M replied carefully, "Yes, he is being released from the hospital today."

"Was it a cowboy horse accident?"

"No, a bad fall while hiking along a steep escarpment on the mountain."

M changed the conversation. "This is Judy, who's Trey's mother. Can you show us all of your new artwork? She's visiting from the YbarC ranch near Telluride Colorado and is a horse woman."

"Follow me."

M and Judy ate lunch on the Taos Inn's patio while waiting for Cookie to pick them up. Judy said, after she put the Taos News down:

"Does the paper cover every accident and rescue in the county?"

M replied, "Yes and usually with a picture. That's an aerial photo of the mountainside of the ranch from newspaper files. I've seen it before. Trey says if the newspaper does not cover a rescue story, then rumors about it fly around the county anyway. That's why we're keeping the real cause of the injury secret or gold treasure hunters would flash mob the ranch."

"Your NO TRESSPASS signs don't keep them out?" Judy asked.

"Not in Northern New Mexico. The Pueblo Indians believe all the land here belonged to them. The Spanish settler's families believe it still belongs to them by land grant deed or no deed even though the king took it from the Pueblos. The federal government believes it owns most of it even though it took it by conquest from Mexico and the Spanish settlers. The sage hippies believe they can squat here and there until someone shows up with a deed and the sheriff to evict them. The eco groups want the federal government to buy it all and put it into wilderness so no one can use it. So, the merry go round goes round and round here. We enforce the ranch boundary fences with cowhands who ride with saddle rifles."

"I guess I kind of knew that when we lived here. That's why Cooper put Maestas in charge so we could move back to the YbarC. Can you and Trey handle it?"

"So far, but I'm worried about Trey's reaction to another drug drop if it occurs on the ranch. He'll shoot to kill and who knows where that spider web will lead to."

Judy replied with a worried look, "I know my son is like his father when Cooper fought to save the YbarC." Judy told M the entire YbarC story over lunch.

Trey and Cooper were riding along the south boundary when they discovered a five-strand barbwire fence cut. Crushed range grass four-wheeler tire tracks guided them to the center of a pasture where the bloody hide and head of a skinned cow elk lay in the grass.

"Looks like a cow elk was poached in the last two days. You have much of that on the YbarC these days?" Cooper asked.

"It's rare but I hear it happens if a local pioneering family needs a meal or to make some cash selling the meat to a local restaurant. Wild game on the menu is a fad these days," Trey answered.

"I thought the restaurants could only sell farm raised game that was butchered in USDA inspected meat plants," Cooper replied.

"That's the law but ignored in New Mexico for wild game," Trey explained.

"You lose cows too?"

"Maestas says one or two a year."

"That's lost beef cash!" Cooper stated.

"That's a tax on ranching around here and keeping the peace with the neighbors. I don't want a bullet in the back of a cowhand riding fence lines over a cow. I told him to call the State Brand Inspector when it happens." Trey added, "The elk is State Wildlife's problem, so I'll have Maestas call it in. I've got a barbwire fence tool attached to my saddle rifle holster. Time to make a father and son repair like in my childhood. You're the free labor now." Trey laughed as they dismounted.

A few minutes later, all ten cut barbwire ends were twisted together and new fence clips were in place on the steel fence posts. Trey took an after IPhone photo to add to the before one for State Wildlife.

Trey informed, "They catch the poacher it's up to a year in jail for cutting the fence and a lifetime elk hunting ban."

"That's a tough law," Cooper stated.

"They seldom catch or charge anyone, Maestas says."

"Why's that?" Cooper asked.

"Maestas won't comment," Trey answered. "But probably because every Spanish person is someone's cousin in New Mexico, so they say. It's not corrupt police and officials like the drug drops but just family food," Trey stated. "Let's return to the hacienda. I'll tell you about my meeting with the Taos Pueblo War Chief in a kiva as we ride back to the hacienda." They became two black silhouettes on the western horizon riding out of the low setting sun.

Over pillow talk Judy reported, "I told M the whole story about our fight to save the YbarC in 1979 and 80. I revealed your battle with the powers to be back then, guns and all."

Cooper asked, "How did she react? Had Trey already told her what he knows?"

"She said he's alluded to it, especially Adrianna's involvement. M was introduced to Joe Bear Spirit Jr. at her office. That seems to be all she knew. Yes, she was wide eyed from some of the details, especially the burning of your mother's ranch house that caused her death. She was not shocked about the Telluride bank's bad behavior or the lynching of Joe Bear Spirit during the Ute water rights fight. Her Apache mother told her that Anglo men rape Pueblo Indian, now called Native American women, routinely and get away with it. Native American men who challenge White men and the federal and state government agents like Joe Bear Spirit did in the Ute water rights fight are routinely found accidently dead. Also, historically they have been lynched on occasion. She says justice seldom occurs on reservations especially if the FBI is involved. M asserted American Indian Movement leaders like Leonard Pelletier are held as political prisoners. She was not surprised about Joe's death and showed no emotion."

"Do you believe she's a strong woman? Is she good for Trey?"

"Emotionally she's a rock. Brave and determined. She drag races cars at 200 plus miles an hour. She rides a horse like a spirit in the wind. She lives in all three cultures in the Four Corners and has no illusions about any of them. She would make a wonderful wife for Trey in the changing global digital world he lives in. I hope he sees that but he's young like you once were when we first met."

"But I figured it out!" Cooper insisted.

"In time you did, and all these years later we are in bed at our son's hacienda," she giggled.

"Trey told me about a meeting with the war chief in a secret kiva last week at the Taos Pueblo. He says the chief told him powerful men are involved in the drug drops, not just the deputy sheriff and the Mexican cartel. It includes the BIA, the FBI, the New Mexico Governor's office, a major Albuquerque banker and more. He says Jumbo Roberts keeps him briefed secretly about law enforcement efforts to stop the drops. Trey and M failed to tell us during our last visit he shot a drug runner during the ranch's drop who turned out to be the war chief's son. The son was hurt and has quit working for the cartel. He's an Iraq war veteran with PTSD who's trying to end drug addiction and reform his life. The war chief wants Trey to help his son set a trap to kill the drug ring's leaders with the Pueblo's Warrior Society's help."

Judy calmly replied, "If Trey decides to help them, he's tough with a moral compass. That's how we raised him. What else did he say about the plan?"

"He's thinking about it. He's waiting to hear from Jumbo when and if there's going to be a big DEA led raid on the next airplane drug drop."

"If no raid?" Judy asked.

"If they drop drugs again on our ranch for any reason then he's all chips on the poker table for the hand."

"You would do the same. I believe M would ride with him if it involves the ranch," Judy stated.

"Then we stay out of it?" Cooper confirmed.

"Yes, but why do I feel your hand inching up my inner thigh under my shorty night gown?"

"Because you wore it on a warm summer night, and I love you."

Cooper and Judy were driving to a lunch meeting with Jumbo Roberts at a café across the border from the hacienda in Manassa Colorado on the drive back to the YbarC. As they passed the modern Mormon LDS Church with its satellite uplink dish on the edge of town a new model white pickup pulled out of its parking lot. They were chatting and did not notice that it was following them. They parked in front of the small cafe and walked into it. Jumbo was sitting at a table in the back corner with his eyes on the door and the room. He did not rise as Cooper and Judy walked up to him, but hand signaled them to sit across from him.

"No names please, the walls can have big ears here. I've ordered us combo plates with tacos, enchiladas and more. The food is some of the best in Southern Colorado and it's only a four-block long town on the state highway. Hard to believe Jack Dempsey, the best boxer of all time, was born and fought here."

Cooper nodded. "We saw his log home museum on the way in. Good to see you but I wish the circumstances were better. My son seems be getting deeper into a fight to protect the ranch from the drug drops. Your take on where this is going to end?"

"Dangerously if he doesn't stand down and let me handle it. He's outgunned and outmanned."

"He probably won't."

"You know more than I do?"

Cooper mostly faded, "No, except he will protect M and the ranch with deadly force if necessary. He believes the corruption that protects and profits from the drugs goes from the bottom to the top in New Mexico."

"I'll continue to keep him in the loop on law enforcement activities, but I may be a step behind these days. I'm like the retired generals you see on cable news rendering an opinion based on information I'm getting from pals still working on the inside. Every year my sources shrink since my retirement." The waitress approached them with a tray full of delicious looking plates of southwest food. "Time to eat and catch up on your lives."

Cooper and Judy paid the check in cash and left after Jumbo. They walked to their pickup and headed west down the state highway toward Romeo Colorado.

Two blocks later, Cooper said, "Don't turn your head but the white pickup that followed us into Manassa is on our tail, about a hundred yards back. If it follows us through the T-junction at Romeo where we turn left to Antonito Colorado something is 'rotten in Denmark'."

"Any police markings?"

"No just a plain white new model. Keep it in your side mirror.

"Roger that, Cooper," Judy replied with concern in her voice.

Five minutes later, they made the left T-junction turn just past the dilapidated adobe bar and the white pickup followed.

Cooper stated, "Hand me the pistol under your seat. Time to end the cat and mouse game." He wheeled the pickup into a tight U- turn and into the white pickup's lane head on. The driver of the white pickup ran off the road into an irrigation ditch to avoid the head-on collision and braked to a muddy, splashing, skidding stop. Cooper U turned again. He pulled up beside the tilted stuck pickup truck and braked to a stop. Judy handed him the pistol as she rolled down her window. He saw a male Mexican brown face stare out of the white pickup's open driver's side window and a pistol came out of it in his hand.

Cooper ordered, "Down Judy," he aimed and fired a shot straight through the white pickup's window, hitting the driver in the left cheek on his gang tattoo. He slumped over the steering wheel dropping his pistol out of the window into the water with a splash. Cooper gunned his pickup's vee-eight motor and it shot down the empty highway. "Put the pistol back under your seat. We're out of here. He's Mexican cartel for sure. We'll drive straight through Antonito to the top of Cumbres Pass. There are two sleeping bags and tent behind the seat in the half cab. We'll find the forest service road at the top and drive down it to a camp site until things cool off."

Judy replied, "M made us a picnic lunch, which we can use for dinner now…get breakfast in Chama early tomorrow. Will he report it to the police if he's still alive?"

"Doubtful. I shot him in the cheek through his gang tattoo. He lost a tooth or two but got a mouthful of blood probably like a bad dentist pulling a tooth. It'll take a tow truck to get the white pickup out of the deep muddy irrigation ditch. He'll tell them his cheek hit the steering wheel. No one's going to ask questions with his gang tattoo," Cooper stated.

"You calling Jumbo?"

"I'll call him and Trey once we're at home. I don't want Trey driving over here. It just confirms what Jumbo told us. These are bad hombres from south of the border in the drug drop operations. Mexican trouble has been spilling across the southern border since Sam Houston's Texas army threw General Santa Anna out of Texas after the Alamo and formed the Republic. Nothing ever changes. Just the players." When they passed by the old, tattered hotel building in the center of town a tow truck with flashing lights headed past them.

Judy said, "Let's motor out of Dodge City to high pass fresh air."

Trey and M were sitting in a pine paneled county courthouse room in Pagosa Springs Colorado. They felt the tension in the air. It was crowded with Land or Death movement members. Four state patrolmen were in bulletproof vests with full SWAT gear. The automatic rifles slung across their stomachs augmented the County deputy sheriff's courtroom deputies. They had been subpoenaed to testify by the county prosecutor against the surviving Land or Death member who had lay in wait to murder them. Instead, he wounded a Pagosa Springs policeman. They had received a death threat by mail at the hacienda a week before the trial. The governor had stationed Colorado National Guard soldiers around the courthouse and throughout the summer resort town that was bustling with tourists and their kids floating down the river on tubes. Trey had checked his Glock 9 at the metal detector station in the lobby. Colorado's open carry law had produced a wall of more than fifty holstered pistols hanging in the rows on hooks. Trey had a new semi-automatic AR-15 rifle in his pickup truck with M's new pistol under her seat. Their eyes were focused straight ahead when they walked past Adrianna who was seated in the back of the courtroom. They were escorted by two of the state patrolmen to the witness bench at the front of the courtroom behind the county prosecuting attorney's polished oak table. It was a highly secured political show trial that had spilled across the New Mexico border. The Colorado state attorney general wanted to send a message to the Land or Death movement to stay the "fuck" out of Colorado. The trial was causing bad publicity worldwide for Colorado's global tourist industry. Jumbo told Cooper the state's legal and business powers were going to bury the defendant in the maximum-security prison at Buena Vista. He added that the Colorado politicians had never given a damn the southern part of the state's Spanish population and its heritage.

The gaunt, white-haired, state-appointed senior judge gaveled the buzzing courtroom to quiet. The clerk called out, "Mr. Trey Stuart please come to the witness stand and be sworn in." Trey rose and started to walk to the stand.

The room exploded into a whispered, "Land or Death" chant. Trey turned around with his back to the judge as he again attempted to gavel the courtroom to quiet. Trey's hand flashed the gunslinger's sign with his index finger pointed at the Land or Death members who surrounded a grim-faced Adrianna with his thumb cocked up with three fingers bent. He snapped his thumb down like a pistol hammer falling. The crowd was stunned with their angry eyes focused on him.

The judge forcefully announced, "If there are any more express or implied threats by the public or a witness then I'll clear this courtroom." Trey turned around and icily stared at him.

After Trey was sworn in, he settled into the witness chair and the greying, experienced, mustached, prosecuting attorney approached him.

He confidently questioned, "Why were you staying at the Hot Springs Motel the night of the shooting, when two police officers killed one man and wounded the defendant after the defendant shot at and wounded a police officer in the line of duty?"

"M and I stopped for a hot spring and dinner on the drive to my parent's ranch near Telluride Colorado."

"What happened after you drove into the parking lot after dinner to return to your room?"

"We saw a restored blue pickup truck that had been parked in the Land or Death Foundation's parking lot across the border at Tierra. We stopped to see an old friend of my father's. Adrianna operates the Land or Death Foundation. We also met her son Joe Bear Spirit Jr. who's the son of a deceased Ute Indian friend of my father."

"Where was the blue pickup parked at the motel?"

"In front of the motel office."

"What did you discuss at the Foundation meeting?"

"My new assignment as operator of the family's ranch in nearby Costilla New Mexico."

"What did she say?"

"Go back to your family's ranch near Telluride where I was born and raised. Continue to let Maestas our local foremen run it and if not sell it. In essence I was not welcome in northern New Mexico."

"And you replied?"

"I planned to operate it."

"Then what happened?"

"The meeting ended, and we departed in our Mustang to Pagosa Springs," Trey asserted.

"Did anyone or a vehicle follow you to Pagosa Springs?"

"No."

"Then how did anyone at the Foundation meeting know where you were staying?"

"We believe a summer local legal intern who attended the meeting heard us discussing where we were staying, and our hot springs plan as we walked to our Mustang. We later saw him in the crowd behind the Pagosa Springs Police's yellow tapeline in the motel parking lot after the shootings. He ran from me when I approached him. I don't remember his name."

"Is he in the courtroom?"

"Yes, he's sitting by the defense attorney in the blue suit." Trey pointed to him.

"Did you meet with or see the wounded and or dead Land or Death members at the Foundation meeting or in its parking lot?"

"No."

"What did you do after you saw the blue pickup in front of the motel office when you attempted to return to your room?"

"We were suspicious about why it was there, so we decided to park away from our room. We decided because the Foundation meeting had gone badly to have M call 911. Then we watched our room door and waited for the police."

"When did the police arrive?"

"In about three minutes two officers in a patrol car drove into the parking lot. They got out of the patrol car and approached our room's door. One was on each side of it. One knocked on it. Suddenly without warning two gunmen came out shooting pistols. The policeman shot both of them. We were told later that they killed one gunman and wounded the other. It was textbook TV police work."

"Had you ever met or seen either gunman?"

"No."

"What happened next?"

"I saw the motel's desk clerk run out of the office door toward a small car parked in an employee space. An incoming Pagosa Springs police car cut her off and the officer arrested her."

"Did you leave your room unlocked when you went to dinner?"

"No."

"Did you give the shooters a key or lose a key?"

"No."

"How did they get into your room and lie in wait?"

"I believe the desk clerk gave them a key because she ran from the motel office when the police arrived."

"Do you believe the gunman intended to murder you and M, your girlfriend from ambush when you opened the motel room door?"

"Yes."

The defense attorney jumped to his feet and yelled, "Objection, Your Honor. That's asking the witness to draw a conclusion."

The judge ruled, "Objection sustained...jury members please ignore the witness's answer."

"No more questions, Your Honor, for this witness."

The defense attorney questioned Trey next. The only contentious question was, "Didn't you threaten Adrianna in the presence of her son and her legal intern when she asked you not to operate the ranch at Costilla New Mexico, which is on a Mexican Government Land Grant made in 1844 that was originally 1.2 million acres?"

"No, I said I would operate it and Maestas would remain foreman as he had been for twenty some years for my father. She knows my family took its legal title from a US Congressional Patent in 1867. Our ranch title is deeded, insured and granted by the US Government not Mexico, which was defeated and tossed out of the Southwest in 1848. She and the

Land or Death movement may not like that but if the Foundation wants the ranch, it can make an offer to buy it. Otherwise, do not threaten me, M or my family or trespass on the ranch. I will shoot to kill any Land or Death member who does so."

The judge said firmly, "One more outburst like that, Mr. Stuart, and I will hold you in contempt of my court."

The defense attorney said, "I have no more questions for this witness."

M was called to the witness stand next and her testimony backed up Trey's point by point. The Colorado State Police escorted Trey and M out of the courthouse and formed a two-car escort that drove them to the New Mexico State line. Two New Mexico State Police cars met them at the line and escorted them to the hacienda. Trey and M called Cooper and Judy to recount their testimony. Both had already seen a reporter's coverage of the trial on the Denver TV news.

Cooper reported, "Adrianna called me. She asserted she couldn't control all of her Foundation members. She fears your threat to kill any of them that tried to attack our family may in fact provoke an attack. There's a sketch by a newspaper reporter's artist of your gunslinger gesture on Denver news. That'll go worldwide on social media your mom says."

"That's why I did it. M said millions could see it on YouTube and be warned don't fuck with the old west. I'm ready if they come at me. Good night. M and Cookie have dinner on the table, and we haven't eaten since breakfast."

Trey and M were on a whitewater raft with a guide in the Rio Grande River Gorge on the west side of the ranch. They had helped carry the inflated raft down an old sheep trail a little north of State Line Road. They were seated in the front of the grey raft with a paddle in hand. The big-chested, ripped, young, dark-tanned guide was in the rear of the raft to steer with his paddle. The raft floated in the weak late summer current of the low river. It was M's first adventure since completing rehab. She looked up as the raft floated toward the flank of the mountain, which was three hundred feet above the steep, dark basalt walls.

"This is an amazing view of the mountain and the ranch's boundary," M said.

"It's awesome. I've never floated the river past the mountain," Trey agreed.

Steve replied, "Just ahead is the confluence waterfall where the Rio Costilla drops into the Rio Grande. It's dry this time of year because the irrigation dam up river on the Rio Costilla diverts the water for agricultural use. But in the spring, after a deep snowpack in the mountains, it runs high and drops into the Rio Grande. Those years I can raft or kayak it to the confluence."

"I've hiked the summer dry riverbed's shallow canyon on the north side of the mountain. There are some amazing petroglyphs on the basalt rock walls in it. I've never hiked to where the confluence is. I hear from my cowhands that there is a cave in the basalt there where hundreds of rattlesnakes ball up for the winter," Trey responded.

"I've heard that too but never checked it out. I don't like rattlesnakes. Too many down here in the gorge on the riverbank's boulders. When I fly fish down here in the winter you have to watch your step. The gorge is warm all winter from the sunlight the basalt absorbs."

"I'd like to fly fish down here in the winter. Can you guide me?" Trey asked.

"Can do."

"That looks like a rattlesnake sunning on that flat top boulder to our left?" M alerted the guide.

"It's a big one," the guide confirmed.

Trey pointed to the right bank, "There's a five-point buck deer grazing in the deep green grass on the riverbank. Do you see many down here?"

"Yes, and more in the winter when there's snow on the mountain. Down river where the gorge is 800 feet deep near Taos the big horn mountain sheep hang out and walk in and out of the gorge on its steep ledge trails. They were reintroduced from near Telluride Colorado years ago. Word up here on the border you're from there."

"I went to high school in Telluride. My parents operate a ranch near there. I used to raft the San Miguel River with friends in the spring and fly fish it with my dad in the summer."

"And you, M, where from?"

"Durango and the Apache reservation at Dulce."

The guide did a double take as his eyes looked up from the water.

"You're my first Apache client. There's a rumor in Taos an Apache woman drag races a black Shelby Mustang?"

"Lots of black Mustangs around. I ride a Paint horse these days on the ranch." The river sounded a late summer low roar in front of them.

The guide alerted, "A bumpy class-one rapid ahead. It's class three when the river is running in Springtime. You'll paddle to help keep the raft straight through it. I advise you sit on its sides to protect your butt."

They bumped and paddled through the rapid, which splashed cool water over the side onto their river sandals. At the end of the rapid they both scanned the mountaintop. They drifted another mile in the slow current, enjoying the canyon's peace and quiet.

The guide alerted them again. "Another half mile is Lee's trail up and out. That's where my friend will meet us with a van. Then it's a bumpy drive out to Sunshine Mesa where your cowhand will meet you all."

M replied, "This has been divine. It's my first adventure since rehab for my broken arm and hand. It's been a treat to look up from the gorge at the mountain. I heard there's a hot spring that flows into the river. Can we stop there and swim?"

The guide replied, "Happy you enjoyed the trip. The hot spring's downriver a bit. Come back next summer and we'll raft to it and do a couple class-three rapids. If I may ask, Trey, does your ranch have Rio Costilla water rights? The rafting companies and fly-fishing guides are supporting running water all summer down it to the Rio Grande."

"It's complicated. We pump 90% of our water from the San Luis aquifer for cattle and hay. The other 10% is ditch water, which, as you know, is diverted from the Rio Costilla at the dam under the 1954 compact between Colorado and New Mexico. It travels down the Rio Costilla from a reservoir. As you probably know the Rio Costilla Cooperative Livestock Association opposes this idea. The ranchers need the water for their hay crops. They graze their cattle on the RCCLA's 80,000 acres of cooperative grazing land. I'm planning to sell my ranch's Rio Costilla water rights back to an original Spanish farmer member. The ranch doesn't need them. So, I'll be out of the game. But my foreman, Maestas, says the RCCLA member ranchers and farmers will never sell their irrigated agriculture water rights."

"Would you sell yours to a River Water Foundation?"

"No, my parents bought the water rights from an original RCCLA member family and morally they'll go back to an RCCLA member."

"Fair enough," the guide replied but he remained silent until the takeout.

On the drive back to the ranch M noted, "We got silence from our guide after the water rights discussion. I don't think we're invited back."

"Cooper and Judy know an artist near the ranch that can guide us. He paints river scenes in New Mexico and Colorado as he rafts and kayaks. They have one of his paintings. Maestas has a neighbor who's a fly-fishing guide. Water is always a dangerous subject in this county and state especially if you own it. The battle over Pueblo, Spanish and Anglo water rights never stops. Lawsuits are always pending. The rafting companies want a longer season to make more money like any other business. They believe the Water Compacts between the two states unfairly tilt to Colorado both for the Rio Costilla and Rio Grande. They also are allied with eco groups who want water taken away from agriculture to restore river flows. Some are anti cows, sheep and growing winter hay for them. I find it odd to be anti-wool and wear oil-based fabric clothing head to toe winter and summer. They don't want the Rio Costilla dried up below the diversion dam each summer for irrigation. Both sides have their agendas. Since our family isn't from northern New Mexico I'm returning our water to a Spanish settler's family. They can fight it out with the Indios they took it from, the rafting companies, the eco groups and the Feds. As for our aquifer well water, it's not for sale unless we sell it with the ranch."

"I understand your point of view as a rancher. The Apache believe water is part of the earth and every being has a right to use it. And that all rivers should be free flowing not dammed. They are the home of fish and water deer, elk and all animals. You are right, water will be an ongoing battle in the West for decades to come. The Utes won a big battle at Durango that restored their Animus River Treaty water rights. It required building a diversion dam there. The rafting companies went to court to try and block it."

"It was part of a dangerous battle that cost my father's Ute friend Joe Bear Spirit his life," Trey sadly reported.

Two weeks later, M and Trey were in Monte Vista Colorado at a hearing for the judge to sentence her father to Colorado State Prison. He had plead guilty to all charges against him for altering her dragster's motor in the vintage drag race and lying about it on the tech inspection report. She had fully recovered from her injuries and was riding the range with Trey.

The presiding judge, a thirty-something, redheaded, local ranch born woman asked M's father a final question, "Sir, how long have you been sober and are you still in AA as this court mandated?"

"Four months sober and the court has my sponsor's AA attendance report. It's perfect."

The judge asked, "Anyone else want to address the court before I sentence the defendant?"

M stood up and said without emotion, "I'm Maria Duran, the defendant's daughter." She deliberately did not use her father's name. He looked down at the pine plank floor as M continued,

"What my father did was inexcusable as my team owner and crew chief. It injured me and could have killed the other driver and the flag woman. It was in violation of the event's tech-reporting rules. He did it drunk but to make sure I won, which had become a family credo. He believed in me as a woman driver when no one else in southern Colorado did. I forgive him and ask that as long as he stays in court monitored AA that you grant him probation with a ban from drag racing for the duration of it. His drag racing license has been suspended for life, but he can appeal it for reinstatement."

The judge looked a little surprised, as did Trey. M had not discussed her sentencing statement with him.

The judge asked, "Maria, you have a restraining order against your father. You have now asked this court to keep him on the streets of Colorado but off its drag racing strips. Do you want the restraining order removed?"

M replied, "No, not during the probation period. If he completes the probation period without drinking, then I will consider the removal of it. He's violent when he drinks and makes bad decisions." Her father stared at her.

The judge paused and then ruled, "This is an unusual request from a daughter of a defendant whose intentional behavior could have killed her. The behavior occurred in an unusual sports event that could have injured or killed another driver, event personnel and even spectators. However, evidence has been submitted to the district attorney that this kind of technical motor fraud is rampant in drag racing at all levels. The tech inspector at the vintage car drag race relied on each team's paperwork and did not make a single physical inspection of a motor or drag racer. The evidence report, overwhelming stated drivers do not question their crew's mechanical preparation with a win at any cost creed. Therefore, since the defendant's daughter, who's also his team driver, has requested probation, then the court orders it for three years with mandatory AA reports. He's banned from drag racing during this time period. I will leave the restraining order in place unless and until Maria Duran also known as M asks for its removal. I will ask the bailiff to hold the defendant in this courtroom for one half hour since he's free to leave now. This will stop any inadvertent contact between the defendant and his daughter, which would violate the restraining order until she can exit Monte Vista Colorado. I so order. All rise, this court is adjourned."

Trey and M quickly exited the courthouse as ordered.

As M drove out of town, he asked, "When did you decide on your sentencing request?"

"When I stood up because I finally realized he's killing himself on the bottle. Probation with AA and a ban from drag racing is his only hope to live. If he breaks it then he'll die in jail. On probation he will not pose harm to me or anyone else."

"And keeping the restraining order in place?"

"I can't totally trust him. If he drinks again, he could beat me to death in a fit of rage. The judge and I gave him a one last lifeline. That's all he gets this time during three orbits around the sun."

"The evidence report stated there is widespread tech motor cheating in drag racing?"

"There is all the way to the National Championships. It always depends on what the definition of what is as President Clinton once said. Also, how much fame and money the driver and crew chief have to cover it up. Isn't it like that in every sport?" M asserted.

"You drove to win with blinders on your race horse?"

"No blinders. I drove to win with the dragster I was given by my crew just like my girlfriend did with the horse she was given by her ranch parents for barrel racing," M stated flatly. "Because if I stopped winning then the dragster would have been given to another driver. There are dozens of boys and men waiting in the stands for that chance to drive a winning machine. This wasn't racing to have a nice family weekend sporting outing. It was for national fame, prize money, media and now the social media that winning brings. It was to sell my father's drag racers and restored hot rods for top dollar to fund the racing and eat. We were close to a national sponsorship for a shot at a top-class championship when he started drinking again. The pits are a village. The drinking was starting to kill our sponsorship chances. Once we finish fall roundup I'll start looking for another ride now that my father's fate is settled."

"That's if the lung doc clears you?"

"Yes."

"I can respect that but you're sure you want to drag race again?" Trey asked.

"Dead sure," M replied firmly leaving no room for a response. She pushed the Shelby Mustang's metal racing accelerator pedal to the floor at the town boundary.

The remainder of the summer passed without incident while Trey and M rode the range together. They stayed within the ranch boundaries and out of Taos and Colorado. M kept her drag racing skills sharp by running late night quarter mile runs on the long straight deserted state highway that passed the ranch's entrance. Trey blocked the oncoming lane with his pickup truck. She had heard about a monthly illegal drag race on the two-lane highway bridge, which crossed the Rio Grande River Gorge where it was 800 feet deep west of Taos.

M and Trey pulled up to the west side of the bridge at two a.m. on a Thursday morning after she received a flash text at dinner. There were already five sets of two cars lined up. She stopped her 1987 Shelby Mustang by a yellow restored 1970 Dodge Charger hemi head. Trey climbed out and put a hundred-dollar bill in a straw cowboy hat by the finish line. He found a safe place to watch behind a low boulder beside the highway, which blocked an old parking area at the bridge's entrance. She nodded thank you to him, flashed a vee hand signal and rolled her window up. The first two drag racers drove their rumbling cars east toward Taos across the bridge to warm up their tires and U-turned them to a stop even with a flag woman. She was silhouetted in their headlights as they raced their engines. Without fanfare she dropped the green flag. The two cars accelerated with tires burning and raced dangerously close to each other across the two-lane black top bridge. The only race rule was the first car across the thick, chalk finish line on the bridge's west exit won the two-hundred-dollar pot per race.

The two high horsepower cars tore across the bridge in about seven seconds reaching nearly two hundred miles an hour top speed. The winner was a hood length in the lead as he crossed the chalk line. The cars passed Trey, back washing him with dust and blowing air. He heard a walkie talkie behind him report, 'No cops have turned toward the Gorge Bridge. We're five miles east of it still. Keep them rolling'. The second team crossed the bridge to the start. Five minutes later, M drove past Trey, her eyes straight ahead with not even a glance at him. He watched the Shelby Mustang as she drove across the bridge, slowly turning her tires to warm them, exited it and u-turned back toward the start line. His heartbeat was fast. The Shelby Mustang looked frail in comparison to the 1970 yellow Dodge Charger Hemi with its supercharger tucked under its scoop centered on the hood. The green flag dropped, and M was a car length ahead off the line as her perfectly timed and clean start beat the spinning smoking tires of the Hemi off the line. She charged to the center of the bridge in the lead, but the Hemi was closing fast. Its front bumper veered dangerously toward her right back fender as Trey stopped breathing. The supercharger exploded and metal fragments tore through the hood as it lost speed. M crossed the line and almost blew Trey over backwards when the Mustang passed him. The Hemi crashed into the bridge's high concrete wall in slow motion and exploded into a ball of fire as the driver jumped clear onto the hard pavement. Trey felt the heat blast on his face. He ran to the teen holding the prize money cowboy hat who gave Trey two one-hundred-dollar bills. M backed the Mustang up and Trey jumped into its front passenger seat for the getaway. M stomped the metal racing gas petal and it accelerated so fast the G force pinned Trey to the black leather custom upholstered seat back.

He jokingly asked, "You always win by blowing up your opponent's dragster? Why did it explode?"

"Yes, on more than one occasion. Men drivers always push them past their motor's redlines not to lose to a girl. He trashed a twenty thousand dollar drag strip motor trying to make up for a slow start off the line. He forgot he was on street tires, not drag strip ones and spun them. The Hemi exploded because he was running alcohol nitro fuel. He may have damaged the bridge, it burns so hot. He'll get a big bill from the New Mexico State Highway Department. We're out of here fast because the State Patrol and Sheriff's cars will close in on the bridge fast. If we pass one coming in from the west and it U turns around then we run. Their cars or SUVs are no match for my Mustang on open roads in pitch black dark."

"I'm just riding shotgun," Trey laughed at his joke.

"No gunfire. Even if they catch us, it's a high-speed ticket and maybe a month in jail if you can't pay off a judge…not a prison sentence."

"Got it. Don't shoot at the posse."

"You watch for elk, deer, cattle and I hear buffalo on this stretch of highway until the turn north at Tres Piedras. Then we run north to the ranch across the southern Colorado line. We're running at a hundred plus with long racing hi-beams. Keep your eyes on the road. This is nighttime rally driving not drag racing."

"Yes, ma'am. I've always wanted to be in the Baja One Thousand Race."

M drove fast through the moonless darkness as it ate the edge of the Mustang's hi-beams. The broken centerline flashed under the Mustang's front bumper like Apache helicopter's Gatling gun tracer fire. Her driving chased the edge of the world as it revolved around the sun. Trey's young, strong, blue eyes locked onto that edge and strained to see past it as the Mustang roared through the night. Eighty minutes later, which was half the route's normal drive time to the ranch M drove through the hacienda gate. The Mustang did doughnuts and braked to a sliding stop throwing up gravel. Trey locked the gate and climbed back into the Mustang. M scrambled over the gearbox console and tossed her jeans and panties onto the dashboard. They made wild love.

Maestas looked at the Mustang, which was parked askew in front of the hacienda with deep gravel circle tire tracks that led to its rear wheels. It was sunup as he walked past it toward the bunkhouse for breakfast. The hacienda was silent and dark. He had learned not to ask why the Mustang was coming and going late at night after he received an icy silent stare from M. He had observed she was the most determined, bone tough, half Apache, reflex quick woman he'd met or heard of. He was happy she was not at war with him at his age and intended to keep it that way. His Spanish forefathers had always feared the Apache and Comanches the most of all the southwestern tribes. They knew both tribes fought to death if attacked and dealt pure torture either quickly or worse slowly until an enemies' death. Their women and girls danced around the victory fires with scalps in their hands. They gave staked out captive men who were being tortured by the warriors just enough water each day to survive for another. It was rumored they severed their sacs and stewed their balls mixed with buffalo.

He had heard M's father was descended from an old Colorado Spanish Conquistador's family from Cortez Colorado, which had been on the edge of New Spain. He had observed M and Trey could turn into a tornado when paired together and if provoked. He kept on walking to the bunk-house without slowing or looking back.

M stirred in the king size bed and blinked her eyes open. A half empty bottle of the most expensive Mexican village mezcal was sitting on her black bedside table by a turned over shallow earth colored clay pottery cup. Legendary Taos artist Ron Cooper, who had hung with Dennis Hooper of Easy Rider fame, distributed it. Judy had bought it for a house present when M spied it on their gallery trip. Her head was splitting as she surveyed the hand plastered mauve-blue adobe walled bedroom. Her jeans lay on the floor by the closed bedroom door. They started a trail of their clothes, which ended with her bikini panties and Trey's briefs. The blue panties were looped around the mezcal bottle on the bedside table. The white briefs lay on a Glock 9 in a black leather hip holster. She lay nude face up on the bed beside Trey who was face down nude. She looked over at the big face electronic clock and it's digital red letters glowed eleven-sixteen. "Shit," she gasped because it usually glowed five in the morning when she first saw it. She shook Trey's shoulders.

He slowly turned over and his barely moving lips uttered, "My brain is split in half and my eyes will barely open. What happened?"

"We drank cup after cup of mezcal while we made love," M answered.

"You are still nude."

"Good observation, Trey. You are too. It's past eleven o'clock in the morning."

"Well that's not really a problem because the cowhands rode out a six a.m. so it's too late to work today. Hand me the mezcal bottle please." M did and he took a big swig.

"Now what?" M asked.

"You." Trey rolled over as she laughed with delight.

After a mid-afternoon lunch chased with aspirin, they opened the hacienda's front door and looked out at the Mustang, which was covered with a thick layer of dust. M pointed to the deep cut circles in the gravel and counted three spinning ones to the Mustang's rear wheels.

She reported very excitedly, "A new doughnut record. Gravel is amazing."

"Yes, it is," Trey agreed. "It sand blasted the adobe wall next to the new picture window, which miraculously survived. Somebody who goes by the name M has a lot of touchup adobe plastering and painting to do."

"I don't paint or plaster. I'm a drag race driver and now cowgirl. So unless you don't want your jeans zipper welded shut, then find one cowboy, Trey." She spun her cowgirl boot heels on the Mexican title floor and walked back into the hacienda.

CHAPTER 13
RIDE THE OUTSIDE CIRCLE

Trey and Maestas were meeting in the blond-pine-paneled bunkhouse foreman's office. It was late September, and the sun was casting long shadows earlier each afternoon and there was a chill in the early morning air. The cowherd was fat from a good summer of grazing knee-deep monsoon grass. The third cutting of irrigated hay was underway to help feed the mother cows over the winter. The calves were starting to separate from their mother's tits and eat grass.

Trey asked, "What date have you usually started the roundup in good grass summers during the past twenty years?"

Maestas thought for a long moment. "Around Oct 15th with normal fall grass like this year. Hard freezes start here in the San Luis Valley as early as late September because on dry clear nights the cold air sinks straight down into it. That's why we started cutting the alfalfa hay last week. Once there's a hard freeze the grass gets dry and even a cow can pull up its roots. Horses are worse and sheep can destroy the roots. By mid-October it's time to cut the herd in half and ship the calves to protect the range. The elk also start to move down into the valley from the high country above 9,000 feet when it first snows. The valley averages 7,000 feet of altitude where they water and eat grass for the winter. By November, the mountain streams and springs start to ice up."

Trey replied, "That's the date we'll start the roundup. My dad and mom want to come for it. They finish roundup at the YbarC in the Colorado high country in mid-September and ship the calves because big snow can hit there in early October. The mother cows are trucked to Arizona winter range. I've ridden in storms two-three feet deep in the high pastures in late October. They held the mother cows on the YbarC and fed them hay the first five winters after they were married but it was nearly a disaster when a couple blizzards hit hard. Fortunately, they had kept my grandfather's BLM leases for winter grazing near Wickenburg Arizona."

Maestas frowned and replied, "I remember those days. Cooper and Judy were squeezing every dime out of the YbarC and this ranch to pay the banks and the cowhands. The winter hay-feeding plan on the YbarC was a risk because deep early or late snow can kill a herd. The cows will stand and freeze if you can't get hay to them. Same true here in the high-country pastures. But on the ranch's high valley rangeland we can feed cattle hay for the winter. It gets light snow mostly less than a foot. Bull elks will herd the cow elks into a line across a ranch pasture. The elk herd will clear the snow off the grass and eat on the move. Snow's never very deep on this ranch because the mountain blocks its storms from the south and west."

"Thanks for bringing me up to speed on the fall weather. I was always here in the summer growing up because of high school and then college. Every microclimate is different. The YbarC is on the San Juan Mountain's west facing flanks, so the winter storm tracks from the Pacific Ocean pass over it on their path to Telluride. Its ski resort gets the most snow of any resort in the Rockies outside of Utah some years."

"I'll post the roundup schedule and the cowhand assignments in the bunkhouse. I'll add Cooper and Judy," Maestas stated.

"And M too. She's wants to ride and learn roundup work," Trey added.

"She's riding her Mustang?" Maestas smiled at his humor.

"No, her Paint horse. It's not as fast but way steadier doing donuts on rough ground," Trey replied with a wink.

Trey walked into the kitchen where M was preparing Spanish Paella with frozen scallops, chorizo sausage and chicken. Its saffron smell permeated the room on the fall afternoon.

"Perfect dinner. Hot news. The roundup starts October 15. I'll call

Cooper and Judy. They want to help this year. Your assignment with your Paint horse is being posted tomorrow by Maestas. He requested you not ride your black Mustang."

M blushed. "I'm all in but I guess he saw the doughnuts in the driveway gravel and noted we didn't show up for range work that day?"

"I'm sure he did but he can only speculate on the rest. He knows the Mustang came in late and hot. He, like everybody else in Taos County, knows a drag race car somehow exploded on the Gorge Bridge at two a.m. on that Thursday morning. So, by deduction I believe he probably figured it out." Trey laughed.

"Will he report it to Cooper and Judy?" M asked, frowning.

"No because he knows I would fire him for that breach. They were as wild at the same age I suspect based on stories I heard in Telluride. A grey-bearded Bluegrass musician named Blue Jay told me some of them when he was drunk in Telluride's Sheridan Bar late one night."

"It's your mother who bought the mezcal for us as a house present not me," M laughed.

"Blue Jay's stories must be true," Trey laughed. "Mom's busted!"

Two afternoons later, Trey and M tied their horses to a tree limb near the mine. They carefully hiked up to the tunnel entrance looking for both human and animal tracks. There were no mountain lion signs but Trey saw a set of men's hiking boot tracks when they reached the tunnel. He noted they tracked down from the top of the mountain.

Alarmed, he said, "M, somebody has been here." He pointed to the tracks that ended at the tunnel entrance.

"Who that could be?"

"Not a cowhand because they are from men's hiking boots size eleven plus. I am size eleven. Let's shine our flashlight into the tunnel entrance and see what it looks like now that the dust has settled."

They walked toward the tunnel entrance but stopped abruptly when they saw basalt rock fall scattered past its entrance. Trey pointed the flashlight into the tunnel, "It's sealed itself and the roof has completely caved in. It would probably take millions of dollars to safely clear the rock fall. John's final report says the wood from the cart dated to around 1680 the time of the Pueblo revolt against New Spain. His second theory is that he believes the Spanish may have used Taos Pueblo Indio slaves to tunnel. The Indio slaves could have killed their Spanish overseers during the revolt. He believes the Indio slaves would have had access to the Aztec parrot feather and placed it through the eyes of the skull to curse the tunnel. The photo of the skull indicates it's European not Pueblo Indian. However, he found no gold in the rock or dust samples from the part of tunnel his team explored. So, the mystery remains why the Spanish miners were tunneling and if they blew the other entrance that may be under the basalt rockslide and why?"

"Any ideas?" M asked as Trey bent down and looked into the wall of basalt rock spilling out of the entrance.

"No but there's a new mystery. There aren't hiking boot tracks out from the tunnel entrance cave in area. So, did the mystery hiker back carefully out in his own tracks or did he crawl into the entrance opening and set off a final roof cave in? Is he buried under tons of rock?"

M replied, "Wow that would be horrible but possible from the curse, which almost killed the mining team. How can we find out?"

"We can't because it's too dangerous and expensive to clear the rock fall."

"Do we report it and to whom?" she asked.

"We wait and see if a missing person's report is posted for this area on the Sheriffs' website."

"If there's no second set of tracks so who would report it?" M reflected.

"Someone close to the person who disappeared if they knew he was coming up here alone. He could have hiked in over the top of the mountain. There's a rough four-wheel drive only road along the Rio Grande River Gorge. I'll send a cowhand to check it for an unattended vehicle or four-wheeler tomorrow."

"Are we done with this cursed tunnel before we get hurt or killed?" M asked with a serious look on her face.

"Yes, forever. Let's walk down to the horses and vamos a la hacienda."

"Perfect!" M replied.

Trey searched the Taos County Sheriff's website for missing persons but found no recent match for a man who could wear size eleven shoes. He dispatched two cowhands on horseback to search the gorge rim road on the west side the mountain for an abandoned vehicle or four-wheeler. Trey also searched the Costilla County Colorado Sheriff's

Department website, which was across the New Mexico border for reports about recently missing men. There were none. He even called the war chief but the Pueblo had no missing men either. About lunch time the lead cowhand called him on his iPhone.

He reported, "We have found nothing near the rough rutted road but three weathered discarded beer cans probably from some hunters during last fall's elk season. The off-road tire tracks here are at least two weeks old. If there's a four-wheeler it's well hidden in the sage, pinion and juniper in five thousand acres along the steep west side of this mountain. It would take fifty men to search it. On the ride over here, we checked the hiking trail entrance that goes up the north side of the mountain for a parked vehicle. Nothing there."

Trey replied, "Good enough. It's like looking for a needle in a haystack. The mountain's rugged and full of canyons, arroyos and thick vegetation. Ride on back. But keep your eyes peeled for anything that looks unusual."

"Roger that, boss."

Trey then called John and he explained the situation.

John stated clearly, "First, if he's a seasoned treasure hunter who heard or read about the medical helicopter rescue, he would have back tracked from the tunnel when he saw the total roof collapse. Something must have spooked him because he didn't sweep them clean with a bush branch. Second, if he was an amateur who heard about the helio rescue and was curious. He may have hiked in from the gorge side of the mountain to avoid being seen and trespassing through your ranch. He might have stupidly crawled into the remains of the tunnel entrance and his vibration set off the final roof collapse. If so, he's buried under thousands of tons of basalt rock. Did you see any blood flow out of the rock pile?"

"No."

"Or a piece of clothing or a finger?"

"No and now that I think about it not even the end of the transmitter's cable we left just inside the tunnel's mouth. Maybe it's under the rock fall that slid out of the tunnel entrance about a yard," Trey mused.

"Don't ever go near it again. A big vibration could cause an additional tunnel collapse and blow out the entire side of the mountain. It could bury you. Put up Danger No Trespass signs around the tunnel entrance at least twenty-five yards out. If he's under that rock fall, he was killed instantly and there's no possible recovery of the body. It's like the coal miners you read about being entombed in mining explosions especially when coal columns are used for roof supports. One happened at Price Utah in August 2007 and not only entombed the miners but a rescue team. No one is ever going into the tunnel on your mountain again."

"Do I report it?" Trey asked.

"No, you can only get someone else killed. Keep checking the missing person's report and call me if there's a match in sex, size, time period or destination. Then I'll handle it."

"Thanks, I'll call if I find anything." Trey found M and reviewed the discussion with John. She shook her head in disbelief and poured them both a stiff Scotch. She silently realized the curse had tried to kill them three times.

It was a warm sunny fall afternoon two days before the roundup. Trey hadn't heard from Jumbo Roberts in a month and no drug drops had been spotted across the gorge or on the ranch. He had kept stalling the war chief who was growing impatient. Cooper and Judy were arriving the next afternoon and they were trailing their horses. Maestas had already started deploying cowhands, and Cookie was leaving with the horse-drawn chuck wagon in the morning. Because of the lack of information on stopping the drug drops, Trey had declined help from neighboring ranchers even though it added three long days in the saddle to the roundup schedule. He only wanted paid cowhands and family members riding in possible harm's way. After he completed washing down and brushing the two Paint horses, he put them in their stalls. He walked over to the hacienda and found M sunbathing topless on the secluded hacienda veranda, which was in the interior of its four adobe walls. Her paperback book was lying on a reddish flagstone She greeted him with a smile as she raised her head, revealing her breasts.

He quipped, "I see you're doing rigorous training for the roundup."

"Busted but a girl has to get the last rays of tanning sunshine before the dusty roundup, which ends with daylight savings time. Roundup jeans, a long sleeve cowgirl shirt, boots, a red bandana and cowboy hat are summer tan killers."

"I understand. I like your very sexy tan lines."

"I know, but please don't drool like a doggie, just pant!" She shook her breasts and then lowered her chest adding. "If your hands are clean then please give me a backrub."

"They are. I just washed and brushed the Paints."

"Don't touch me, and go straight to the shower!"

"Boo, you're no fun."

"I can be. Meet you in the shower in five minutes. I have to wash the suntan oil off."

"And dinner?"

"Cookie's last night for hacienda dinners...steak, baked potato and beans. I'll cook dinner for Cooper and Judy tomorrow."

"I'm out of here."

"Remember scrub down hard. No sweaty Paint horse smells."

Judy and Cooper were seated on the leather couch in the hacienda's viga supported high ceiling living room.

Trey was finishing his roundup briefing for them. "Maestas will ride out with the cow hands at 6 a.m. tomorrow morning. They'll start the roundup on the southeastern pasture first. The cowhands will gather an eighth of the herd or about 75 calf cow pairs. M and I with you all and two cowhands will move the herd back to the cross-fenced headquarter pasture near the hacienda. It'll be slow dusty trail work. We ride at seven am."

Cooper replied, "Let's get at it. We haven't been on a roundup here in almost twenty years. We only have come down after the herd was gathered at headquarters for the final count and to oversee the calf shipping and mother cow culling."

M walked into the great room as Trey added, "I haven't heard from Jumbo in a month. He's gone dark. Have you all?"

"Not since we had lunch with him in Manassa Colorado when we drove back to the YbarC last visit. It was mostly to catch up on life. He did say he was concerned about any potential interaction that you, M, or the cowhands might have with a drug drop. He says they are not only Mexican cartel but their reach maybe high into the New Mexico's law enforcement, business and political world. He said his information about the drops is getting thinner since many of his state police contacts have or are retiring on both sides of the border."

M was all ears as Trey replied, "And then his ability to get timely information to me is waning, which elevates the level of danger on our western pastures by the gorge. I hope we can complete the roundup without a drug drop. After it's over we are off the west pastures until next spring."

"So do your mother and me. Please update on the old mine tunnel?"

Trey answered, "It's over. We were up there after you left, and it's totally caved in. John said to post No Trespass signs twenty-five yards out. If it caves in again its basalt rock fall compression could explode a hole in the side of the mountain that could send rock flying out that far." Trey left out the hiking boot footprints since no missing persons had turned up in sheriff's reports on either side of the border.

M announced, "Finish your drinks and follow me to dinner. Grilled salmon, fresh fall hashed Yukon potatoes with a late fall garden salad. Starting tomorrow its Cookie's steak, hash brown potatoes and baked beans at the chuck wagon."

Four sets of hooves thundered as Cooper, Judy, Trey and M with their tanned faces rode with the rising warm east sunrays on their shirt backs. Trey could see his breath as he surveyed the browning dry grass pasture, which had seeded. It felt good to be working the roundup with his parents. He knew it would invigorate them. They would ride and work from a lifetime of roundup memory and reflex. He wasn't concerned about M's riding ability but her lack of roundup experience was problematic. Things could go wrong very fast when cows, calves and cowhands on horses interfaced with each other. Thousand-pound animals could do enormous damage to humans when spooked, angered or just plain out of sorts. He had seen a cowboy at a YbarC roundup trampled and nearly killed when a charging mother cow suddenly surprised his young horse, knocking it down. It was hard, tough and sometimes almost blind dusty riding on dry fall rangeland, especially in wind. Good roping was often your best defensive friend. M had never roped during her riding life and didn't have a lariat on her Paint horse. Normally Trey would not have let a rider without roundup skills work but he knew she would not take no for an answer. He had been in the saddle on a ranch since three years old so today was M's probation day. He planned to monitor her carefully and he knew Cooper and Judy would too. If she put herself in danger, then it was roundup with Cookie at the chuck wagon.

An hour later, they arrived at the southeast pasture where the cowboys were halfway through gathering the first seventy-five cow calf pairs. The calves were squirrely because they were used to trailing their mothers spread out on the range not in a loose single file. They were being compressed into a herd and sometimes becoming separated from their mothers. Some were bawling for help. The older mother cows also knew something was up because it reminded them of the previous fall separations from their calves. The first-time mothers were simply confused as they had been since birthing their first calves in the spring. The cowhands and their experienced well-trained horses created order out of potential chaos. Maestas's old blue heeler dog still moved agiley around and through the herd. The bone tough dog lived to help herd cattle on roundup days. He would drop dead on the job rather than quit it. Watching the cowhand's veteran horses work smoothly Trey wished Cowboy Singing Star his first and only round-up horse was under him. Cooper had given the two-year-old copper brown quarter horse to a blond haired, crewcut Trey when he was eight years old to ride during his first YbarC fall roundup. Cowboy had to be put down when he broke a leg on a roundup while Trey was away at college. It was Trey and M's Paint horses' first roundup so both were also on probation. If either one faltered on the day one trail drive back to the hacienda's pasture he would replace them day two with experienced quarter horses. They tied their horses to fence posts and chatted quietly among themselves while the herd was approaching from downwind.

Trey asked M, "You and your Paint horse ready to herd the pairs back to the ranch?"

"We are in sync, but I wasn't prepared for the calf chaos I'm watching. When we checked them on our range rides they were nursing or following their mothers around quietly. So, I'm a little worried about that."

"Fair enough for your first roundup but we're not gathering them. They'll come through this pasture gate mostly in single file calf following mother. You and I are at the head of the herd with one of us on each side. I'll ride down the line if necessary and you will stay lead always. Only gallop your horse fast out of the way if the herd stampedes behind you. Otherwise, it's slow a trot back to the ranch. You'll get the hang of it with your Paint. She's smart. I'll keep an eye on you two."

"Good. I want to learn how to help roundup the cattle. It'll make me feel more part of the ranch and your heritage,"

"That's great. In about half an hour before our work starts. Cookie has some sandwiches you can have now for an early lunch, or you eat in the saddle. Once we start moving the herd back to the hacienda we can't stop. We don't want to scatter them and start all over. Our job is to keep their cow and calf minds on walking back to the headquarters' pasture to graze and water."

"Roger that, I'll eat now," M replied.

The cowhands herded the pairs in a loose single file through the pasture's sixteen-feet-wide open red gate. The calves were learning to concentrate on their new job without stopping for a milk snack whenever they wanted one. The older mother cows remembered their trail etiquette and fell in line. The first-year mothers copied their behavior but walked in a more choppy line. Trey's crew waited for the first three pairs to exit the red gate then M took the left point side, and he took the right one. When half the line was through the gate Judy fell in line behind Trey, and Cooper behind M. After the last pair exited the gate, a cowhand swung it closed. The two cowhands who were riding drag fell in behind the herd's uneven line. M started to realize this was going to be a long day on horseback. She had never clocked how slow cows walked. She quickly learned she could not take her eyes off the herd. A few minutes out of the pasture gate a calf started to stray from the herd. She slid her horse back down the line and pushed the confused calf behind its mother. Trey signaled well done with a slight nod of his red bandanaed face. The crew had a rainbow of colored ones pulled up over their noses to block the fine dust the herd's hooves churned up. Trey, Cooper and Judy slid their horses easily up and down the line pushing errant calves and an occasional cow back into line. The cowhands worked harder and faster in drag to push the trailing cows with their calves. One of the cowhand's blue heelers moved up and down the head of the line to help keep it moving with nips on cows' hoofs. Everyone worked in silence except the cows and calves, which mooed and bawled messages and complaints into the rapidly warming morning air under a deep blue cloudless western sky. M mentally noted she was happy to be a drag race driver. Riding two or three miles an hour while staring at bovines was not exciting work. Trey watched her whenever possible and hoped she would concentrate only on the herd. Danger and disaster lurked only a minor mistake away. A spooked bolting cow and calf could lead to a riding mistake that could lead to a stampede that could take down a horse and rider. That result could be a dying or dead trampled rider worst case.

The herd was nearing its holding pasture by the hacienda and it had been an uneventful day. The cowhands riding drag had lassoed a young mother cow that had panicked and broken away with her calf following. Another mother broke away on a dead run with her trailing panicked calf in danger of tripping and breaking a leg. The chasing cowhand let the pair go and made a note of their location in his shirt pocket size notebook. Trey rode ahead of the herd, dismounted and opened the red gate to the pasture. He remounted and signaled M to ride away from the herd. He knew the cattle were thirsty and would smell the water in the pasture's sleek green fiberglass stock tank. The water was pumped from a well by the nearby bluish solar panels that were starting to reflect the late afternoon low fall sun. After the cattle finished funneling through the gate into the pasture, Trey and M galloped toward the hacienda. They rode through its open gate and dismounted at the front door, tying the Paint horses to the Spanish wrought iron, black hitching-post rail.

She said, "I'm saddle sore and stiff. Your cows are slowpokes. I'm starved too. I'll eat in the saddle tomorrow. How'd I do? You and Cooper watched me like a toddler!"

"A-plus as usual. You kept your concentration and slid down the line like a pro to restore order. You and your Paint horse have good chemistry and she works to help and protect you."

"Do I get another assignment tomorrow?"

Trey replied, "Yes, it's another very long day. We're bringing in two hundred and fifty or so pairs from the west pasture along the gorge. The cowhands started rounding them up this afternoon. We'll have more help on the trail drive too."

"That's the pasture with the green gate that the deputy and the drug runners in the topless brown Bronco came through, right?"

"Yes. Jumbo has been silent, so I want to move the west herd back now. It's the biggest one. The shakedown drive went well today."

"Good thinking. Move it while we're all fresh, including the horses," M agreed.

"You want to ride back out to cow camp, eat Cookie's dinner, listen to roundup songs and sleep in a bed roll under the stars?" Trey deadpanned.

"Not tonight. I'm taking a hot tub after I hose and brush my Paint. Another night for the songs and a bedroll."

"Works for me. I'll drive the red pickup out to camp and go over the

day with Maestas. Get set for tomorrow. I'll drive the chuck wagon dinner back in for us all. Cooper and Judy are aging and will want a guest
room bed tonight, not hard ground. Can also you hose my Paint down too
and brush him? Feed them both lots of oats?"

"Roger that. When I worked at the stables as a teenager, I did a dozen
horses some late summer afternoons."

"I'm out of here."

"Don't I get a kiss?"

"Yes, but only after you have a hot tub and a shower to knock off the
trail dust and sweat."

"Touché. I'll have a cold margarita waiting for you."

Trey turned and walked to the pickup. When he arrived at the chuck
wagon the cowhands were singing while waiting for supper. The song was
'Ride the Outside Circle' that was about the youngest cowboy on a roundup. The boss always assigned him to ride the widest circle around the herd
as it was gathered. His job was to turn the strays back to the herd and with
a rope if necessary. It was the most exhausting riding job on the roundup
with the most hours in the saddle. Trey's memories came flooding back
because at fourteen his father assigned him the job. He joined into the song
with the cowboys as one of them strummed his worn Gibson guitar.

The southeast sun was in the late morning sky when the two hundred and
fifty pair's herd was gathered. The calves were getting more and more
chaotic. Two Blue Heeler cow dogs were running non-stop. The crew had
to move the cattle from near the green gate by the gorge across the vast
western pasture to the hacienda's holding corral.

Trey rode up to Maestas. "The west pasture herd always this squirrely?
I know it's a lot of pairs, but we seem undermanned and late moving them
this morning."

Maestas answered, "We are a bit of both, but you decided not to use
ranching neighbors' help this year because of the drug drop danger. Two
hundred fifty cows with their calves are always tough to herd. I agreed with
you partly because our cowhands have workmen's comp insurance, health
insurance and unemployment insurance. Most of our ranching neighbors
are smaller don't carry anything except maybe family health insurance. I
figured we could handle it today unless the weather was bad. It's blue skies
with light to no wind predicted. We can always cut this herd in half like

yesterday and move the rest tomorrow. Your call."

"Let's take perfect weather and so far, it's all quiet on the drug drop front. Move them out of here. What are my family's assignments today?"

"You and Cooper take the head of the herd. Put Judy behind Cooper on flank. They're used to riding together and have experienced roundup horses. M should ride the outside circle because she's the youngest cowhand, but you know that's not possible. She can't rope. Why don't you send her to Cookie to ferry lunches for us to eat in the saddle even though that leaves us another cowhand short."

"That's not possible. She wants to work the roundup."

"Then put her on flank behind you and I'll put a very good swing cowhand behind her. You're responsible for her safety. Let's get moving. The cow dogs gonna have a heart attack holding this herd."

"Roger that, thanks Maestas, you're on tail?"

"You bet. I'll eat some dust, but I want to see the herd from tail to head. Kind of like a QB in football. I want to see it, sense its energy and keep it moving. I've got the best old horse too...right up there with Cooper and Judy. Why are you on that big Paint? He hasn't done no roundups. Besides he's an Indian pony."

"Fair question. Cowboy Singing Star, my first and only roundup horse broke a leg and had to be put down while I was away at college. I've mostly ridden the Paint all summer and he's strong and smart. He got me through a running gunfight on the drug drop. He's quick and sure-footed. Must have some Comanche blood in him. He has earned the roundup."

"Comanche horses the best fighting mounts the Spanish conquistadors ever fought. That's your call for the roundup. Let's head 'em out."

Maestas rode back to the tail of the herd, checking final assignments. Trey rode toward the head of the herd to order family assignments. The Paint trotted sure-footed with grit up the side of the herd. The roundup crew began to shape the herd and move it. Cowhands with experienced horses pushed the cow and calves slowly back into a double or triple pairs line. It was like a three across stock car race restart except at three miles an hour with half of them rookie drivers. Trey guided M to her assignment and then rode up to the front of the herd across from Cooper. The two of them began to shape the front of the herd and set its pace. The sun was heating up the late morning still air. Trey began to sweat as he rode. M moved her Paint horse well, but her lack of roundup skills showed as the herd continued to bulge sometime five pairs across at her spot. Trey and the swing cowhand behind her had to slide their horses back or up to help her. Their constant motion was unsettling the head of the herd and forcing Cooper to keep it moving on its route toward the hacienda's pasture. Trey and M were between the herd and the gorge. He knew the crew had to keep it moving away from the gorge for the next two hours. He couldn't risk even the slightest chance of the herd turning and stampeding into the gorge and sweeping M into it with the herd. One of the Blue Heelers had sensed the problem and moved up from the tail of the herd to help M. The dog darted along the flank and moved errant cows or calves back into the line. M's Paint worked well with the Blue Heeler, but she was not in sync with them. Trey noted the crew needed couple more cow dogs but without the neighbors helping they were at their ranch houses. Slowly the roundup crew settled the herd enough for the cowhands who had been working since sunup to start eating lunch in the saddle one at a time as Cookie delivered them on horseback. Cooper signaled Trey all was well, but he didn't return it. Trey was very worried about M.

M was struggling in the saddle for the first time in her life. She silently prayed for the Virgin Mary to guide them safely back to the hacienda. The cows and calves did not behave like a dragster running in a fast straight line. The calves wandered erratically around their mothers causing the Blue Heeler to dart around her and the Paint that adjusted in unison. Intellectually she understood their teamwork but physically she was not in control and her body felt out of balance. She over corrected the Paint instead of letting her body flow with its instinctual moves to herd the cattle. She waved off her lunch when Cookie rode toward her.

When he rode up beside Trey to deliver his lunch he whispered, "M's in trouble."

Trey nodded and took his lunch. He took the first bite of a roast beef and Swiss cheese sandwich with mustard on fresh sourdough bread when his iPhone vibrated in his grey denim shirt pocket. He answered it with his other hand letting his horse work.

Jumbo said, "Listen up, I'm approaching the other side of the Rio Grande River Gorge across from your ranch at 100 miles an hour lights flashing and siren on. I got a call twenty minutes ago that DEA intercepted a drug drop text message. It's in ten minutes. DEA agents from

Alamosa Co are almost there. FBI on its way from Santa Fe by chopper. Colorado and New Mexico State Patrol on the road too. But all Northern New Mexico and Southern Colorado County and Town law officers firewalled out because of suspected corruption. Stay put at the hacienda. Pull your cowhands in."

"Too late for that. Its roundup and we're moving 250 pairs from the west gorge pasture right now. Cooper, Judy and M helping Maestas and the cowhands. If the drug drop crosses the gorge to the ranch and spooks the herd it could stampede into it."

"You're in deep cow shit. What can you all do?"

"Keep moving them three miles an hour east to the hacienda pasture."

"Do it. I'll text you when I reach the drug drop zone."

Trey Rocky Talkied Maestas, "Trey, over."

"Roger that Maestas, over."

"Just got word there's a drug drop in ten minutes across the gorge from us. Law enforcement on the way to ambush and arrest them. There'll be gunfire for sure. Send a cowhand up the southwest side of the herd and I'll slide down the northeast side to warn everyone. We have to keep the herd moving to stop a stampede if shooting starts."

"Roger that, boss." Trey tossed his roast beef sandwich and the Blue Heeler raced up and caught it in the air. He U-turned the Paint and trotted down the side of the herd but skipped M. He alerted the three cowhands on the flank of the herd. He rode back to alongside M.

"Jumbo called. A cartel airplane drug drop is in five minutes across the gorge. Massive law enforcement converging on it including an FBI helicopter. We have to keep the herd moving to stop a stampede if there's gunfire. I won't be able to help you. Ride away from the stampede's direction at full gallop if it starts."

"Roger that but if I can't?"

"Try and swim your Paint on the edge in the stampede's flow at speed. Like skiing an avalanche. Stay on her. Keep her up. When you get outside the edge, vector gallop away from the head of the herd."

"If that doesn't work?"

"You're maybe trampled dead. Make it work. I love you." He kissed her cheek and spurred his Paint up the line. He hand-signaled Cooper across the herd after Maestas had alerted him. They both knew deadly reality of what might come and were ready.

wo minutes later, Trey heard the drug drop plane's twin motors as it
flew low on the opposite side of the gorge. He turned his head and saw
its silver body glint in the sun. Suddenly he heard automatic gunfire from
across the gorge. It banked, changed its course and started to fly across
the gorge toward the herd. The cows and calves stirred as they the heard
the roar of its powerful twin motors and more rapid gunfire. The herd got
restless as the flank cowhands worked their horses to keep it moving. The
roar of the motors increased as the plane came straight toward Trey at 200
feet over the edge of the gorge continuing to lose altitude. He pulled his
new semi-automatic AR-15 rifle from his saddle holster and aimed it at the
right wing's gas tank. The herd kept moving. Spooked cows and calves
were braying. The silver bodied airplane brightly reflecting the south sun
came straight at Trey as it crossed the ranch's barbwire boundary line
fence along the edge of the gorge. It was still dropping when Trey sprayed
the left fuel wing tank with salvo shots that riddled it. Three large bales
were thrown from the plane and landed yards from the edge of the herd
behind M. The wing burst into flames as Cooper rode around the head of
the herd to help Trey block a stampede toward the 400 feet deep gorge's
edge above the Rio Grande River. Trey saw the pilot's face and eyes as
he fired another salvo of shots through the windshield and blew his head
apart. Both Trey and Cooper heard a helio coming up from the south low
and fast not from across the gorge. The smell of fear rose from the herd
while the ballet of the cowhands' horses worked to hold it together. The
crippled airplane dipped straight toward the ground as it flew over M, Trey
and the herd. The prop wash almost knocked them off their Paints. It pivoted sideways a hundred yards from the herd and its burning wing hit the
ground as it cartwheeled. It exploded into a fireball.

The helio flew low up the ranch side of the gorge. Trey watched the
cowhands, Cooper and M ride hard to hold the herd, but its patience was
overdone like burnt toast. The cows with their calves following them
turned in chaos and stampeded toward the gorge away from the airplane's
fireball. M and Cooper peeled away from the head of the herd at full gallop. The flank cowhands galloped toward the tail where Maestas and his
old cow dog fought to turn the stampede. Trey wheeled his Paint, snapping
in a fresh ammo clip into the AR-15 rifle and rode straight for the gorge
to intercept the helio to hand signal it to bank and turn across the gorge.

He hoped the cowhands, the cow dogs, Cooper and M could turn the herd north along the ranch's barbwire fence by the gorge. As he raced toward the thick blue plastic-wrapped bales in the grass, he saw the door was off the helicopter too late. An automatic rifle opened fire from the helicopter as bullets whizzed by him. He realized it wasn't the FBI helicopter too late. It was flying to provide cover for the drug drop pick-up. His Paint galloped sure footed as he raised the AR-15 rifle to his shoulder and fired a salvo of shots at the shooter, killing him. The Mexican cartel gunman tumbled forward through the helio's open door and fell twenty-five yards in front of Trey. The pilot flew the helicopter in low, aiming its skids at Trey's cowboy hatted head. He aimed and fired the entire clip of bullets through the bubble windshield killing the pilot as the left skid missed his head by ten feet. The pilotless helicopter nosedived fifty yards in front of the charging herd and crashed. The blades churned up grass and dirt. It exploded into a fireball that turned the stampeding herd north up the side of the ranch's fence line along the gorge. The flank cowhands all peeled to the tail's safety to regroup while Cooper raced to the herd's head.

Trey heard two vehicle motors and looked south. A topless brown Bronco raced through the green gate, carrying a shooter with a rifle holding on to its roll bar. It was followed by a logoed Rio Arriba County New Mexico's Sheriff's white SUV.

"Oh shit," he shouted as he turned his part Comanche Paint horse straight toward M to help her. The gunner opened fire from the brown Bronco. Trey wheeled the Paint horse again and galloped straight at it with his AR-15 rifle blazing bullets from its red-hot barrel. The driver zigzagged the high wheelbase Bronco as much as he could without tipping and rolling it. That caused the shooter to stop firing while he fought for balance as the Bronco bounced and turned on the rough grassy pasture's surface. Trey's Paint horse's gallop was smooth and sure-footed. Trey stopped shooting and mentally calculated the speed of the left to right apexes of the brown Bronco's swerves. He raised the rifle to his shoulder ready for the vehicle's next swerve's left apex. He fired a salvo blowing the gunman out of the Bronco when the bullets cut him in half. He landed hard and bounced to a rolling dead stop. When the open top Bronco returned to its right apex, he hit the driver with another salvo of bullets. He slumped over the steering wheel and the Bronco kept turning at high speed until it rolled, looped two times and came to a rest on its side.

Trey glanced over his shoulder as he slowed the Paint and saw M and Cooper galloping in the smoke from the explosions, struggling to stop the head of still stampeding herd on its trajectory north along the ranch's barbwire boundary fencing. If the herd turned west toward the gorge again it could pin their horses to the five-strand barbwire fence. Then kill them when it tore down the fence and charged over the edge of the gorge. Trey heard the pop of a pistol fire. He saw a deputy sheriff driving the white SUV full speed toward the blue bales. He was shooting wildly at Trey as his pistol bounced in his hand that was out of the side window. Trey calmly ejected the empty clip and inserted a full one onto his rifle. He guided the Paint with knee pressure. The gait was smooth as it courageously held the point of attack while DNA remembered some Comanche war. Trey raised the AR-15 rifle to his shoulder and sprayed the front tires and grill with a burst of bullets. The radiator exploded into a cloud of steam that blocked the deputy's view. His next shot hit the deputy's pistol hand and the gun dropped into the pasture grass, bouncing away behind the SUV. The front tires started losing air and flattening quickly on the rough pasture's surface. The SUV skidded sideways and the deputy braked hard too late. It rolled onto its side plowing up dirt and grass. Trey slowed the Paint to a trot to rest him and started a long turn back to the herd, which was a half-mile away. The Paint was breathing hard and sweating. Trey knew he could kill him if he rode at speed, but he had no choice. He spurred the Paint to close the gap to the herd and help M and Cooper.

His Rockie Talkie, which was attached to his cowboy belt with a carabineer crackled. Jumbo reported, "I'm on the FBI chopper and we're lifting off from the Lovato bridge staging area to fly across the gorge. We've heard continuing gunfire. We see two black smoke columns."

Trey pressed the send button on his radio's side, "Galloping full speed north up the ranch boundary fence line along the gorge to help stop the stampede along it. Do not fly the helicopter from the bridge over the gorge directly into the head of the roundup herd. Vector it way south of the herd. The helicopter could spook the herd and could turn it west again toward the gorge pinning the flanking roundup crew to the barbwire boundary fence. If it races over the 400-foot edge of the gorge it will take the cowhands with it. May be M and Cooper. Over and out."

"Roger that, Jumbo out."

Trey spurred the Paint to get his last mile an hour of speed. He closed fast on the gorge side tail of the herd where Maestas and a cowhand were struggling to keep it shaped and heading north. Their horses were feet from the panicked mother cows and calves. The Paint started to turn through braying dying trampled calves and a few mother cows standing with broken legs. He heard the chop of helicopter rotor blades and looked up at the eerie, clearing, smoky, pale-blue sky. It was too low on a vector across the gorge on a path toward the head of the herd.

"Fucked," he softly whispered to the Paint. "It's survival warfare now. I know you can gallop like the wind with me. We save the roundup crew first and then the cattle." He rode toward Maestas as the helicopter banked hard away from the herd's head too late. The braying cows and calves panicked, started to turn the stampede west toward the gorge again. Maestas and a dusty resolute cowhand rode to the edge of the wave of turning cattle to stop it. The entire herd turned like a surfing wave breaking front right to left. Trey kept the Paint on a vector to the fence line trying to outrace the herd's stampede into the four hundred feet deep gorge. He saw Maestas become engulfed in the stampede's sea of cattle. Without warning his old horse went down throwing Maestas off his saddle into the stampeding cows and calves. Trey and a strong young cowhand nearer to Maestas were both out of position to help him. His battered white cowboy hat came off as he disappeared into the herd. It hung on a cow's horn like a ghostly grave marker. The young cowhand continued to handle his horse with precision to stop the breaking wave. He flowed along the edge of the herd like a surfer on a board crossing a breaking wave. The helicopter continued a sharp turn away from the herd flying away from the gorge with the motor's whop whop sound diminishing with each rotor turn.

M fought with all her skill and strength to keep her Paint up as the wave of cattle engulfed her. Cooper galloped his horse down the front of the oncoming wave of cattle to save M. Judy watched helplessly from the back side of the herd as it started to engulf M and then her lifelong husband. Her heart stopped beating and she stopped breathing. Suddenly she saw Trey's Paint racing up the fence line toward the point where M and Cooper were struggling to keep their horses up. She was relieved but not surprised he had survived the last volley of gunfire, and took a deep breath through her bandana. She prayed silently the exhausted Paint could reach M and Cooper in time. She and Cooper had raised Trey to ride like the wind, shoot from horseback at full gallop and be brave on the range. Trey at full gallop turned his horse away from the fence line toward M and his father. In the thickening dust storm he saw them engulfed by the herd. He saw the other west flank cowhands trying to turn the stampede back north as the helicopter's rotor noise subsided and the cattle started to slow. He rode straight into the edge of the chaotic braying exhausted cows and calves. M's young Paint started to go down. She saw Trey's Paint maneuver past a panicked mother cow and close in against her horse's left beside her. When her Paint fell awkwardly to the right she athletically slid onto the back of Trey's saddle. She wrapped her hands tightly around his waist like a Hollywood stunt cowgirl in an old western movie. She did not interfere with his arms and hands as he worked the reins with his tarnished silver spurs to guide the Paint. He calmly maneuvered the strong young horse to the edge of the herd.

The cowhands started to turn the slowing cattle north again as the barb-wire fence line loomed at the gorge's edge. Trey rode M out of the herd but could not put her down on the pasture grass safely to ride back to his father. The cattle were too close to be on foot. He turned his head and watched Cooper's experienced but older horse continue to struggle. It finally died on its four hooves from exhaustion and went down. Cooper disappeared into the herd. Judy watched in horror but could not ride across the herd to help her husband while tears welled in her brown eyes. She continued to use all her roundup skills to work the head of the herd to save it. Trey rode with M holding on to his waist, helping the cowhands finally turn the entire herd fifty feet from the fence line. Dust-caked and exhausted it slowed to a walk. It was the best roundup crew disaster stampede work that Trey had ever imagined could happen. His sad eyes showed his concern for his father who he couldn't reach until the herd moved past the point where his horse died. He waited for the last cow and calf to pass and then he U- turned his Paint to ride back to search for Maestas. His gut told him all was lost. They found Maestas as the dust settled but it was range ugly under a sunny blue sky. He was trampled badly and lay still. The top of his skull was missing. His old Blue Heeler cow dog was standing guard over his listless, dusty, torn-clothed body. M teared up but did not cry. Trey U-turned the Paint toward where his father was last seen and reined the Paint to a trot behind the herd to wait for it pass over Cooper in its exhausted slow walk. The cowhands were shaping the herd again on both flanks and Judy was calmly controlling its head with her experienced horse. She looked back at Trey when the dust settled. She hand-signaled she would stay on point. Trey signaled he would stay on drag replacing Maestas as trail boss but ride to the place Cooper went. She bravely signaled back thumbs up.

When the last trailing calf passed, Trey dropped M near the fence line, "I'm riding up to where I last saw my father's horse take him down." He handed her his pistol. "Use this if anyone tries to approach who's not law enforcement."

M started crying. "Cooper and his horse went down trying to help me. I'm so sorry."

"I respect your thought but don't be sorry. It's a cowhand's roundup duty to help save another cowhand in trouble unless it's a suicide mission. You were on the inner edge of the herd, and he should've gotten you out safely. I saw his old roundup horse falter and probably die from exhaustion. I almost killed my young Paint because he worked at a gallop so long in the dusty heat. He's just now cooling down and starting to breathe normal for a three-year-old. I didn't ride in after Maestas. He was too far away, and it was too late to help him."

His Rockie Talkie crackled, "Jumbo over Trey. Sorry about our pilot error. We flew from the Lovato Bridge staging area and the pilot's vector was off and low. Did you hold the herd...you there?"

"Trey over. Your too low helicopter's rotor noises turned the cows and calves and they stampeded toward the gorge. We just slowed and turned the herd back north along the fence line maybe fifty feet before they ran through it...dropped into the gorge. Your pilot a city boy?"

"Denver's State Patrol headquarters and ex-military chopper pilot... he didn't know his low vector could start a stampede. Your roundup crew ok?"

"Negative on that. Maestas our ranch foreman is dead. Cooper went down on his old horse in the stampede riding to help M. I saddle to saddle rescued her like I practiced with my teenage pals growing up on the Yba-rC. Once the herd clears the place where my father went down, I'll ride to him. Judy and the cowhands all ok after amazing roundup work."

"Oh my god, Trey not both Maestas and Cooper. We see two burning aircraft and a turned over brown Ford Bronco and white deputy sheriff's car with a uniformed officer limping toward three blue bales that were dropped!"

"I shot down the drug drop airplane and a helicopter covering the drop with my new AR-15 rifle from my Paint horse at full gallop. The helicopter had a gunman who fired on the cowhands and me. I killed him and the pilot who aimed a skid at my head. The Bronco gunman fired at me too. Both he and the driver are dead. I charged them on my Paint horse to stop the drug pick-up by the herd. This Paint's gotta be part Comanche. The deputy fired at me as he raced to pick up the bales. I shot his tires out and then a pistol out of his hand. You need to pick him up ASAP. The Mexican cartel owns him."

"Roger that."

"I'm galloping up the fence line. Land your fucking chopper until I radio you the herd is safely out of its rotor noise range after I find Cooper. M is standing on the fence line in a white cowgirl hat and blue western shirt. Please don't let your FBI sniper on the helicopter shoot her. Over and out."

"Roger that. We all heard you loud and clear."

Trey's burning eyes pierced the settling trail dust as he rode in behind the slowing, braying, still-frightened herd with his red bandana pulled up over his nose to breathe. The bone-tired cowhands and their horses were continuing to shape it before they turned it toward the hacienda's pasture an hour away. A dust-caked bleeding horse lying on its side started to come into view. Trey heard the FBI helicopter cut its engine silencing its rotors two miles behind him. He slowed the Paint to a trot as he approached the fallen horse. He saw a thick dust-covered man's body curled against the horse in the grass with one leg under it. He was not moving. He reined the Paint to a stop and jumped off it. He raced across the trampled pasture to his father whose straw cowboy hat was plastered onto his head.

He knelt and carefully removed it. "Dad, you alive?"

There was no reply, so he felt Cooper's wrist vein and found a low pulse. He got his canteen from the Paint and washed Cooper's bloody face. Cooper's eyes blinked open and blurrily looked up at Trey.

"It's a bad horse wreck, son. He died under me but protected me in death. The cows ran around him but a few three-hundred-pound calves stumbled and fell over him onto me. I'm broken up bad. Bleeding inside maybe."

"Cowboy up, Dad. I'll get help."

Trey iPhoned Jumbo, "I'm with Cooper. A bad horse wreck but he's alive. Trampled some and broken up. Get the Taos Medical Helicopter up here with a paramedic."

"Already called it and it's airborne ten minutes out. We have the deputy sheriff from Espanola. He's refusing to tell us why he's out of county with a busted-up SUV and a half shot-off hand standing by three bales of drugs. A Colorado State Patrolman is walking up the fence line to bring M safely to us."

"She has my pistol. Make sure he's clearly ID'd in uniform."

"He is. They know each other from her state patrol high speed driving class. He's amazed that she's standing by a fence post, wearing a cowgirl hat at the tail of a stampede. She never mentioned she could ride a fast horse."

"I'm staying with Cooper and have a first aid kit in my saddle bag. I'll patch up any bleeding, but he says some is internal…the worst kind. Send the medical helicopter straight to us. Don't stop it at Maestas…he's dead. Use my Paint for the LZ marker. It's the pilot's second medical recue on the ranch. He'll be fine. Please do not move the FBI helicopter until the medical one is out of here and the herd has turned east on its way toward the hacienda pasture. Don't route law enforcement vehicles into the hacienda or across the ranch from it. You could start another stampede. Bring them through our north gate on the State Line Road and down the ranch road along the fence by the gorge. Please no flashing lights or sirens. After the herd is secured in the headquarters' corral by the hacienda then you all can use the ranch's main gate but no sirens. Tell M her Paint is not on the ground where it stumbled and went down. It may be running with the herd. I'll ride her out. Please get Maestas out to a morgue. Cut his downed horse's throat to make sure it's dead. I couldn't because of the stampede was full on. I'll take care of Cooper's horse after we get his leg out from under it. No shots."

"Roger that, Trey. You know we'll need a full statement from you."

"Talk to me tomorrow after breakfast at the hacienda or the Taos Hospital. We're suspending the roundup for a couple days after we bed down the herd tonight. I don't want tired cowhands and horses killing each other. I'll be easy to find. Either with my father at the hospital or at the hacienda until the roundup starts again. Over and out."

Trey turned into the open ranch entrance gate after driving back to the hacienda at sunup from the Taos Hospital. He had a few hours' sleep on a blue plaid, coffee-stained, aging lumpy couch in the visitors' lounge. His father was in ICU recovering from emergency surgery for internal bleeding caused by a now missing appendix and spleen. His collapsed lung had been reinflated and he was on a ventilator. His shattered left leg was in a cast. He was expected to make a full recovery albeit a slow one, the surgeon reported. Judy had stayed at the hospital with him. M had stayed at the hacienda to manage the ranch with Larry the thirty-six-year-old, blond, lead cowhand who Trey had appointed to be the foreman. Larry had grown up on a New Mexico Ranch near Santa Fe that his parents sold to a subdivision developer. He parked the red pickup up at the hacienda steps where M met him. She threw her arms around him and kissed him hard.

Trey said, "That's the best greeting I've ever had."

M replied, "Not every day that I get rescued wild-west show style by the best cowboy on the American range."

"Speaking of the rescue did your Paint horse show up?"

M smiled. "She did with the herd. One of the cowhands brought her to me after they bedded it down last night. She was disguised as a thick dusty-brown-colored quarter horse. I gave her the best bath and brush down of her life and a double bucket of oats. She's resting in her stall. I took care of your Paint too. He was dusty, dirty exhausted."

"Does Larry have a cow and calf count including causalities?" Trey asked.

M frowned. "Total bedded down 463 with 22 calves counted dead on the range and 17 mother cows put down with mostly broken legs. The cowhands were able to gut 13 calves and all the mother cows in time to truck them at sunup this morning to the slaughterhouse in Manassas. An ambulance picked up Maestas's body after you left for the hospital. I called his family and expressed our condolences and told them you were at the hospital with your father who was badly injured."

"Good work. Maestas's loss is tragic. That'll fill the bunkhouse freezers with beef. We'll give a quarter side of beef to each cowhand for their family freezers. We'll ship the cowhides to a tannery to replace the old worn-out ones in the bunkhouse and the hacienda. Law enforcement still in the west pasture?"

"Larry's out there now with the New Mexico State Patrol, the Taos County Sheriff, The DEA, the FBI and he says the FAA is on the way because aircraft were downed. Jumbo checked on me before he went home and had a couple shots of the good Scotch Cooper brought you." Trey's iPhone chimed. "Speaking of the devil it's Jumbo. Thanks for checking on M. Hope you enjoyed Cooper's Scotch. He's in ICU as a precaution but will recover fine sans a spleen and appendix with a lot of rehab for a broken femur with 16 pins in it. He'll need a lot of Scotch too."

Jumbo replied very relieved, "I prayed Cooper cowboyed up out there and survived."

Trey replied, "He did but his old horse mostly saved him. Pinned his leg but blocked the mother cows off him. Most of his damaged was from frightened calves, that didn't even know they were in a stampede, that stumbled and fell on him. His horse still had a slight pulse when I put him down. All four legs were broken. So, when do I make a statement?"

"Today. You at the hacienda?"

"Yes, and to whom?"

"The New Mexico State Police, the FBI, the DEA and the Taos County Sheriff's department. Tomorrow it's the FAA because you shot down two aircraft. Tell them all the same straight story that you told me. You were attacked during the drug drop, and it was self-defense. The drug drop airplane set off a stampede when it flew across the gorge over the roundup. You and your cowhands saved the herd."

"Got it. Send them over. You coming down too?"

"No, I'm retired they say. Call me if anyone gets heavy. Don't shoot one of them, please."

"Got that but I'm not happy with the FBI helicopter pilot. I'll spend the day on it but back to work tomorrow. Which of the law enforcement groups removes the burned-out drug plane and helicopter off my pasture? Or do I send the ranch's D-8 cat down to bury them?" Trey asked.

"I advise you to keep the FBI chopper pilot thought to yourself. Turns out he's a newly hired city boy ex-military pilot with no rural or ranch over flight experience. The FAA probably with the FBI will remove the aircraft for investigation and evidence. Don't you or your cowhands cross the yellow tape or bother anything in the wreckage."

"Got it. Roger out."

"That was Jumbo. I'm making statements to law enforcement agencies all day in the hacienda. You work with Larry and make sure the herd's settling and resting well."

M asked, "Is this over after you make statements to law enforcement?"

"Who knows? It's self-defense, protection of the roundup crew and herd as far as I see it. We'll see if a Mexican cartel kingpin with their New Mexico helpers get arrested and the drug drops stop. I'll settle the score if they don't," Trey stated.

"With the war chief?"

"We'll see. I'm hungry. Where's Cookie?" Trey changed the conversation.

"Bringing the chuck wagon back to the bunkhouse. I'll make you breakfast while you take a hot shower. Your face and arms are still dusty with blood streaks."

"Roger that."

Trey was sitting behind his father's antique, hand-carved wooden Spanish desk in the hacienda office. He sat in a western-style, high-backed, brown-leather, office chair facing one DEA and two FBI agents across a worn cowhide rug. They were seated on a brown leather couch with green painted spoke wagon wheel arms. He had just answered their questions about how and why he shot down the two aircraft with an AR-15 rifle.

He added, "Both drug drop aircrafts started the stampede during the roundup which resulted in the deaths of 37 mother cows and calves, the death of Maestas, our ranch's foreman since my family purchased it 22 years ago, and injuries to my father who is in the ICU unit at Taos Hospital. Count my family very unhappy that we were only notified about the drug drop ten minutes before law enforcement converged on it, which pushed it across the gorge during our annual fall roundup. I heard gunfire across the gorge just before the silver airplane banked during its low flight path and turned toward the herd. Which one of your federal agencies or state patrols fired those shots, or did a gunman on the drug drop plane fire at you all first?"

"A retired Colorado state patrolman warned you against our black out rules. He won't be involved in any more of our DEA drug enforcement operations. We're conducting an internal investigation and cannot comment on those alleged shots you heard. Or if you actually heard shots," The DEA agent stated.

Trey snapped, "You and the FBI cannot ever comment on anything you're investigating. Did one of your trigger-happy federal agents or a rogue local lawman fire the shots? Or maybe shoot to warn the drug drop plane you all were waiting below it to seize the shipment, which then diverted it across the gorge over my ranch and the 500 plus roundup herd."

The DEA agent pushed back hard, "You accusing one of my agents of conspiring with the drug cartel, Mr. Stuart?"

"Are you investigating that possibility?"

An FBI agent stated, "We are, Mr. Stuart, and we're investigating whether you or one of your cowhands angrily fired at the drug drop airplane when it flew low up the other side of the gorge causing it to turn."

"If you actually think me or a cowboy in the roundup crew whom all use hand signals to communicate would fire a shot knowing it could set off a deadly stampede into the 400-foot-deep river gorge then fucking get out of my office now. It's clear you don't know anything about roundup operating procedures."

The FBI agent angered said, "It's an offense to swear at a federal agent in an investigation. Do it again and I'll arrest you and hold you as a material witness in jail."

Trey countered, "Do you know who the Mexican cartel kingpins and their New Mexico helpers are? Are you going to arrest them or just waste time investigating my roundup crew, their horses and the cattle that survived the stampede to cover for the cartel? How much were the drugs in the blue plastic bales worth?"

The DEA agent took the bait and snapped back, "Ten million dollars on the street for the coke, fentanyl, meth and oxy we estimate. No pot. The Mexican cartel business model has morphed to hard drugs led by the highly profitable fentanyl since most states have legalized marijuana for recreational or medical usage."

Trey countered, "So it wasn't the low-level morons in the airplane, helicopter, and Bronco who planned the drop and control the profits, was it? They don't in the cartel drug movies. Once more whom are you investigating at the top of the drug food chain in New Mexico, Colorado and or the real Mexico that run the drug drop operations and banks the money? When will you arrest them to stop the drops on or across the gorge from my ranch and my neighbors' ranches Is that the right question?"

The senior FBI agent stated, "We're here to ask the questions, not you. You're not cooperating."

"Get out of my office then. If you want to ask me another question, call my attorney. And after your agencies and the FAA get the burned aircraft and vehicles off my ranch do not come back without a search warrant. That's all. I've got a roundup to restart and cattle to ship in a week. I'll escort you out the hacienda's front door. Adios." Trey stood up and walked to the heavy pine office door and opened it.

The senior FBI agent aggressively warned, "I'll be back. If and when you talk to the Taos News or any national news outlets since this is already on the AP wire and you allege law enforcement corruption or ineptitude, then we'll arrest you. And I repeat hold you as a material witness." Trey turned his back to the agents and walked toward the hacienda living room as M joined him in the hallway, which was filled with Western art. As the agents passed them to exit through the open front door, he scrolled through his iPhone text messages.

"You're right. Here's a call from an AP reporter. Guess this a big story. Here's one from a Hollywood reality TV producer. He wants to film the rest of the roundup while the burned-out aircraft are still on the ranch. Here's one in Spanish, which I happen to speak, threatening my life and the roundup crew too for screwing up the drug drop and shooting his brother who I guess was one of the gunners or pilots. I think I'll call the AP reporter first. If the brother comes at us on this ranch, he'll die in a hail of plain old western ranch trespass bullets. I'll pass on the reality TV show because the filming could set off a stampede. You can read my interview via AP tomorrow. Last time I checked, the first amendment was still the law of the land." He slammed the hacienda door behind them and turned to M. "Check the tape recorder you set up in the bookcase in my office. Please make sure it's all there and put in a new tape for the New Mexico state patrol and the Taos County Sheriff's meeting this afternoon. We'll tape the FAA on Monday too but they're here to file a report on why the airplane and helicopter crashed and burned. That's easy. I shot the birds' wings out of the sky and blinded their eyes."

"I gather no one in the room would reveal who funded and runs the drug drops since all the peasants are dead. What about the deputy sheriff they arrested? Did he talk?" a worried M asked.

"No one mentioned him. The DEA confirmed the drugs were worth ten million dollars on the street. Bet the sheriff may dodge that one too. He and the state patrol are batter up. Let's eat lunch before they descend on us. I'll fire up the gas grill and put on a couple rib eyes."

"I already made some potato salad. Cold beers are in the fridge. The sunny veranda beckons. Oh, Judy called. Cooper's out of ICU. He's listed in serious condition. She's ducking reporters and says a TV truck is headed up here. She'll sleep in his room tonight," M reported.

"Thanks. I'll take him the good Scotch tomorrow. That'll get him out of his serious condition faster than any medicine."

Trey's iPhone rang just as he and M were finishing lunch. Trey checked the number and answered.

"Guess I got you banned from future drug raids this side of the border."

"You did. I can live with it, but you and M may not be able to. The cartel may come after you all for costing them a lot of money," Jumbo stated.

Trey interrupted him, "Ten million dollars I'm told plus a plane, helicopter, rigged to run Bronco and guns."

"And you pissed off both the DEA agent and the FBI so expect no future warnings or help from them."

Trey replied, "I hear my family has bad history with the FBI, so I expect none. Everything I've heard about the DEA in Mexican border states like New Mexico says some of their agents are on the cartel take. That true?"

Jumbo hesitated. "Yes, some but no mostly."

"At yesterday's drop?"

"If you spin the bottle maybe. I believe a DEA agent fired the first salvo of shots that missed the airplane. The FBI didn't. I was on their chopper. Neither the New Mexico nor Colorado State Patrol had reached the staging area. The Taos County Sheriff's Department was cut out of the operation."

"Is the deputy sheriff I wounded from Espanola New Mexico talking? ID'ing the kingpins?"

"No, he's lawyered up and not even suspended from the department."

"So, the corruption goes deep in his department?"

"Historically, yes."

"And my strategy this afternoon?"

"Refuse their interview until you have an attorney present. But tomorrow cooperate with the FAA. They only want to determine why the airplane and chopper crashed and exploded."

"I'll call the Taos ranch attorney?"

"No, call Cooper's attorney."

"It's all interconnected here?"

"Mostly."

"I'm calling now. He can charter fly down. Thanks. Adios, amigo."

At eight a.m. Trey was in his hacienda office with William Alexander the Ybar C's attorney when M led two New Mexico state patrol detectives and the county sheriff into it. M stayed for the investigation meeting, and it began with Trey repeating the facts of the downed drug drop airplane and helicopter. He recounted in detail the shootout with the brown Bronco and the deputy sheriff. He vividly described the herd's stampede that resulted in Maestas's death, M's rescue and his father's injuries. When he was finished, his attorney asked:

"Anything else you need to know from my client?"

The hard eyed, crewcut, senior New Mexico state patrol detective stated, "We're developing a full report in conjunction with the Colorado State Police. The initial field report by our first responding patrolmen states that they were not present on your ranch during the airborne drug drop, the vehicle shootouts and the resulting cattle stampede. That's because they had responded to the DEA call for help from Highway 285 on the west side of the Rio Grande River Gorge. They did not reach the DEA drug drop interception staging area until after the silver bodied twin engine airplane had crossed the gorge into the airspace over your ranch. They also reported they did not hear any gunfire on the east side of the gorge as they sped toward the DEA agents with their siren on but without flashings lights. Is that your and M's recollection?"

Trey replied, "Yes. I only saw their black SUV and the Colorado State Police SUV on the ranch during day two of the roundup after the shootouts and the stampede. That was during the Taos medical helio's pick-up of my injured father."

M replied, "I don't remember seeing their SUVs on the ranch during the shoot outs and resulting stampede. I had trouble handling my inexperienced roundup Paint horse so my attention was totally focused on the stampede. A Colorado state patrolman who I know, secured me when I was on foot by the ranch's boundary fence near the gorge. My Paint horse went down during the stampede, but Trey rescued me saddle to saddle. Thankfully, my Paint recovered her footing and ran into the stampeding herd and returned to the hacienda."

The detective asked, "Did either of you talk to them?"

Trey replied, "No they were at least a half mile south of me at the deputy sheriff's rolled over white SUV when I first saw their black SUVs. I had ridden north along the ranch's fence line as soon I could to rescue my father after the stampeding herd cleared the area his horse went down in."

M stated, "Yes. I was standing a quarter mile away from the rolled over white SUV at a fence post when the Colorado state patrolman reached me. Trey had ridden to search for his father who was trampled by the stampede."

"That confirms their report."

Trey's attorney asked, "Sheriff, do you have any questions for my client?"

"Yes, I do. Why were you riding the roundup with an AR-15 semi-automatic rifle, not a cowhand's saddle rifle? Were you looking for trouble?"

Trey answered, "My entire roundup crew was aware of the drug drops across the gorge from the ranch. There had already been one drug drop early spring that was on my ranch. A deputy sheriff in uniform driving a white SUV covered the pick-up of a large bale covered in burlap in the west pasture near my boundary fence by the gorge. I could not identify the county seal logo on its doors. It departed following a topless metallic brown Bronco, which picked up the bale. That same brown Bronco entered the ranch during the day two of the roundup. A gunman in the Bronco during the first drug drop fired shots from a semi-automatic rifle at M and me as we galloped away on our Paint horses. Did one of your deputies report the pick-up of the drug bale to you or the New Mexico State Patrol or the DEA? Or was it the out of county deputy sheriff that was arrested yesterday?" The two state police detectives looked at the sheriff with frowns on their faces.

The sheriff questioned, "You make this story up to defend your actions yesterday? You have a witness to this allegation?"

"He said he does," answered M. "I was riding the range on my Paint horse with Trey when the first drug drop happened. We were checking the west pasture cattle."

The sheriff snapped back, "You covering up that you shot at my deputy?"

William Alexander stated, "Trey you don't have to answer that unfounded allegation. Sheriff, how would you have known if Trey shot at one of your deputies at the first drug drop if there is no police report filed about it?"

The senior state patrol detective asked, "Did your deputy make a report to you and file a report with us? You are on the DEA task force to stop the drug drops and arrest the perps. We haven't seen a report."

The sheriff stalled, "We did not send it to you because it's not State Patrol business."

The senior detectives asserted, "It is, sir. Mr. Stuart has made a very serious allegation regarding one of your deputies if he was at the alleged first drug drop and helped pick up or seize the drugs."

William Alexander asked, "Did your office or the New Mexico State Patrol question the out of county wounded deputy in the rolled over white SUV? He was arrested by a Taos County deputy at the scene of the roll over and after the DEA agents seized the drug shipment?"

The junior state patrol detective answered, "We made a request to do so but the Taos County Sheriff's office stated he had been released in custody to the Rio Arriba County sheriff to return to duty pending an investigation. I called the Sheriff's office in Espanola to set up a meeting and was given the deputy's attorney's phone number. He has not returned my call."

Trey angrily snapped, "No one has questioned the deputy who shot at me while he was trying to pick up the three bales of drugs during the stampede? And he's back on patrol."

The sheriff stated, "We're leaving it up to his boss the Rio Arriba County sheriff at Espanola to conduct the internal investigation as a matter of courtesy."

Trey countered, "So the cover up is on to protect two crooked deputies in two counties who were illegally on my ranch for two diverted airplane drug drops from across the gorge. During the first drop shots were fired at M and me from the same brown Ford Bronco that fired shots at me during the second drop, which stampeded my roundup herd. Both times the Bronco and white SUVs entered through my ranch's west pasture's green gate?" The two detectives stared coldly at the sheriff but remained silent playing for time.

The sheriff snapped, "I should arrest Mr. Stuart and M for fabricating a lie about my deputy to bolster his story about provoking a series of shootouts during the roundup drug drop on his ranch. He knew law enforcement was across the gorge waiting to intercept it."

Trey's attorney stated, "Do you have an eyewitness to corroborate M and Trey's allegations about the first drug drop on the ranch. If it was your deputy that saw a gunman in the brown Bronco shoot at M and Trey, then why didn't he intervene? He should have arrested the shooter and the driver. Instead, he presumptively covered the drug pick up by the Bronco of the alleged drug bale?"

The sheriff snapped back before thinking, "Because Trey fired shots at the brown Bronco."

"I did in self-defense," Trey stated.

The senior state patrolman asked, "Sheriff, how do you know that fact if there is no field report by your deputy and if so where are the drugs your deputy helped pick up? Your deputy's name please? We need to interview him ASAP."

The sheriff angrily said, "The deputy in question is dead. He was shot and killed by a Land or Death movement member at the Water Association damn standoff near here. This meeting is over."

The two detectives stood up and the senior one said, "Sheriff, you are under arrest for criminal felony conspiracy to conceal and failing to report a criminal drug seizure by your deputy. Also, for refusing to reveal the location of the said drug drop shipment as evidence. Hand over your sidearm." He drew his pistol. The junior detective read him his Miranda rights.

"You'll regret this, Detective, after I call the governor's office your career is as done as burnt toast. As for these lying Colorado ranch stray dogs Trey and his half breed Apache girlfriend M my department and the DA will deal with them later."

Trey's attorney said clearly, "That's threat to harm my clients."

The senior detective said, "Sheriff, I advise you to remain silent and hand over your firearm gun barrel first." The sheriff slowly drew his gun but at the last instance pointed it at the junior detective who was waiting to take it. The senior detective fired a shot into the sheriff's shoulder and he dropped the pistol. The junior detective kicked the pistol away from the sheriff and handcuffed him. The room was silent as all the parties realized the cartel drug drops and their tens of millions of dollars of profits had been protected by law enforcement.

M broke the silence, "Someone call 911 for a paramedic. The sheriff is bleeding from the bullet wound in his shoulder."

After an all-day State Patrol crime scene investigation in Trey's hacienda office, M very shaken, called Judy at the hospital to check on Cooper's condition. She also gave Judy a heads up on the wounding of the sheriff. While that was happening, Trey met with the FAA investigator and repeated his story a third time. Then came an hour of matter-of-fact aviation related questions, which were carefully asked to establish Trey's salvo of shots brought down the two aircrafts and not mechanical failure or pilot error. When the session was completed, the investigator stated the FAA was having the wreckage trucked to a warehouse in Alamosa Colorado.

Trey asked, "If you can please tell me who owned the airplane and the helicopter as you call it? My new foreman could not find a tail number on the airplane and the helicopter number was partially burned off."

"I can because it will be a matter of public record and the news media will broadcast it live by satellite TV when I exit your ranch gate. The airplane was reported stolen from a general aviation airport near San Antonio Texas two years ago. Since the tail number was removed, I assume it has been in Mexico and has flown drug drops across the US border including the ones over your ranch. The A-Star helicopter is owned by the Third State Bank of Albuquerque New Mexico. It's operated under a lease to a local aviation company, which charters it when not in bank use. It was on a private charter when it crash-landed on your ranch by an off shore company registered in the British Virgin Islands named SAD LLC. DEA believes that SAD stands for South American Drugs. They provided an insurance rider from a broker in the BVIs, which was backed by Lloyds of London in the amount 2.5 million dollars for the helicopter and 10 million dollars in property damages because SAD LLC provided their own pilot. His name listed on the flight manifest is Juan Riviera. The FAA license he presented is counterfeit. There was no flight plan filed. That's all we know at this point."

"That's a lot of good info, sir. Can my ranch claim property damages, medical expenses, loss of life damages, interruption of business damages etc.?"

"Generally, yes, on this type of blue chip aviation policy rider. You will need an attorney and a CPA to handle this matter for your ranch. However, this is a first of a kind investigation for me at the FAA. Usually, a helicopter clips a building or power line then crashes. I've never investigated one that was shot down over a roundup of stampeding cattle and allegedly dropped three bales of drugs. Plus, a passenger on board the helicopter fired shots at a ranch roundup crew. That's like a Hollywood movie I saw. However, it wouldn't surprise me that the FAA accident report files show low flying aircraft in the Western US may have set off cattle stampedes."

"I'll get my CPA and attorney to work on the ranch's legal damage claims. Call me on my iPhone or text me if you need any more information. Thanks."

Trey met M sipping white wine in the late afternoon sun on the veranda and he asked, "You ok?" The Scotch bottle was on the turquoise metal-rimmed round tempered glass-topped table too. He poured a double shot of it into a crystal glass tumbler neat and took a solid drink.

"Mostly but did the fucking corrupt sheriff have to start a shootout in the hacienda's ranch office?" M asked.

"He must really fear the Mexican cartel and what the Taos locals call the Espanola New Mexico drug mafia in or out of prison. Our problem is the death of the deputy at the first drug drop in the white SUV who escorted the metallic brown Bronco off the ranch conceals the name of who received the drugs. He may have helped deliver the drugs to someone with the Bronco's driver. The war chief's wounded son was dropped off at the Pueblo for medical treatment before the drugs were delivered. The sheriff, if he knows, won't reveal who received the drugs from the first shipment dropped on the ranch. That person or persons can still come after us. We have to assume they are Mexican cartel."

M replied, "Then there was the deputy that followed us from Taos to the ranch."

"Do you remember what he looks like?"

"A little, I only saw him in the side mirror at a distance. He wore a uniform shirt and had an official tan cowboy type hat. He was clean-shaven. He had expensive aviator sunglasses like deputy sheriffs on TV," M replied.

"Well since he looks like most of the deputies in the West, we'll be on the look out for him." Trey laughed. "Let's take the red pickup and go visit Cooper at the Taos hospital. We'll get my mom a room by ours at the La Fonda Hotel after a good dinner. We have another day before the roundup restarts. The FAA is moving the wreckage of both aircraft to an Alamosa warehouse tomorrow."

"Great idea. I love you." M gave him a long kiss.

CHAPTER 14
THE MOON AND MILKY WAY

Trey wheel chaired his father out of the Taos Hospital door on a sunny, cold, early-November day. The calves had been shipped and the new foreman was managing the ranch's winter operations. Maestas's memorial service the week before had drawn over 250 plus relatives and friends to the historic adobe Catholic Church in Garcia Colorado. The 1850's crumbling and mostly abandoned historic adobe house plaza was just across the Colorado border from the ranch. His interment was in the cemetery nearby where dozens of his family members were buried. Festive, colorful, artificial flowers decorated the wooden and stone grave markers. Small American flags on sticks decorated the graves of veterans from every war since 1852. When the sun hit Cooper's cowboy hatted face his mood changed and he smiled for the first time since the roundup. Trey helped his mom load Cooper into their pickup truck for the trip back to the YbarC. He put the folded up wheelchair with Cooper's aluminum crutches in the half cab and closed all the doors after Judy climbed in.

She said, "Thank you, both, from the bottom of my heart for helping Cooper during his hospital recovery. I'll get him through his four-month rehab in Telluride. He'll be ready to ride the range by spring."

Cooper added, "Thank you for all your support even though I wasn't always a perfect patient. I've never spent three weeks inside a building or even a house. It's great to feel the sun again."

Trey replied, "Mom, are you sure that you can drive him back to the YbarC alone?"

"I'll be fine. It's good you and M are escorting us out of New Mexico. I won't feel safe until I'm in Colorado, with still no arrests in the drug drop case."

M replied, "Don't worry, Trey has a saddle rifle in the red pickup plus a small pistol arsenal. Your loaded Glock 9 is under your center console. We'll both miss you all. We love you all."

"Dad, the Rockie Talkie I gave you is on channel 140. Just press and call M if you need to talk to us. We'll get it back when you stop for gas in Alamosa Colorado. There's a change in your usual route back home so you don't drive through Tierra Amarilla where Adrianna's Land or Death Foundation is headquartered. You'll go north from there to Gunnison Colorado and on to the YbarC. If Judy gets tired of driving, you can overnight in Gunnison and have a good dinner. Let's hit the road."

Trey and M talked as they led Judy north on highway 522 past the ranch and across the Colorado border.

M asked, "You want to spend a peaceful night at the hot spring motel with the yurts? It's forty-five minutes north of Alamosa? We need some time off from the ranch and family."

"Perfect idea. My gold card is restless in my wallet. The calves shipped and the payment arrived by wire transfer yesterday. Let's start spending it on ourselves. You earned your ranch work and roundup pay dodging gunfire and a stampede. It was like the old west in the late 1880s when my great grandfather operated the YbarC."

"Good, I packed a bikini and a swimsuit for you in my day bag and two tooth brushes. That's all we'll need. We can stop in Alamosa at the liquor store near the college for Scotch and white wine," M suggested.

"Good idea."

"You think Cooper can really work the range again?" M asked.

"At almost sixty-five he'll ride the range but mostly in a pickup. After the horse wreck and trampling he suffered, his body is battered. Doc said his spine got stepped on and is a mess. With pins in his shattered leg, it is going to be a tough rehab just to walk without a limp again. Bouncing on a horse will not be good for it or his back. Tasks like roping are over. Arthritis coming too from the injuries and years in the saddle."

"So, will he retire? Leave Western Colorado's cold mountain ranching and move to the YbarC's warm Arizona winter grazing lease Judy told me about?" M probed.

"Not for a year or two until the pain makes it not worth saddling a horse winter or summer. Judy, Tommy Lee, the foreman since before I was born, and the cowhands can wrangle the YbarC. When he retires to Arizona then Judy goes with him. She's eight years younger, a smoother rider than dad and has always worked in the ranch office running the books and money. She's less range beat up by years. She can ride the warm flat high desert land down there in her sleep. He can drive it in one of these big new comfy air-conditioned pickups.

"Do you take over with the New Mexico ranch now and the YbarC then?"

"The short answer is yes. They will probably deed me the New Mexico ranch at Christmas. They will deed me the YbarC when they go to Arizona but keep the house and land there, which is mostly a BLM grazing lease until they die."

"Is there a long answer?"

"Of course, there always is. You are the 'it' factor in the short answer. Will you be a partner in that life with me?" Trey asked.

M did not hesitate, "I will but on the condition that's a marriage proposal. And that you and I mutually consult each other on intentional decisions that can lead to our deaths. You good on that?" M asked.

"If you mean like me joining the war chief on his proposed mission to rid northern New Mexico of the Mexican cartel drug drops or you racing two hundred plus miles an hour in dragsters then the answer is yes."

"I love you, Trey. I accept." M threw her arms around his neck and kissed him hard as the pickup almost swerved off the road before she caught the steering wheel with one hand.

The Rocky Talkie crackled, and Cooper said, "Can you two please stay on the highway?"

They laughed and said in unison over their Rocky Talkie, "We're engaged."

Judy replied, "It's about time. Way to go, M. Lassoing a Stuart is hard but a good life's work and love."

"Thanks, Mom," Trey replied.

"We'll spend the night and celebrate it with you in Alamosa," Cooper replied.

"Thanks, Dad but we're checking into the hot spring motel north of Alamosa and it's not on your route," Trey replied.

Judy replied, "Perfect. I've got Cooper covered."

"Over and out," M replied smiling.

Trey and M were chatting with the desk clerk at the Valley Hot Springs resort while a housekeeper was finishing cleaning their room.

He reported, "Water is a perfect temperature right around at 102 degrees. You can spring until 10 p.m. Robes and towels are in your room. I recommend flip-flops for our wood plank walkways. Our view of the Crestone Peak is always breathtaking at sunset."

M asked, "Do you have any loaner flip flops?"

"No but we have them for sale on the shelf behind you at our cost, ten dollars a pair."

M and Trey walked over to the shelf, and each found their size. M walked over to a long glass-topped antique oak merchandise case next to the shelves and looked into it. A minute later, she said, "Trey, please come over here. There is some amazing handmade silver jewelry with a pale blue turquoise I have never seen before."

He walked over to look at it as the desk clerk came over with a key. The clerk opened the case and handed M the bracelet and necklace that she had pointed to. M tried them on, and the pair looked fabulous on her.

Trey asked, "Where is this pale blue turquoise mined? I've seen western turquoise all my life but never this tone of blue."

The clerk answered, "The mine is ten miles from here."

M peering into a small mirror on the wall next to the counter, asked, "Who makes it? This is not Pueblo Indian."

"Actually, my aunt, an old hippie silversmith who originally lived on the Buffalo Commune near Taos in the 1960s. She lives down the highway at Crestone in a straw-bale house now. She was at the commune when Dennis Hopper filmed Easy Rider there. She claims she smoked pot and slept with him when he later moved to Taos and lived in the Mabel Dodge Luhan house. She says she's in a documentary film shot there and was nude in the bathtub with another woman who was an Apache girl. The documentary she says has never been shown in theaters or on TV."

M surprised, replied, "Great story. Trey doesn't know this story. My mother was the other girl in the bathtub. She's Apache and was in Taos after high school graduation on a trip with my grandmother who was delivering handmade baskets. She met some hippie girls at the Kit Carson Park in Taos, which borders the Luhan house and the Pueblo. They invited her over to the house where she says Dennis Hopper was editing a motion picture 'The Last Movie'. It was a crazy scene for a 17-year-old reservation girl. There was a camera crew from Hollywood filming the editing and the party, or 'happening' as the hippie girls called it. She smoked pot for the first time and drank wine with the other girls. They convinced her to stay for dinner and afterwards a blonde girl, probably your aunt, took her up to the bathtub where Dennis was bathing. They took their clothes off and joined him in the tub. Then the camera crew came in and filmed the wild hippie scene. Afterwards she dried off, dressed and walked back to the Best Western by the Pueblo where my grandmother was staying. Before she left, the director of the film crew gave her a printed paper form to sign but she only printed her name and res address in a in a blank and refused to sign it. A month later, he showed up at the res and found her. He gave her $500 to sign the release. She knew no one on the res would ever see the film so she took it to buy an old pickup truck. Six months later, the director called her and invited her to a screening of 'The American Dreamer' in Taos. She got a ride with a friend going to Taos to deliver his silver jewelry to a gallery on the Plaza. She went to the screening, but the blonde girl wasn't there," M said a little sad for her mother.

The clerk replied, "My aunt left for Afghanistan before the documentary was shown. I'm sure she would love to see your mother again. She's in Bali now where she goes each fall to meditate. If it's OK, I'll take your information and have her call you when she returns."

"Yes, please do that please. I'd love to talk to her, but my mother died of breast cancer recently. Trey, I want the necklace as a gift for my grandmother when we go to the res to tell her we're engaged. I want the bracelet for myself."

Trey asked, "What's the price please?"

The clerk responded, "For the matched pair from the same turquoise slab $2000.00 less 10% for friends and family."

"Wrap them up. Here's my Gold Card again. We shipped calves this week. They're uniquely beautiful."

M whooped, "Yes," and kissed Trey

The clerk winked at Trey and quipped, "Your hot spring vacation will be a ten. My aunt always says silver and turquoise is a woman's best friend."

Then a housekeeper walked into the office and said, "Room seven is ready."

Three days later, Trey was driving the red pickup with M at his side on New Mexico Highway 64 about ten minutes from the Jicarilla Apache reservation where M was born.

He asked, "An old blues song asks if you feel like 'go in home'?"

"I do. It's been too long since I've seen my grandmother."

"Why's that?"

"Partly because how I got banged up in the dragster, which would have set her off against my father. She might have started drinking again, which is the Res cure all for anger and depression. Also, it's better to visit her now that you are a permanent part of my life. Too many white boys play with pretty Apache girls and disappear once a parent finds out."

"I can see her logic. She wants to protect you. How will I be received?"

"We'll find out. Our engagement means I'll never return to the Res to live. You're not welcome to live there even part-time. I won't be there to help her in old age like her friend's daughters or granddaughters. Once she finds out you're from a big ranching family, maybe very negatively. You family is ranching on a lot of stolen Indian land. She might wonder if you'll stick with me in sickness as well as health. Or at the end of the day whether you and your family will accept mixed blood children."

"Wow, that's a laundry list. Why so long?"

"Because it's the hard truth history of the treatment of Pueblo Indian, now Native American, girls and women by white boys and men in the west. Renaming us Native Americans hasn't changed anything. My Spanish blood is a curse second only to white blood as far as the Apache are concerned. We almost became extinct fighting both races. So please don't expect a hero's welcome for being a big ranch boy that is stealing my maidenhood and taking me off the Res. It'll be one step at a time for you over many moons. The necklace is a peace offering from me to my grandmother for bringing you onto the Res. It's not like the old days when mountain men traded bead necklaces for squaw wives in the Western movies," M said smiling at her quip.

Trey quipped back, "So beads this trip but what's your dowry? Is it horses like the old Western movies or some cattle? Maybe Winchester rifles for the Res warriors to raid my ranch and burn the hacienda?"

"Touché, but probably a new house for her on the Res with modern everything since I won't be returning to help her in old age. I don't have a brother or sister either."

"Are you serious?"

"Sí, amigo."

"When should I build it?"

"After the wedding and before our first child is born."

"You're in charge of the plans, the contractor and furnishing it. Get your research started when we return to the ranch."

"Perfect. There's the casino on the right so turn left two roads past it and I'll tell you when to stop."

"Anything else? She may choose to speak to you only in Jicarilla Apache even though the Res school taught her English, so I'll translate."

"Why?"

"She's old school. More time to read you. More cultural nuance for me. Turn here. It's five houses down on the right with peeling, baby-blue paint." Trey parked in front of a small worn clapboard house with a sagging porch roof. He took a deep breath and decided to leave his black cowboy hat in the pickup and wear his ski logoed baseball one. M squeezed his hand and opened her door.

They were driving west past the Dulce town limit sign as they exited the Res. They were on the way to Bluff Utah for a couple days of R and R in the still-warm, fall, red rock desert country.

M volunteered, "You did well."

"I couldn't tell since I don't speak the language. I assume your translation was spot on."

"Mostly but I'm a little rusty since I don't speak it every day and may have missed some nuances," M admitted.

"You got your looks from your mom and grand mom too. She's still movie-star beautiful at her age. I saw the touch of the French trapper in your Apache family that you mentioned. Why hasn't she remarried?"

"Because most of the available Apache men her age are either married with grandchildren even great grandchildren or if widowed, drink and now gamble too much. The casino is a curse for lonely Res men."

"I gather she liked the necklace and asked you to call the woman who made it to set up a visit to Crestone."

"Yes. She said my mother told her the hippie girls at the actor's hacienda in Taos were the only teenage white girls who were ever nice to her. She remembered my mother talking about the blonde girl fondly, and would like to meet her. My mother said the blonde girl kept the actor separated from her in the old-fashioned bathtub because he was very high on drugs and drunk. He didn't touch my mother. Another black-haired hippie girl took her place in the bathtub when things started to get sexual. My mother was still a maiden when she married my father even though my grandmother opposed the marriage. She is happy the universe gave her me. She asked me to be very sure about you."

"You left that part out."

"I'm very sure about you."

"So I heard her accept the new house," Trey responded.

M laughed. "You were right about the westerns movies. I left some translation out. It's not only a new two-bedroom house but also new used car not horses for her. Plus, five young mother cows and a hunting rifle for her brother who must approve my marriage."

"Why the car too? Does she think I'm rich?"

"The car because you have taken my maidenhood before marrying me. The cows and rifle are for her brother because I'm very beautiful like my mother, so he needs a proper dowry to approve the marriage, or he'll lose face in the tribal council. He knows you're rich in land. He's the tribal member on the Board of the New Mexico Cattlemen's Association. Your family's ranch is well known."

Trey teased, "I thought you freely gave me your maidenhood on a blanket by the Hesperus River. It was life changing. The only mention of a car was driving the Maserati. On the easy to look at part of the dowry it's too low. I got the best deal in the history of the West."

"I did give you my maidenhood freely by the river so turn right about four miles from here when we see a gravel road with a cattle grate. I know a spring with a west facing afternoon sunny grassy spot a couple miles up it. I packed us a lunch with a bottle of red wine. I put my panties in my handbag when I was in my grandmother's bathroom. Giving her a car means you can take my maidenhood by customary tribal tradition. That's lucky for you because you may take it again today." She took his right hand and pulled it up between her open brown thighs.

"Keep your eyes on the road and left hand on the wheel. No need to speed. We'll be there soon. I'm so ready to lose my newfound maidenhood the Jicarilla Apache woman way with my life warrior."

M climbed out of the noon-sun-drenched swimming pool at the Recapture Lodge just off the Utah State Highway that divided the town of Bluff in half. Trey looked up from a tattered USGS topo map as water dripped off her bikinied figure forming a wet spot on the warm concrete. The distant red rock cliffs and giant monument formations teased their eyes under a deep blue sky. The cottonwood tree's yellowing dry fall leaves sang in a light breeze. The San Juan River's low current flowed by the Inn.

He said, "I propose we follow your swim with a sandwich plus white wine at the picnic table in front of our room. After lunch, drive the pickup to a trailhead where we can hike into an Anasazi ruin before sunset. We'll dine at the café under the red rock formation a half-mile down the highway tonight. The Navajo fry bread and food is always delicious there. After dinner it's back here for a hot tub under the Milky Way."

"I can't think of a better afternoon. I have to be careful not to disturb the ancient's spirits at the Anasazi site. I can't touch or remove anything, not even a pottery chard," M stated.

"But you're Apache."

"That makes it even worse. The Pueblo Indians are the ancestors of the Anasazi. There are Anasazi ruins on the Jicarilla Apache Reservation, so I was raised not to interfere with the ancients. It can bring death from their spirits."

"Do you even want to hike into a ruin?"

"I'm curious about it so yes, but just to look not disturb it," M replied picking up her rainbow-colored beach towel to dry off.

M and Trey had parked the red pickup under a lone cottonwood tree beside the bone-dry, deep-rutted, rocky road and were bushwhacking across a dry arroyo bed. They scrambled up its steep, unstable, red clay soil bank and continued hiking through thick brush on both sides of the narrow trail. It tore at their western shirts' cotton sleeves and ranch boot cut jeans. Finally, they reached an almost white moonscape smooth rock outcropping and hiked up across it for a quarter of a mile in the mid-afternoon low sun. On the other side of the outcropping a trail led them into a narrow canyon with a trickling stream. It was barely flowing between small puddles. They saw the dry grass outline of Anasazi irrigation ditches that diverted water from the stream's banks that once watered a maize crop. Scattered small cottonwood trees with yellow leaves lined the low stream banks. When they rounded a slight bend in the grey-white, rock-walled canyon an alcove appeared in the high steep cliff wall. It housed the 1000-year-old ruins of stone-walled, multi-storied houses and granaries in various states of disrepair.

Trey asked, "How close do you want to hike to the ruins?"

"So far so good. I sense no evil here only a feeling of ancient dwellings that housed happy people who lived in the warm sheltered rock alcove, grew and stored corn, hunted, made pottery, and raised children. I can see the black smoke stains on the ceiling of the alcove from the women's cooking fires. I'll lead you up the narrow trail to the first two-story stone house. The rock path will be slippery smooth that crosses a thin ledge to it. Watch your footing in your cowboy boots," M warned.

"Now I see why you wore your beaded leather moccasins with their deerskin leggings. You can grip the smooth stone with your toes."

M stepped onto the worn rock ledge trail and led him across it toward the stone walled house. He followed M across the trail until she paused. He watched M fit her hand perfectly into a rock handprint carved into the alcove's back wall. Under it laid broken pieces of pottery and there were dried corn kernels in a chipped Anasazi bowl. A dried Aspen pole that still had one ladder-rung lay beside the stone house's front wall. The dry desert air had preserved a village of stone buildings, broken pottery, corn and wood for ladders. If the Anasazi men and women that once lived in it returned, they could rebuild the village and grow irrigated corn again.

Trey was amazed at what he saw. "It looks like they only left decades ago not eight hundred years or so. Why did you touch the carved handprint in the alcove's rock wall?"

"The handprint beckoned me because it was mine from another lifetime. The ancients' energy field here is earthy and friendly. The people here were not involved in the decline and collapse of the Anasazi spiritual center at Chaco Canyon near my Res where their priests practiced cannibalism and sacrifice. The Aztec priests taught it to them to stop the drought that lasted four hundred years. Follow me into the low door and duck."

M led him into a narrow room with the alcove's smooth rock as its floor. The stone walls of the two-story house were still strong. Its open window looked out over the small canyon into a dried-up pool where water cascaded from the mesa above it during the winter snow melt and summer monsoon seasons. M closed her eyes and sang an Apache language chant from a childhood memory for several minutes. She opened them:

"The ancients bless our coming marriage. They want us to live in peace with all people of the Four Corner's South West. They say we must kill the new Aztecs who bring drugs of death. They are the same as the ancient sadistic raiders and priests from the south who sacrificed corn maiden girls by cutting and pulling their hearts out while they were alive. The Aztecs never found this village. The people here lived and farmed in peace until the water from the rain and snow stopped coursing down from the mesa top. Then they walked up the nearby big river we call the San Juan by our Inn and over the summer passes of the snowcapped mountains to one of the longest rivers on mother earth. That's where they built new Pueblos to live in and to grow blue corn. We call it the Rio Grande River today. The Anasazi people who left this place never returned."

"The ancient spirits spoke to you?" Trey exclaimed.

"Yes. The Aztecs are now the Mexican cartel that drops the drugs on our ranch. You must help destroy them and their allies to protect me and all other peoples. They murder, rape women, and poison the earth and all its families."

"That's a strong message from the ancients!"

"True, Trey, but you must trust their spirits. I'm going to place my hands on the rock windowsill and then focus my gaze on the water in the small stream below, which gives all life. After I set my hands then raise my skirt and make love to me. This will consummate our love in this ancient sacred chapel and my pledge to the ancient ones to help protect all peoples." Trey honored her request from the Anasazi spirits with strength and absorbed their courage through love that radiated from M.

Trey and M were sitting on the veranda of the café down the highway from the Inn. They felt the warmth radiating on their faces from the giant five-story red rock monument near the veranda's edge. The sun had set but they could see a thin line of pale orange twilight light on the far western desert horizon. The blazing ball was speeding toward the California coastline to fall into the Pacific Ocean at the end of another day in their young lives together. M gazed into Trey's blue eyes as she finished the last bite of her pinto beans and spiced ground lamb on fry bread with fresh salsa.

Trey commented, "The ancients made you hungry. You wiped your plate clean. There's nothing left for the grey cat on the railing by the cafe door."

"It was actually swimming, hiking and erotic desert sex. The cat could miss a meal or two," M said with a smile.

"My Navajo fry bread spicy lamb tacos chased with a cold Coors longneck was five-star. You can't beat sitting by a sun-soaked, high desert, red rock that warms you while you dine instead of an overhead propane patio heater. The warm rock's heat is sustainable for a million years. I'll pay the cashier inside. You want a dime round mint chocolate in a shiny wrapper? We hot tub under the stars next."

"Two of them. One for dessert to energize me in the hot tub so I can talk to the stars. And one when I get in bed to energize us."

"Then it's four." Trey smiled as he walked toward the café door to pay their check. He reached to pat the cat on its head with his empty hand. It swatted a paw at him, so he quickly jerked his hand back.

M laughed, "Don't pat me on the head empty handed either, cowboy. I can taste those mint chocolates already."

As the cooling high Colorado Plateau night air sunk into the hot tub Trey and M quietly stared at the Milky Way. Its bright starlight was hypnotic and pulsed into their optical nerves. It was a natural meditation that was so powerful Trey remembered it from the first time his mom showed him the Milky Way while riding the range late one summer night. It always affected him the same way whenever he gazed up at it in the vast, empty west's, clear night sky. It was an awesome reminder that a man's life was a pebble in a timeless Universe so he should use it wisely to help not injure the earth and its people.

M's mind took her on a much different march through her mother's Apache origin myths. The light rays that traveled twenty-five million light years to her brown eyes reminded her that the Universe was forever and always present. It saddened her that mankind could be so cruel to the earth and each other. Why were the Native Americans still treated so badly in her lifetime like her ancestor's life times? Why couldn't human beings see there were more stars co-existing in the Milky Way than people living on the earth? She pledged to herself to help stop humanity's war against humanity. She squeezed Trey's hand to signal her partnership on this mission. He responded with a knowing squeeze back.

A few silent peaceful minutes later they walked back to their room with colorful beach towels wrapped around their bodies that caught the starlight. After entering the room, they toweled each other dry. Both stood silently nude in the rising full moon's light that flooded through the window. Its soft light outlined the curves of their strong bodies. It aroused a sexual tension from a quarter of a million miles away. M unwrapped the silver covering of the two mints, which glistened in the moonlight. In an act of communion, she slipped one into Trey's mouth and one into hers. She smiled as she pulled him onto the moonlight-soaked white bed sheet and pressed her body against his. These moments she knew would strengthen them for the hours and days ahead. The Aztec evil was an old and dangerous force that destroyed all peoples it touched. She and Trey had not sought it, but it now sought to destroy both of them and people around them...Anglo, Spanish, Apache, and Pueblo Indians. She bent her mind waves into Trey's as they both disappeared into the ecstasy of the moment under the pure moonlight beams.

CHAPTER 15
THE LAST POW WOW

A week before Thanksgiving Day, Trey and M drove toward Taos. A red-orange, multi-layered, Thunderbird sunset lit up the western sky on a quickly cooling late fall night. They talked quietly as the red pickup swept them through the now silent winter ranches, farms and villages. Lights from adobe houses and doublewide's windows dotted the landscape with occasional TV screens flickering in their windows. A motley crew of pickups and one-ton flatbed trucks rested by houses and steel-sided barns. The shiny metal roofed hay sheds were full to the rafters with cattle and horse feed for the winter. The irrigation center pivot rigs with their long-nippled tubular arms were silently paused. The centerline highway stripes shot under the pickup at sixty miles an hour as M watched for elk and wild horses that might cross the empty highway at dusk now that the herds were grazing in the valley. Sweet-smelling Pinion wood smoke curled from kiva fireplaces and wood stoves. Cords of stacked firewood stood tall beside the houses in easy reach of backdoors. Pickups had snowplow blades mounted on their front suspensions. Rural Northern New Mexico had started to settle in for the twenty-degree-below nights and snow that came in December. The Arctic fronts' air sunk on clear night onto the San Luis Valley's seven-thousand-foot-high floor. Snow already tipped the twelve-to-fourteen-thousand-foot mountain peaks that surrounded the valley.

M asked, "Did you talk to Jumbo again today for the latest update on the drug drop arrests?"

"Yes. He confirmed there have been no arrests. Also, the deputy who was arrested during the roundup was found dead in his SUV with a gunshot to the head with a scribbled suicide note. The county coroner ruled it a probable suicide. The Colorado state patrol does not believe it was a suicide. They were never able to question the deputy. I sense Jumbo suspects I know more about the drug drop el jefes. He may think I'm looking for a way to retaliate for Maestas's death and my father's near fatal injuries so I broke off the call. I didn't want him to call Cooper."

"Have the cowhands reported any more sightings of airplane drug drops across the gorge?" M asked.

"The short answer is no visual sightings, but they are not riding the west pasture on the gorge's rim now with the mother cows in the hacienda's pastures eating hay. Two of them were elk hunting near a water tank on the mountain's flank last week and thought they heard a low flying airplane at sunset across the gorge. They could not see it," Trey reported.

"So let's go over the Operation Aztec plan for tonight one more time," M requested.

"We're checking into the hotel and then I'll slip out of our casita around seven o'clock. I'll drive the pickup to the Pueblo's tourist parking area. The war chief has agreed to an eight o'clock meeting with the Albuquerque banker, a governor's aide, a major liquor distributor, a cartel guy from Mexico and a local businessman. They are pressuring him to move the drug drops to Pueblo lands. His son's life has been threatened. BLM ordered their rangers to monitor the federal land across the gorge from the ranch 24/7. The war chief alleges they told his son there's a cartel $50,000 bounty for my head. He has kept BIA, DEA and the FBI out of the loop."

"And the logistics?"

"The meeting is in the information center on the public edge of the Pueblo near the parking area. The war chief's son will place me plus two Pueblo ex-army Rangers at ambush points. All of them have either sniper or advanced weapon's training. Their rifles have night vision scopes and laser beam scopes with silencers. The line of fire is into the lighted entrance area of the info center. When the Mexican cartel gang approaches the door of the center we will take them out. After I arrive there a Pueblo member will return my pickup to the hotel parking lot. The chief's son will have a horse ready for my escape. He'll guide me across the Pueblo land to the edge of our hotel's back entrance. I'll put my rifle back into the ranch pickup and slip into our casita. You'll alibi that we spent the night making wild love. When we return to the ranch tomorrow at sunup my rifle will disappear forever."

"It sounds straight forward but where will the bodies go?"

"The chief said to a sacred place for enemies that have departed the earth, which cannot be discovered by white men."

"The Apache have those places too," M stated coldly.

"His son warned me war is hell and everything on a battlefield can change instantly no matter how good the intelligence and planning are."

"I get that. It's like going off the line in a drag race. You can win a perfectly planned and driven race, or your engine can blow you up in a nitro fuel fireball. It's key to have the plan to execute the mission. I only wish I could help more."

"You're helping by alibiing me. You don't have the rifle or horse skills for tonight. I'll leave a Colt .45 pistol in my overnight bag for you. It's loaded so just aim and pull the trigger. Use it only to kill. Tomorrow you're doing the driving. There's a wrinkle you're not aware of. I rented a garage for the winter near our casita for the Maserati. I had Cooper send two cowhands to deliver it there a few days ago. I told him we were going to use it to vacation in warm southern New Mexico and Arizona for a month this winter. We'll switch the pickup for the Maserati at sunup. There may be police roadblocks out of Taos tomorrow when or if any of the drug gang members are reported missing or escape alive. We're not pulling over for a county sheriff's SUV, a town marshal's patrol car or the FBI. I'll handle the firearms and you are the wheel woman."

"I'll visualize the drive while you're at the Pueblo and be ready for up to 180 miles an hour." M smiled like a fox that just caught a jackrabbit.

Trey eased the red pickup out of its parking place behind their casita and drove up Passeo Del Norte toward the turn to the Taos Pueblo. It was a quiet pre-Thanksgiving night. The shops and galleries were closed along his route, but a couple restaurants and a gas station were open. A few vehicles were on the Passeo where traffic could back up a mile in the summertime coming into the historic Taos Plaza. The tourists were gone, and the winter skiers had not arrived yet. He savored the rare ancient peaceful feel of the 400-year-old town. But he knew bloody Taos was anything but peaceful. It had been founded after the Spanish conquest of the Pueblo in 1615. The Pueblo had survived Apache and Comanche raids before and after the conquest. In 1680 its cacique Popay had led thirteen Pueblos along the Rio Grande River in a revolt. The Pueblos' victory caused the death of Spanish settlers, Catholic priests and the destruction of all things Spanish throughout all of New Spain now New Mexico. Sixteen years of independence was ended in 1696 with the re-conquest of Taos and the Pueblo by DeVargas a Spanish conquistador. He burned the revolting Pueblos along the Rio Grande River all the way to Taos. His armored soldiers cut off the right arm and foot of any male Pueblo boy and man who opposed his army. Later the Utes and Navahos raided for and sold slaves to the Spanish merchants and hacienda settlers in Taos. The Army of the United States arrived and conquered Taos in 1847 defeating its Mexican garrison. The occupying US Army bloodily suppressed a revolt by some of Taos's Spanish population and the Pueblo Indios. The soil he planned to fight the cartel and its allies on tonight was drenched in blood. The darkened adobe Catholic church near the information center was an illusion of spiritualism that had fostered war against all of mankind for two thousand years. He knew tonight was just another chapter in the book of the 1000-year-old Taos Pueblo's defense against the world. He was honored to be trusted to play a bit part.

He turned into the Pueblo's entrance road and drove by empty winter grazing pastures. He passed the Pueblo's small casino with its lights and quarter full parking lot. He drove past a few houses and turned into the public visitor's parking lot. He mused except for tonight he would always be a paid visitor, but this night would be dangerously special in the defense of this 1000-year-old United Nations Heritage site where its farmers still grew blue corn. He remembered M's long goodbye kiss as he cut the headlights. A minute later, there was a knock on his window. He slid out of the cab with his rifle and handed the key to an old ponytailed Pueblo man with a black bandana around his forehead. He pointed for Trey to cross to the Pueblo side of the information center, but they exchanged no words. He gave off the silent power of being a warrior in his youth. He was armed only with an elk horn handled knife that was tucked into a buffalo hide belt with a square silver buckle. The logo of the Army's 101 First Airborne Division had been hammered into the buckle by a Pueblo silversmith. Trey crossed the gravel road as the dark shadowed hulk of the adobe church loomed on his right. The burned-out adobe walls of the Pueblo's first Catholic church, which the American Army destroyed by cannon fire during the 1847 rebellion was behind the information center. He had come to a killing field to hunt the new Aztecs and their allies.

Trey walked past the closed ticket and information windows of the building and turned the corner. The war chief's son and two young Pueblo members were standing there in faded camouflage Army fatigues with military issue automatic laser night scoped rifles cradled in their hands across their chests. Their faces were blacked out and they all had black bandanas across their foreheads. Their long black-haired ponytails signaled their strength and power as members of the Warrior Society, which protected the Pueblo. In ancient times they protected the Pueblo's farmers and its stored blue corn from the raiding Utes, Apache and Comanche. The deep Rio Grande River Gorge to the west of the Taos Pueblo and the high mountain range on its east backside were nature's geo protection for it. Its enemies from the southwest were funneled into the steep-walled, narrow, Rio Grande River canyon. Its enemies to the north and east had to cross high mountain passes, which were blocked by avalanche prone snow eight months a year. Enemy raiders were sitting ducks for ambush in the river canyon or on the passes for the Pueblo's warrior's arrows.

Jonathon in an almost whisper said, "At 20:00 a group of eight to ten men, depending on the number of the Mexican cartel leader's security gunmen, and including his New Mexico allies, will arrive. They'll park by this side door staff entrance to the building. I don't know how many vehicles they will have. I am on a walkie-talkie headset to a warrior on the Pueblo's entrance road just past the casino. Once I have a vehicle count, I will hold up the number with my fingers. Keep you scopes on me. I will take vehicle one and my two Warrior Society members will take vehicles two and three. Trey, you will take vehicle four if there is one. Let the occupants all exit vehicles before you fire at will. When the first one walks toward the side door, I will open fire. Take kill shots only and through the vehicle windows if necessary. Once all the vehicles pass through the Pueblo gate, another warrior will close and lock it behind them. This is your silencer, Trey. I'll attach it to your AR-15 rifle. Kill all the Mexicans because we will not know which one is head of the cartel. Assume the cartel security men will have heavy automatic weapons and that could include a machine gun or Russian made RPG rocket launcher. They are highly trained in heavy weapons fire fight techniques by South African mercenaries. We know our positions, Trey. Mine is from the burned-out church. If you miss my hand signal, then fire on the last vehicle in line after you hear the first shot. You are firing from behind the low adobe wall corner at the front east side of the parking lot. If any of them cut and run toward your wall for cover, shoot them. When it's over I'll meet you at your position, Trey, and guide you out of the Pueblo on horseback. Any questions?" Deadly silence enveloped the mission at hand.

"Then disperse to your positions. It's 19:45. Check your watches. Cell phones off. Here's some black for your face, Trey. Finally, if anyone is wounded you will only be treated in secret on Pueblo lands. When you're in position check your rifle's sight lines. The wind has dropped to one mile an hour," Jonathon concluded.

Trey walked to his position behind the thick adobe wall. He practiced scoping the side door area of the building getting the feel of his rifle with a modern, very-light military silencer on its barrel. Its scope's software calculated wind drift. The lighting fixture over the side door provided him good vision at thirty yards. He noted he could use the top of the low adobe wall as a tripod, but his face would be exposed when he fired shots over it. He marked Jonathon's position. Seconds now seemed like minutes. Minutes seemed like hours. He looked at his Rolex Explorer watch's bevel at 19:55 and sighted in on Jonathon's position to wait for his vehicle finger count. He sent one more silent I love you through the ether to M. Suddenly without a hand signal from Jonathon five black SUVs sped through the Pueblo's main gate toward the information center.

The two lead SUVs raced past Trey and turned toward the side of the building. They parked beside the employee entrance. Two of the trailing three SUVs formed an inverted T behind the ones by the building's side door entrance and blocked Trey's line of sight to it. The fifth trailing SUV suddenly turned, entering the parking lot and started a counterclockwise sweep toward Trey. A passenger door flew open, and a warrior's body was thrown out. It skipped violently across the gravel. Trey guessed it was the lookout who never radioed the vehicle count to Jonathon. The SUV's bright headlights swept toward him. He heard automatic rifle fire from the cartel gunmen near the side door as the warrior's silenced rifle bullets tore at metal and shattered the glass of the SUVs by the building. He stood, turned, and fired a salvo of semi-automatic bullets into the SUV rounding the parking lot just before its headlights beam hit him. Behind him all hell broke loose with machine gun tracer bullet fire arching from the other four SUVs in all directions. Trey's semi-automatic fire shattered the oncoming black SUV's windshield. It killed its surprised driver and the passenger before they could return fire. The Mexican round-faced driver slumped over the steering wheel as it careened ten feet away from Trey and crashed into the parking lot's low adobe wall. Its bumper hit the wall so hard it front flipped over the wall and landed on its top.

Trey dived for cover at the wall's corner when Jonathon yelled, "RPG incoming." Rapid automatic machine gun bright white tracer rounds filled the night sky. Trey raised his AR-15 rifle and fired a salvo into the upside down SUV's gasoline tank and it exploded in to a fireball. An RPG round hit the corner of the wall just as Trey ran toward the back of the parking lot using the fireball as cover. When the RPG rocket grenade hit the thick adobe brick wall it blew it into fragments as Trey dived onto the gravel and skidded. Scorched adobe brick parts blew over his head and splattered into everything within twenty-five yards. He maneuvered on his belly, back toward the parking lot's entrance as machine gun tracers flew over his body at the wall's height. When he reached the adobe wall at the parking lot entrance he stayed in a prone position. He peered out to survey the battlefield. The two SUVs at the building's side door were burning and the other two were riddled with bullet holes and blown out windows. Bodies and body parts surrounded the SUVs. There were still tracer rounds outgoing from the two SUVs that were not burning. Then he saw another RPG rocket launched toward Jonathon's position at the old burned-out church. It exploded and he saw a body fly through the air. Suddenly a man crawled out from under the bullet riddled SUV in front of him with an Uzi machine gun. He reacted and fired a salvo at his head, which exploded into pieces before he could fire at Trey.

He took a deep breath to clear his head, but the night air was filled with smoke, and gagged instead. He saw the two Pueblo warriors running toward the back of the two SUVs in front of him, firing point blank finishing shots into bodies on the ground. Trey stayed in prone position

and raised his rifle as a badly wounded Mexican cartel man in a custom
tailored blue British suit rounded the left SUV's front bumper running
to escape the two warriors. Trey sighted a shot at his heart and squeezed
the trigger three times as his head snapped back. He kept coming toward
Trey, firing an Uzi machine gun wildly. He was the Aztec chief. He staggered and fell ten feet in front of Trey. His black eyes pupils locked on
Trey in a rage of ancient hatred. He pointed the Uzi machine gun's barrel
at Trey with all the strength he had remaining in his life. Trey aimed his
AR-15 rifle between his eyes and a salvo of shots blew his head apart
at ten feet. The Aztec's blood exploded into the air in all directions. It
covered Trey's forehead and dripped down his blackened cheeks. Trey
relished the moment of the Aztec's blood sacrifice. As fast as the firefight
had started it ended. Trey carefully stood in the silence of the burning
SUV's light fields. One of the warriors in camouflaged fatigues walked
up to him with his blackened face dripping blood.

He said simply, "I'm in command now. The RPG round killed Jonathon. You are a good warrior. Go now to the back of the parking lot. The
oldest warrior of our society who returned your pickup to your casita has
two horses. He won the Medal of Honor in Vietnam. He will guide you
safely out of the Pueblo. You can never return here to be linked with the
Warrior Society's fight for the Pueblo tonight. In the war chief's and my
heart you will always be a member of our society." Trey watched as he
turned and stopped at the cartel's leader and pulled a black military knife
from his ammo belt. He cut the cartel's leader's heart out with a series
of precise knife thrusts and held it in his raised hand. He stuck it into the
black SUV's special radio aerial and slipped away framed by the burning
vehicles against the night sky.

Trey met the old warrior and mounted his horse. They rode to the Rio
Pueblo River.

The old warrior simply said, "Wash the blood and the black war paint
from your face. Then we will ride to the Pueblo's edge by your casita."
Trey rode in silence behind him and did not turn on his iPhone to report he was safe to M. He did not want his cell phone call signal traced
to the Pueblo. The night sky darkened as they rode away from a battle,
which never happened. Trey used their secret two knocks followed by one
knock on the casita's heavy, brown-stained, hand-carved, wooden door.

M opened it with her Colt .45 pistol pointed at him. He closed the door behind him as he gently pushed the pistol barrel away from his stomach.

She breathlessly said, "Sorry even an Apache girl can't be too careful these days." She softly laid the pistol on the dresser's wooden top.

"You certainly can't with me in your life," he replied deadpan. M threw her arms around him and kissed Trey hard. She stepped back and looked him over.

"What's with the black eye shadow and speckled dried blood on your face and neck? Your hands are skinned up too. Your jeans and shirt are caked with bloody dust."

"Just the traces of a dogfight in a graveled parking lot. I need to get out of these clothes ASAP and shower from head to toe. I don't think we were followed here. My Indian pony was an amazing night ride. He never stumbled or made a sound. I'd buy him if I could. I'll tell you the entire true west story at the ranch. The walls have ears in Taos. Put more pinion on the fire and burn my clothes. Then join me in the shower. My whole body needs a soapy hot water scrub and a rub down."

"Where's your rifle?"

"It returned with my guide to the Pueblo. We'll never see it again." Trey stripped down. M winced when she saw dried drip lines of blood down the center of his chest. He put a single finger over his mouth signaling silence. He headed through the bathroom door and turned on the tub shower full blast. M gathered his clothes and fed them an item at a time into the kiva's blazing pinion fire. When all of Trey's clothes were burning, she stripped down and walked into the bathroom. She stepped into the bathtub and pulled the shower curtain closed. Trey's body was shiny wet. M skipped the full body massage but not the sexual part of it. Moments later, their wet bodies coupled as her breasts pressed against his chest. Their orgasms were wildly animalistic as the night's tension exploded into sexual passion. It was her Apache scalp dance solely with Trey.

D awn came early as they silently finished dressing, packed and double searched the casita for any personal evidence that they had stayed there. Trey sifted the cold ashes in the kiva and used a fireplace shovel to put them in a plastic laundry bag he found in the closet. Wordlessly they carefully and quietly opened and closed the door. They walked down the sidewalk toward the red pickup truck. Trey dropped the plastic bag of ashes into the bear-proofed opening of a trash container. Their eyes scanned the parking lot and its high brown adobe walls for any sign of life. There was none. Even the birds had all gone south for the winter. He opened the driver's side door of the pickup and pulled the keys from under the matt. He climbed into it and leaned over to open M's door. His cowboy booted foot hit a hard object at the edge of the accelerator. He pulled it back and looked down. The east light from the rear window highlighted an elk handled hunting knife. He smiled as he picked it up carefully. Its razor-sharp blade glinted in the low sun.

M asked, "Where did that come from?"

"A trade for a rifle and for my secret honorary membership in the Pueblo's Warrior Society. I'll hunt with it with for life."

He started the motor and once it had warmed up, backed out of the parking space. His eyes continued to survey the parking lot as they drove into the alley behind the casita. Almost a block down it he stopped the pickup short of a brown adobe garage with a tin roof. M hopped out, unlocked the padlock and started to pull open the old-fashioned faded turquoise painted double wooden doors. They both heard the roar of a high-powered supercharged car turn into the alley and head toward them. When their heads snapped around, they saw a yellow, 1970 hemi head Dodge Charger coming fast toward the pickup. M reached into the waistband of her leather driving pants and pulled out the Colt .45. Trey reached to open the glove compartment of the pickup to get his Glock 9. The yellow Dodge braked hard sliding on the cracked gravelly pavement. M moved toward the front fender of the pickup. The Mexican driver of the Dodge Charger reached out his side window with a pistol in his hand and aimed it at Trey's heart. M stepped in front of the pickup and aimed the Colt .45 with her outstretched arm at the Dodge Charger's driver. At a hood's length from him M fired five shots one at a time into his head that burst into a fountain of blood. His shot ricocheted off the pavement and his bullet disappeared into the adobe garage's wall with a thud. He dropped the gun onto the alley's broken pavement. Trey, happy to be alive signaled her with a V for victory. He looked down at the dead Mexican hit man with no remorse. M opened the garage doors and climbed into the Maserati. The Vee-eight motor rumbled into life as she backed it out of the garage and around the pickup. Trey stuck the Glock 9 into his cowboy cut, brown leather jacket's side pocket. He pulled the pickup into the garage, jumped down out of the cab and retrieved their two pieces of luggage from its half cab. M pushed the trunk lever button and he put the luggage into the Maserati. He closed the garage doors and snapped the padlock shut. The yellow Dodge Charger's hemi engine was still rumbling when Trey walked past the pool of blood from the Mexican cartel's hit man's head. He slid into the passenger seat of the Maserati and snapped his seatbelt on. M carefully pushed down the accelerator knowing the tires were cold. She did not want to spin it. She U turned back down the alley toward the casita and drove past it toward a street entrance.

She asked, "A cartel hit man?"

"A Mexican one. Great shooting. He had a bead on me. I stupidly left my Glock 9 in the glove compartment."

"I know. I saved my favorite heart. How did he know where we were picking up the Maserati?"

"Only way I can figure is that he followed the old Pueblo warrior last night to our casita when he dropped off the pickup. The cartel gunmen also found the Pueblo warrior scout near the entrance and killed him. The hit man watched us stop this morning after we drove up the alley from the casita's parking lot. He was in a parking place out of our view. Then he exited the ally here and doubled back around to us at the garage," Trey replied. M turned onto the Passeo North toward the ranch. A police car with its siren wailing came toward them and sped past. It turned into the street that the hit man had used to enter the alley.

"Shit," Trey said. "Someone living near the garage heard the shots and phoned the Taos police. Drive as fast as you can without drawing attention until we reach the last light before the run to the ranch."

"I'm on it. Do we have radar? Trey opened the glove box and found it. He set it up. The hi-tech radar ran through its memory list after he plugged it in. The tension mounted as M pushed the town speed limit toward the last light. A few early-morning workers passed them coming into town. Near the last stop light the radar went off and voice signaled hi-tech state patrol radar. They both held their breath as a siren came toward them with a black state patrol SUV flashing its lights. It roared past on the empty road.

"He's responding to the shots fired call...not looking for speeders this early. But in case the caller or someone saw the Maserati I'm flooring it after the light before they can set up a roadblock or put out an all-points bulletin for a black Maserati sports car," M stated calmly.

"Good plan. You learn their procedures teaching them at high-speed driving school?" Trey asked. M passed under the green light and floored the Maserati's race metal gas pedal.

"Yes. Watch for animals on the roadside wild or domestic. It's early still. The wild ones may be returning to the mountains at sunup." Trey glanced over as the Maserati hit 140 miles an hour.

M quipped, "We'll be at the ranch in twenty-two minutes."

"That's half our normal pickup drive time," Trey replied.

"Exactly half." M smiled.

"That's fast."

"Our lives will always be fast." M laughed.

ABOUT THE AUTHOR

Tom Tatum is an author and accomplished film and TV producer/director. He is the founder of Tatum Communications, inc., which has produced, directed, and written over 400 TV, documentaries, video segments, VHS/DVD's, commercials, and Motion Pictures. Tatum's work has been seen by a worldwide audience and includes notable titles like Double High, Winners Take All and Greenpeace's Greatest Hits. Tatum Video's indy action/extreme sports program library spans 40 years and is one of the largest in the world.

Currently, Tatum operates his Ute Peak Ranch in New Mexico, and is "lead sled dog" on many multi-million-dollar solar projects via his company Ute Peak Solar, Inc. An avid advanced skier, he is married to well-known Colorado and Taos, New Mexico artist, Kathryn Tatum.

9 781647 347376